The

Temporal
Trinity

Book Two of the

Jared Kitchens

For my wife, Jenny.

Without your words of encouragement, proofreading, and tolerance of mundane tasks, this book would be just bytes on a computer.

You're the one I want to go through time with.

SCHEDULE

Part One

Priori, Father Time

Chapter 1:00

Retrospective Perspectives
by the Historyteller

In the first book of the *Anachronist Chronicles*, I, as Historian of the planet Aia, told the story as I remembered it—which was incredibly well, considering my psychic ability to see into the past. As an *Everseer*, I have been both blessed and cursed with temporal omniscience. However, 90% of the *Everseers* who attempt to foresee the future go completely insane. Those with hindsight, however, are 90% sane. I'm not as popular at parties as a fortune-teller, but I like to think I'd make a rather nice History teacher.

At any rate, in my last tale, the planet Aia met its doom due to rapid age and decay. This story will eventually take a group of several Aian survivors to a very similar, yet far away planet called Earth.

Now, you may be familiar with much of Earth's history already. If that is so, I ask you this: What if someone made that story up just to entertain others? What if everything I wrote in the first book had been completely fictional and not actually from post-cognitive visions in my head?

Historians today use artifacts found by archaeologists to understand time-periods before their births. They rely on

3

documents and carbon-dating to find their stories, but the general public also pays close attention to the legends and lore that have been passed down by word of mouth for centuries.

There is a fine line between History and Legend. It's difficult to know where a story ends and history begins. How much of what we learn as History was actually just made up by whomever survived some particular invasion, siege, or catastrophe? What about the history of those who didn't? Furthermore, legends and lore have intermingled with History such that children believe George Washington actually cut down a cherry tree and could not tell a lie.

As our heroes, heroines, and anti-heroes move through history in this story, please remember that *I* am your Storyteller, and *you* are my faithful reader. You may have several textbooks or documents that contradict the events in my story. However, how many of your so-called "Historians" have the *Eversight* to see visions of the past?

Chapter 1:01

Out of Time, Out of Space

"Stop it, Aori!"

"Quondam, please try to get along with your uncle."

"He started it. He won't stay on his side of the room."

"Quondam, this is his house. Albeit, it is a large house that is currently rocketing through outer space, but it is still his house. Besides, he is just a child."

Quondam seethed. Asalie always took Aori's side. Everyone seemed to love the child, even though he had very recently destroyed the planet Aia—their home. Quondam saw himself as the hero—the good guy—and yet, his fellow passengers tickled, baby-talked, and fawned over the former-man responsible for irrevocably altering time—in other words, the bad guy.

"Just because he changed into a baby, doesn't mean we have to treat him like one. He's still a villain. Doesn't anyone remember what he did?"

In our lives, we struggle to meet deadlines, make appointments, and try to work in some "me" time in between our numerous scheduled events. Every so often, a moment

5

arises when the breakneck speed of what we have to get done falls away, and we can enjoy a brief period of quiet reflection.

The passengers aboard Aori Timister's clock-tower-come-rocket, having no deadlines or appointments scheduled, struggled with the enormous amounts of quiet reflection one can only understand on a seven-year trip through space.

Seven years, of course, is only an estimate. When your planet has been destroyed, and the next one is several hundreds of light-years away, you're what we might call, "in-between-home-planets." Aia no longer kept her roughly 360-day orbit around her sun, and without such orbital repetition, how does one keep track of time?

The people of Aia had no stake in the argument between metric and standard measurement, as they used neither. Instead of saying, "I live 4 kilometers from town," one might say, "I live 30 minutes from town." This form of measurement has also been used in big cities such as Los Angeles, where a simple, two-mile journey could take hours depending on traffic.

The Codan people of Aia, whose last surviving members made up most of the passengers on Aori's clock-rocket, used units of measurement similar to those found in music. They used meters (or beats), measures, and bars.

> The light-year, though it contains the word "year," does not refer to time. Rather, it's the distance light can travel in one year. Science fiction spacecrafts often travel at the speed of light, which is approximately 9.46 trillion (9.46×10^{12}) kilometers or 5.88 trillion (5.88×10^{12}) miles in one Earth year.

Of course, this system of measurement also depended on time; a measure might be the distance one could travel in four beats. The complicated system often caused many Coda to be late for appointments, especially those requiring more than a day's walk.

In order to make the long trip from Aia's solar system to the one composed of Earth and eight other planets, Aori's clock-rocket had to travel faster than light-speed. Otherwise, many of its passengers would die of old age before reaching their destination.

Fortunately for most of them, the god of Time had bestowed upon them certain advantages. The average Coda lived hundreds of years, and the occasional extension on that lifespan was not uncommon. Though it was rare, some Coda were occasionally given an *encore*, or a second chance on life.

The Coda named Emmeleia D'Aeolian joined her people, whom she had recently freed from their prison on the 22nd floor of the tower. She preferred to go by her traveling, or stage-name, Lithe. As she and her people played the traditional Codan song of mourning, Lithe's homemade mandolin itched to play along.

The lamentation called for the playing of pipes or flutes, and the music sounded similar to the bagpipe-elegies played at Irish funeral processions. In order to fit in with the rest of the ensemble, Lithe's mandolin underwent a few changes. The instrument, having been constructed, or rather grown, from the seed of a very old, very famous tree called the *asa*, frequently exhibited marvelous magical properties. It could become any instrument required for a particular song, and it often seemed to have a life of its own.

The wood of the *asa* tree also provided the very structure of the former clock tower in which they now lived. Mystical energy reverberated in its walls, which seemed to change shape in order to provide the best acoustics for the Codan lamentation.

Though Aori's choice of building material had made him many enemies, many of those same enemies owed their lives to the construction. While Aori had designed and created many fantastic inventions, he could not have built a safer rocket for traveling through space. Even the space-age construction materials of Earth's NASA program could not have provided for the passengers in the way that the wood of the *asa* could.

At timed intervals, which the passengers came to refer to as seasons, the clock-rocket produced fruit. The nutberries of the *asa* nourished them, while the natural respiratory cycles of the plant provided air for them to breathe. Amazingly, the ship seemed to live, without roots or leaves, and asked nothing of them.

"It is a symbiotic relationship," Asalie explained. "We provide air for the growing vegetation, just as it provides for us. Fortunately for us, the vessel does not need sunlight or nutrients from the ground."

Though Quondam often listened to Asalie intently, his more mature, rational selves required less-mystical explanations. "How can it survive on air alone?" he asked in the raspy voice of a much-older version of himself.

"It feeds off the energy of the spiral," she said with a smile, as if the answer had been obvious. "The death of Aia has provided the energy for many new lives."

"How can you smile in the wake of such destruction?" Quondam asked, brusquely. "At least the Coda mourn its loss; you carry on as if nothing has changed."

Asalie stood up, stretching to all of her four-foot height, and yet still her presence was intimidating. "You are still young, Quondam, and so such impetuousness is to be expected, but do not take me for some addle-brained, old woman! I know more about death than you shall ever learn, boy."

Taking her long, gnarled staff in one hand and Aori in the other, she began to walk away from him. "Quondam, *everything* has changed. I have just accepted that life begins anew."

8

Aori looked up at the goddess of life through a sphere of amber that had become his favorite toy ever since his regression to infancy. Its value to Aori had developed from spite, having recovered it from Pyrite Pettifogger, who had mined and subsequently stolen it from Aori's mine.

Any geologist could tell you that amber forms from tree sap that has been compressed and heated for millions of years. Unbeknownst to the infant Aori, he now held a clue to the age of his home planet. The bubbles in the amber held air that had cycled through the atmosphere of Aia long before any humans existed on its surface. Any microscopic entities that had been trapped inside the amber were preserved for all eternity within those bubbles.

Though he could not yet form the words to comment on the subject, Aori's expansive brain wrapped around the endless possibilities within those bubbles.

As Quondam sat alone, gazing out into the vast nothingness of space, he took a moment to reflect. In his short life, which was technically only approximately nine years, regardless of his ability to change his age at will, Quondam had experienced more than his share of loss. His parents had died when he was very young, and he had never really understood why they had perished, or why he grew up in an orphanage instead. Whenever he thought of them, and the pain their death had caused, the older parts of his mind took over and dulled the pain. Just as he could shift to other ages to heal physical injuries, his mind shifted accordingly to protect itself.

To think, all this started to bring Munder back to life.

Quondam looked at Munder, and the emotions he had felt seemed lifetimes away. The timepiece that gave him his abilities had also caused Munder to fall, seemingly to his death. If not for the time-god, Toki, what would have become of the giant? What would have become of the world?

9

If Munder had not arrived at the precise second he did, and if he had not given Aori a timepiece that turned him into a child, what might have happened? Quondam knew that Aori would have done something horrible, but it just didn't make sense. He believed that the villain had tried to destroy the world by altering time, but Munder stopped him and the planet was destroyed anyway.

It's not fair, he thought.

Children often believe that the world should be fair, and while there exist many natural, supernatural, and unseen forces that strive to bring balance and harmony to the universe, sometimes *fair* and *balanced* are in opposition. The mechanisms employed to bring about harmony in nature—for instance, the deaths of children or loved ones—hardly seem worth the lives that may be created in their absence.

"What're you looking at, runt?" Munder walked up to Quondam and poked him in the chest.

"Stop it, Munder." He knew by now that even though Munder had been raised in a different time by a manipulative, possibly evil god, they were still friends. And even though Munder had come back with a large army intent on capturing and probably hurting him severely, he knew that Munder's repeated poking him in the chest was just a childish, playful taunt.

"Stop it, Munder," he repeated. When a giant pokes you, even if he doesn't mean for it to hurt, it doesn't exactly tickle. "I wasn't looking at you, so go away."

Munder poked him again.

After struggling to his feet, Quondam asked, "How did you know to give Aori the timepiece? How did you know that would stop him?"

Munder poked him again.

10

"Stop it, Munder." Quondam poked him back. "Aori was after my timepiece, so when you showed up and just gave him yours…" His finger hurt.

He fell backwards, having been poked a bit harder. "…We all thought you had gone crazy and joined Aori—ow – but it was all a plan to turn him into a child. Brilliant."

Munder just smiled and kept poking. "Yep."

"Munder, stop it. By the way, what did you do with that timepiece, anyway?"

Munder stopped poking. "Why?"

"Look, I'm not threatening to take it away, so don't go falling off any cliffs or anything. I just think we should all know where it is, in case Aori grows up and tries to use it again."

"It's mine, Quondam. I worked hard to get it, and I deserve it." Munder poked a little more angrily this time.

"Ow, Munder!" Quondam's voice changed, as if he had grown out of the playground antics. With the strength of a man much older than nine, he grabbed Munder's finger. "I did not mean to imply that you were using the timepiece for evil purposes. However, you must understand that it is not a toy!"

Their argument had caught the attention of several other passengers, who gathered around as spectators would at any playground confrontation. These particular on-lookers, however, fought their urge to shout, "Fight!"

Lithe stepped between them, and her long arms kept them well separated. "Quondam's right, Munder. We got that timepiece from Emperor Saturn."

"An evil emperor, I might add," added Quondam.

"Well," said Lithe, "actually, he was just trying to help his people."

"He was subjugating his people and forcing them into a class-based system of government in which he ruled with an iron fist! That's evil."

11

"From a certain perspective, I suppose." The differing perspective in any argument regarding evil usually came from Finis, the self-described Living Embodiment of Death. Like Asalie and Aori, Finis was a mortal imbued with the powers of a god. As a deified man, his responsibility was similar to the night manager for the graveyard shift, except he actually watched the graveyards. Death incarnate resented the common misconception that Death=Evil, and he had spoken with Quondam on the subject numerous times.

It is often easier for children or those with narrow minds to see all conflict as simple as good vs. evil. However, conflict exists in every part of our lives—God vs. man, natural vs. supernatural, man vs. woman, yin vs. yang, etc. The conflict can lead to harmony or discord, depending on any number of circumstances, but as in the yin/yang example, the preferred state is balance.

Furthermore, those with differing perspectives often use the label *evil* as propaganda to draw in supporters for their side, just as Quondam hoped to do. Ignoring Aori's perspective takes far less energy than accepting and understanding it. Pointing a finger at a so-called *evil* removes guilt from the pointer and places him or her in the role of *good*.

More than an opinionated public speaker, Finis was the End of All Things. Obviously, he had a certain flair for ending an argument. His was often the last word in any discussion.

"I was quite enjoying the Requiem for Aia, people. Did we have to interrupt it with more bickering?" Despite his small stature, Finis shared Asalie's commanding presence.

Quondam and Munder both lowered their heads in shame and reverence.

"Quondam, if I might have a word with you, in private…?"

Finis led him to a quiet room down the hall, which also had a spectacular view of the infinite landscape, or lack thereof. Through the windows, which Aori had invented himself, stars twinkled in far off galaxies. "They say," Finis began, "that some of the stars have already died in the time it took for the light to reach us."

Quondam made an interested, yet barely audible, response. He felt as if he had just been reprimanded by his father, and he predicted the forthcoming lecture would be unbearable.

"It's a bit sad, when you think about it. Imagine no one knowing of your glory until well after you had already died."

Quondam thought for a moment. "Who will tell our story?" He had grown up with legends of brave heroes doing valiant deeds, and he had always longed to be one.

"The Coda, I suppose. We are fortunate that Aori captured and imprisoned them here."

Groaning, Quondam launched into his tirade. "All I hear about is Aori, and how fortunate we are. How fortunate that he committed those atrocious acts against the Coda, so that they can be around to sing for us now!"

"Many opportune events occurred, Quondam. The outcome could have been drastically different if not for...."

"Aori. And if Emperor Saturn hadn't been trying to speed up the growth of his larvae, Munder wouldn't have the timepiece. And if you hadn't killed every baby, wilted every beautiful flower, and took my parents away from me, what? What good came out of that horrible evil, Finis?"

Finis closed his eyes, as parents often do in a half-hearted attempt to calm their children. "It's not my job to show you the positive to every negative. Ask Asalie your question."

"I can't. She's playing grandma to an evil timelord."

"There you go again with the *evil* nonsense," grumbled Finis. "I think you use that word a bit much."

Tears welled up in Quondam's eyes as they reverted to an appropriate age. In his emotional, self-centered state, he

13

shouted, "How could Asalie betray me like that? I *worshipped* her!"

Finis had never had a knack for consolation. He often faced the drama of the dead person who felt quite emotional upon having died. Crying and carrying on made little difference in that particular situation. The songs and lamenting wails of the Coda, however, tugged at his heartstrings. He wasn't an unfeeling corpse; he just didn't know what to say to make people feel better.

"I'm pretty sure she's crazy, if that makes any difference." Finis patted the boy on the shoulder. "She's also dying...but I guess that doesn't help."

Quondam sniffled. "No, it doesn't. You'll just take her away from me too."

"Listen, kid. I don't take them away, and I certainly don't take them away from *you*. And Asalie isn't betraying you by mothering Aori. Kids need nurturing, and you'd understand that if you'd stop acting like a child."

"I am a child," Quondam whined. "And I never had that...nurturing."

Again, Finis faced the very real struggle between wanting the child to stop crying and his own inability to comfort. "Your mother," he began, "I remember the day she died."

"You knew my mother?"

"Of course I did. I'm Death incarnate. She was dead." Realizing his words could be a bit less harsh, he added, "She loved you. I could tell. She begged me to help you... to watch over you..."

Quondam swallowed the lump in his throat, but his eyes still felt heavy with tears.

"Of course, I'm not accustomed to watching over the living. However, I felt somehow that you did need protection. Have you ever wondered how you might have ended up, if you had gone to live with Aori and your grandparents, instead?"

14

"It couldn't have been worse than the orphanage," Quondam mumbled.

Finis gazed into the darkness, as if he were looking directly into the past. "Oh, I think it could have. That is why I think you are too narrow-minded when it comes to Aori. I believe he has been manipulated, just like the rest of us."

Quondam shook his head. "Manipulated? He's the one with all the machines... and machinations. Nobody forced him to cut down a whole forest."

"Speaking from experience," said Finis, "the gods often act through men. If not for the will of Death, do you think I'd hang out in a mausoleum surrounded by corpses? Do you think I would kill babies, as you so eloquently expressed?"

"The Timisters have always served Time, Quondam." Asalie stepped out of the shadows, and a dim light filled the room. She still held the child Aori in her arms. "Aori was but a third of the temporal trinity—god, man, and zeitgeist."

"Father, son, temporal spirit," echoed Finis.

Asalie continued, "It is hard for you to accept, Quondam, but your uncle did not wish to destroy the world. He began just as you did, with a fool-hearted and vainglorious attempt to fix time to his liking and change what he saw as the evils of Death and Time."

Quondam attempted to argue with her comparison, but the words just rotted on the vine. Asalie continued, "Just like your quest to save Munder, Aori enacted his own futile quests to resurrect his friends and family. By meddling with the forces of time, he became nothing more than a puppet for Toki, the Time god."

Quondam stopped glaring at the child and turned his gaze back to the stars.

Finis cleared his throat. "What happens to the Dying Embodiment of Life when everything dies?"

"She dies, I suppose," said Asalie. "We are both connected to Aia, Finis. We are nothing but disembodied

15

gods now. What happens to the Living Embodiment of Death when there's nothing left to die?"

"Maybe I'll live?" Finis's voice was optimistic. After having killed his own daughter and then himself, the mortal Finis had been doomed to an unending life as Death's incarnation on Aia. "If my work is done, maybe I'll just live a normal life. The curse is broken."

"Tragic death follows you everywhere, Finis. You cannot escape it. I am sorry."

"But, I haven't killed anyone," Finis countered, now feeling the emotion he had rebuffed in Quondam. He even felt the indignation of the child's sense of justice. "It truly isn't fair."

"Aia has died, Finis. Everyone has died. Nothing could be more tragic."

Unlike Finis, Asalie possessed, among her many magical abilities, the kind of hug that drives away gloom and sets the world right. Setting Aori down for a moment, she took Finis and Quondam into her warm and pacifying embrace.

For that moment, the world was right… except they were in-between-worlds at the moment.

Chapter 1:02

Stages of Development

Dirge touched his sister's hand, making a gentle vibration that only another Coda could have perceived. Able to pick up the slightest of sounds, Lithe could decode and interpret exactly what her brother was trying to communicate.

"We're not sure what day it is," she told him. "It's difficult to know without the cycles of the sun."

The young Codan boy vibrated a response.

"Oh Dirge, don't worry about that. We can celebrate your birthday any day of the year."

He didn't seem satisfied with her answer. When he had tried to take his own life using a piano chord, Dirge had been a little more than five years old. Now, he felt much older. Of course, psychological damage takes its toll. Besides the fact that Dirge had always been a solemn, melancholy youth compared to other Coda his age, he had also injured his vocal chords to such an extent that he could no longer speak. To a Coda, the ability to sing was vital, and the vocal chords were the most sacred of body parts. From a Codan perspective, Dirge's life was already over.

To occupy his time and get his mind off his psychological pain, Dirge worked with Notturno and other Coda in the

17

art of designing instruments. The ship provided many of the raw materials for woodworking, and Asalie assured them that the ship would not mind if they borrowed some of its wood. They gave back to the cycle, she told them, by creating new instruments and music.

Dirge fashioned a guitar similar to one he had owned before war devastated his hometown of Solace—before Aori's clockworkers captured him with the rest of the Coda. It had been an electric guitar, and despite the fact that electrical outlets had not yet been invented, he had used it to create stirring solos that might have been described as "death metal," in another time.

Dirge's new guitar, however, was acoustic. Though it sounded drastically different from his previous instrument, he still felt reluctant to play it. The last music he created also resurrected his family, an army of undead Coda, and a very important little girl named Harmony. Though Lithe often praised him for having restored peace among the various factions of Coda, he knew necromancy was a black art not to be taken lightly.

"Necromancy," Finis had told him, "uses magic to animate the dead. By calling on the forces of Death, the necromancer gains untold power. It is best to leave that kind of work to the professionals. Death is part of the great cycle, and you should never meddle with forces you do not fully understand."

Finis had always watched over Dirge, seeing as how most of the boy's music had been directed towards him. Since stopping Dirge's suicide attempt, the two had become almost inseparable. While they could not communicate by speaking to one another, Finis loved listening to Dirge's music, and Notturno would often sit in with them and interpret.

"They are kindred spirits," Notturno said of Dirge and Finis.

Lithe frowned. "Yes, I know."

18

"That troubles you?"

"I suppose it does," Lithe admitted. "I was gone for most of Dirge's life. This is our chance to reclaim all those lost years."

"He's growing up, Lithe. Young boys often dislike feeling watched over or coddled by their older sisters. Imagine what it has been like for him, growing up in your shadow."

Lithe parried and lunged at him, but offensive moves against Notturno were like trying to hit shadows. In fact, his skin itself somehow dodged the light in the room. Shadows clung to him like clothing. He evaded her attack and repositioned himself for a counter move.

"I coddle him?" Her question sounded more offended than angry, contrary to her actions.

"We all do. He is a child, and he has been through great stress at such a young age." Notturno pushed against her staff with his, causing Lithe to lose her footing.

Resuming her balance, she huffed, "I can help him cope with the loss of our family, as I have."

"Being a stone like your father is not coping, Lithe."

His words distracted her. She had not thought of the Odestone for some time. She had discarded it out of anger after learning that her father had been serving the Time god. In spite of her anger toward her father, the Odestone's current whereabouts concerned her.

Notturno's staff slammed into hers, shocking her out of the depths of thought. She backed away and bowed respectfully. "I'm sorry," she said. "I was distracted."

"I know," Notturno said. "Perhaps you are not coping as well as you believe."

"Perhaps you are right," she admitted, "but at the moment I'm preoccupied with what has become of the Odestone. I have to find Munder."

"Lithe, we are not done with your training," Notturno said.

Notturno was the leader of the Symphony, a secret organization made up of Codan warriors and spies. Lithe had worked all her life to be admitted to the organization, and she felt fortunate that Notturno was still around to teach her their ways. Most of the members of the Symphony had died, either in the Battle of Solace or with the destruction of Aia.

"This is important. I am sorry."

Munder stared at his wristwatch, which had formerly given him the ability to travel between time to a dimension appropriately called Tweentime. Trips that normally would have taken months became instant. In the future, the process is known as teleportation. Nevertheless, Munder missed that ability. The watch beeped sporadically, and digital numbers flashed upon it now and then, but it seemed, by and large, very dead. Uncontrollably, Munder did as many watch-owners futilely do; he tapped on the face watch. Obviously, nothing happened.

"Stupid watch," Munder muttered. He refocused his attention on his other timepiece—the one he had taken from Emperor Saturn of the Fellfalla. Being careful to hold it by the chain in order to prevent some sort of strange metamorphosis, Munder studied the pocket-watch. This timepiece, too, was broken, and its tick sounded something like a very confused drum major leading an even more confused percussion section.

Numerous and seemingly unconnected events had brought the timepiece to him. The Emperor had tried to develop an army of Fellfallan soldiers from the newest batch of larvae, but ended up being locked in a chrysalis state instead. The chrysalis was in turn eaten by Munder's pet caterpillar, Brahma, whose strange metamorphoses allowed Munder to travel across the world to Aori's tower just in time.

"Stupid worm," Munder muttered, referring of course to his quasi-friend and mode of transportation. "If you hadn't eaten the clock, Brahma, I might not have had to kill you."

"So that's how you got it?" Lithe had walked in so quietly that the ticking of the clock drowned out her footsteps. "I was afraid that you would resort to killing to get it, but I hoped that you had changed."

"I did," Munder stuttered. "I am. I changed." He had been caught off guard by her sudden appearance, and Lithe had always had a way of making him flustered.

"What about Daphni and the other Fellfallan knights?" Lithe continued to grill him. "Did you kill them, too?"

A bead of sweat pooled on Munder's forehead. He removed his helmet, which had been constructed for him by Brahma out of chitin, exoskeleton, or some other insectoid material. It had two long, spiraling horns, which very closely resembled those of the caterpillar form of Brahma. As if the helmet had protected him from remembering, Munder suddenly grimaced at the mental pain of memory.

Certain families in the hierarchy of Codan society share special gifts that set them apart from the general population. The Aeolian family, from which Lithe's mother descended, had always had a proficiency for controlling wind and air. Lithe's father came from the line of Dorian, who had made some unknown, and probably dark, pact with Tempo, the time god. In order to achieve immortality, those from the line of Dorian could also sing their souls into inanimate objects. Ode sang his into a stone, hence the name *Odestone*.

"I don't think I actually killed any of them. A couple fell into the Dead Sea, but I really didn't have anything to do with that. The stone told them to."

Lithe's concern doubled. "The stone? The Odestone? You mean, you still have it?"

"Yeah," answered Munder. "It tried to convince me to jump in the water also, but I couldn't. I had appointments to keep. Miles to go and all that."

"It's here? My father is here?"

Munder pulled the Odestone out of his pocket. "It's pretty quiet now. Maybe it's dead."

"It's a rock, Munder. Of course it's dead." Quondam entered the room and took the stone from the giant's hand. He looked it over, and tossed it back to his friend.

"Give it to me, Munder," Lithe tried to sing the command, but it came out more like a grumble.

Munder tossed the stone back to Quondam, thus beginning the playground game that would one day be called "Keep Away." It requires two very childish individuals to keep something away from another, always more logical and mature individual, who never enjoys the game.

Lithe stomped her foot. "Quon, please. Am I surrounded by children?"

"Pretty much," said Quondam. By this point, his base state had aged to roughly ten years old, which meant that his already self-centered immaturity had led him on a more callous path. Perhaps the act of his older selves' insulating him from mental pain had also desensitized him to the gamut of human emotion. Then again, perhaps kids are just cruel at that age.

"That is my father, Quon."

"Your father is a rock?"

"Yes."

Quon was confused. "I met your father. He was a bit old and stodgy, but he was a human, or Coda."

"I'll explain it to him later," said Munder, reveling in the fact that, finally, he knew more than his friend. "It's a long story, and it might be a bit painful for Lithe."

The friends had always harbored similar feelings of boyish attraction towards Lithe, with each of them trying to one-up the other to show off for her. Quondam detected the sycophantic nature of Munder's comments and shot him a dirty look.

22

"Stop trying to kiss up, Munder. You were just throwing her dad around the room."

Lithe sighed. "More importantly, Quon, Munder may have murdered good people because the stone told him to do it."

The news shocked Quondam out of his ten-year-old persona into an older, more serious expression. "You're evil again?"

Munder shoved him up against a wall with more force than he meant to exude.

"Obviously so," Quondam hissed through the pain, "Since you're trying to break my spine. I should have known you were evil, since you're so intent on keeping that timepiece."

"Stop. Both of you." Lithe's song immediately made them cease all action. "Quondam, you are not helping matters. I was interrogating him just fine on my own."

"Is that what this is," questioned Munder, "an interrogation? You guys going to lock me up in the tree's dungeon?"

"Munder, sit down," Lithe commanded. "Let's talk about this. First, let me have the Odestone. I promise I will return it if you so desire."

Munder set the Odestone on the table and sat in a wooden chair that was excessively small for him. Despite his immense weight, the *asa* wood stood firm. "Ask away."

"I don't have to. My father was a loremaster, and the stone picks up the vibrations of everything around it. In a sense, it gathers stories and allows him to retell them." Lithe held the stone in her hands and instantly learned everything that had transpired with the timepiece, the Fellfallan knights, and Munder.

"Well? Am I a murderer? Do we need to find some wooden handcuffs?"

Lithe gradually withdrew from her thoughts. "The matter with Brahma remains between you and your

23

conscience, Munder. From what I have gathered, you did not actually kill any of the Fellfalla. The fact remains, however, that tragedy follows that timepiece. By carrying it, you carry also death and destruction."

"Kinda fits my style, I'd say."

Quondam stepped away from the wall, which had been supporting the weight of his broken spine while it shifted to a sturdier state. "You could have picked a less dangerous accessory to your outfit."

Lithe set the Odestone on the table in front of Munder. "If it is important to you, take it. Personally, I want nothing to do with my father. I doubt I will ever understand his involvement with Tempo, nor can I feel comfortable with him around." She turned and left the room quickly.

"Way to go, idiot," Quondam said as he followed Lithe out of the room.

When he caught up with her in the corridor, he asked, "Do you think we should lock him up, just to be safe?"

Lithe kept walking. "I do not know."

A thought flashed in Quondam's mind, and he stopped in his tracks. "Do you think the Odestone told him to stop Aori?"

Lithe kept walking. "I do not know."

"If so, then maybe it was a good thing."

Lithe sighed impatiently. "We need to talk to the gods."

A Handy Guide to Whatever Everyone's Calling Time These Days

- Time, Lord of Time, Father Time, god of Time, etc.
- Toki (in the Orien language)
- Tempo (Codan)
- Priori (meaning "first" or "before," as opposed to Aori)
- Quartz Thymegarden (Gnomish)
- Aeon (occasionally used by Asalie and others)
- The Great Manipulator
- Various Expletives (mainly Munder)
- Chronos (Greek)
- Saturn (Roman)
- Heh or Huh (Agypsian / Egyptian)
- Timey McTimingham

Chapter 1:03

Ch-Ch-Changes

The gods, along with several of the other passengers of the ship, currently gave all their attention to the complete sentences from the mouth of babes—or in this case, one toddler by the name of Aori.

"Time still flows while we are on this trip," said the boy, "and while most of you have aged around two years, I have aged four."

"He doesn't sound like a four-year-old," grumbled Quondam.

"You would know, child," Aori retorted. "I have retaught myself to speak in the same manner I have taught myself everything else—time, diligence, and repeated trial and error."

"Good. You can speak. So tell us why you wrecked time and destroyed the world. And make it quick—I'm not getting any younger." As a punch line for his joke, Quondam shifted to his base age of ten.

Seldom amused by jokes, Aori chose to roll his eyes instead. From the perspectives of most of those in the room, the action looked horribly cute in the face of a four-year-old.

However, the tension in the room could be cut with a chainsaw.

"I did not destroy the world," Aori insisted. "The guilt for that act must solely weigh on your conscience, Quondam."

"Blithering fool," Quondam responded. He had shifted to an older age so that his oration and vocabulary would be more adult. "I'm the hero here. How could I have had anything to do with its destruction?"

Aori's eyes closed, presumably to shut out the memory of Aia's doom. "You prevented me from saving it."

"Poppycock! You wanted my timepiece because you feared that I would take your place as Father Time's favored son!"

"You didn't know how to use it properly. With that artifact, which was so foolishly given to you instead of me, I could have reversed the damage I had done to the planet. I could have saved the world, if not for your stubborn pig-headedness!"

At this, Finis chimed in, "Perhaps that was part of the Timelord's plan all along."

"Yes," Asalie assisted, "by separating the tool from the master, Time ensured that Aia would die. However, we cannot continue to quibble about who could have done what to save the planet. It was part of the Great Spiral's plan for Aia to die. It is all a part of the cycle."

"Is anyone else getting tired of hearing that?" Munder joined the rest of the group in his usual, uncouth manner. He looked down at the toddler in the center of the room. "Hey, Aori. How were those terrible twos? Must've been a bad couple of weeks for you. And who wants to go through teething a second time?"

Aori grinned sarcastically. "Ah, Munder. I've waited long for the ability to express my feelings toward you for sweeping in just in time to ruin everything. But it looks like the guilt has already wreaked havoc on your physical form."

28

"What?" asked Munder of the puzzled looks around the room. "What's he talkin' about? Did he just call me 'ugly,' with those high-dollar words? Well, at least I'm not a dumb kid."

"Munder…" Quondam stared up at Munder in mute wonder.

"Sorry Quon; I didn't mean no offense at that. I meant Aori was a dumb kid."

"I know, Munder. That's not it. You…you're a … monster."

"Now who's being offensive? I know I did some bad things, but I ain't no monster."

"One moment," interrupted Notturno, who had been keenly observing the entire conversation from the shadows of the room. "I know a song that might provide some illumination here. It is a glamour, of sorts."

The dark-skinned Coda began to play music that sounded very similar to something by David Bowie. As the music drifted through the room, glowing particles of magic gathered in a long oval shape. The song continued, and soon a mirror-image of Notturno appeared before him. In fact, all who looked upon it could see their image projected in the magic mirror, regardless of where they were positioned in the room.

When Munder gazed into the mystical energy, he saw a beast with dark fur and large horns that twisted in upon themselves in a spiral. In place of hands and feet, he had hooves; his wooden arm now had a wooden hoof. A snout had replaced his mouth and nose, but he retained his long, braided beard. Despite his beast-like form, he still stood on his two hind legs. With a voice that shook the walls, he yelled, "Stop that devil music!"

"It's not the music, dear," said Asalie. "I believe you have transformed into what is called a *ram*. Apparently, this is part of your personal growth cycle."

29

Munder interrupted, still shouting, "Cut it out with the 'part of the cycle' crap, lady. We've all had enough."

"Munder," Quondam tried to calm him.

"No. Anyone who is not a ram right now needs to just shut up. I've heard about all of your problems." In a high-pitched, mocking tone, he added, "'Asalie loves him more than me,' 'Dirge needs to lighten up,' 'I might be doomed to keep committing atrocious acts and then commit suicide...' Okay, that last one is a bit worse than this, but come on people! Can we just focus on me for a second—that is, without pointing fingers and calling me a murderer?"

"How did this happen, Munder?" Lithe moved closer to inspect his bestial form. Suddenly, the Odestone's account of Brahma's transformations clicked in her head. "You used the timepiece, didn't you?"

Munder turned toward a wall and rammed his head into it as softly as possible. The action, which signifies, "I can't believe what I just did," usually does less damage to the wall.

"I thought it would just change my age, like with Quon."

"Obviously, this timepiece works differently," said Lithe. "I suggest you never use it again. You might turn into something... more hideous."

"Thanks," said Munder.

Chapter 1:04

Never the Tweens Shall Mate

On Earth, when one travels across the International Dateline, yesterday waylays today, steals its credit cards, and commits identity theft for as long as it takes for the traveler to become accustomed to that "new time." In actuality, that imaginary line is humanity's arbitrary attempt at manipulating Time itself and harnessing a god's power. Nonetheless, it does tend to boggle one's mind when you arrive before you even left.

While the magic of time zones and datelines on Earth depends on the existence of watches and such, it really means nothing to primitive people who don't rely on such man-made contrivances. The magic that happened on the Woodship Timister, however, was honest-to-god (albeit, the god of Time, perhaps) magic.

On his eighth birthday, Aori focused intently on the wooden candles currently charring upon his cake. A remarkable choir of Codan well-wishers sang him their traditional birthday song, which was strangely very similar to the traditional American one. However, as with most Codan songs, a deeper power emanated from its performance, and most birthday-boys and girls found that wishes made while blowing out candles usually actually came true.

In Aori's case, his mind was elsewhere, or else*when*. As he focused on the eight flaming twigs, he imagined what the flames had been before—moments before a magical prelude to the Birthday Song had sparked them into being. He thought about the ever-changing flames, and how they never seemed to take the same shape twice. What shape would they take in half a breath's time? How long did the flames have before they would just sputter and die?

Aori's thoughts were the thoughts of a man contemplating more than just eight years, some presents, and a wish made upon exhale. The flames had become metaphors for—

"Blow out the candles already!" shouted Quondam, whose patience had just sputtered.

Munder joined in, "Please. The sooner you get it over with, the sooner they'll stop singing!"

Aori took a deep breath in, preparing himself for one of those exasperated sighs that he had grown so accustomed to making around his traveling companions. In the time between his inhale and exhale, however, he took the time to harness that universal, honest-to-Time-god magic. Instead of blowing out the candles, he focused intently on the flame, created a small bubble around the candle, and temporarily displaced it from its own time. When it came back, the candle was two minutes older than the rest of the inhabitants of the ship, and the flame had gone out.

Aori exhaled with a long sigh. For the last four years, Aori had been teaching himself how to use his Time-god-given talents, and trips to Tweentime had become almost as simple as walking through a door. Furthermore, by working problems in Tweentime, he was able to avoid the rapid aging he had experienced on Aia. In fact, sometimes he had to remind himself to age.

Of course, four years had passed for the other travelers as well. Quondam's base age of fourteen had developed him into a troubled teen. For one reason or another, he was always storming out of the room and slamming doors. Though he had passed into stages of development that are traditionally held to be less ego-centric, pubescence had dulled his ability to see multiple perspectives. In a nutshell, despite his mystical, magical age-changing powers, he had not actually changed much at all in the last four years.

"I'm so sick of celebrating birthdays," Quondam complained to anyone who was listening, which really amounted to no one. "Years don't even exist anymore. We're telling time by the rings of growth on a tree that doesn't even need the sun to grow. How do we know it's not *my* birthday today? I'd like a cake too, please. Where's my---."

Quondam stopped abruptly, because in less than a second, his tongue left its timeline, dried out a bit, and phased back into his mouth. He no longer had anything to say because his tongue had already finished his rant in Tweentime.

Meanwhile, Aori smiled at his accomplishment.

Wiping a bit of sweat from her brow, Asalie went back to work baking another birthday cake. According to her personal philosophy, life begins with the dawn of each new day. Regardless of the fact that dawns and dusks were unnoticeable without a horizon, she held firm to her beliefs. Every day, someone on the ship had a birthday, despite the fact that no one remembered the current date.

She had always fit the role of the archetypal grandmother, so spending all her time baking just made sense. Plus, the cyclical repetition of the task comforted her and took her mind off other things. Of course, she never ceased in her mantra, "It is all part of the cycle."

That particular cake had been specifically designed for Dirge, with the shape of a guitar and eleven wooden candles on the top. However, despite his age, Dirge still appeared to be five years old. While the rest of the ship's passengers had grown older around him, he had not aged a day since his attempted suicide.

Everyone tried not to talk about it, but the passengers often found themselves whispering their concerns to Lithe. She always tried to remind them politely that, though he was mute, he could hear even the faintest whisper. In truth, the ship's perfect acoustics ensured that every sound vibrated clearly in his pointed, highly-specialized Codan ears. Tuning out the incessant chatter of his fellow passengers had become Dirge's greatest concern, and he could find solace only in playing his music loudly.

When he wasn't brooding alone in his room, he was staring out into the dark void with Finis. Dirge found the company of Death incarnate to be a breath of fresh air, so to speak, because Finis had lived his life in silent tombs. It is said that there is no silence like that of the grave.

When he spoke, Finis addressed Dirge directly, rather than speaking about him in hushed whispers as the other passengers did. He listened when Dirge played his requiems and threnodies, and he appreciated them in the way Marilyn Monroe must feel when she hears "Candle in the Wind."

"Your life has not ended, Dirge," said the living representation of Death.

Dirge continued to play his guitar, as if that was his way of contributing to the conversation.

"I know what you felt that day, when you took your own life."

His song became slower, with prolonged sustain on each note.

"I have been inside the heads of all souls in that hour of desperation." Finis struggled with his words, as positive affirmations had never been his style. "You did a truly noble thing in sacrificing yourself so that your powers could not be used for evil."

Dirge struck a wrong note.

"However, I know that you truly wanted to die that day."

34

He stopped playing.

"You wanted to end it all, and embrace the comfort of nothingness. In the void, there is no pain, thought, or feeling. I understand, Dirge, because I have felt it too."

The two kindred spirits stared out in the vast blackness of space. Finis continued, "It no longer comforts me, Dirge. The veil of death does not keep me warm; it smothers me. I want my existence to mean something more, Dirge. You are blessed, because obviously you were meant to survive."

Dirge turned his gaze from the nothingness of space to the nothingness of the Death god. Something clicked inside him, and he felt pity for the deity. He knew that Finis could no longer serve as the physical embodiment of Death.

"It is not usually my place to convince people to live. Usually, I welcome them with open arms. You have a purpose, though. You have a reason to live, and gods help me, I wish I could show you how."

Dirge wrote a new song that day, which made them both feel better. It may have been humanity's first anti-depressant. Of course, as many commercials for such medications also indicate, there are often side effects.

"Come on, Munder," Quondam urged. "It will be fun."

"For you, maybe," Munder grumbled.

"I'll even make myself a little kid so I'm not too heavy."

"You're *acting* like a little kid."

"Just give me a ride, Munder."

"Promise you'll shut up if I do?"

"Promise."

They gave each other the same kind of mischievous grin that used to be a harbinger of every bit of trouble they caused together at the orphanage, and Quondam jumped on his back.

Meanwhile, Aori stood at the window of his room and examined it closely. The longer he stared, the more frequently he glimpsed flashes of the window's history. He saw it as super-heated sand particles, as thousands of shards as Crowfoot crashed through it, and finally he watched it magically grow back just as the atmosphere thinned around them. "Asalie was right. Even the window exists in a cycle."

Though he knew his patience had improved considerably, Aori felt that the trip was taking far too long. He wasn't sure where they were headed, but the voyage had already gone on for several years, and it didn't seem as if they were getting any closer to anything.

He sat down in front of his *Epic* game board and studied the pieces. The game reminded him of his old friend and mentor, Bertram. He had been so single-minded in his goal to resurrect his friend that he didn't realize all the suffering he had caused around him. Countless innocents had been dragged out of their homes by his clockworkers just to serve his selfish schemes.

Holding the game-piece of Bertram in his hand, Aori whispered, "Old friend, wherever you are, I hope you are finally at rest. I toiled for so long to bring you back, but maybe Asalie was right about that, too. Your energy is out there in the Great Spiral, waiting to be re-manufactured into something new."

Aori surveyed the rest of the game-pieces he had carved so long ago. One, which he now recognized as Munder, had taken on the giant's new animalistic features. Though he had not known Munder at the time of its creation, Aori assumed that the magic of the *asa* wood had played a part in their shaping.

Next to Munder, as always, was the game-piece for Quondam. It currently looked like a small child, and though it pained Aori to hold such feelings toward one who appeared so young, he could not contain his bitter resentment. He felt better knowing that the feeling was mutual.

"So, you're my nephew," Aori told the game-piece. "I wonder now, in what ways Father Time would have manipulated you, had your mother not hidden you from the family. Would you have been able to withstand the temptations I could not? If you had been given my power, would you have caused such utter destruction?"

As he focused on the game-piece, a bubble of Tweentime formed around it. As the object popped out of real-time, an idea suddenly popped into Aori's head. With the deepest concentration, he cupped his hands into a bowl shape. Eventually, a sphere flickered into view in his hands, and a beautiful blue energy swirled throughout the shape. If his thoughts broke away from the sphere for even a second, he knew it would pop, and he wasn't sure what would happen if it did. He tried not to think about what might occur and chose to just focus on making the bubble bigger.

A distant sound, similar to thunder, caught his attention and the spheroid shape wavered ever so slightly. *Focus*, he thought. *It's just the Codan marching band.* With a bit more intense thought, he got the bubble to reach to the ceiling. At that point, it had already absorbed a few objects in the room, and Aori could see the objects swirling inside his sphere.

Boom. The surface of the sphere rippled.

Boom. The sound was getting louder, and the ripples were turning into waves.

BOOM! Pieces of Aori's door exploded across the room, and a large, black thing crashed through the doorway. Aori looked up from his task just in time to see Munder's horns coming right for him. He shouted, and in his anger, he lost control of the sphere. The bubble burst, and everything the blue, swirling energy filled the room.

"Munder! You idiot! What did you do?"

Momentum carried the giant forward, but he no longer felt anything substantial beneath his feet. A bluish-white glare invaded his sense of sight. "Hold on. I think we're going to crash."

37

Nervously, Quondam replied, "I think we already crashed."

"Maybe we're dead," Munder suggested.

Aori sighed. "I should have known you'd be involved as well, Quondam. Couldn't you children have played in a different part of the tower? It *is* rather large, you know."

"Sorry," Quondam said. "Where are we?"

Aori looked around. "I believe we're in Tweentime."

"Looks different in this part," Munder mumbled. "Where's the ground?"

"Well, we're in the middle of outer space at the moment… or in between this moment and the last one." Quondam felt uneasy. "Can… Toki find us here? Does he have some way of detecting intruders?"

"I don't think so," said Aori. "I've been here before, and I never even saw him. Of course, I suppose that doesn't mean he wasn't aware of my presence."

Quondam's uneasiness persisted. "Can you get us back?"

"I think so. I've only been here in astral form; it may be different with physical bodies."

"…And three of them, at that," muttered Quondam.

"Oh, it's not that bad," said Munder. The others eyed him suspiciously. He continued, "I used to take large groups through all the time. You know, Quon. Remember my battalion? Ah, those were the days."

"Yeah…Could we stop reminiscing about the good old days of trying to kill me and focus on the now, please?" Quondam punched him in the arm.

"Well, I always used my watch to travel between here and…there, but it's very broken."

"Wait," Aori butted in, "when you used Tweentime to travel, did you come out at the same place you entered?"

"No, I could pretty much go anywhere, as long as I knew how long it would take to travel there. It was really confusing at first, but--."

38

"This is perfect!" Aori shouted excitedly. "Of course, we don't know how long it will take to get wherever it is we're going, but we can assume that in an hour, we'll be closer to our destination, correct?"

Quondam and Munder nodded. The confusion bounced between them like a match of ping-pong.

"Think about where we will be in five minutes if we keep traveling on this course," Aori instructed them.

Munder raised his hand. "Um... I'm going to venture a guess and say... space."

Aori closed his eyes. "Just concentrate." As he imagined the deep vastness of space, he felt another sphere growing in between his palms. As he looked inside it, he could see the great wooden rocket, surrounded by utter darkness. He stretched his mind and the sphere stretched with it. It seemed easier to enlarge the bubble when inside Tweentime.

Soon, the bubble was large enough to encompass even Munder's massive bulk. Slowly, Aori let the surface of the sphere wrap around them, and then they were looking out at the blue, swirling energy of Tweentime from inside the bubble.

The air was very thin, and getting thinner. Aori's concentration waned and the bubble popped, leaving them stranded in the middle of outer space. In the distance, he could see the wooden ship, but he knew it wouldn't reach them for another five minutes.

"Brilliant idea," Quondam tried to shout, but in space, no one can hear that sort of thing.

Chapter 1:05

Across the Universe in Two Shakes of a Ram's Tail

"Oh dear!" Asalie sprang from her bed and ran to a window. "Are you sure they left? I can't see them anywhere," she spoke aloud, but no one shared the room with her.

She gently caressed the wooden wall surrounding the windowpane. "I understand. We have to help them." As she touched the wood, the skin tone of her hand gradually grew to match the dark red color of the *asa*. In a matter of minutes, her whole body seemed to be a part of the ship. She walked into the wall and it absorbed her.

From Aori's perspective, the structure of the wooden rocket appeared to change. Of course, it was all he could do not to implode, so he didn't fully appreciate the long branch growing from the tip of the rocket.

Had Aori and the others noticed the new growth, they might have felt that warm feeling one gets when recognizing an old friend in a time of need, as the branch looked exactly like Asalie. She stretched her arms out as far as they could go, and the branch of the rocket stretched with her.

41

Instinctively, Aori built another sphere and wrapped it around them. Through the swirling surface of the sphere, he could see the Asalie-shaped branch growing towards them. Fortunately, the sphere protected them and prevented their eminent suffocation, but it also meant that Asalie wouldn't be able to see them. He would have to get the timing just right to break the bubble just as the branch reached their position.

It took quite a bit less than five minutes for the rocket to reach them, due to the growth rate of the Asalie-branch. As soon as Aori felt that he could reach out and grab her, he grabbed Quondam and Munder, popped the bubble, and fell into the warm safety of Asalie's gentle, yet wooden, arms.

Immediately, the three of them experienced a strange wooden taste in their mouths. They passed through the wooden walls of the ship like plant cells moving through phloem by osmosis. Munder was used to looking at his wooden hand, but he did find it a bit disconcerting when his entire body appeared to be made of fibrous plant tissue. He could feel water and nutrients passing through his body on their way to the rest of the tree, which created in him a very strong urge to go to the restroom.

When Munder passed through to the other side, that wooden feeling subsided, and he felt his body returning to its normal (though still ram-shaped) form. When he tried to move his wooden arm, however, he was shocked to discover that it was still embedded in the wall. He pulled at it with all of his strength, but it wouldn't budge. Apparently, it wanted to return to its roots, so to speak.

"Hey," Munder shouted. "I need my arm back, thank you!"

Quondam couldn't help but laugh. "Did you try pulling it out?"

Munder shot him a dirty look. "It's not funny. I'm going to be stuck like this forever."

"You could always hack your arm off. Want me to go get your axe?"

42

"Yes!" Munder shouted. "Do it!"

Quondam laughed. "Just wait. I'm sure Asalie can help."

Aori tried to explain his plan for quicker travel to Asalie, but she was understandably leery of anything involving Time magic. Besides, his last attempt to use Tweentime to travel almost killed him and the others.

"I could put a sphere around the whole ship, Asalie. It would work. I know it would."

Asalie smiled at him, as a grandmother would smile at the fool-hearty ideas of her imaginative grandson. "Aori, you must be patient. We will reach our destination soon enough."

"This time, it's not about my impatience. I predict that this journey will take longer than the span of our lives. Many of the Coda are already old and decrepit."

"Aori. If we are meant to die of old age on this voyage, then that is what the Great Spiral intends. We are but a part of the...."

Aori stopped paying attention before she even got to her favorite phrase. He was already working his plan over in his brain. If he could take the entire ship through Tweentime, he could shorten their trip by a fraction of its duration. It would be like taking a shortcut.

Quondam walked up in time to overhear most of the conversation. "How will we know how long it will take to get to ... wherever it is we're going?"

"I'm working on that. I just need to do a few more calculations."

"Take your time," Quondam mumbled. "We're not going anywhere."

That night, they scheduled a meeting in the large common room for all of the passengers to attend. Asalie, who was otherwise very open-minded by nature, just stood by the wall like an old, unbending oak tree. She seemed to be

43

mumbling softly to herself, though she might have been talking to the ship.

The Coda mostly sat together, but Dirge chose to sit next to Finis. Notturno sat in front of the group, as he was usually their spokesman and leader in most affairs. Lithe, who had always had trouble sitting still for too long, paced across the room. She avoided Quondam and Munder, as she had already chastised them earlier for getting into an adventure without her.

Munder chose to stand very close to the wall, since his arm had not yet been dislodged, and Quondam forced himself to sit very far away in order to keep from giggling at his friend's misfortune.

Aori stood in the center of the room and tried to look as tall and important as possible, despite his youthful appearance. His top hat, which had come to feel like an extension of him, no longer fit his head. He had it stuffed with scraps of fabric to keep it from slipping down over his eyes.

He told the group about their recent experience and explained Munder's past travels through Tweentime in a much less confusing manner. "Time and space work differently in Tweentime, so you could make a two-day trip in a quarter of the time."

"The problem," Quondam added, "is that we have to know where we're going, and how long it will take us to get there."

"Obviously we do not wish to end up in the black void, as you did," Notturno pointed out. "Can we stay inside the ship?"

"Yes," Aori assured them. "I believe I can create a sphere that will take the entire ship through Tweentime and take a shortcut."

"A shortcut to where?" Ever the pessimist, Finis asked, "What if it is a dead end, Aori?"

Lithe chimed in, "What happens if we return from Tweentime in the middle of a planet or star? I'd say *that* would be a dead end."

Mumbles of dissent undulated through the crowd. Everyone shared a collective anxiety, though many of the Coda knew very few words in the Common language. The tension in the room was palpable, and it transcended the confines of language barriers.

Aori tried to speak, but the clamor of the crowd drowned out his voice. The noise chipped away at his patience and eroded his temper. He shouted, "Silence! This is my ship. I built it, and I will decide its fate. You all can either come along for the ride or stay right here."

The crowd got very silent.

Quondam stood up and moved to the center of the room. He shifted to an older, more respectable age. "Look," he began, "you all know that I have not seen eye to eye with Aori very often, and I still don't really trust him. He's probably going to kill us all someday, but…."

Aori stared at him blankly. "Is this your way of helping?"

Quondam continued, "If he was truly as evil as I believed he was, he would have killed me in my sleep long ago. I guess that really struck me when we were out in space. He could have just left me out there to die, or locked me away in Tweentime for all of eternity. I, for one, would like to hear the rest of his plan."

Aori took a deep breath to calm his nerves. "We know that we have been traveling for roughly six years. Since we don't see any nearby planets, we could assume that we're at least six years away from anywhere. We don't know where we'll be in six years, but we know we'll be closer than we are now. We just have to take a chance."

Quondam raised his hand. "If you agree that we should travel through Tweentime, raise your hand." Giggling hysterically, he added, "…unless your hand is stuck inside a wall, that is."

"Funny," Munder grumbled. He raised his remaining hand.

Lithe looked over at Dirge, who was trying to convince Finis to raise his hand. She stretched her arm upward and her long arm came close to touching the ceiling. Dirge smiled at her and raised both his hand and Finis's.

Notturno touched the Codan woman closest to him and vibrated the proposed vote to her in Codan. This manner of communicating took far less time and got the message across more completely than even his most poetic of words could have done. The group of musicians collectively raised their hands in agreement.

Asalie spoke in a deep, solemn voice that was almost mumbling, "I will go wherever the Spiral takes me, but I fear for what will happen to the *asa* when Time steps aside to make room for us."

"I will keep us shielded from the effects of Tweentime, so that our personal timelines will not be affected," Aori promised. "The *asa* will experience only a brief period of displacement, and we should all only age a few days in the entire six-year trip."

Asalie hesitantly raised her hand. "Let us pray that you have the power to keep your promise."

Aori created a small sphere and gently moved his hands inside it. Instantly, he could feel a tingle in his fingers, as if they had suddenly become mixed up with the fingers of one second ago. He stretched out the bubble so that it fit around his entire body. Once in Tweentime, manipulating the energy took less mental strain, and he was able to wrap a thick layer of magic around the entire ship.

The displacement of such a massive object resulted in the creation of a black hole in the space where it had been.

The phenomenon would make for a very interesting tale, but it actually plays no part at all in this particular story.

The passengers looked out the windows into the violet swirls of Tweentime. "Amazing," remarked Notturno. "We have escaped the confines of Time itself."

"Well," replied Aori, "I believe we are actually sneaking around between the minutes, or measures."

"Yes, I'm sure we are very stealthy and inconspicuous in a giant clock-tower rocket-ship," Munder harrumphed. His arm remained firmly stuck inside the ship's wall; therefore, his disposition remained firmly stuck in the negative.

Quondam gazed out into what appeared to be an infinite amount of nothing. "So…How are we all going to focus on the same unknown destination?"

Aori walked over to a dark window on the other side of the room. "If we just imagine covering a lot of distance, we will hopefully see any approaching planets through this window over here. This is our view of the space outside of Tweentime."

Quondam tried to picture a planet inside his mind, but Aia was the only one he had ever seen. Calling on the memory banks of his future selves, he tried to predict what would one day be his home. Still, he pictured the dense forest of the Nutberry O, the not-quite-bustling city of Auldenton, and all the other land features of his former home planet.

"What's that?" Lithe peered out the window at a small speck in the distance.

The other passengers rushed to join her. "It appears to be a small moon."

"That's no moon," said Quondam. "It's Aia."

"It can't be," Lithe argued. "We saw it crumble."

Aori stroked his beard, or the beard he should have had, had he not been currently eight years old. "Perhaps we are

47

seeing the Aia between its current state and its past. It is very intriguing, but what is it doing here?"

Quondam swallowed hard. "I think I may have brought us here."

"What? How?"

"I tried picturing the planet of our future, which I should have been able to do, since my future selves are currently living there, theoretically, but I guess I couldn't do that because all I really know is Aia, so my frame of reference is limited in scope, and... I'm sorry."

Aori sighed. He snapped, "Quondam, that means we just backtracked the entire distance it just took us six years to travel!"

"I know," Quondam buried his head in his hands. "I'm sorry."

"How could you be so vastly ignorant? You, of all people, should have had the foresight and presence of mind to avoid such a grievous error! Didn't your future self mention something about not ruining our entire trip?"

"Hey now," interrupted Munder. "Tone it down, Gramps. Only I can insult Quon like that."

Quondam began to sob softly into his hands.

"Surely you must understand the temporal magic you possess, Quondam. Why the god of Time entrusted such power to a child, I shall never understand."

With that, Quondam ran out of the room crying. Appropriately, his body shifted to an age that was more accustomed to bawling.

"Aori," Lithe shouted in a melodic note that ceased all sound within the room. "That's enough! Aia is all that any of us knows. We probably all pictured our home at the same time. There is no need to be so harsh."

Sobs sent shockwaves throughout Quondam's shoulders. He gave in to the force of the emotions; his younger selves had needed a good cry for a long time. "Everything is all my

48

fault," he sniffed. As young children often do, Quondam let himself get caught up in the dramatic exaggeration.

"I was the hero. I was going to save the world, and instead I just got in the way. And now, I've led us right back to my failure."

He felt a hand on his shoulder and instinctively jumped. Looking around, he noticed that he was all alone in the darkened corridor. "Who's there?"

"Just you," said a gruff voice.

"Who are you?"

"You. You remember me. I'm the you that you will one day be."

"So, in the future I talk in circles?"

The voice laughed. "In the future, everyone talks in circles. It's the coolest."

Looking at his reflection in a window, Quondam saw the old man who had spoken to him previously, during his trip to the underworld and in this very corridor, before Aia's doom came to pass. "I don't understand how I could be talking to myself, when you won't exist until I'm much older."

"People with dissociative identity disorder often have conversations with their multiple personalities," said the old man condescendingly.

"Oh. I see. You're what happens to me in the future, after my mind fractures?"

"In a sense, I suppose. However, I can feel your mind breaking a bit right now."

"Of course," said Quondam. "They say you're not insane if you talk to yourself—only if yourself talks back to you."

To make matters worse, the old man suddenly appeared next to Quondam in the reflection. Quondam tried shaking his head and rubbing his eyes, but he still saw double images of himself reflected in the glass.

"You look like you could use a hug," said the old man. He spread his arms wide and embraced Quondam.

49

"If you can't hug yourself, who can you hug?" Quondam smiled, as he had to agree that he had needed that hug indeed. "Do multiple personalities always manifest in the physical realm?"

"Maybe," the old man shrugged. "You should start studying that now, so that I'll know the answer. Then, I could tell you all about it."

"Good idea," said Quondam. His head hurt.

"Now, to solve your problem: I know where you're headed."

"You do?"

"Of course, silly. I lived there for most of my life, remember?"

"Actually, I don't remember, but I'll take your word for it." Quondam rubbed his throbbing temples.

The old man walked past several of the corridor's windows, which made them spring to sudden life. They looked like television sets, and each showed a different image of land features that vaguely resembled Aia. Quondam had seen the windows used in this manner before, on his first visit to this corridor. The old man had activated them at that time, too.

"Is that Aia?"

"No, idiot. Aia's dead."

"Excuse me," Quondam glared at the old man. "I don't believe I would insult myself like that, in the future."

"You're right," said the old man. "I'm sorry. I just forgot how ignorant... how little I once knew." He awkwardly patted Quondam on the back. "There there. Feel better now?"

"I would also hope that I'd be more comforting in the future."

The old man gave a listless, half-roll of his eyes. "Well, I've been through a lot. May I continue?"

"Please do."

"The planet you see in the images is called Earth. Memorize it, so that you can fix your mistake and get back into the good graces of your group. They need you to be their hero. Aori cannot save them. Only you are powerful enough to turn the tide."

"What tide?"

"Just focus," the old man replied. "Be the hero. Get your team back on track."

"What track? Are you saying we're just following a predetermined path?"

The old man started walking away, down the spiraling staircase at the end of the corridor. "Do you really think the ship just flew itself for six years? Now, go back to your friends."

Just as Quondam returned to the common room, Aori noticed the approaching blue, green, and white planet in his view-screen. "We made it!"

"It's called Earth," Quondam announced. "I thought of it, and here we are."

The others gathered around the view-screen. Lithe kissed him on the cheek. "I knew you could do it, Quondam. All you had to do was stretch your mind."

A smile spread across the hero's face, and he felt better than he had in six years.

Chapter 1:06

The Landing

"It's beautiful," Lithe remarked. "It looks just like Aia."

The Odestone vibrated in Munder's pocket, causing him to jump. "Apparently your dad has something to say about that."

The smile left Lithe's face. "Give it to Notturno. He'll translate for us."

Munder threw the stone at him, and Notturno began to translate the vibrations into spoken language. "Ode says that there was an old folktale on Aia that had been handed down from generation to generation about the creation of twin planets. He speculates Earth and Aia were those twins, and that they were apparently separated at birth."

"Lovely story," said Aori, who took little stock in the lore of man. He approached the world from a more scientific viewpoint, which he also saw as more reasonable and logical. Being a writer himself, he felt that he could have just as easily written a similar far-fetched story to explain the things he had already discovered through science.

Asalic muttered something inaudible under her breath. She sat in a darkened corner of the room, rocking back and forth in a wooden rocking chair that the ship had apparently grown especially for her. Aori's opinions often differed from her own; she loved the way that stories grew upon each other and evolved into similar tales for a different civilization. However, in her current state of mind, she could not have argued that point.

"Hey hero," Munder muttered. "You know so much about this Planet Earth, so tell us—how does it feel to crash into it?"

Still riding high on having saved the day, Quondam shrugged off his friend's taunt. "I don't remember that it kills us all, so it couldn't be that bad."

"As long as we are in Tweentime," Aori assured them, "we should be able to control how fast we reach the ground."

"We hope," said Munder.

As the ship descended through Earth's atmosphere, Aori concentrated on their destination. Through the windows, the passengers could watch as the purple swirls of Tweentime reorganized into what looked like clouds.

It continued to rocket towards the surface of the planet, as if its travel was stuck on "fast-forward," and in many ways, it was. Finding the violet, swirling view a bit nauseating, several of the passengers decided to assume a more comfortable crash-position elsewhere in the tower. However, Quondam and Aori remained in front of the view-screen as they watched a large body of water get closer and closer.

At this point in time, the waters of the Persian Gulf reached much further north, engulfing much of the Tigris and Euphrates Rivers and stretching relatively close to the Red Sea on the west. The waters had been receding for hundreds of years since the Great Flood.

"Brace yourselves," Quondam shouted. Panic spread through the passengers, and the tension stretched like a rubber band about to snap.

"In the unlikely event of a water-landing," Munder added, "your seat-cushion can be used as a flotation device."

"Munder, you're not helping!" Lithe tried to clear her mind and think of the song she had played previously to slow a fall. Clouds whipped past the view-screen, and sweat dripped from her forehead. As faithful readers may remember, Lithe's Lyric of Levitation, which her mother taught her long ago, simply contained the words, "la la la."

Whether by the magic of Lithe's song or the temporal fluctuations of Tweentime, the ship froze just inches above the surface of the water. A collective, audible exhale of relief filled the room.

Aori released the bubble from around the ship and it fell the last few inches into the water. Obviously, since it was a wooden ship, it floated. If any onlookers had seen the ship floating there, the sight might have reminded them of a story about a similar wooden boat that had existed in these parts just a few hundred years before this time.

As the ship had landed in an upside-down, but upright position, it bobbed like a cork for a while before finding its center of gravity. The rocking motion soothed Asalie, but many found it rather sickening. When it had settled, it floated at an acute angle with the surface of the water, with the heavier base of the tower submerged somewhat. The angle made walking in the ship a bit of a hassle, but the younger passengers (except Aori, of course) saw it as a fun challenge.

The strain of maintaining the bubble for so long had severely taxed Aori, so he excused himself to his room. Of course, the frequent rocking of the ship had toppled many of his belongings, and he had to set his bed back on its feet before crashing into it.

The other passengers followed suit, assuming that the ship would continue to pilot itself. Lithe and Quondam,

55

however, stayed behind with Munder, whose arm still held securely inside the wall. That particular wall currently served as the ceiling, so he hung from that point like a chandelier. With the weight of his giant body pulling against his arm, he felt considerable pain.

"At least you didn't get all jostled around like the rest of us," Quondam tried to mollify the angry giant.

"I'm sure Asalie could help get you out," Lithe assured him. "I don't know why we didn't think of that earlier."

"*I* know why," Munder snapped, in an accusatory manner. "You guys wanted me here. This is my prison. You thought everyone would be safer if the animal was chained to the wall."

"Well, it's not really a chain…" Quondam muttered, "…and now it's the ceiling."

Lithe gave him a look and tried to defend herself. "Munder, do you really believe we would do that to you?"

Munder just looked away.

"Let's go find Asalie," suggested Quondam.

Left alone with his pain, Munder could feel the roots of his arm growing. With his arm upright, its natural geotropism meant that roots would grow in the direction of the pull of gravity. They were spreading across his chest and shoulder, which felt like a large animal's jaw closing on his bones. Blood oozed out from the places where the roots took hold, and the giant screamed in agony.

Upon hearing Munder's scream, Quondam and Lithe quickened their pace to Asalie's room. When they got to her door, they exchanged puzzled looks. "That wasn't there before, right?" asked Quondam.

Due to the angle of the ship, the entrance to the room was positioned on the floor, and it no longer even closely resembled a door. Where the door had been, a large tree grew. Moss and vines covered its bark, but the trunk of the tree itself looked rotten and dead.

56

Lithe knocked on the mossy bark, but it barely made a sound. "Asalie? We need your help. Could you open your door, please?" They heard no response, so they both banged on the wood loudly.

"I have an idea." Quondam unsheathed his sword, which had remained wooden and non-lethal ever since he had tried to use it against Aori so many years ago. "I hope this doesn't hurt her," he said as he stabbed the sword into the trunk of the tree.

As soon as the sword touched the wood, it began to grow. As the wooden composition of the sword spread up his arm, Quondam felt as he had when Asalie had pulled him through the walls of the ship. Eventually, his whole body felt as if it were made of wood.

Unfortunately, whatever disease had turned the bark of the door-tree black and rotten also spread through the sword and into Quondam. He felt woozy and nauseous, but he knew that he couldn't vomit with a wooden digestive system. He tried coughing, but his lungs wouldn't cooperate. It seemed that a black cloud of haze was overtaking him, and the rotten wood around his ears eventually muted Lithe's worried screams.

Just as he felt the growth overtaking the last of his humanity, Quondam felt a tugging sensation at his roots, or feet. His body shortened, and he ended up in Asalie's room, just below where he had been standing.

Spasms convulsed throughout his body, and he coughed up twigs and moss. Slowly, he felt his skin and bones returning to normal. His lungs went back to breathing oxygen instead of carbon dioxide, and his sword no longer looked rotten and black.

Looking around the room, he noticed that the roots of the door-tree took up most of the space. They stretched down from the ceiling, crept outward to all the corners, and attached, at their thickest point, to the withered and rotten body of Asalie.

The shock of the image knocked Quondam almost to the floor. "Asalie?" he whispered, in the type of voice one would expect from vocal chords that had recently been plant tissue.

She tried to smile, but it looked more like wrinkled bark.

"What is happening to you? How long has this been going on?"

Asalie spoke, and it sounded like trees creaking in the wind. "Hundreds of years, child."

Suddenly, Quondam remembered what Finis had called her: *the dying embodiment of life.* "But, you were fine a few minutes before the crash. Why the sudden change?"

"Whatever disease grows inside me was abated while we were in Tweentime. We skipped six years' worth of traveling, but I'm afraid the time has caught up to me."

"Are you…" he choked on a lump in his throat, "…going to die?"

The roots in the room embraced Quondam in a gentle hug. Asalie whispered, "I hope not. I sense that there is much to discover on this planet, and our journeys begin again here."

The child in Quondam spoke up. "I don't want any more journeys. I'm sick of adventures." Tears streamed down his cheeks.

She wiped his tears away with dried leaves. "No matter what happens to me, child, I will always be with you. I will grow in every leaf, every blade of grass. This is not the end."

"I have so much more to learn from you. I wasted the last few years being mad at you for spending so much time taking care of Aori, when I should have been taking care of *you.*"

At this, Asalie laughed. The roots shook with her laughter, and the trunk swayed on the floor above them. "You may still get a chance to care for me, child. I apologize for neglecting you in nurturing your uncle, but I hoped to raise him up right this time. You grew up just fine without my help."

Quondam wiped away his tears. He wrapped his arms around the fibrous growth that had once been Asalie's body, and he squeezed as hard as he could. The tighter he held her, the more tears flowed out of his eyes. When he opened them, everything was a blurry mess.

Through blurred vision, it appeared that the roots were withdrawing back into Asalie. The trunk of the tree above him got smaller, and the mass of her body diminished. Pride swelled up inside him, as he felt that he had once again saved the day.

However, as he held her body in his arms, he noticed that the entire room was changing. The wood of the walls was gradually turning into brick. Quondam rubbed his eyes, thinking the blur of the tears had played tricks on his vision. With the tree gone and the walls turned to brick, it seemed as if he was in an entirely different room. Even the position of the door had changed back to where one would normally find a door.

It opened, and Lithe stood in the doorway. "What happened?"

"I have no idea," he answered.

"Is… she…"

Looking down at Asalie, Quondam could tell that her chest was moving. Whatever happened had probably saved her life, but she was no longer conscious. "I think she's alive."

Chapter 1:07

The Tower

The entire ship had changed. As he carried Asalie down the hall, the complete lack of anything wooden struck Quondam as very confusing. At the end of the hall, they could see sunlight pouring in through windows. Plants hung from the ceiling, and beautiful flowers grew in a garden between the slabs of dried brick.

"This seems like a good place for her to rest," he said as he set Asalie down among the flowers.

"Will she be okay if we leave her alone?" asked Lithe.

"I think she needs good soil and healthy plants around her more than she needs us."

Lithe grabbed his arm. "Did you hear that?"

"No, what was it?"

"It sounded like voices," Lithe whispered.

"We're not exactly alone on the ship. It could have been anyone."

"No… they spoke a different language, and I think I would recognize any of the voices of the passengers."

The sound of footsteps got closer and closer, so that eventually even Quondam could hear them. Quondam drew his sword, just in case. Lithe tensed up like a cat, ready to spring.

Two men with dark skin and flowing robes came around the corner. They both had black beards, and they wore sandals. One can imagine their surprise when they saw the strangers, clad in otherworldly garb, one with pointed ears and a tail.

"Who are you?" one of them asked, and much to their surprise, both Quondam and Lithe could understand their words.

"Who are *you*?" asked Quondam, with attitude. "This is our ship."

"Ship? This is no ship," said the other man. "It is a tower."

"No, it was a tower," Quondam corrected. "Now it's a rocket."

Lithe interrupted, "No, Quon, I think they are right. It's a temple of some sort." She gestured for him to look out past the garden. There were windows, but they no longer had any glass in them. Through the openings, they could see several steps leading down the side of the temple, and droves of people walked all around the building.

Quondam sheathed his sword. "I think there has been some sort of mistake."

The men continued to eye him suspiciously. "Perhaps; we must take you to our king. He is both wise and powerful. He will sort this out."

When they arrived in the throne room, many of the other passengers were also there. Lithe ran over to Dirge and hugged him. "Are you okay?" she asked.

"What about me?" asked the king in a booming voice.

Everyone, including his servants, gave him a very puzzled look.

The king stood up, and he towered over them. He wore leather armor and a loin cloth, and a scraggly, black beard

62

tangled into his long, curly hair. Muscles seemed to burst out of his wide frame, and his presence was very intimidating.

"Don't I get a hug?" he asked.

Everyone froze.

"Wasn't anyone worried about me?"

At this, the king's servants sycophantically obliged him. "Why would we need to worry about one so powerful as you, oh great and...powerful Nimrod?" They cowered at his feet.

Nimrod ignored them and walked down the steps from his throne. He had to tiptoe in order to avoid stepping on his loyal subjects. "Fine, I'll hug you!"

Lithe cringed as the giant king bounded toward her. She braced for impact and closed her eyes as she was lifted into the air. She held tightly to his arms, and noticed that one felt quite unlike skin. Knocking on the arm created a dull thud.

"Munder?"

"Yep."

She whispered, "How? Are you in disguise? Are we prisoners? What is going on here?"

The giant king set her on the ground, walked over, and poked Quondam hard in the chest. "I don't think we're prisoners. Apparently, I'm the king."

"Ow," Quondam whimpered.

Aori circled the giant for a closer inspection. "You used the timepiece again, I suppose?"

Munder's eyes shifted from side to side. Despite his large size and daunting presence, he looked very much like a child who had been caught breaking the rules. "I thought it would help me get my arm free."

"Apparently, it worked," said Finis. "I am afraid I am still quite confused, however."

"Yeah," Quondam added, "how did we get inside this temple?"

Aori put it all together. "His arm was stuck inside the ship, so the timepiece affected it as well. I find it all very fascinating. Apparently, you shifted into someone who already exists here—their king."

"And apparently they can understand us," Finis surmised, "because they look a bit upset."

One of the servants picked up a spear. "What have you infidels done with our king?"

"Nothing," said Aori. "He's right here."

"You just said that someone took over his body." Another of the servants pointed a spear at Munder.

"Look," Munder grumbled, "regardless of whether I'm your king or not, I still have all the power here, so back off!" He snatched up the spear and snapped it like a toothpick. The rest of the servants ran out of the room.

"Great," said Quondam. "You just scared off the only ones who could answer our questions. For example, what is this place?"

"I think I know who can give us the answers we seek," Lithe announced. "Give me the Odestone, Munder."

"No need," boomed a voice that echoed off the stone brick walls. "You can all understand my vibrations now, just as you can understand the speech of the native Earth-dwellers."

"What is this place, father?" asked Lithe.

The Odestone bellowed, "It is called the Tower of Babel. It is a ziggurat, something like the pyramids we saw in Agyp, on Aia."

"How does he know so much about this place?" Aori questioned.

Lithe explained, "My father is a loremaster. He gathers stories from the people in the area. If it's been spoken aloud, he knows it."

The Odestone added, "These clay bricks have a story all their own, and they have absorbed the tales of these people. They built this tower as a safeguard, in case their god brought another flood. They hope that it is tall enough to tower over the deepest water."

Aori cleared his throat. "Another lovely story. Why would their god want to drown them all?"

Finis added, "It happens. We all know I have taken some lives in my day, and I'm not a bad guy."

The Odestone rumbled. "He is not just 'their god.' He is *the* god. These people are at a crossroads. They believe, but Nimrod has come and shaken their faith. Many of them now worship him, and he has built this tower in order to defy God."

"A tower to stretch to the heavens," mumbled Munder.

"By the way," Quondam mentioned, "I just want to say, Nimrod is a perfect name for you."

Munder poked Quondam and knocked him to the ground.

The group decided to have a look around to explore the tower. As they walked, the Odestone served as their tour guide. "There is magic in this place. People from all over come here to trade and learn from the university. Despite their different backgrounds and languages, they all come together here and cooperate. They study the stars and try to predict the future. They provide for themselves by growing their own food and herbs in the gardens. There is even a library, so that the people can record their history and keep their stories alive."

The words struck a chord in Aori, who had tried to do the same by building his own library. These people seemed to have a lot in common with him, despite the fact that they were from completely different planets. "In being creative and self-sufficient, they, too, defy their creator. It's as if they are trying to usurp their god's power to create. Now, if you'll excuse me, I would like to peruse their library."

"Be careful," warned Quondam. "We are outsiders, and they might see us as enemies."

The Aian refugees then split up to explore the tower further. Notturno and several of the other Coda chose to inspect some music they had heard down the hall, while

Quondam and Lithe returned to the garden to check on Asalie.

"Where is she?" a panicked Quondam exclaimed. The garden where they had left Asalie was empty. Even the flowers were gone. "This is the same garden, right?"

"I think so," answered Lithe. "I usually have a very good sense of direction."

"There aren't any footsteps in the soil."

> The creative power of language, you may remember, served as a topic of discussion in the first book of the *Anachronist Chronicles*, with the creation of Toki's crystal palace by song. In a well-known Earth book called the Bible, God created everything by speaking it into existence. Thus, it follows that a people's ability to cooperate and build via their common language would, in fact, seem like a seizure of that creative power.

Lithe grabbed a handful of dirt. "The soil is looser here, in the spot where we left her. If only I could gather the story of what happened from it, as my father does."

"We need to find Munder, and bring the Odestone here, then."

However, at that time, Munder was beginning his own, separate adventure. Upon returning to his throne

> The story of the Tower of Babel is well known among many cultures and religions. Scholars believe its location to have been the area of the Middle East later known as Iraq. According to the story, the people who built the tower all spoke the same language. If you are familiar with the story, you may be able to predict how this will turn out for our heroes.

room to finish a well-deserved meal of roasted pork (anything other than the home-grown food that the ship had provided was a welcome feast), the king's loyal subjects once again fell to their knees in prayer and idolatry.

A member of the king's council, whose name was Sham, was also Nimrod's distant relative. He begged, "Please, O great king, we need your guidance!"

Munder took another bite of food. "Fine. Next time, don't cook the pork so long. I like it a little bloody."

"My lord, your heretical diet is not the issue; you are the only one who can save us."

One of the king's other advisers added, "A vast army approaches from the north, and you are the mightiest hero in the land."

Munder pictured himself as a hero and pride swelled in his chest. "I'll be your hero," he vowed. "Bring me my axe." As he marched down the steps on the northern side of the ziggurat, the Odestone vibrated in his pocket. "Munder, perhaps you should wait until I have more information on this approaching army."

"They are threatening my people!"

"*Nimrod's* people. This is not your fight."

"Look, Odie," Munder grumbled, "I have been cooped up in that ship-tower-rocket for six very, very long years. I need this fight, no matter whose it is."

Munder charged. A few of the soldiers fled before him, but many were trampled in his initial onslaught. Even more fell with the first swing of his axe. His bloodlust raged like the storm that brewed overhead, and his opponents fell with the drops of rain. Thunder shook the sky down to the earth in a completely figurative sense, but the fleeing soldiers would later tell legends of the battle and credit Nimrod with the fury of the storm.

Finis stood on the uppermost level of the tower and surveyed the land below. "Death has followed us here, Dirge. Even as we speak—or I speak, and you listen—a battle rages below us. I can feel their deaths, but they are not my responsibility."

67

Dirge continued to play his guitar, as if the mayhem below did not concern him.

"Yes," Finis went on, "I am the living embodiment of Death, but surely people died before I came here. There must be someone else to handle the job here."

The music from Dirge's guitar seemed to speak to Finis more so than it ever had before. It moved him to tears, and feelings of immense guilt festered inside him. "I know that I am abandoning them, and I do not know what will become of their souls without me as their custodian."

Dirge's music seemed to reply.

Knowledge, they say, is power. The God presiding over these events had already warned his people about avoiding the Tree of Knowledge, but curiosity is a powerful temptress. Perhaps the pursuit of knowledge in the Tower of Babel served to further label them as sinners. While my temporal omniscience grants me visions of the past, it does not allow me to see into the minds and motives of deities. I don't think I'd want to cross that line, anyway.

"You are right. I am abandoning them as I abandoned Aia in its Death. But, what service could I provide, that your people's threnodies and requiems could not? The Coda ushered their souls back into the Spiral. My work was done. I ended it all."

Finis listened as the music continued to speak to his very soul. He looked at Dirge quizzically for several minutes. "How is it that I can understand you?"

The music answered.

"Of course," said Finis. "The magic of the tower has broken the language barrier for us all. How marvelous! I was afraid that my mind was playing tricks on me!"

Dirge continued to play.

In the library, Aori rushed from book to book like a child in a toy-store. The excitement drove him to read faster than he ever had before, and he was finishing a book every second. The text on the pages had been written in a language that was foreign to him, but the magic of the tower allowed him to understand every word. As he read, he picked up on the pattern of the written language, and in less than an hour, he had mastered it.

The history of Nimrod and his ancestors unfolded before him, and he learned that the king descended from the line of Ham, son of Noah. According to the literature, Noah made a covenant with God, and so blessed his whole family. Apparently, however, Ham had been the less-favored son of Noah after seeing his father naked and drunk. For that reason, Nimrod felt like an outcast from the chosen people of God.

"That explains why he would covet the power of his distant relatives and their god," Aori surmised.

When the sun began to set, Aori continued to read by torchlight. He found books written in many different languages, from different cultures and faraway lands. Potential knowledge of this strange, new world fueled his curiosity, and he read with crazed fervor.

As the sun set, Munder returned to his meal in the throne room. The blood of the fallen soldiers soaked his leather armor, and a wild, untamed spark burned in his eyes. He tore through the meat like an animal, pausing only frequently to bask in the glory of his victory.

Lithe found him in the midst of his violent feast, and the image disturbed her. She and Quondam had witnessed much of the battle from the vantage point of the garden, and they feared their friend's bloodlust had overtaken him.

"What has come over you, Munder?"

"Ah, Lithe," Munder said through a mouth full of food. In his feeding frenzy, he had just noticed them standing in front of him. "When I called for women, I didn't know they'd bring you."

Lithe's eyes widened as her intuition kicked in and she understood what he meant. "I assure you, that is *not* why I am here."

As his innocent brain wrapped around the words, Quondam fought the urge to punch his friend in the face to defend her honor. "Munder, if I didn't know better, I'd say that you returned to your old ways. Or, will you just say that you're once again under the influence of others? Did the Odestone feed your frenzy this time, or was it someone else?"

"I assure you," bellowed the Odestone, "I had nothing to do with this."

Lithe grimaced at the voice of her father. "Do you know who did?"

The walls vibrated with the Odestone's voice. "Nimrod himself, I believe."

Suddenly remembering her greater concern, Lithe said, "Munder, we need the Odestone. Something has happened to Asalie. She's disappeared. We fear she may be in danger."

"Fine," Munder grumbled. "Take it."

Lithe hesitated. "I…would rather you carry it. We may need your strength, also."

Suddenly, a loud rumbling shook the walls.

"Oh, don't get all offended, Odie. She didn't mean nothin' by it."

"That's not my father." Fear cracked in her voice.

On the roof of the ziggurat, Finis had watched as the sun set. On Aia, the sunset was his symbol, and many cultures had believed that he was solely responsible for the apparent, daily death of the sun. He saw it as just another negative thing for which the blame had fallen on him.

"I am moving on Dirge. I have sensed my own death for some time."

The music took on a solemn, dolorous sound.

70

"With my death, my curse will be lifted. No longer will I be reborn just to commit atrocities and die by my own hand. I have served my penance.

A few notes sounded a little sharp.

Finis understood, and the music hurt him deeply. "You're right, Dirge. It will never end. As long as I live, people will die."

The living god of Death looked at Dirge through tear-soaked eyes. The music echoed in his ears. Turning away from the child, he walked to the edge of the roof, leaned forward, and allowed himself to fall.

The instant that his body struck the stone bricks hundreds of feet below, the entire building began to tremble.

Dirge continued to play.

As books tumbled off the shelves around them, Aori scrambled to reach every word, every bit of knowledge they had to offer. "Not yet," he shouted. "Just let me finish the books first. There are so many answers to be found here! So many truths lay buried within these pages! They are not conspiring against you; they are just spreading their knowledge. Why do you want to keep them in the dark?"

Aori believed in the

Now, as the story goes, God, or similar supreme beings in other versions of the story, destroyed the Tower of Babel and scattered the people to the winds. He confused their languages, so that they could no longer understand one another. From then on, the people of Earth disagreed about almost everything, which resulted in many wars and lots of death. The word "babble" actually originates from the name Babel, which originally meant "Gate of the God" in Akkadian. The word later came to mean, "to confuse" in Hebrew.

gods. Even though he refused to believe that Asalie made the sunrise and Finis made it set, he could not deny that they

71

existed. He had just spent six years living with them. Now, he also believed in a vengeful, jealous god who had caused a good bit of destruction to the planet He had created. Aori predicted that more destruction wold follow.

Bookcases toppled over, and a strong gust of wind forced its way into the library. Books flew off the shelves and worn pages of papyrus whipped about the room. Aori jostled about trying to grasp as much of the literature as he could.

Brick by brick, the walls disintegrated under the force of the strong winds. Through the openings, Aori could see that the sand only seemed to be blowing in and around the tower. Even the nearby ocean seemed still by comparison.

Since our heroes were aberrations on this planet, they were not only scattered to different parts of the Earth, but they were also scattered throughout time.

I feel I should also point out that this is not the only tower story in the world. Various stories descended through the generations in Central American civilizations, and the events of the stories match closely. How could two different cultures on opposite sides of the world have such similar structures and legends to accompany them? Some scholars believe the lore passed to the Americas by way of explorers or conquistadors. Of course, my visions of the past suggest otherwise.

Far from the shifting sands of Babylon, Aori's other tower met a similar fate. Its inhabitants, who included Connery, Caitlyn, Asia, and several Fellfalla, were similarly scattered across the world and throughout time.

Part Two

Aori, The Wayward Son

Chapter 2:00

Retrospective Perspectives
by the Historyteller

Despite the fact that historians throughout time have recorded events in various cultures around the world, much of the "history" traditionally taught in schools is a tunnel-vision of the past. World History lessons in America have always been shown through red, white, and blue-tinted glasses. Historical accounts depend on the historian's frame of reference, which has been rather limited in some cases.

Children already find multiple perspectives of an issue sometimes difficult to see, which is compounded by the presentation of one-sided stories or histories. For example, children were taught for centuries that Christopher Columbus discovered America, completely ignoring the historical fact that the people living there had discovered it long before him. History often paints the explorer as a hero while white-washing his crimes of murder, theft, trespassing, kidnapping, and human trafficking.

A young child, with a limited worldview and frame of reference, accepts the Cowboys vs. Indians perspective on history in general. Throughout time, there have been good guys and bad guys, and they are fundamentally opposed. This attitude creates an in-group / out-group phenomena that permeates every aspect of our culture. "We" won the war against "them."

In America, children are taught about the Revolutionary War, and that colonists were fighting back against oppression from a tyrannical king way over in England. How is that same historical event taught to British students? In German history textbooks, how are the atrocities of the Holocaust portrayed? Is there a big caption that reads, "Our bad?"

This black and white viewpoint hits a wall when history lessons focus on civil wars, in particular. For instance, if you're a child growing up in the American South, it's difficult to side with the Confederates when hearing stories about their fight to keep slavery. It requires a bit of re-scripting in one's schema of who is "us" in the "us vs. them."

A similar feeling arises in the Biblical stories that will be addressed in the next few chapters. Those of the Jewish or Christian faith believe in an infallible God, so if He tells you (even if it's through an intermediary such as a prophet) to kill every man, woman, and child in a village and salt the earth, then by God, you better do it. At the same time, however, it's difficult to justify the killing of children, even with a black-and-white, us vs. them mentality. When faced with such moral dilemmas, most people just say, "Well, the Lord works in mysterious ways." In other words, don't think about it too much.

While we're on the subjects of religion, history, and narrow frames of reference, let's discuss how Jesus and numerous other Biblical characters are always represented as white people. They lived in the Middle East, escaped to or were enslaved in Egypt for centuries, and undoubtedly got exposed to the tanning effects of the sun throughout their lives, but in movies, they're played by white dudes with British accents. It's no wonder children grow up with such limited perpectives on historical events, when even their religious stories are presented with blind spots and tunnel-vision.

Chapter 2:01

Better Late Than Never

Amidst the swirling tornado of sand, Munder could not help but be reminded of a movie he had seen on one of Toki's televisions during his formative years. As he lost sight of his companions, he shouted, "There's no place like home!"

Sand filled his mouth and choked him. As his body flailed about uncontrollably, the timepiece whipped about on its chain around his neck. He reached for it and immediately felt the sweeping uneasiness of the artifact's magic coursing through him.

When the winds and the magic abated, Munder opened his eyes just in time to see a boot coming towards his face. Instinct took over as the giant moved to the side and grabbed his assailant's ankle with his wooden hand. With his other hand, he grabbed the man by his brightly-colored vestment and held him above his head.

The crowd went wild.

Munder gazed around him at the droves of spectators watching him fight. The bright lights dazed him, but through squinted eyes, he could see that the crowd surrounded him on all sides. He appeared to be in some kind of arena in which people came to watch men brawl for sport. Of course,

Munder had seen this sort of thing before, having watched lots of television while growing up in Tweentime.

"Put me down, you big oaf!"

In his state of wonder, Munder had forgotten about his opponent. With a spinning motion like that of a shot putter, the giant hurled his foe out of the ring. The crowd erupted in mixed cheers and gasps from those close to the action.

Three ropes bordered the ring, which was not, by the way, at all ring-shaped. He crawled over the ropes and moved in to finish off his adversary, when he noticed that the man with the brightly-colored clothing was bleeding and slowly backing away.

"You're crazy!" the man shouted. "Stay away from me!" In a panicked and hoarse voice, he whispered, "This wasn't part of the show. I was supposed to win!"

"Show?" Munder pondered. His voice sounded strange and foreign.

"Somebody help me! This moron's going to kill me!" A slightly pudgy man in a black and white shirt stood between them, shielding Munder's foe with his own body. While he was distracted with the man in black and white, his opponent blindsided him with a steel chair. Blood poured from a gash in his head, and the room suddenly began to spin around him. Each individual light above him gradually fused together into an oppressive brightness. Just as Munder considered complaining about the lights, they faded to darkness.

As he slipped into unconsciousness, he was vaguely aware of several hands dragging him across the floor. Weighing the agony in his head against the comfort of unconsciousness, he chose the latter.

"You awake?"

"No," grumbled Munder. He tried to open his eyes, but the oppression of the bright lights continued.

"That was some match, mister."

80

"Match?" Slowly, his eyes focused on a small boy in a light green hospital gown, who was standing at the side of his bed.

"Yeah. I know you had that jerk beat. That was a cheap stunt he pulled, whacking you with that chair. Everybody knows Andre the Giant's the best wrestler ever."

"Who?"

"You, silly!" The boy gave him a dubious look. "Did you get amnesia when you got hit with that chair? I seen that in a cartoon once."

Munder rubbed his head, as if that would make everything seem clearer. It didn't. "I've been stabbed, shot full of arrows, and I survived a fall that would'a killed a normal man, but I just got knocked out by a chair?"

"We think it was actually your heart that caused the problem," said a professional-looking woman in a white coat. "Hello. I'm Dr. Burke."

Munder grumbled, "Heart? I was pretty sure I didn't have one of those."

The doctor laughed politely. "Complications with the heart are quite common among those with your condition."

Condition? Again, Munder felt lost in confusion. He decided to play along, so as not to seem like an imbecile in front of a woman. "Of course, my condition."

"I'd like to run some more tests," she continued. "Would you mind sticking around for a few days, or do you have some big wrestling match coming up?"

Munder looked at the boy, as if he was the one with all the information.

The boy spoke up, "You can't miss Wrestlemania! It's the biggest show of the year!"

The doctor patted the boy gently on the back. "Davey, maybe you should go back to your room so Mr. Roussimoff can get some rest." She ushered him out of the room, while Munder looked around for a Mr. Roussimoff.

81

Something vibrated on his bedside table. "You *are* Mr. Roussimoff, Munder," sang the Odestone. Though they were no longer within the magical walls of the Tower of Babel, Munder could still understand the vibrations of the Odestone.

"You were born Andre Roussimoff, but your working name is Andre the Giant," the Odestone sang in a low, monotone voice. "You are a wrestler by trade, which means that you spar with others for money and renown."

"And apparently I'm dying," Munder grumbled.

"I'm afraid so, yes."

"Looks like I picked the wrong body to shift into this time." He looked around the room, taking in the modern conveniences such as electricity and indoor plumbing. A television hung from the ceiling across the room. "What year is it?"

"I haven't gathered that information, yet. I learned what I told you by listening to your own personal song, and the words of those around you."

Munder gritted his teeth. "I don't have my own personal song."

"Of course you do. You just don't sing it."

The giant rolled his eyes. "Whatever."

"Your condition is called acromegaly, or giantism. This was not the first time that your heart gave out under the pressure of your large body."

"Look, Odie. I've always been a big guy—bigger than I am now, in fact—and it never killed me before."

The Odestone solemnly sang, "I suppose your heart is weaker now."

Munder fiddled nervously with the buttons on his bed. After changing the position of his bed several times, he eventually came across a button that turned on the television. Though the set showed only static, it triggered a memory of a program he had viewed in Tweentime, many years ago.

"I'm guessing that every time I use the timepiece, I'll shift into someone else's body...."

"It appears so, yes," the Odestone vibrated.

"Then maybe I'm here for a reason... to set things right."

The Odestone hesitated. "I have not gathered any lore on that. I believe your metamorphosis is not random, but I have no way of knowing your destiny."

"Any oracles or seers here in... where are we?"

"This is a healing-house called a hospital. I am afraid the walls carry no songs of the land outside, however."

Munder sat up in his bed. "I guess we'll just have to take a walk outside, then. T.V.'s broken, anyway."

"The doctor said that you need rest, Munder," the Odestone protested.

The giant walked over to a mirror mounted on the far wall of the hospital room. In his reflection, his eyes looked sunken and tired. He had a rather long face, and the overhang of his brow reminded Munder of the Neanderthal Prochrons that had served in his battalion on Aia. He was tall, but not quite as tall as his previous incarnation. He did, however, have to duck his head as he walked through the doorway.

The Odestone vibrated in his sweaty palm. "Please do not strain yourself, Munder. Remember, this is not your body. If the wrestler dies, what will become of you?"

Munder turned around and headed back towards the bed.

"Thank you, Munder," sang the Odestone. "You are a reasonable fellow, after all."

The giant gently set the stone back on the bed-side table and left the room.

"Munder!" the Odestone rumbled. "Come back! I need you to help me gather lore about this place!"

As the room vibrated, the television tuned into a local station and the static subsided.

Munder stomped past the room of the boy he had met earlier. The boy noticed him and called out, "Hey. You can't sleep either?"

He hadn't even noticed that it was night-time. The bright lights of the hospital had screwed up his sense of time.

"Just walking."

"Wanna watch T.V?" Davey asked.

Munder stepped into the boy's room. "What'cha watching?"

"Bert and Ernie. They let me use the VCR and everything."

The giant sat down next to the little boy and was soon engrossed in the program. The fuzzy people with large, round noses bickered like he and Quondam often did. After they had resolved their argument, or more precisely, the taller, yellow one had given up and decided to bang his head against the wall, Munder lost interest in the program.

"Do they have to sing so much?"

Davey laughed. "I think so."

"So," Munder hedged, "are you dying too?" Barbarous, ex-villainous giants aren't too tactful with their words.

"I dunno. Maybe," the boy answered. Gloom set about his face like a dark cloud.

"Anything I can do to help?"

The boy looked up at Munder with the eyes of a much older, wearier man. "I feel a lot safer with you around. You're big enough to beat up anyone."

Pride swelled inside the giant. "That I can do, kid."

After the boy fell asleep, Munder went back to his own room. Excitedly, he told the Odestone about the boy. "I think I found my purpose here. I'm just here to protect that little boy."

The Odestone was preoccupied with listening to the television.

"I think there's someone bad...who has done...bad things to him." The excitement in Munder's voice dwindled, and he stared off pensively into the darkness outside his window.

"You could be right," said the Odestone absently.

"He needs somebody like me to protect him, because I didn't have somebody like me, and... look how I turned out." Something caught in the giant's throat and stung in his eyes.

As soon as he picked up the Odestone, his emotions leveled out and he resumed the personality of a mental patient on lithium. His grip muffled the vibrations of the stone, so he held it in his palm.

"The people in this contraption are telling a very interesting story, which I would like to hear, Munder." The Odestone was about—no, exactly—as sensitive as a rock.

Munder watched the television, but all he saw was a boring news story. "News? Nobody watches the news. Change it."

As he fiddled with the controls on the television, the story caught his attention. According to the news reporter, a man had driven his truck into a local eating establishment, in Killeen, Texas. He massacred 23 people and injured 20 others. The gravity of the report struck him heavily, as if the truck had hit him instead.

"Was this some sort of battle?" Munder asked.

The Odestone dropped to the floor. "No."

"Did those people kill that man's family?"

"No."

"What did they do to him? Why would he do something like that?"

The Odestone vibrated against the tiled floor. "Perhaps Finis was mistaken when he said that men are not evil."

Munder's jaw clenched and his eyebrows formed a tight, straight line as he glared at the television set. "That's what I'm here for—to put a stop to his madness. I will go and make his death long and excruciatingly painful."

85

"Too late," said the Odestone. "He put a stop to it himself."

A knot twisted up in Munder's face. "How could I be late? I'm always right on time!"

He kicked the bed, accidentally tore out his I.V., and threw a bedpan across the hall. It landed in another patient's room, who looked quite angry about it, until he noticed the size of the giant across the hall.

"What the hell am I here for, then? Why would some higher power or whatever send me to the future just a few hours too late? It doesn't make any sense!"

He slammed his fist through the plastic casing of a wall-mounted clock. "You did this," Munder shouted at the clock. "You always made sure I got everywhere at the right time! What did I do wrong?!"

Tearing the clock from the wall, he threw it on the floor and stomped it into millions of miniscule pieces. "I'm done with you," he grumbled. "Forever."

As he renounced the god of Time, the timepiece around his neck began to burn his skin. He reached for it, but stopped himself just before touching it. As his skin smoldered under the metal watch, he growled and writhed in agony.

A nurse ran in and looked like she was looking at a train wreck heading towards her. "Sir, you're going to have to calm down!" She escaped down the hall, shouting for the other nurses to call security.

The Odestone rumbled on the floor. "Munder, be mindful of your heart condition. If you get too excited, you could…."

As if on cue, Munder collapsed.

When enough strength resumed within his eyelids to open them a crack, Munder could not quite understand why a very small man was standing on his chest. Assuming he had shifted into a much larger giant, he swatted the tiny man away like a bug.

"What'd you do that for?" Davey scampered around the room, picking up the action figures that Munder had scattered.

A smile grew on Munder's face, which was a rare occurrence. "I was scattering them to the winds, because they tried to build a tower to the heavens."

"What?"

"Nothing." Munder sat down on the floor and picked up one of the action figures. "Mind if I play?"

"Nope," said Davey. "I was wondering how many army men I could fit in your nose, but you woke up before I could figure it out."

"Sorry," Munder laughed.

As the child and child-like giant played with their toys, the Odestone rested upon the television set and listened to the lore of the early 1990's in America. It learned that musicians, rather than traveling from village to village to share their songs, now broadcast them via music videos. He enjoyed the music, but he gathered little lore from it, except for the fact that a certain knight had quite the fondness for big butts, about which he could not lie.

The news channels provided more information on current affairs, but Munder simply would not tolerate more than an hour of CNN a day, and he only permitted the music videos because of the preponderance of scantily-clad women. Cartoons and extremely violent action movies, both of which Munder preferred, offered very little to the stone loremaster. However, once *Sesame Street* had ended each day, the Public Broadcasting Network provided very rich, historical information.

Unfortunately, television served as the only medium for the sharing of lore in those days. Radio stories had gone by the wayside, and no one had gathered in Ye Old Taverns to share folktales for hundreds of years. The Odestone found that, despite the variance in medium, many of the stories had remained the same; a good hero fought some evil, and many of those heroes just happened to also be orphans.

Only seemingly by coincidence, two such orphans currently battled one another via action figures on the floor of Munder's hospital room.

"So, lemme get this straight-- they're ninjas *and* turtles?"

"Yup."

"And they're also teenagers?"

"Yup. And, they're mutants. Mom told me what that means, but I don't remember."

Munder examined the humanoid turtle action figure closely. "We had creatures like this where I'm from, but we called them Murtles...or Mortoises. I think they were like the lords of the turtles or something."

"Were they ninjas?" asked Davey.

"I don't think so, but I never really met any."

Tact once again left the giant, as he blurted, "How come your parents never come see you? Are they dead?"

Davey looked down at the toys in his hands solemnly.

"I'm an orphan too," said Munder, trying to smooth over the subject. "I don't even know what happened to my mom and dad."

"Mine were shot."

"I thought so," said Munder. "In that cafeteria?"

"Yup," said Davey. Tears welled up in his big eyes.

"But you weren't hurt?"

"Nope."

Munder twisted the head off of one of the action figures by accident. "Sorry," he mumbled. As he tried to fix it, he continued to apologize, "I would have saved your parents if I had got here in time. And I would make that bad man pay for what he did, but...you don't have to worry about him anymore. He can't hurt you ever again."

"He'll hurt people again someday," said Davey.

"No," said Munder. "He's dead. It doesn't work that way. Well, except when people thought I was dead, and I came back...but that was different."

"He's gonna get born again."

Bewilderment, which was really Munder's natural state, resurfaced. "What? How could you know that?"

The boy continued to play with his toys, as if the momentous information he presented could not possibly be as important as who would win between Leonardo and Raphael. "The same way I know that you weren't always Andre the Giant."

"And how's that?"

"I dunno," the boy casually brushed the subject aside. "This turtle is my favorite."

"C'mon, kid. Put the toys down and talk to me."

Davey smiled. "You used to look like a big goat."

"A ram, actually. How do you know that?"

"I dunno," Davey said. "I just see stuff...like who people were before they were born."

"That's a pretty cool trick."

"Yup. By the way, I think the old man sitting on the TV wants you to change the channel."

Munder fiddled with the buttons on the television set. "He just wants to watch the news, I bet." He picked up the stone and set it on the floor next to Davey's toys.

"Can I see it?" asked Davey. In the language of children, that meant, "May I hold it in my hands, play with it, and possibly borrow it for a week or two?"

The Odestone vibrated a greeting into Davey's hand, and it tried to offer condolences for the boy's loss. Unfortunately, Ode was never very good at comforting those in need, so his song just dulled the boy's senses a bit.

Davey told Munder and the Odestone all about the past lives of his favorite nurses and doctors, while the Odestone

89

told the story of how they got to Earth and how they had been separated from all their friends and family.

"Have you ever seen anybody around who could change his age?" Munder hoped to find Quondam and the others in this time period.

"Nope, but I think you and I fought a long time ago."

"Really? Why would we fight?"

"I dunno," said Davey. "God told me to, I think. I heard about the story in Sunday school. I shot you in the head with a slingshot."

"Funny," said Munder. "I don't remember that."

Davey pointed to Munder's chest, where the timepiece had burned a hole in his hospital gown. The metal of the pocket-watch had melted into his skin, similar to the way Quondam's timepiece had grown into his chest.

"Is that the thing that turned you into a ram?" asked Davey.

"Yup," answered Munder.

"Why's it stuck to you like that?"

"I dunno," said Munder, borrowing the boy's answer for difficult questions. "I guess Time wanted to let me know who's the boss."

"Tony Danza," the Odestone mumbled. Apparently, he had gathered lore from 80's reruns.

"Can I see it?" Again, Davey meant that he wanted to hold the watch, play with it, and possibly borrow it for a week or two. Of course, Munder didn't realize that until it was too late. Davey had touched the timepiece, and in an instant, they were gone.

Andre the Giant suddenly found himself sitting in the floor of a hospital room, surrounded by toys. Obviously, this came as quite a shock to him. However, by suffering the brunt of his episodes with heart failure, Munder had bought the wrestler a couple more years of life. Sadly, he passed away in 1993.

Chapter 2:02

An Eddy in the Timestream

As the winds tore through the walls of Babel's library, Aori scrambled to gather all the books. Sand swirled around him, and the stones that made up the walls of the tower crumbled and joined the sandstorm. A piece of the bookshelf broke off in his hand as the wind carried him into the air. Soon, Aori could see nothing but sand in every direction.

Something seemed to tug at a part deep inside of him. He felt the temporal spirit within him churn and swirl, as if he were caught in an eddy in a river. "Are we such a threat to you, that you would scatter us through space *and* time? I am the living Son of Father Time! I will not be cast away like some feather on the wind!" Yet, the roaring wind and sand drowned out his defiant shouts.

Tapping into the temporal magic that spiraled around and inside him, Aori funneled himself between the drops of the time-stream and entered a bubble of Tweentime. Purple spirals whorled in the background, outlining the shapes of sand dunes and faraway mountains.

He still clutched several books tightly in his arms, afraid that they might slip from his grasp if he let go. The books were precious refugees from a catastrophic tragedy, and Aori held them as sacred texts. A small piece of the bookshelf still remained in his hand, and even though it had been a part of a library on Earth, he believed that it was all that was left of his once great clock towers.

As he placed the broken wood on the ground, Aori hoped that new *asa* trees would grow on Earth, everywhere the brick-dust of the tower had been scattered. He placed the books gently on the ground next to the wood, and he could feel it slowly growing. "Protect these books, lovely *asa*," he whispered to the wood.

Still harboring some of his characteristic impatience, Aori decided to have a look around while the bookshelf regenerated itself. Though the environment in Tweentime appeared to be a reflection of the landscape on Earth, it was barren and quite lonesome. Aori found himself longing for the companionship he had taken for granted aboard the Woodship Timister.

Reaching out his arms, he could see the purple energy twirl around his fingers. "Temporal Spirit, what has become of all the others?"

Ripples circled outward from his fingertips. In the whirling energy, he saw several images that overlapped in circular waves. There were so many images and so many ripples that Aori had trouble distinguishing his companions from all the other Aian refugees on Earth. There were hundreds of Coda, Fellfallan moths and butterflies, Ori, and Agypsians who had traveled to Earth.

In one ripple, he saw a large soldier who towered above his army. As Aori suspected, the giant had one wooden arm that was barely hidden under his bronze armor. *Munder.*

As soon as Munder became aware of his surroundings, he felt that familiar feeling of leading an army into battle. Much to his surprise, however, the foe he faced this time was a young child. Before he could speak or even think, he noticed a small, polished stone hurtling towards his head.

The stone hit Munder directly between the eyes, and the pain knocked him off his feet. Lying on his back, the stone tumbled onto his chest. It gently vibrated, and the pain faded away. "Odie?"

Munder saw the child approach with a sword that was almost too big for him to carry. "Davey?"

The child did not answer, but Munder managed to grab the Odestone and touch the timepiece on his chest before the sword came crashing down on Goliath's neck.

Aori tried to follow Munder's image as the giant shifted forms, but he just seemed to fade out of reality. Suddenly, he sensed the giant's presence in Tweentime. "He's here, isn't he? He has to travel through here in between forms."

Another ripple spread outward from his finger, and he caught a brief glimpse of Munder passing through Tweentime. "Wait," he commanded. Munder, the ripples, and all of the purple swirling energy stopped suddenly.
Touching the frozen ripple in the fabric of Tweentime, Aori passed through the circling waves and immediately stood right next to Munder.

"Aori?"

"Yes. It is good to see you."

"Where am I?" the giant asked. "Am I dead?"

"No, but I believe that particular form is now headless. You are in Tweentime. Apparently, you pass through here instantaneously as you shift to other forms."

Aori took Munder back to where he had created the ripples, and he showed him the overlapping images of their fellow Aians. Munder felt a slight discomfort at seeing the boy carrying the head of the giant away from the battlefield.

"I can't believe my higher purpose was to get hit in the head by a rock," grumbled Munder disappointedly.

In a low, monotone voice, the Odestone sang, "In the few seconds we were there, I managed to gather a few pieces of the story. You were Goliath, the leader of the Philistine army. You were slain by a boy named David, who was on a mission from God."

"Davey?" Munder deduced.

"So it seems," the Odestone vibrated.

"You knew that boy?" asked Aori.

"Yeah, I remember him from a future life."

The Odestone vibrated and filled in the gaps for Aori briefly.

"You have seen the future?" Aori surmised. "This is amazing. Do you see the possibilities here?"

"We could place a bet on this wrestling match I lost," suggested Munder.

"No," said Aori, shaking his head. "Well, yes, but that's just the beginning. There are no limits to what we could accomplish."

"Well, we're a bit limited to the T.V. schedule," said Munder.

"What?"

The Odestone vibrated, "Most of the lore I gathered was from a device called a television. I learned nothing of what happened, or will happen, to you or any of the others."

"I see." Aori gazed into the rippling images. "I see them, but I have no way of knowing where—or in what time period—they are."

"Where is Lithe?" asked Munder. "And Quon?"

"As you can see, the images are a little blurry." It was like looking at one's reflection in the rippling surface of water, and the images ran together like a washed-out watercolor painting.

"I think I prefer Toki's televisions," said Munder.

"Do not say that name!" shouted Aori. "Not here. This is his home. Do you really want to let him know we're here?"

"He probably sensed us long ago," warned the Odestone.

94

Aori looked around nervously. "You're probably right. It is not safe for us here. You two need to keep moving. Don't stay in one form for more than a week or so."

"What about my higher purpose? Surely I'm not just skipping around through time for no reason," grumbled Munder.

"I agree. It seems unlikely that things would be so random. Keep shifting, and keep an eye out for other Aians. We need to find the others and gather as much knowledge as we can."

"How will we communicate with you?" asked the Odestone.

"Hopefully, you will gather lore about me, if I can somehow strike out and make a name for myself in this world. However, maybe there is another way. Munder, give me your watch."

Munder eyed him suspiciously. He backed away and prepared to guard the timepiece with his life.

"Not the timepiece, Munder." Aori fought his impulse to use the term *idiot*. "I might be able to fix your wristwatch so that we can use it as a communications port between Tweentime and Earth."

As Munder handed over the wristwatch, he grumbled, "Take care of it. That was a gift from…you know who."

"Yes, I know, and I will," Aori promised. "It will take me a little while to fix it, so you should go on to your next life. I should be done with it by the next time you need to shift."

Munder turned to leave, but stopped. "Could you also watch over Davey?"

"The boy who just killed you?"

"Yes. I think I was sent to take care of him."

Aori nodded. "I'll see what I can do."

With a somewhat awkward goodbye, Aori released the spell that had stopped the swirling energy of Tweentime. Munder faded, and Aori was once again alone.

Chapter 2:03

All the Time in the World is Not Enough

As always, Aori had all the time in the world. He could settle down with a few good books and while away the hours learning everything there was to know about life in the last millennium of B.C. time. However, without the raw materials necessary for his tinkering and inventing, he found that boredom made the days creep by even more slowly. Loneliness seeped in through the cracks between the hours, and Tweentime felt like a barren wasteland. For one who had always had more tasks than time, it was torture.

With but a thought, Aori once again felt the wind swirling sand into his eyes. Remembering his half-hearted promise to Munder, he set out to find the boy called Davey. He knew he was close, because he had witnessed the battle between the boy and the giant from his vantage point in between time.

As he walked, he heard the sound of women singing. His thoughts drifted back to the days of listening to the Coda sing on the journey to Earth. These women sang of the boy David, who had slain the giant Goliath. They played instruments and danced like the waves of heat emanating from the hot sand. Their songs told the tale of David killing ten thousand of the Lord's enemies compared to King Saul's meager thousand slain. Knowing the baser qualities of men's souls, Aori assumed that this would not sit well with the king.

"Excuse me, ma'am?" he spoke to one of the singing women in his best Hebrew, which was quite adequate considering that he came from an entirely different planet. Somehow, the magic of the Tower of Babel had endured the Scattering.

The women all wore cloths around their heads and faces, presumably to shield them from the frequent sandstorms. The woman Aori addressed, however, had a familiar-looking mark on her forehead. It looked like a plus-sign with a circle around it. Obviously, this woman was either one of the Coda from the journey to Earth or a direct descendant of those Coda.

"What are you doing out here, child?" asked the woman.

Aori had all but forgotten his current age, as the time since his rejuvenation had seemed like much more than a mere ten years or so. Rather than trying to explain to the woman, Aori chose to assume the role that his physical age implied. "I am lost," he whimpered. "I came out here to see the famous young boy who saved us all from that evil giant."

"We are headed to Jerusalem, to sing the praises of the boy David," she said. "We can take you there, if you wish."

Aori joined their group, although his singing and dancing were quite pitiful compared to the women's. He enjoyed their company, after spending so much time alone. They were not far from the city gates, and already the citizens of Jerusalem gathered around to hear their song. In the hubbub of excitement awaiting David's arrival, Aori managed to blend in with the crowd, which was fortunate, since his light skin and prematurely grey hair made him look rather odd.

Once they passed the city gates, the dancers entered a large courtyard area. At the far side of the courtyard stood a magnificent dais with an ornate throne. King Saul sat upon the throne, looking none too pleased.

"Stop singing at once!" shouted Saul.

The music stopped abruptly, and all eyes turned to the king.

"They have ascribed to David ten thousand, and to me they have ascribed only thousands. What more can he have, but the kingdom?" He spoke the words to his advisors who stood around him, but everyone could hear in the uncomfortable silence of the crowd.

Aori whispered to the Coda, "Perhaps it is time for the musicians to make their grand exit. I don't believe it is safe for us here."

Together, they wove through the crowd into the relative safety of a deserted room. Once indoors, the Coda removed the covering from her head. Sure enough, she had the pointed ears of her Codan heritage. She saw him staring and tried to cover them again.

"Please, don't," said Aori. "I am accustomed to the features of the Coda, believe me."

She looked at him quizzically. "How could you know of the Coda? There are so few of us left, and the bloodline has thinned so…"

"I know much that people of Earth do not know," Aori said.

"You…" she stammered, "You come from Aia, the birthplace of my great-grandmother?"

"Yes," he smiled. She was the sure cure for his homesickness and loneliness. "What is your name?"

"I am called Tehilim," she said.

"Pleased to meet you," Aori bowed low. "My name is Aori Timister."

As a sign of submission, she lowered her eyes to the floor. She was not used to being treated with such respect by the men of these lands. "Thank you for removing me from

99

the danger outside, but now I fear for the safety of my fellow musicians."

Aori peeked out a window. "I think they took a cue from us and scattered amongst the crowd. Hopefully, the king will not take out his anger on them."

"No, but David is surely in danger," she said.

"Very likely," Aori agreed. "I must find him. I have sworn an oath, of sorts, to watch over him."

"I may be able to help you. I have been traveling with him, writing songs about his labors for the Lord. He is camped not far from the city, but word of King Saul's displeasure has assuredly reached him by now. That explains why he has not followed us into town."

Aori stared off into space, obviously working through the mechanics of some sort of plan. "What can you tell me about this King Saul?"

"Oh, there are many tales about the king, but people do not sing of him as we do about David." She stopped, lowered her head, and continued, "Please do not take my words as disrespect for our king. I should not have…."

"Please, Tehilim, speak freely. I want to know everything."

"King Saul has been a good leader, but I have heard tales that he has fallen out of favor with the Lord. The prophet Samuel anointed a new king of Israel, and we all believe it to be David."

Aori chose his words carefully, for he himself had apparently fallen out of favor with the Lord. "What exactly did Saul do to displease the Lord?"

"According to the stories I have heard, the prophet told King Saul the Lord's orders, and they were not followed. He was to destroy the enemies of the Lord and burn their cities, and instead his men took some food for themselves."

"Were his men hungry?"

"They were starving, it is said," answered Tehilim.

"So, they chose to go against the divine commands, as opposed to starving."

Tehilim showed discomfort with Aori's words, which might have been seen as blasphemous to some. Taking notice of this, he continued, "Obviously, Saul has made grievous mistakes. I assume there were other times that he defied orders?"

"That is what I have heard," said Tehilim, not wishing to speak out against either her ruler or the Lord. "He has also been conferring with magicians, it is said."

Aori decided not to reveal that he, himself, might be considered a magician, what with his proficient use of temporal magic. He wondered what other qualities he possessed that would brand him a heretic in this time and place. Certainly, his role as the mortal form of the Time god might raise a few eyebrows.

"Perhaps I should have a talk with the king," Aori suggested.

"You are a child. I do not think he will wish to speak with you."

Aori smiled. "Ah, but I have a plan."

Those who have read the Bible or been to Sunday School may already know how this particular story turns out. Such knowledge allows for a convenient foresight, or hindsight, as the case may be, but obviously the Bible did not include the part that Aori played.

Nonetheless, as the story goes, King Saul's son Jonathan had befriended young David, and he saw the value in the valiant deeds David had done for Israel. He went behind his father's back to warn David that Saul wanted him dead. Jonathan repeatedly pleaded with his father to spare David's life, even though the threat to Saul's kingdom was also a threat to the kingdom Jonathan would have one day inherited. Obviously, Jonathan's siding with his enemy caused some friction between the father and son.

It is also important to note, once again, the importance of lore. As Tehilim indicated, there were far less songs and tales about the exploits of Saul than there were about David, even though Saul had once been the favored and divine choice for king of Israel. The songs about David presented him to a large group of people in a very positive light, much like P.R. consultants did for politicians and celebrities in more modern times. Even if Saul had actually been an okay guy, he had already lost public approval simply because he hadn't hired the right P.R. musicians.

As Aori approached the king's chambers, he muttered, "I have a bad feeling about this." In what he considered to have been a long life already, he had rarely, if ever, placed himself in such a dangerous position solely for the benefit of another. Most of his actions had been predominantly self-serving, albeit with the best intentions in mind. Had he realized that, by altering time, he would eventually bring about the destruction of all of Aia, he might have chosen a different course of action.

A large guard wearing bronze armor stopped him at the door to Saul's quarters.

"My name is Aori Timister. I am a magician, and the king seeks my counsel."

"You are a child," said the guard.

"Of that, I am aware. And yet, I am more powerful than you can possibly imagine."

The guard pointed a spear at Aori's throat. "Do you threaten me, boy?"

Aori stood so motionless that it seemed as if he had stopped time. Instead, he was concentrating on speeding up time. As he focused intently on the spear at his throat, the metal of the spearhead began to rust. The wooden handle rotted, and in a few seconds, the weapon crumbled to bits of dust and rusted bronze.

The guard froze.

"Now," said Aori. "Let me pass, or the same fate shall befall you."

Before the guard could even speak, Aori had passed through the doors and into the king's chambers. An ornately-robed man knelt at the king's feet. As Aori approached, all eyes turned to him, and he could see star charts in the man's hands.

"Astrology?" asked Aori. "Did the stars foretell my coming, O grand seer?"

The robed man stared at him with his mouth open wide.

"Who are you?" shouted Saul. "How dare you barge into my home?"

"I am Aori Timister, sire. Do people use the term, 'sire,' here? At any rate, I am here to guide you through this turbulent time."

"What do you know of my life, boy, that you may give *me* guidance?"

Aori spoke in a solemn tone. "I know that you have lost favor with the Lord, and that your future as king is very short."

"Lies!" shouted the king.

"You have heard the words of the prophet, O King. You know that the one called David fights with the Lord on his side."

The king cursed David aloud and threw a spear at the wall. The image of the spear pinned to the wall triggered something in Aori that can only be described as the opposite of *déjà vu*. He knew that he would see the image again, in the future.

"My king, I have seen the future, and I know now that you plan to kill David. You wish to pin him to the wall with your spear. If I am right, you will try, and you will fail."

Sure enough, Aori's prediction did come to pass. Upon returning from a suicide mission to bring Saul proof of a hundred slain Philistines, the king did, indeed, attempt to pin

103

David to the wall with the spear. David dodged twice. Along with having the Lord on his side, David also had help from the harp of his favorite musician, Tehilim. On Aori's advice, she had been singing prayers and playing songs that would make David dodge more deftly.

For whatever reason, Saul's obsession with David became increasingly more violent and fanatical. Everywhere that David fled, the king sent soldiers to hunt him. Heeding the warnings of his friend Jonathan, David took all the soldiers who were loyal to him, left Saul's kingdom, and went to Nob, which was in the land of Benjamin.

Among those loyal followers were Tehilim and her fellow singers. As they traveled, Tehilim wrote songs detailing the tragic tale of the friendship between David and Jonathan. He loved her singing, and she inspired him to write his own music as well.

When they came to Nob, they sought sanctuary in the temple of a priest named Ahimelech. In addition to feeding David and his men with holy bread from the church, the priest also gave David the sword of Goliath, which had apparently traveled almost as much as David had in the years after slaying the giant.

Unfortunately, one of the servants in the temple, whose name was Doeg the Edomite, was loyal to Saul. Word of David's whereabouts soon spread to Saul, who had taken up the hunt personally. Aori traveled alongside the king, though his allegiance traveled elsewhere.

The tedium of travel on mules and camels severely taxed Aori's patience. Concern for David and Tehilim weighed heavily on him, and he knew that he could warn them if he took a shortcut through Tweentime. However, as the king's main advisor, it would be difficult for him to escape undetected.

"My king…" Aori trailed off. Despite his vast intellect and Time-god-given talent for manipulation, Aori was at a loss. "What's that over there?"

King Saul looked in the opposite direction just long enough for Aori to vanish in a bubble between time.

Aori had studied enough maps of the area to understand where he was headed, and the magic of Tweentime allowed him to travel there instantaneously. When he rematerialized outside the temple, he rushed over to greet Tehilim.

"Aori! How did you get here?" she exclaimed with surprised joy.

"No time to explain," he said quickly. "Saul is on his way here. David must leave quickly."

"He left days ago, towards Gath," said the Coda.

"Good; then he is safe. But what about you, Tehilim? Why did you stay behind?"

Tehilim's face fell. "I wished to go with him, but the path ahead is not safe for women, it is said. He said that, as long as I traveled with him, I would be in danger."

"That is probably true," said Aori. "Nonetheless, I must find him. He needs to know that Saul himself hunts him, and the king has gone completely mad."

Aori looked out to the horizon and tried to gaze into the future. He saw only a sandstorm, which was a pretty safe prediction, since they happened almost daily here. "You said he was headed for Gath, correct?"

"Yes," answered Tehilim.

He stared off into the sand surrounding him, which looked identical in every direction. "Could you show me where that is, on this map?"

Once she had shown him the destination, Aori vanished in a bubble of Tweentime. In an instant, Aori entered the town of Gath, a day before David would arrive.

Just as David arrived in town and met King Achish of Gath, Saul and his army rode into Nob. The king sent for Ahimelech, and his soldiers brought the priest to him by force.

105

Saul questioned him at length, "Why have you conspired against me, you and the son of Jesse, by giving him bread and sword, and by inquiring of God for him, so that he has risen against me, to lie in wait, as he is doing today?"

Ahimelech answered, but by that time, Tehilim had utilized her innate ability to block out any sound, for she did not wish to hear what transpired in the next room. Rather, she hummed a hymn that she and David had written together.

"You shall surely die, Ahimelech, you and all your father's house," shouted Saul.

Though his soldiers refused to raise their swords against the priests, Doeg the Edomite carried out his master's commands. Eighty-five priests died that day.

Then, the entire town of Nob was "put to the sword," as it is written in the Bible (1 Samuel 22: 6-19). When towns are put to the sword in this day and age, it means that every man, woman, child, and animal is slain, and no living thing is left to tell the tale.

The hymns that Tehilim hummed that day to block out the dying screams of innocents would one day become the part of the Bible known as *Psalms*. The word psalm comes from a Greek word that was translated from the Hebrew version, which was called *Tehilim*. Sadly, its Codan namesake did not live to see the psalms collected.

Chapter 2:04

Once is Chance,
Twice is Coincidence...

Whenever writers indicate that some horrific event left no one to tell the tale, it is usually an exaggeration for effect. After all, if no one survived, how would anyone else in the story know what happened? In the massacre at Nob, a son of Ahimelech named Abiathar escaped just in time and ran to find David.

By the time David arrived in Gath, Aori had already visited their library, which was really a church, and he had read every scroll of text. The genealogy of who begat whom in the ancestry of Gath did little to relieve his incredible boredom. He found only slight diversion in counting the letters in the text, ascribing numerical values to the letters, and then deciphering the underlying meaning between the lines. This painstaking process was later known as numerology and has been practiced by Hebrew scholars for thousands of years.

Aori greeted David and his men right outside the city walls. With a respectful bow, he said, "David, son of Jesse, I have important news for you. My name is Aori Timister, and

I am a friend of your musician, Tehilim. Might we speak in private?"

"You are known to me, Aori. Let us walk and talk together, for I may have important information for you, as well."

The two young men walked down a barren, dusty street, and Aori told David everything he knew about Saul's whereabouts, intentions, and madness. The solemn, serious look upon David's face belied his youth.

"You have come far in a short time to deliver this grim news, Aori. While I do not understand how you could have possibly arrived here before us, I will not question the Lord's blessing."

Though Aori's pride almost led him to reclaim the credit for his timeliness, prior experience had instilled the fear of God in him. "I have found that some supernatural occurrences are better left a mystery."

"So it seems. And here is another mystery for you, Aori Timister. The man named Saul has committed grave acts of violence in the past, and he will continue to do so in his next life."

Aori remembered what Munder had told him of the boy Davey and his gifts. "You can see the king's former and future lives?"

"It is more of a feeling," David said, "like when the Lord speaks to me. I know not what Saul will do in this life, or where you will find him in his next life, but it seems that he is forever cursed."

"This is very intriguing information, indeed," said Aori. Deductions and calculations of two and two cranked like gears inside his brain. "I will need some time to think this over."

"And I have much to discuss with King Achesh. May the Lord bless you, Aori."

"And you, David."

Abiathar arrived with the news of what had transpired in Nob late that night. An uneasy feeling roused Aori from his meditation just seconds before the priest's son crashed through the door. As he explained the grim details of the massacre, Aori cursed the king and himself. If he was truly the mortal form of the Time god, why had the temporal spirit not given him the clairvoyance to prevent the heinous incident?

The fate of Tehilim struck him the deepest. Though he had not known her for long, she had been a pleasant reminder of Aia and better times. He blamed himself, but he could not have known that Saul would take out his anger on anyone even remotely connected to his enemy.

With emotions swirling within like the sandstorms all around him, Aori set off into the desert alone. He had had his fill of Earth and all its evils. Lonely solitude would be better than the grief he felt for those who he had only slightly known.

Tweentime became his hermitage, as he turned his back on that time period. He kept his promise to watch over David only by occasionally checking bubbles in the time-stream. In the bubbles, he saw David win multiple battles against faceless enemies, and Aori could not determine what they had done to incur the wrath of the Lord. He wondered if either side in the battles really knew why they were enemies. The holy wars he witnessed were just the beginning of an eternity of wars over religious differences.

Though he had washed his hands of all this, he still watched Saul through the bubbles as well. Each time he gazed through the rippling time-stream, he hoped to see Saul get what was coming to him. He watched in utter disbelief as David, when given the opportunity to get revenge on Saul, instead chose twice to spare his life.

Finally, in a tragic battle with the Philistines, Saul's kingdom crumbled around him. His son and heir, Jonathan, perished in battle, which was unfortunate, but it left David (who was his son-in-law) as the next in line for the throne. Saul's soldiers fought off the onslaught as long as they could, but it soon became obvious to the king that, without the Lord's blessing, he would most assuredly lose the fight that day. In a final act of desperation, Saul begged his few remaining soldiers to kill him, as he could not bear to die at the hands of the Philistines, who would have had no mercy in mutilating his body. Fearing the consequences for killing the king, his men declined his request. With the heathen enemies fast approaching, Saul took his sword and threw himself upon it.

Unblinkingly, Aori looked on, completely devoid of compassion for the dying king.

Chapter 2:05

Children 2, Giants 0

"You'll never believe where I was a minute ago," said Munder after Aori caught him in transit to his next life. His tone of voice sounded excited, but he maintained his characteristic annoyed grumble.

"Well, I saw you falling from some great height," Aori replied.

"Yeah. I've decided that I'm doomed to just keep getting killed by some little runt."

Aori could not contain his smile. "Perhaps that is your higher purpose, then."

"To die repeatedly?" Munder folded his arms across his chest and glared at Aori.

"If at first you don't succeed, try, try again," laughed Aori.

Munder scowled. "I sure hope, when you finally grow up, that you're big enough that it won't feel like an uneven fight when I smash your face."

"Ah, Munder," Aori sighed merrily. "Once again, you've come at just the right time. I seriously needed that laugh. Now, let me hear your tale."

"I'm done talking to you," Munder grumbled. "Odie, little Grampa wants a story."

The Odestone practically purred with excitement. "This is a grand story, Aori. Even I enjoyed it, and believe me when I say that this old fossil has not smiled in centuries."

"I believe it," said Aori. Feeling like a boy at story-time, he sat down cross-legged on the floor to listen to a tale told by a rock.

"Once upon a time," began the Odestone, with a flourish that contrasted with its usual stony demeanor, "a giant lived in a large castle."

"That was me," said Munder.

Aori's voice dripped with sarcasm. "No, really?"

The Odestone sang, "The castle was so high up that clouds surrounded it on every side. The giant had hordes upon hordes of gold and other riches stashed away inside his castle."

"Tell him about the goose," Munder interrupted. "You won't believe this."

Aori, who had read, translated, and written comparative analyses on the folklore of Aia, was quite familiar with the fantastic events of such tales. "Try me."

"It laid eggs made of gold," said Munder excitedly.

Aori's face contorted as he tried to imagine how that was physiologically possible. "Is the gold in a molten, liquid state while it is inside the goose?"

Munder stared blankly. "Um... yes. Go on, Odie."

The Odestone continued, "Despite the improbability of having a goose that laid golden eggs, it was obviously the giant's prize possession. Since gold is actually a rather soft and malleable metal, the giant could reform the eggs into necklaces, rings, and even calves."

"Calves?" Aori checked to make sure he had heard correctly.

Munder answered, "Calves. You know, like baby herbovines? You'd be surprised at the market for golden calves in this—well, that—day and age."

The Odestone continued, in detail that bordered on boring, about the physical properties of gold, its uses, and even the temperature of its melting point. While the Odestone had slightly jazzed up its storytelling ability, it was, after all, still a rock. Even when it had been a flesh-and-blood Codan man, his stories had still put people to sleep. It was trying to change—the best that rocks can change—but it was a slow process that would take multiple eons and lots of heat and pressure.

Aori shut his eyelids for a split second, but in that time he managed to drift into a rather deep sleep. Anyone who has ever fallen asleep in public—for instance, in a crowded classroom—is undoubtedly familiar with the sensation of nodding off and jolting awake. Aori looked around to see if anyone had noticed that he had fallen asleep. He also checked his chin for drool.

"Amazingly," the Odestone droned on, oblivious to its drowsy audience, "the giant had also managed to forge harp-strings out of gold, and they were tuned to perfect pitch upon a golden harp."

"Which is odd," Munder added, "because the giant hated music, and he felt a particular nausea at the sound of harp music."

"Munder," said the Odestone, "please do not project your own feelings into the role you assumed. Obviously, the giant was a very reasonable individual who appreciated fine music."

"Right," said Munder. "Now get to the part where he eats children."

The Odestone shook irritably. "According to the harp, which held vast amounts of lore in its... curvaceous and magnificent frame, the giant did, in fact, eat humans. Of

113

course, he was large enough that he could swallow them whole with little chewing, so it was probably rather merciful."

Munder added, "He also had a mill that ground human bones into flour so that he could bake bread out of them."

"Gruesome," Aori commented.

"Indeed," said the Odestone.

"Indeed," Munder repeated with an evil grin.

"Apparently," the Odestone continued, "the giant enjoyed a relatively fulfilling existence with his wealthy goldsmith business. He could have lived happily ever after, if not for the intervention of a young boy named Jack."

"The runt had help, though," Munder grumbled. "Tell him about how Asalie betrayed me and almost got me killed."

This caught Aori's full attention. "Asalie? She was there?"

"Munder is merely speculating," said the Odestone. "The boy said he had been given magic seeds, which subsequently grew into a colossal plant that reached up through the clouds to the giant's castle."

"That does seem within Asalie's abilities," agreed Aori, "but I can't see any reason why she would want to get involved."

"Nor could I," the Odestone concurred.

"Look," Munder snapped, "she was obviously going nuts, and she disappeared right before we were all scattered. She's probably just roaming around, handing out magic beans all willy-nilly."

"While that is a sound theory, Munder, I would like to hear the rest of the story."

"And I would like to finish," the Odestone rumbled.

"Fine. Don't mind me. I'm just the star of the story."

The Odestone might have rolled its eyes, if it had them. "Anyway, Jack climbed up the enormous plant and into the clouds."

"…Where he burglarized my castle…"

"Jack entered the castle and heard the giant's snoring, which drowned out the lovely music of the harp…"

"Thank goodness for that," added Munder.

"Apparently, the sweet, melodious tunes of the beautiful and shapely harp had put the giant to sleep…"

"That, or your stories of everything we could make out of the gold…."

"And while the giant slept, the boy discovered the various items being manufactured out of gold, and he was most certainly impressed with the multitudinous practical uses for the Earth's precious ore."

At this, Aori had to interrupt. "Ode, surely you aren't suggesting that making jewelry is a practical use of natural resources. While I'll admit that rings are attractive, they hardly serve a practical purpose."

Munder rolled his eyes and sighed. "Can we get on with it, please?"

"Of course," said the Odestone, "and I should clarify that not all the items that were mass produced in the giant's factory served a practical purpose."

"Thank you," said Aori.

"As it were, Jack began concocting a plan to transport the golden objects back down the plant to his house. It seems his family was very poor, and he had been instructed to sell their only herbovine, but instead he traded it for the magic seeds, and…"

Munder interrupted once again, "We don't really need to hear his side of it, Odie. Just let me tell the rest." With his wooden hand, he pantomimed strangling someone very short. "That little runt started rerouting the conveyor belts in my factory so that they'd move my treasure down his stupid plant to his stupid house."

"Wait." Aori interrupted the story for clarification. "He took apart and rebuilt your entire factory?"

"Yes."

"And you slept through the entire dismantling and reconstruction?"

Munder grimaced. "I was bewitched by that horrible, evil harp."

"That harp was absolutely not evil, Munder. Obviously, the giant was the only true evil in this story. That's why the boy had no qualms against stealing everything from him, and anyone who ever hears this tale will most assuredly see things from the boy's point of view."

"Anyway," Munder grumbled, "I guess it wasn't enough for this pipsqueak to steal everything I owned, including my *extremely practical* gold-plated toilet, so then he also stole the golden goose itself!"

Aori frowned. "Munder has a point here. I'm thinking this story should never be told to children. This boy does seem rather greedy."

"Yes," the Odestone agreed, "and his greed seemed to be his downfall, for when he attempted to steal the golden harp, it stopped playing its wondrous music."

"When I woke up," Munder continued, "I saw that everything was gone, and I could smell that little twerp. Of course, my first impulse was not to eat him, but I did want to grind up his bones. I believe that was my right as a home-owner."

"The boy escaped down the plant and, without thinking, the giant made the foolish mistake of following the boy down the stalk."

Munder gripped the Odestone tightly. "Keep it up, and you'll be Odie the pile of pebbles."

Aori shook his head, laughing. He had to wipe the tears of laughter from his eyes. "I think I can figure out the rest. I assume he cut down the plant, and you engaged your timepiece just before falling to your death?"

"Yup," said Munder.

"You were right. That is an unbelievable story."

"Oh, it gets better," said Munder.

"It does?" asked the Odestone.

"Yup." He reached into a satchel he had draped about his waist, and from it, he presented the golden harp. "I may have climbed down the vine without thinking, but I'm no fool. Gold's gold—even if it is a dumb, old instrument."

· The violet, swirling energy of the temporal spirit swirled around the Odestone, forming the ghost of a smiling, old man. Ode ran a finger down the harp's strings with a gentle, loving caress.

"I thought it'd make a nice gift for Lithe, if we ever find her," Munder said with a dumb grin.

As he looked upon the ethereal phantom of Ode the Elder of the House of Dorian, Aori felt that the weight of the grief he had carried with him had lifted. Perhaps not everything in this world was cruel and ugly.

Chapter 2:06

The Newly Improved Tweenticker 2000

As the golden harp played softly in the background, Aori tinkered with some finishing touches on Munder's wrist-watch. The technology surpassed Aori's vast knowledge of clockwork, seeing as how it involved microchips and batteries rather than cogs and gears. However, all of the bits and pieces seemed to fit together as Aori figured they should, and he could sense a kind of inaudible hum of temporal magic within it.

"It's been a learning experience, working on this watch. I think all it needs is a bit of a boost to jumpstart its magical energy stores."

Munder put the watch on and tapped its face in that futile way watch-owners often do, even though they know it won't do anything. "Can you do that?"

Aori scratched his chin in thought, even though he no longer had any facial hair there. "Yes, I think so. But when I do, it may transport you out of Tweentime. We have more to discuss before you go. I'm hoping that it will allow you to travel to and from Tweentime at will. That way, I won't have to catch you in between shifts."

"And how will we communicate with you?" asked Ode, still swirling in the form of a temporal spirit.

"I have considered that, as well. Come—let me give you a tour of my library." They took a few steps over to where Aori had placed the book and pieces of the bookcase from the Tower of Babel's library. "Keep in mind that these pieces came from the tower, which was somehow sharing time and space with my own tower. I am thinking my tower's powers of growth may still reside inside it. Fortunately, you get to be here for the experiment."

Munder tried to mask his boredom with a polite smile. "Oh, yay."

Aori closed his eyes and focused intently on the so-called library. "Nothing grows in Tweentime, because this plane of existence does not have the same boundaries as Earth or Aia. I am hoping that means that I can bend those boundaries."

"I don't understand any of that. Could you just do it?" Munder asked.

Aori smiled. "I'm going to make the library remember just how old it is."

"Um... okay." He still didn't really understand, but he figured Aori would keep explaining it until he agreed.

The metaphorical son of Father Time then reached out and harnessed the temporal energy that swirled around them. Though it had seemed rather complicated, as he had tried to explain the process, he found it rather easy to give the library back a few hundred years of its "life." Right before their eyes, the bookcase began to grow shelf by shelf, until it was about four feet high. The book that Aori had taken from Babel had gone forth and multiplied in the time that he had bestowed upon it, and it now had lots of other books and scrolls to keep it company. Upon perusing the new editions, Aori found that he had already read the texts. By simply visiting the library at King Saul's palace, he had updated his own magical library outside of time.

A smile spread across his face, as his experiment had been a complete success. "Just as I hoped—the library will continue to grow as we read more of Earth's literature. That means all you have to do is visit libraries throughout time, collect books for me, and in that way, I shall have the knowledge of the future right here in this time between time."

"That's great," said Munder, "except I... I'm not a very good reader."

"I don't think you will have to. The Odestone should be able to gather lore from the books, and it will act as a conduit for transmitting the lore here. I realize it is difficult to understand, since we are working mainly with the abstract constructs these books represent."

Munder tried to massage away the pain in his skull. "I think I'd rather be out getting beaten up by some little runt than here, getting a headache from listening to you ramble on about... whatever."

Aori laughed. "I'd also like for you to look for more signs of the other Aians. I'm afraid we may all be in danger as outcasts among these violent humans."

"Yeah," Munder said, "I usually get a real kick out of violence, and even *I* find this place a little brutal."

"That is simply because the violence is all perpetrated against you by small children," the Odestone vibrated. Its delivery of the joke was rather flat and stiff, but Aori laughed nonetheless.

"Anything else I need to know before I go find a deep lake and watch Odie sink?" growled Munder.

"Well..." Aori's expression turned somber again. "I'm still gathering data, but there is obviously some connection between the massacre in your future time and the one I witnessed recently. In both cases, the murderer also killed himself."

"We will gather all the information we can, Mr. Timister," the Odestone vowed.

After the giant and the stone had departed for unknown places and times, the barren isolation of Tweentime resurfaced. Aori even missed his clockworkers. Though he had no emotional attachment to the machines to speak of, he missed the services they provided. Before, he could send the clockworkers to find books for him, and they would. The option of going back to Earth to search for literature irritated him immensely. He wanted nothing to do with humans and their drama.

Of course, the last time he commanded his clockworkers to find him books, they ended up burning libraries, killing innocent civilians, and kidnapping whole races of people. Aori had deduced that the machines had had some other programming, presumably by Toki, the Time god.

The problem Aori faced affects many people with extra time on their hands. He had time to do any number of tasks, but he would far rather delegate the responsibility to others. If you had all the time in the world, what would you do? You would probably complain about being bored. If someone suggested a craft or something to keep you busy, you might be as listless and lethargic about it as Aori was feeling at this time. One might call him "lazy," which is a word that never would have related to him before, as he was always fastidiously inventing, synthesizing, and otherwise creating in such an efficient manner. However, many of the tools and resources he required were not currently available to him, and the workshop that had been part of his tower had scattered with the dust from the Tower of Babel.

He tried keeping himself busy by writing a book on the physics of travel to and from Tweentime. The fact that Munder took a shortcut between now and then in the process of transforming intrigued him. He theorized that the

122

psyches, or perhaps astral forms, of the beings whose bodies Munder assumes must also travel through Tweentime.

Reaching out his mind, he tried to sense the presence of other beings who might be temporarily caught between time. Though Tweentime looked like a vast wasteland of emptiness, it was infinite.

Suddenly, his search turned up a familiar face in the emptiness.

"Pettifogger?"

"Nothing!"

Aori looked around him. His surroundings had changed, but they were even more barren than before. Apparently, he had traversed millions of miles across Tweentime during his mental exploration. Now, he sat before his former protégé, who he had left for dead on Aia.

The gnome now had little hair left on his head, but he had a long, white handlebar mustache that curled up to his cheekbones. A sharp, angular beard pointed down from his chin like a spearhead. Though he still wore the goggles he had stolen from Aori's workshop, a wrinkled brow and crow's feet now snaked out around them. The years had taken their toll on Pyrite Pettifogger.

Though to the casual observer, Aori appeared as a young child, the magical spectacles showed his complete timeline in multiple flickering frames per second. The filmstrip-like perspective took some getting used to, but the gnome easily recognized his former mentor.

"Is it truly you, Pettifogger?"

"Yes, but…"

"I didn't accuse you of anything." Sitting cross-legged, Aori's eyes were level to those of the gnome. "I am glad to see that you survived the destruction of Aia, Mr. Pettifogger."

Pettifogger looked very nervous. "Yes, I survived. We all survived."

Aori gazed around at the nothingness surrounding them. "There's no one with you, Pettifogger."

123

"Oh no, they're back… back home, of course. We escaped here just before… before…"

Pangs of guilt hammered at Aori's conscience like underground miners chipping away at rock. "I'm sorry, Pettifogger. I tried to save the planet, but I didn't work fast enough."

"It's all in Time's hands now," said the gnome.

"Yes, I suppose. I suppose it has always been."

An awkward silence oozed out between them like a puddle of sludge or slime.

"You serve him now?" Aori cut through the sludge. "Toki the Time god?"

"… No more than you have ever served him, Mr. Timister."

"But, you did betray me to him."

"Correct."

"And you stole from me."

"Correct."

"I always knew you were pilfering gems from my mines, but what else did you take?"

Pettifogger seemed to be staring out at nothing, but the goggles allowed him to see parts of Tweentime that Aori could not. "These goggles…"

"I see that."

"Some clockworkers…"

"That explains why they suddenly seemed to stop taking orders from me."

"Your washing machine, a magic-steam engine, a few other trinkets…"

"You always did seem to have a fondness for my inventions." Aori's brow furrowed, and he stroked what used to be his beard. "I sense there's more."

Pettifogger protracted a prolonged pause. "Power," the gnome whispered, as if saying the words softly would make them go undetected by his own conscience.

"The power to come here," Aori deduced.

124

"Yes."

"You can steal power, as well?" While the feelings of betrayal stirred again within him, Aori could not contain his childlike sense of wonder. "Have you stolen abilities from anyone else?"

Pettifogger looked at his own wrinkled hands. Through the spectacles, he could see how they had looked before. "I tried."

"You attempted to steal from Toki?" Aori suggested.

"Yes," said the laconic gnome.

"I assume, by your current appearance, that you were discovered."

Pettifogger nodded.

He cleared his throat, as if to say something important, but then just stared off at the nothingness again

Aori reached out mentally through the swirling temporal energy, searching for some sign of what Pettifogger saw that he could not. "What are you looking at, Pettifogger?"

"Aia."

"The glasses allow you to see it for what it once was, I assume?"

The gnome cleared his throat, paused again, and finally said, "This was once my hideout... where I came to escape Aia, and all the destruction I caused..."

"*You* caused?"

"Now, this is my prison. He aged me, and left me here to look out for eternity at the world outside."

"Wait. Pause for a moment, Pettifogger. You mean to tell me that you were responsible for Aia's destruction?"

Pettifogger paused for several moments.

"I'm not to blame?" Anger suddenly faded from Aori, as relief swept over him.

The gnome looked at him, and through the goggles, the image of Aori the Elder superimposed onto his current, youthful appearance. "I'm afraid we are all to blame, Mr.

Timister. I tinkered with the machinations that you had already created."

Aori could not fault the gnome for sharing his foolish zeal for controlling time. "We were puppets, Mr. Pettifogger. We thought that we were in control, but all along, we were in his hands, as you said earlier."

Pettifogger's goggles fogged with the vapors of tears.

"I accept your unspoken apology, Mr. Pettifogger." He patted the old gnome on the back. At his current age, they were roughly the same height. Though it was a bit awkward for both of them, they shared in what onlookers might have called a half-embrace.

Behind them, the rusty mechanism of a revolver cocked into place. The sound echoed through the void like the ticking of a clock.

Aori wheeled around and time slowed as a bullet exploded from the revolver with a flash. The bullet approached them, and Aori could see it tearing through the ether of temporal energy. It paused in mid-air, and Aori caught a glimpse of the gunman. He was a Metachron, one of Toki's soldiers stolen from another time. He wore a brown leather vest and a wide-brimmed cowboy hat, suggesting that he had been stolen straight from a 50's Western.

Aori quickly snatched the bullet from its fixed location in the air and deflected its course out of harm's way. Before the gunman could think, Aori had taken the gun and turned it on him. "Who are you?" he asked the gunman.

Confusion stunned the gunman, as he tried to figure out how he had lost his weapon.

Aori sighed. "It appears I am doomed to have one-sided conversations all day. I will presume that you work for Toki."

The gunman nodded.

"Brilliant. You and my terse friend here should have a lengthy conversation, consisting entirely of nods and shrugs."

Pettifogger and the gunman looked at one another and shrugged.

Aori took a second to admire the craftsmanship of the revolver. "'Tis quite similar to my Aorimatic Alternating Arrow Apparatus, don't you think?"

Pettifogger nodded.

"Whatever your name is, I think you should go back from whence you came."

"I'm suppost'a take y'all with me," drawled the gunman.

"How profound," Aori muttered with one brow crinkled. "Unfortunately for you, we simply refuse. And since I now have your weapon, I believe I am in control of who will be coming and who will be going. You, sir, are free to return to your home."

Aori turned to face Pettifogger, and the gunman vanished. With the gun now pointed at him, Pettifogger cringed.

"My apologies, Mr. Pettifogger." Aori pointed the gun elsewhere. "I didn't mean to frighten you. I only mean to suggest that we make haste, and you perform one of your infamous escape tricks."

"I can't go, Mr. Timister."

"Pettifogger, don't be daft. You cannot stay here, with danger lurking in the very ether. Toki obviously knows we're here, and I'm afraid neither of us is in a position to have a civil discussion with the old codger."

Concern trickled from Pettifogger in beads of perspiration, but he remained steadfast in his position. "I have to stay here and watch."

"Poof! The curse is lifted. You may now freely go as you wish, so let's go, before more of his soldiers arrive."

"It's not that simple, Mr. Timister."

127

"Look; I am the mortal portion of the Temporal Trinity, little gnome. If I say you can go, you can go. Didn't you see me bend time just now?"

Pettifogger looked back at the nothingness. "Remember when I said *we* all survived?"

"And I thought you were just insane, yes…"

"Well, my family is out there."

"In the void?" Aori squinted to see through the vast, swirling energy.

"No, beyond the void."

"Outside of Tweentime?"

"Yes," muttered Pettifogger.

As they discussed the issue, the Army of the Anachronist approached from a distance. Some road horses, while others drove futuristic motorcycles.

"Fine, Pettifogger. I will build you a spyglass that will allow you to monitor them from afar… but we need to go, *now*."

In a blink, they disappeared and teleported back to Aori's library. Only, it no longer looked like as it had before. It had grown, as children do when you have not seen them for a long time. He remembered when his library was knee-high to a grasshopper, and now it stood at least two stories high. However, unlike your average building, it hovered in the ether and had roots growing from its foundation.

"Not as you remembered it?" asked Pettifogger.

"There were only a few shelves when I left. I don't understand it. I thought nothing could grow here. Time is meaningless…"

"Time *is* meaningless here, but that doesn't mean that time doesn't exist. It just pools up or creates eddies. It's more random here—more chaotic. This is time in its most primordial form." Suddenly the monosyllabic gnome had become rather verbose.

"Mr. Pettifogger, I believe that's the longest string of words I have ever heard you assemble as long as I've known you."

"I never thought you were listening, before."

Aori frowned. "I suppose I didn't have the time, before. I'm sorry. How is it that you know so much about Tween-time?"

Pettifogger smiled, which he had not done in what seemed like a lifetime. "I have had countless years to just sit and watch the temporal flow. Besides, gnomes have a strong connection with the natural order of things, so chaos draws my attention."

He reached in a coat pocket and pulled out a small golden seed. "The natural order is for things to be born, grow, and then die. Tweentime tends to muck up the order of things. Do you remember Daisychain?"

"Your sister? Why yes, I believe I do." Aori smiled. "I still have the flower she gave me. It's here somewhere…"

"You see, Mr. Timister, we are the link between everything natural and everything manufactured. This seed is actually mechanical, but it looks like something from nature. Watch." He coaxed the seed to open and sprout a tiny golden plant that looked like a jumble of wires and sheets of metal. Soon, shiny golden flowers blossomed at the top of the stem. He placed the plant on the doorstep of the library. Immediately it took root and began reproducing. More seeds sprouted and soon Aori had a garden growing in front of his library.

"Goldenrods," said Pettifogger with a bittersweet smile.

"Thank you," smiled Aori. "It's amazing."

"I owe you, Mr. Timister. For my life, for betraying you, stealing from you…."

"I am not without guilt myself, Mr. Pettifogger. We both have some penance to do. I think we can help each other in that area. I have a job for which I believe you would be perfect. My library needs books, and I believe you're just the scoundrel for the job of stealing them."

An uneasy look spread across the gnome's face.

"We'll return them later, after I've read them," said Aori, to assuage his concern. "While you're gone, I will work on your spyglass, if you'll let me use the lenses from those goggles you stole. Although, I still don't quite understand how your family could be outside of Tweentime. Are they on Earth?"

The gnome handed over the stolen spectacles. "No," said Pettifogger, "Aia."

Aori's face contorted in confusion. "You'll have to explain that to me later, Mr. Pettifogger."

"I shall try," he answered.

"I suppose you'll have to steal my power again so that you can travel in and out of Tweentime. Good luck—and if you find any materials that we could use for inventions, please bring some back. I'm afraid my resources are rather low at the moment."

"Yes, Mr. Timister." The gnome grinned. "But, sir, you're forgetting the limitless supply of gold in your garden."

Aori looked down at his new garden and smiled. When he looked up, Pettifogger had vanished. Shaking his head with a smile, Aori went about harvesting ore from the plants. Without the forge he had built on Aia, he would have to devise a new method for refining and smelting the metal. Deep in thought, he didn't notice Pettifogger pop back in through the ether. "Oh, I forgot…" he said in his squeaky voice.

Aori jumped at the sound. "Pyrite Pettifogger! Don't sneak up on me like that. I may be young now, but I could still have a heart attack!"

"Sorry, sir. I just thought I should tell you: it's Fool's Gold."

Aori's face tightened for but a moment. Then he shook his head, laughing. "Scoundrel!"

130

Chapter 2:07

Attack of the 50-Foot Munder

"Munder, you need to control your rage. You know what tends to happen when you get angry," the Odestone vibrated in warning.

Flies buzzed around Munder's head, and he swatted at them blindly. The blood pounded through his skull, drowning out the sounds of the Odestone chained around his neck. Something stung at his face as another annoying insect flew past. He grabbed it with his clawed hand and squeezed. The buzzing stopped, but now the insect smoldered in his palm. Upon closer inspection, he realized that the explosive insect was actually a tiny jet.

He also realized that his skin was a dark shade of purple. Looking down, he noticed cloven hooves where his feet should have been. Two enormous wings extended from his shoulder blades, and a spiked tail whipped around behind him. As it whipped, buildings crumbled at his feet. As usual, he had horns on his head; only this time, they were much longer and they weighed down his forehead considerably.

Tiny tanks fired up at him from the street level, and when they fired, it felt like being hit with a baseball. With a powerful stomp, he smashed a tank into bits.

In his current form, the tallest of skyscrapers came up to the middle of Munder's chest. His weakest kick shattered the steel girders that served as a building's skeleton. He uprooted one building from its foundation and used it as an improvised club against the next squadron of attack helicopters. The wanton destruction only served to fuel his bloodlust, and any semblance of rational thought fell by the wayside.

"Munder! You are destroying the city and injuring innocent bystanders," boomed the Odestone, but his words were lost in the cacophony of devastation.

Faintly, as if through earmuffs, Munder believed he heard orchestral music swelling up in the background. The music sounded rather heroic, and it made Munder feel as if what he was doing was a truly noble deed. "Be gone, evil buildings! I shall topple you with my purple might!" His voice came out raspy and strangely demonic.

The valiant soundtrack heralded the arrival of a massive ship that flew in the air by means of rocket engines and propellers. Cannons fired and actually did damage to the monster's thick, purple skin. Three individuals leapt from the ship's deck as if connected by some sort of wire-and-pulley system. One spiky-haired kid with a huge sword lunged straight for Munder's eye. The assailant connected with blow after blow with the massive weapon, and Munder was surprised as to how much it actually hurt. He tried to fight off the attack, but his tiny enemy just bounded from body part to body part, inflicting as much damage as possible.

As the swordsman showed off his acrobatic prowess, one of the others shot at Munder with a futuristic-looking rifle. She appeared to be a woman with space-age armor. The shots exploded on impact with his kneecaps, which disoriented the giant and made it difficult to stand. He reared up a leg and stomped on the woman with a satisfying crunch.

Before he could turn his attention back to the swordsman, he noticed the third enemy, who was a young girl, creeping up to her fallen comrade. A blinding white aura

132

surrounded her, and suddenly the armored woman was back on her feet.

Munder bent over to get a better look, as the young girl seemed to be saying something. He couldn't quite make out her words, but magical energy seemed to swirl around her. Light gathered from all over and fixed upon her in a large sphere. The sphere got larger and larger, until it was roughly half Munder's size.

Suddenly the orb burst open in a blinding flash of light and a brightly shining figure of a woman with white, flowing robes stood in its place. She had hair so white that it hurt to look upon it, and she hovered in mid-air in front of Munder.

The bright lady shouted something in Japanese, which Munder somehow translated to mean, "White Shining Fists of Brilliance!"

Before he could figure out why she shouted that, white shining fists of brilliance knocked him onto his back. Through the blinding light, he swore that he saw a four-digit number appear above his head.

Completely incapacitated, Munder chose to remain in the more comfortable position of flat on his back. Again, he had assumed a new incarnation only to get trounced by a smaller opponent. Surely, some gods somewhere had it in for him.

The young girl walked up and whispered in his ear. He couldn't make out the words, but he suddenly felt that they were responsible for taking away all the pain and chaos of the world. He drifted off into a peaceful sleep.

When Munder could finally reopen his eyelids, the Odestone immediately vibrated with a fervent rumble. "Ah, I see how it is. I try to calm you down for over an hour, but as soon as some cute, little girl whispers in your ear, you do whatever she says."

"Sorry, Odie. I got carried away again, I guess." Munder's head pounded, and his eyes were sore and blurry. "Where am I?"

"Tokyo, Japan," the Odestone answered. "Or what's left of it. You did quite a number on the downtown area."

"That sounds like a movie I saw once."

"Exactly," said the young girl. She was teenaged, and she wore brightly-colored clothing that Munder guessed was extremely trendy and modern. "I promise; Tokyo wasn't always like this. Giant monsters used to only attack in bad science fiction movies."

"Who are you?" Munder tried to shield his eyes from the light that radiated from her.

"Name's Sunny. I'm the spunky teenager of the group!" She gave a huge, fabricated smile and flexed a muscle, as if she were posing in a comic book. She even froze in that position for a good five seconds or so.

Munder looked around the room for cameras.

"Y'see, we used to have a pretty peaceful city. There was crime, sure, but no giant monsters rampaging through town... except in movies and video games. Ever since they re-released those cheesy sci-fi movies on HaNGDiVMoG, it's like the monsters took on a life of their own."

Munder sighed. "What the heck is a hangdivmog?"

"Hallucinext-gen-digital-video-movie-games. I thought everyone knew that. I guess, since you're an Oni from a demon dimension, they don't have them there, eh?"

"Of course. I'm from a demon dimension. Perfect." For some reason, his headache just wouldn't go away. It could have been the strain of holding up his massive horns, but he thought it might be due in large part to the spunky teen.

"I'm whatcha call a Caller. I call other-worldly spirits from... other worlds...."

"...So they can fight your battles for you?"

"Yep!" Sunny said in a manner that clearly illustrated the word *spunky*.

"So did you call me?" asked Munder.

134

"No, but somebody must have. It was probably the dragon. They say he's trying to raise an army to destroy all of Asia. But we're gonna put a stop to that!"

"That's super," said Munder. "I guess I'll just be going, then…." As he got up from the table, his head spun. He noticed that he still had the purple demon appearance, except now he was a much more convenient size.

"Hold on there, Mister!" The spunky teen stood in his way, with her arms akimbo. "We defeated you in battle, so now I'm your master! You're gonna have to fight alongside us now!"

Munder rubbed his forehead with both hands, trying to knead out the craziness like lumps in dough. It didn't work. "Okay, I'm assuming that this is the future, and this is what has become of the world. Normally, I'd be all excited to be inside a movie, even a bad sci-fi one, but it seems like all I ever get is a major beat-down. I'm getting just a bit tired of it, and some spunky little teenage girl isn't going to stop me!"

"Then how about me, Demon?" The swordsman stepped into the room with all the bravado of someone who knows he's the main character and hero of the story. Although, the word *swordsman* applies rather loosely here, as the spiky-haired individual had a rather effeminate demeanor, and Munder was only slightly sure that he was actually a male. He wore a bright yellow shirt that cut off to show his midriff, and he wore superfluous suspenders that unnecessarily accessorized his black leather pants. Large necked boots and gloves rounded out his garish attire. If not for the giant sword that took up most of the room, Munder might have died laughing.

"Let me guess, you're the brooding, young hero whose father left him a giant freaking sword with some as-yet-unidentified mysterious power. Your name is Storm, and you usually speak with just dramatic pauses."

"…" said the hero.

135

"That's amazing," said the third member of the team. "But his name is Arashi…which translates to *storm*, I guess." She was an adult, roughly in her late twenties, and she no longer wore the futuristic armor. A pair of glasses hung purposefully on the tip of her nose, and pencils stuck out of an uncomfortably tight-looking bun atop her head. She wore a white lab coat that clearly defined her as the scientist of the group.

"This is Hatsumeika," said the spunky teen. "We call her Meika for short."

"She's the inventor of the group, I assume. Are you currently working on an unstoppable super-weapon that will nullify the dragon's powers and allow you to defeat him?"

Meika's mouth fell open. "I—I hadn't even mentioned the plan to the others yet… but you're correct! How did you do that?"

Munder rolled his eyes. "Let's just say I've played this movie-game before."

"This isn't a movie-game, Bucko," said Arashi gruffly. "It's the real world, so you better start gettin' used to it!" To punctuate his point, he made a flourishing sweep of his sword and posed dramatically.

"Well, fine. If this is the real world, I've got a jaunty band of adventurers of my own to find. You guys wouldn't happen to know a half-Orien kid named Quondam, would you? Of course, he might be an old man, instead of a kid."

The spunky kid huffed. "Excuse me," she said sassily, "but we prefer *Asian*, not Oriental. Rugs are Oriental."

"Excuse *me*," Munder said. "That's not exactly what I said, but whatever."

"How would an Oni from a demon dimension know the hero Quondam?" asked the androgynous swordsman.

"For starters, I'm not really a demon. The name's Munder."

"Ha ha ha! You make me laugh, demon!" The hero made another fancy movement with his sword and posed with the sword behind his back and one finger on his other hand pointed upward, like a gun. It was, quite obviously, an unnecessary gesture.

"Almost every giant monster we have fought has tried to say they were the great giant Munder, trapped in another body," explained Meika.

Munder sighed. "That about sums it up, though. How d'you guys know me?"

Sunny said, "There's an old folk tale about how the hero Quondam saved all of Asia from the dragon."

"The same dragon that threatens to destroy Japan even now," said Meika.

"And other stories about Quondam also mention his giant sidekick, Munder." Sunny said perkily.

"That's me, but *he's* the sidekick," Munder grumbled.

"Well, in some stories," Meika explained, "he's more of Quondam's pet."

Munder grumbled. He pulled at Arashi's suspenders until they snapped hard against the swordsman's chest. "Look, kiddies. I'm the hero. Tell them all about it, Odie."

"Munder, please don't bring me into this," the Odestone sang. "I feel like I'm only barely holding on to the shreds of my sanity as it is."

"Sing them the ballad of my great deeds, minstrel," Munder bellowed.

The Odestone laughed, and tried to turn it into a cough, but it's difficult for a rock to pull off such a save. "Right. I will do what I can, Munder." The stone sang of the many adventures Munder had blundered his way through, and it only lightly touched on the murderous rampages, bitter betrayals, and uncontrolled bloodlusts.

When the song was over, the three heroes were visibly moved. Arashi even wept a little.

"Would you like to access the airship's chrono-records?" Meika offered. "They might give you some indication of where your friends are now."

137

"If I had a clue what that was, I might."

"They're computer files, silly!" laughed Sunny cheerily.

The Odestone spoke up. "These records—do they have some audio component, or would my obtuse companion here have to read them?"

Munder grumbled.

"Oh sure!" Sunny exclaimed. "Who has time to read anymore?"

The chrono-records told of Quondam's numerous acts of heroism for the Asian people, as he apparently single-handedly drove off the Huns, forced the Mongols out of China, protected merchants on the Silk Road from demons, and defeated the dragon Jaaku.

"Look up my name," commanded Munder.

"Munder," the Odestone hummed, "it is important that I gather as much lore as possible in this time-period. This machine could give us all the information we need. Try not to be so self-centered."

"Fine. Look up 'how Munder saved the world even though his stupid rock was only interested in reading and junk.'"

Meika typed in Munder's name, and the following text surfaced:

> …Munder the Giant resurfaced briefly as
> the dim-witted Gore, a member of the
> vampire group called the Blood Brothers. He
> narrowly avoided a severe trouncing by his
> once and future friend, Quondam, when…

"That's enough," said Munder, banging on the computer. "I'd rather not hear countless tales of how many small weaklings have beaten me over the years."

He removed the Odestone from around his neck and placed it next to the computer's speakers. "I suppose you think this is funny, Odie. Well, you can just stay here and gather as much lore as you want. I'm going out to save the world from a dragon!"

Munder stomped out of the room and through an electronic sliding door. As he walked through, the door caught on his tail. Several curse-words echoed throughout the halls of the airship.

"We aren't prepared for the final battle with Jaaku just yet, Munder. To fight him now would just be suicide," said Sunny with her usual sunny disposition, despite the looming chance for death in their near future.

"That's fine," said Munder. "You kids would only get in the way... and annoy me. I'll just do it myself."

"That, my son, would be a foolish idea," said a raspy voice.

Munder turned in the direction of the voice and saw a very short, very old man with a wide brimmed, bamboo peasant hat. He had a long, white Fu-Manchu-style beard that stretched down to his waist.

"I can't believe I forgot the obligatory old man with sagely advice in a time of need..." Munder mumbled.

"I am Mukashi," said the old man. "I was there for the last battle with Jaaku, four hundred years ago..."

"Wait a second," interrupted Munder, "—how did I know that word, 'obligatory?'"

"You must have read it somewhere," said Mukashi, a bit exasperated, but still maintaining that sage-like, wise-old-man-voice.

"No, that can't be it," said Munder dismissively. "I don't read."

"You mean you really can't read?" Sunny laughed.

"First of all, shut up. Secondly, I just said that I don't read. I probably could, if I wanted to. And finally, say one more thing about it and I'll break your cheery, little face."

Sunny shut up.

139

"Hang on one more second—how is it that you were at the last battle? You're 400 years old?"

"Impressive math skills, giant one, but I'm actually 408. I was a child when I helped Quondam fight Jaaku the first time."

"Gotcha," said Munder. "Whatever. Now that we have our old man, who I predict will die just before the final battle but only after giving us one last piece of wisdom that will save the day, let's go slay a dragon!"

He started walking off again, but Sunny jumped in front of him. "It's not time, yet. Meika's still working on her ultimate weapon, and Arashi is still learning more about his innate powers by training with Mukashi."

"Of course," said Munder. "Hope the old man doesn't die before finishing the lesson."

Sunny's cheerful smile contorted for a fraction of a second. "Besides, Munder—you can't go without me; I'm your Caller now, remember?" With a sprightly bounce, she gave him a playful punch on the arm.

Munder smiled that polite smile one gives when a small, annoying child is stepping on your toe repeatedly and giggling as his mother looks on and does nothing. Then, he punched her back.

When Sunny woke up, Munder was gone.

Fortunately for a would-be heroic dragon-slayer, said dragons are relatively easy to find. They often leave a large path of destruction. Unfortunately for Munder, he was leashed to a certain area due to the fact that his Caller was unconscious on the airship. He was also much smaller than he had previously been, and the dragon towered high over the tallest of skyscrapers.

Jaaku more closely resembled the dragons of Asian lore than the beasts of fantasy literature based in other geographical areas. He had a long body like a snake, four smaller limbs, and a large head. Flames ornamented his face in the appearance of a long beard, mustache, and eyebrows. Fire also erupted from the end of his tail and in even intervals along his back, giving the appearance of spines.

The dragon had coiled itself around Tokyo Tower, which is 333 meters tall and was modeled after the Eiffel Tower in Paris. A ride to the observation deck cost around 1500 yen at that time, but all the visitors had either fled or been eaten. Pretending to be undaunted, Munder leapt from the airship's deck in the direction of the dragon, assuming his purple wings would allow him to fly. Instead, he dropped about 4 meters before being called back to his Caller. He was instantly teleported to Sunny's side.

Her characteristic cheerful face was marred by a swollen, purplish-black eye. "Couldn't stay away, could you?"

Munder grumbled. "How many punches in the face would it take before you stopped being so freakin' cheery?"

She stopped smiling briefly. "As you can see, we need more time. Meika is working on weapons for us based on what Mukashi remembers of Jaaku's weaknesses."

"Super," said Munder. "I'll need a really big axe." Pausing and posing dramatically, he flexed his enormous muscles. "Bigger than Arashi's sword."

Sunny giggled.

Munder grumbled.

"Whenever we need to learn a lot of really hard skills, build something that would take many months, or—in your case—go from being a jerk to a nice guy in a very short amount of time, there's only one thing to do…"

"Let me guess: A montage."

"Exactly." With a peppy bounce in her step, she led him down the hall to what looked like an engine room. There were many technologically advanced machines in the room that looked extremely complicated to Munder.

"This," Sunny continued, "is the Montagenerator. It's one of Meika's greatest inventions. Of course, she had help

141

from Mukashi. He's a master of temporal magic, whatever that means."

Suddenly, Munder became interested. "That explains why he's been able to live 400 years."

"Four hundred eight years," Sunny corrected giddily.

All of the deductive, inductive, and productive thoughts that had been slowly forming in Munder's insufficient brain fell by the wayside in place of much more violent thoughts involving Sunny and a very large axe.

The second that they activated the Montagenerator, motivational music began to play. Despite Munder's distaste for all things musical, he could not deny the fact that it had a strong effect on him. He could already feel himself getting really pumped.

As he didn't plan to grow, progress, or learn anything during the time, he just sat back and watched the montage unfold. Meika worked on their ultimate weapons, Mukashi trained Arashi in some mystical fighting techniques, and Sunny helped the Odestone navigate the computer's history databanks. The Odestone was in lore heaven.

By the end of the inspirational song, each member of the party had a weapon of ultimate power. Munder looked at his, which looked like a metal pole, compared it to Arashi's huge, gleaming sword, and mumbled a string of expletives under his breath. "Thanks for the stick," he growled. "Why are we using swords and stuff in the future, anyway? Don't we have laser blasters or something?"

Meika huffed. "It's not just a stick. Press the button on the side."

Munder pressed the button, and the stick extended another three feet. "Oh, it's a long stick. My apologies."

"Press the other button."

Munder pressed the other button, and the stick emitted a purple glow. Two wide bands of purple light shot out of the end of the stick in spiraling arc-shapes, forming an S-shaped axe blade. The arcs of energy buzzed and sparked, but despite the obvious danger, Munder could not contain his curiosity. He lightly touched the axe-head with the end of his finger, and suddenly he had one less finger. Several loud curse words filled the room.

Meika forced a face of slight concern. "I forgot to tell you—don't touch it, idiot. It's a laser axe. The longer handle allows it to double as a halberd."

Fighting back tears, Munder whispered, "I love it. Thank you."

The party of heroes hurried toward the now-devastated Tokyo Tower. It looked like a matchstick burning in the night sky, which contrasted with the uncharacteristic darkened state of the cityscape. Downtown Tokyo had been lit up by neon and electricity for many years now, making it look even flashier than New York's Times Square or the Las Vegas strip combined. Now, however, the city appeared as if technology had taken a turn to the dark ages.

The dragon wormed its way through building after building, setting the structures ablaze and rupturing gas lines throughout the city. Munder looked on in awe at the holocaust before him, and he gripped his axe tighter. "So, what are his weaknesses, O wise sage?"

There was no response.

"He does have weaknesses, right Mukashi?"

"He's gone," said Sunny.

"Our spiritual guide and mentor figure left us before the final battle? Is he on his deathbed? Is he planning on sending us some psychic message during the fight?"

Meika pointed up at the smoke-filled sky. "No, I think he stole our airship and made off with our only chance for escape."

Munder cursed repeatedly, opting to include as many slurs against the elderly as possible.

143

"Maybe he's just getting the airship away from the flames, so it doesn't explode," Sunny attempted to lighten the mood.

"No, he's betrayed us," Munder snarled through clenched teeth. "I've been around betrayal enough to know it when I see it."

Meika tried, as always, to fix things. "You were around him more than any of us recently, Arashi. Did he seem strange at all?"

Arashi was silent for a moment, and then said, "He did seem rather preoccupied with the time. He checked his watch a lot, as if he had an appointment or something."

Rusty gears and sprockets scraped against one another inside Munder's brain. "Toki. I should have known."

Toki is the Japanese word for 'time,' so the reference to the god of Time meant little to the others. Munder clarified quickly, giving a brief synopsis of each dastardly deed Toki had committed. "And now he has the Odestone, too."

Since rescuing the stone from its burning Aeolian home years ago, Munder had only let it out of his grasp for brief periods of time. The two had become inseparable, and even Munder understood the ramifications of losing their best source of Earth's lore.

As the airship disappeared into the smoky, crimson-tinged sky, the words of his companions stopped making sense. Without the Odestone to act as a constant translator, the Japanese language sounded like gibberish to him.

Jaaku the Dragon shot through a nearby building like a rocket, causing debris to fall all around them. The team sprang into action, each performing their usual tasks; Sunny healed their wounds, Meika fired volley after volley from her hand-cannon, and Arashi hacked and slashed.

Munder stared up at the sky. He figured he could still catch the airship if he tried, and in the grand scheme of things, the Odestone was by far more important to him than Tokyo was. He wasn't used to facing such dilemmas.

Usually, he solved most of his problems by choosing to kill something.

As he weighed his options, it grew more and more obvious that his teammates were losing the fight against the dragon. Sunny had already had to cast a resurrection spell on her teammates, and none of her light magic seemed to have any effect on Jaaku. Still, Munder's ties to these people, especially the more annoying ones, were flimsy at best. Torn between his desire to maim and his loyalty to his stone friend, he chose to follow the ship.

Unfortunately, Munder was rarely in the position to make his own decisions. As soon as he spread his wings and leapt from the roof of the building, the leash of his Caller snapped tight, and he was teleported to Sunny's side.

"Oh brother," sighed Munder.

Sunny shouted something in Japanese, and Munder assumed that it was probably some sort of peppy battle cry to cheer him on through the fight.

As it turns out, it was probably more like a summoning spell for invoking the purple Oni's true form. Munder grew to the size of the buildings around him, and suddenly the fight seemed a bit more even.

He grabbed the dragon by the tail, spread his wings, and launched into the fire-lit sky above. Assuming he could still only travel a limited distance from Sunny, he swept down and scooped her up in his other hand. Her body appeared lifeless, but he figured she had to enter a trance in order to call a monster to fight for her.

Higher and higher he soared, straining his eyes to see through the dimly-lit smoke. The airship was nowhere in sight, but the thinner air was effectively extinguishing the dragon's flames. He knew the ship could not have made it so far in such a short amount of time; "With Toki aboard, though, it would be plenty of time to escape," he deduced.

Looking down at his watch, he realized his only choice would be to follow Toki to Tweentime. However, he didn't want to just abandon Sunny and the dragon thousands of meters above the ground, and he sure didn't want to take the annoying, spunky teen along with him.

"There's no rush," he told himself. "Once I enter Tweentime, I can make up for lost time." The dragon writhed and twisted, trying to free itself from his grip. "But first, I suppose I'll have to dispose of this problem."

Munder swung the dragon by its tail in three wide arcs before letting it go. As the dragon struggled to right itself with gravity working against it, Munder pulled the axe from its place behind his back, pressed the button to activate the laser, and sprang upon the falling Jaaku.

With one swing of the axe, he hewed the dragon in two. The smell of burning dragon flesh billowed up around them as the two halves of Jaaku fell lifelessly towards the Earth. Still unsatisfied, Munder dealt several more blows to each half of the dragon, leaving little more than a few charred chunks to rain down on the city below.

By the time he found his companions and landed, his size had once again reduced to more like what he was accustomed to in his original body. Sunny groggily opened her eyes and said something cheery in Japanese.

Meika rushed over to Sunny and Munder, attempting to capture them in a congratulatory embrace. Munder dodged, but he had to admit a feeling of pride had swelled up inside him. This time, he was the hero, without double-crossing anyone else or attempting to seize the role from another by force or murder. The pride only lasted a few seconds, before extreme irritation usurped its seat of power.

Arashi shouted something in Japanese, leapt into the air, and came crashing down on Munder. The others stood back in confusion as Arashi's huge sword hacked into Munder's flesh.

"What are you doing, Arashi? Have you lost your mind?" shouted Meika.

Trying to remain positive, Sunny yelled, "We're all friends here, Arashi!"

Of course, Munder understood none of this, as his only source of knowledge in the Japanese language was currently a prisoner of a mad god. "Forget this," he grumbled, as he made a conscious decision to give in and let his mindless rage take over. What was the point of trying to understand, anyway?

The purple Oni kicked out with his hooves, knocking Arashi into the side of a building. Munder got to his feet and surveyed the damage to his body. He had several chunks cut out of his flesh, but his wooden arm had protected him from most of the blows.

Small beads of light gathered around him, and the pain slowly faded. He turned and noticed Sunny casting a healing spell on him. As much as he could in this situation, he smiled.

Arashi shouted something in Japanese, and if Munder could have understood, he would have known that Mukashi, or Toki, had planted information in his head regarding Munder's timepiece. While the others were working on their own projects during the montage, Toki had been working on another of his schemes, and Arashi had been growing puppet strings. Despite the language barrier, Munder could tell that the swordsman was focused intently on the timepiece.

Suddenly, he reached for the object, which activated its temporal magic. The instant that Arashi lunged at him with his giant sword, Munder vanished.

In Greek mythology, the god Zeus had a habit of cheating on his wife, Hera. On one such occasion, he fell in love with with a nymph named Io. In order to protect her from Hera's wrath, Zeus turned Io into a heifer. What a flattering transformation that was.

Hera asked Zeus to give her the heifer as a gift, since she was onto him. She then appointed a giant named Argus

147

Panoptes as a sort of private detective to do surveillance on the heifer and guard her from any visiting gods with a passion for cows. Panoptes was a good choice for this job, as he had one hundred eyes scattered over his entire body.

In retaliation, Zeus sent Hermes to sneak in and rescue the heifer. Hermes was famous for his swift running speed, but even he could not slip past one hundred eyes. The messenger of the gods then decided to enlist the help of Orpheus, a mortal musician who was, without a doubt, a Coda. The Coda gave him a lyre and several songs.

Enter Munder, just in time for the show.

Munder slipped into the body of Argus Panoptes and immediately wanted to shut his eyes. He could see in every direction, and it hurt his brain to look himself in the eyes. It is common knowledge that Munder's mental functions are somewhat limited anyway, but combine that with the processing power needed to take in sensory information times 100, and he just couldn't take it.

Just as he was considering gouging out his own eyes, the sound of soft, sweet music entered his ears. That made him also consider gouging out his ears, but he wasn't sure that was possible.

"Nope," he grumbled, and pushed the button on his watch.

As Munder transcended time and space to Tweentime, the hundred eyelids of Argus Panoptes began to droop. Hermes swiftly snuck in, slew the giant with a large crescent blade, and rescued Io.

Chapter 2:08

The Sandbox

Aori's sense of time had skewed slightly in the last few days... or years. He had no idea how many minutes had passed since Pettifogger left to find books for the library, but it felt like days. "Why, when the isolation already bothered me, did I send him away on an errand?" he muttered to himself.

Listlessly, Aori sifted through the library's books, scrolls, and sheets of papyrus. He had already read all of the text in his library, and nothing had changed in the last few minutes (or hours). With no clocks or sun to show the time of day, Aori found it incredibly difficult to stay focused on tasks. He wandered from one thing to another, but he felt as if all his research and work had led him nowhere.

"Come on, Aori," he said to himself. "That spyglass isn't going to build itself."

As if to mock him, the walls and floor of the library suddenly began to creak and hum with life. The floor cracked a little, and a small wire sprouted up from the floorboards. Aori gazed on in wonder. "Perhaps I was wrong...."

The sprout grew fatter and eventually encased itself in a thin skin of rubber, so it looked more like a power cord to some electronic device. Small, metal buds opened up to form leaves. Instead of the veins one would find on a natural leaf, this one appeared to consist of transistors and silicon. Aori lost himself in the magnificent show of nature and machinery combined.

Though no name for the contraption came to mind at that time, Aori assumed it grew in response to something his friends had found in the real world. In fact, the growth had begun the very instant that Ode started working on the computer.

In spite of the buttons, circuits, and screens it sprouted, however, Aori could not get the device to do anything. Though satisfying, punching all the buttons as a child or elderly person might do served absolutely no purpose. Nonetheless, the machine-plant captivated and amazed him.

He was so preoccupied, in fact, that he did not hear the cries of help coming from outside the library. The door swung open, and the minute form of Pyrite Pettifogger tumbled into a bookshelf with a loud crash.

Quickly, Pettifogger slammed the door shut behind him. By that time, he had created enough noise to distract Aori from his trancelike state. He rushed down the stairs to see what had happened, and found Pettifogger braced against the door and panting.

"What is going on here, Pettifogger?"

The gnome could not catch his breath.

"Are you hurt?"

Pettifogger managed a quick shake of his head, then put his slender finger to his lips. "Quiet," he whispered. "Maybe they'll wander off."

Panic and puzzlement butted heads inside Aori. "Who? Toki's men?"

"No, these are from Earth. They are Persian soldiers."

"How did they get here?"

Pettifogger shrugged. "I suppose they followed me."

Aori gently pushed a curtain aside just enough to see out the window. Several Persian soldiers stood upon a winding walkway that had grown in front of the library. They currently fought against thick vines and brambles made of Fool's Gold.

"It appears," whispered Aori, "that your garden is keeping them at bay for the time being."

"Sorry," the gnome whispered back. "For what it's worth, I did manage to escape several other bands of soldiers in my quest."

"Well, at least you made it out alive," said Aori, displaying a compassion that Pettifogger had seldom seen in his dealings with his master.

The gnome stared with wide eyes at Aori. "What?"

"I expected you to ask about the books before my health, Mr. Timister."

Aori cleared his throat. "I keep trying to tell everyone, I'm not a heartless, evil despot. I was just really, seriously preoccupied with myself for a long, long time. Now, did you get the books?"

Pettifogger smiled. "Yes. I traveled over much of Asia Minor, through Alexandria, Anatolia, and I visited King Solomon's library in Jerusalem. You're going to love what I found."

"Well done, Mr. Pettifogger!" Aori started to embrace the gnome, but a loud crash against the door saved them both from what might have been an awkward hug.

"They're at the door now!" Pettifogger panicked. Aori listened to the thuds against the wooden door, but despite his vast and incredible power over time, he simply could not devise a plan for surviving this attack. "Shall we stay and fight, or run and hide?"

Pettifogger glanced at his companion from head to toe, which currently measured something around 4 feet. Quickly, he marveled at Aori's slowed aging process over the span of time he had been absent. "Well, since you are still a child, and I am a wee, tiny person, I should like to suggest that we run."

They managed to make it to the second floor by the time the Persian soldiers had hacked their way through the door. The boy and the gnome hid in utter silence and listened for the footsteps of the warriors below them. Instead, they heard the sounds of battle. Swords clanged against each other, and grunts and screams echoed through the library's walls.

Finally, the sounds of battle faded and the footsteps continued; only this time, they were much louder, as if all the soldiers stomped up the steps in unison. Aori held his breath and closed his eyes, waiting for the inevitable axe to fall.

Instead, the axe just lightly brushed up against his shoulder. "You can come out now, pansy."

Aori looked up, and the monstrous figure of a three-eyed giant towered before him. The extra eye bulged and stared at him mockingly. "Munder?"

"Of course. I'm your bodyguard, ain't I?"

"I suppose," said Aori. "Why do you have three eyes?"

"Well, I was born with two of them. I guess you could say I checked out of my last job a little early, and I guess I got to keep part of the... perks. Have you always had a weird outline of an old man around you?"

Pettifogger came out of hiding and interrupted. "Did you see a large band of Persian soldiers downstairs?"

"Yep," said Munder.

"Are they still down there?"

"More or less." Munder turned to Aori. "Who's the runt?"

"Munder, meet Pyrite Pettifogger. He is a gnome, and a... friend."

Munder smirked. "Pleased ta meet ya." He held out a finger for the gnome to shake.

"When you say 'more or less,' Munder," stammered Aori, "does that mean I'm going to be cleaning bloodstains off my bookshelves for the next three months?"

"Some are still breathing, I think."

"Ah," said Aori, as he crept down the stairs. "This gives me an idea, Munder. What if I trained my own Anachronistic Army, built from the soldiers we encounter as we traverse the ages? Similar to my library, this army would grow, and eventually it might rival even that of Toki. One day, we would be able to overthrow him and restore order to the timestream."

"That would be great, but we need to overthrow him tonight," said Munder.

"What? Why?"

Munder stretched his back, as if he were already preparing for another fight. "He stole the Odestone."

"Toki?"

"Yep."

"How?"

"Long story."

Aori sighed. "We have time. We have all the time in the world, actually."

"I'm not really the storyteller, you know. After I rescue Princess Odie from the castle, he can tell you all about it." He headed toward the door, axe in hand.

Aori stood in the doorway, as the door currently rested in pieces on the floor. "Munder, you can't possibly be serious."

"Look, kid-gramps, I'm not asking for your help."

"You certainly can't overthrow the god of Time all by yourself!"

Munder grumbled. "I don't have to kill Toki. I just have to get the Odestone. Take a second to think about what Toki would do with him."

"He would have the lore of the ages at his disposal... but he probably already knows everything already."

"More importantly," said Munder, "he's keeping us from having that information."

Aori took a minute to marvel at Munder's newfound vision and insight. "It's amazing what one extra eye can do."

Munder's face tightened up. "I don't think you really want to keep standing in my way."

"No, I don't. I want you to reconsider. I want to put a stop to Toki just as much as the next guy, but we cannot simply rush in and hope for the best. Give me time to develop a plan, and I promise you, we will return your friend."

"He's not my friend. He's just a rock," grumbled Munder.

"Hmm," said Aori. "Nonetheless, I need you here to train these soldiers. You will be their captain, just as you once led the Army of the Anachronist."

Munder rolled three eyes. "Fine. Plan." He stormed out the broken door, dragging two soldiers along behind him.

"It will take many more than five beaten, bloody soldiers to rescue your friend from Toki's castle," suggested Pettifogger, as they watched Munder train the injured men.

"You are right about that," Aori agreed.

"They don't even understand what he's saying."

"I think they understand the fear he's put into them."

"I think I do too," Pettifogger gulped.

As Munder barked orders in a foreign language his men could not comprehend, Aori studied the books Pettifogger had acquired. He hoped that they would include some clues as to the whereabouts of the other Aian refugees, or at least give him a working knowledge of his soldiers' language.

Aori learned Persian fairly quickly, which surprised even him, as he assumed most of the residual magic from the Tower of Babel had faded away long ago. As best he could, he explained the situation to his new squadron. However, when the situation deals with a pocket dimension between

154

time, a living library whose owner is from another planet, and an impossible battle with a god of Time, something always gets lost in the translation. Basically, the men understood that if they didn't do as the large man said, they would wind up in very small pieces.

.

"Let's go out and recruit more men," Aori announced after several days of training the army. "We will need more swords if we are to have any hope of even making it to the castle."

"Well, I'm staying here," grumbled Munder.

"Munder, I may have need of your... expertise in coercion."

Munder didn't understand the words *expertise* or *coercion*, but he figured it was a compliment. "I've had enough of Earth; all the little twerps of the world seem to have it in for me. I hate kids."

Aori laughed. "Well, I will do what I can to grow up, but in the meantime, I will try to protect you from the world's children."

"Good luck with that," said Munder.

When Aori's bubble of Tweentime settled on the hot deserts of Israel once again, the boy sighed heavily. "Please tell me that there is more to Earth than just sand."

"Oh yes," said Pettifogger. "There is marvelous beauty here, Mr. Timister. I have seen rolling plains of the greenest grass, oceans bluer than the sky, and...."

"Look," Munder interrupted, "I hate to interrupt this pansy-talk, but I've been thinking."

Pettifogger muttered an inaudible insult.

Aori smiled. "I'll try to refrain from making some jest about the idea of you thinking."

"Great," said Munder. "But first, could you please pull yourself together?"

"Pardon me?" asked Aori.

155

"Remember that outline of the old man I saw around you earlier? Well, now it's following you, along with a weird, swirling, purple ghost."

"Hmm," said Aori. "What do you see when you look at Pettifogger, or the soldiers?"

"I see a tiny nuisance and a bunch of wimps."

Pettifogger muttered another inaudible insult.

Aori moved back and forth as Munder's third eye followed him intently. "I believe it's your third eye. Perhaps it allows you to see more than meets the eye."

"You mean, like robots in disguise?" Munder snickered.

Aori gave him a puzzled look. "Perhaps.... What is it you were thinking, earlier?"

Munder cleared his throat. "Okay, follow me on this one, because I know you're going to think it's a crazy idea, and everyone's probably going to say 'Munder, you're such an idiot...'"

Pettifogger muttered an inaudible, but obvious, insult.

Munder continued, "Aori... what if you *are* Toki?"

"What?"

"Look, you're starting an army with me as the captain. So did Toki. Is that a coincidence, or some sort of weird screw-up of time?"

"So," said Aori, "you're saying I will eventually become Toki, travel back in time, and give myself the power to alter time?"

"I know. It's stupid."

Aori rolled it over in his brain. "It's a conundrum and an enigma intertwined in a Gordian knot, but I find the idea intriguing, nonetheless. If I am Toki, and I change things— make different choices—perhaps I could somehow find a way to set everything right."

"It would also explain why your powers are getting stronger, and why I see that old man following you." Munder looked like the thinking hurt his brain. "Maybe..."

156

"I hate to interrupt," said Pettifogger with the hidden smile of someone who didn't mind interrupting quite so much, "but does anyone else see a little boy sitting in the sand over there?"

"A boy?" Munder tried to hide the panic in his voice. "Where?"

"Over there."

Munder squinted. "All I see is a light that hurts my eyes."

"I see him," said Aori mystically.

A small boy sat cross-legged in the sand at their feet. He had constructed an intricate sculpture made of sand, consisting of several buildings making up a large city. In the shifting breeze, Aori swore he saw small figures made of sand moving about in the sculpture.

The boy wore ragged and brown peasant clothes, and he had dark brown hair and skin that had been tanned by the bright sun. Despite his meager appearance, Aori sensed a strange aura about him, as well as a sort of kindred spirit.

Aori approached the boy and sat down, and as he did, he saw a brief glimpse, superimposed on his current form, of the boy as a man with a crown of thorns. He had an unmistakable presence and spirit radiating from his core, and Aori believed that he knew who the boy was, or would one day be.

"Nice sandbox you've got here," said Aori.

"It is a desert," said the boy.

"You'll have to work on your figurative language. That was a metaphor."

"The world is my sandbox."

"You'll have to work on your down-to-earthness, kid," said Aori. "Mortal men don't really talk like that."

The two children played innocently together in the sand, in perfect contrast to the immense power they represented. The paradox continued to unfurl, as they shaped and molded the sand sculpture of the city; the boy built and Aori renovated, while time, the elements, and erosion slowly ate away at their work of art.

As they played, Aori brooded like a teenager on the pressures of being the mortal incarnation of a god. He ranted about the sins of the father in the trinity with son and temporal spirit. He tried to sound sage-like and give the boy advice, but his emotions got the better of him, in the end.

"I've been the scapegoat for all the things *he* does. I'm supposed to add a more human, mundane aspect to the temporal spirit, but he's the one who acts like a kid at play with his toys. You'll see, kid. In the end, when you need Him most, He will forsake you. Toki could have stopped time and saved the world, but he just let it fall apart around me."

When he was done with his rant, Aori had aged several years. He was now roughly fifteen years old. "The beauty of all this is that storytellers and historians can just skip whole sections of time in just a few lines. We can always gloss over this time in your life."

At last, the boy stood up and brushed the dust off his clothes. He, too, had aged to his mid-teens while they had played. He looked down at the sculpture they had created. "This is the city where I will die."

A sudden gust of wind blew the sand away, marring the image completely. The young man walked away, saying, "God be with you, Aori Timister. I have much to do, and I have wasted too much time already."

"Then, may Time be with you," said Aori.

When the young man had disappeared over the horizon, Aori once again noticed Pettifogger and the others. "Have you been standing there the whole time, Mr. Pettifogger?"

"Well, I did have time to go get some mules for us, but I swear I wasn't gone long enough for you to age as much as you have!"

Aori laughed. "Mr. Pettifogger, you are quite the resourceful gnome!"

"I got us more soldiers," grumbled Munder.

"Well, praise be to you too, then, Munder. Perhaps you should go back and begin training them."

"Yeah," said Munder. "I'm sick of this place. There's too much war."

They all had a good laugh at the irony of Munder disliking a place for its violent content, and the giant went on his way back to Tweentime to train his battalion.

Chapter 2:09

Of Pedantry and Pedestals

Roughly around the time Pettifogger set foot on Earth the first time, which would have been approximately 900 BC, iron had become the most common metal for crafting weapons and armor. The Iron Age began around 1200 BC in the Middle East, but the metal was even more expensive than gold at that time. Obviously, the armies that could afford to implement the stronger metal dominated those that still used bronze.

Aori and Pettifogger decided, then, to go to Anatolia, or Asia Minor, where the practice of smelting iron had begun. The name *Anatolia* is Greek for "the rising of the sun," but this should not be confused with the Land of the Rising Sun, which would have been much further east. The name *Asia*, of course, came from the Aian woman who came from her doomed planet bearing the souls of her lost people with her. The name spread along the Silk Road into Asia Minor, or modern-day Turkey. The Greek language incorporated the word as a description of any land to the east, where the sun rose.

At the time of their arrival, Asia Minor had just become a Roman province. The Roman Empire stretched to just about every piece of land that touched the Mediterranean Sea, and, more than likely, continued fighting to get the rest even as Aori and Pettifogger traveled.

As you might have already surmised, this did not mark the most interesting period in the lives of Aori and Pettifogger. They mainly went from town to town recruiting soldiers and sending them to Tweentime to be trained by Munder.

The duo also traveled through Macedonia, Greece, and other Roman provinces in search of clues to the whereabouts of their fellow Aians. While they heard no news about Quondam or Lithe, they did find Ionian, Aeolian, and Dorian Greeks scattered throughout that republic. These people had quite obviously intermingled with the Coda, as evidenced by their use of the three main houses of Codan society. As faithful readers may remember, Lithe's mother, Aria, was from the Aeolian line of nobles, while her father had Dorian ancestry.

While Aori tried to bolster up his forces and gather raw materials for his inventions, Pettifogger often spent his time wandering through the marketplaces and picking pockets. Many items of considerable value could fit inside his pack. Of course, this was due in large part to the fact that Aori had enchanted the pack to send items directly to his library in Tweentime. Aori called it the Timister Totebag of Unfathomable Depths. Pettifogger just called it a bag.

Even though the townspeople hardly noticed him, what with his small stature and keen knack for evading sight, Pettifogger felt uneasy as he meandered through the shops and crowds. Almost every shop contained shelves and shelves of clay pots, urns, or bowls for sale. As he examined them closely, Pettifogger felt as if even these inanimate objects were watching him.

"It's just this heat getting to me," he muttered to himself.

Several urns in particular caught his eye, however. The Greeks often recounted stories in picture form on their creations, yet these artifacts seemed to depict events from another world. Pettifogger recognized a large moth with his arms outstretched, standing over a massive crack in the ground. Another urn showed two large towers grown together at the base, covered in an overgrowth of burning thorns. Careful to avoid detection by the merchant, Pettifogger pilfered one of the jars and sped off to find Aori.

Outdoor markets contained all manner of artisans peddling their wares, and Aori flitted around like a moth from booth to booth. The metalworkers in particular caught his attention, as he needed supplies for his gadgets. He found that gold had very little value when compared to iron, and weaponsmiths seemed to be the most popular amongst the craftsmen.

As he perused the latest and greatest items for trade, he felt disappointed in the lack of innovation. He had seen it all before – and no one had even thought of anything like the devices he had built back on Aia.

Then, a marvel of modern technology seized him and sparked his curiosity. It almost looked more like a moving sculpture than a practical machine, and yet, it intrigued him like nothing else he had seen on Earth. A fire at the bottom served to heat up a sealed cauldron filled with water, causing steam to rise up through pipes. The pipes then connected to a rotating sphere. On opposite sides of the sphere, two more pipes jutted out at a slight angle. As the steam propelled out of the tilted pipes, the sphere rotated faster and faster.

"A steam engine," Aori remarked with a wide grin.

"It is called an aeolipile," the merchant told him. "Hero of Alexandria invented it, they say. I wish he would come and tell people what its purpose is, because nobody wants to buy it."

Aori smiled. "I could think of a thousand uses! I built something like this years ago to run my train, factories, and clockworkers...."

The merchant's quizzical look gave Aori pause. He had forgotten that he currently looked like a fifteen year old boy. Before he could explain, however, a commotion distracted both of them.

A large group of Roman soldiers ran right towards them, chasing after a very short, white-haired man with a pointed beard and mustache. The crowd of merchants and traders parted to make way and watch the spectacle.

Instinctively, Aori slowed things down around him so that he could process what was happening. Once he recognized Pettifogger and hypothesized that the gnome had undoubtedly pilfered his way to the wrong side of the law, he should have just teleported them safely back to Tweentime. However, something inside him – perhaps a developmental deficit in the risk-avoidance portion of his teenage brain— made him run headlong into trouble.

"Pettifogger, duck!" Aori yelled as he tossed a bubble of temporal magic at the Roman pursuers.

The other Romans stopped dead in their tracks as they watched their compatriots just pop out of time and space. Hesitantly, they inched forward, with spears and swords at the ready.

"Sorry, Mr. Timister," Pettifogger muttered. "I don't know why I ran—I guess I just panicked."

"No worries, my good gnome. We came here to recruit soldiers, and you've brought them right to us. Of course, I don't think we'll escape without a fight."

The gnomish thief pulled out his dagger and stood back-to-back with Aori. "Do you have a weapon?"

"Not at the moment, but I'll improvise."

The Romans surrounded them, which served to bolster the soldiers' courage. They closed in their ranks and the circle tightened around Aori and Pettifogger. As they charged in toward the duo, time screeched to a halt.

Like yarn through a loom, Aori and Pettifogger weaved between the seconds and the circle of soldiers. Occasionally, Pettifogger would take a cheapshot or two, slicing the hamstrings or removing the coinpurses of the soldiers. Meanwhile, Aori teleported from booth to booth, tossing pottery or other random objects at the enemies. The spectators in the crowd didn't quite know what to make of it, as they continuously disappeared and reappeared all over the market.

Due in part to his inexperience with all-out brawls, in addition to his overexertion of temporal energy, Aori's pace eventually slowed. Exhausted, he slumped to his knees, while a Roman soldier grasped him firmly by the shoulder.

The soldier spoke in Latin, which was one of the languages Aori had already picked up in his journeys. In fact, he had already translated several works of Greek and Roman literature into the Common tongue of Auldenton and Codan. However, he had nothing to say to prevent the inevitable beating he would soon face.

First, the back of the Roman's hand struck against Aori's jawbone. The skin of his cheek burned, and the force of the blow knocked him to his knees. Despite his ever-expanding knowledge of temporal magic, nothing sprang to his mind in the milliseconds before the next blow struck.

As blood escaped from a large cut on his brow, Aori wondered how long it would be before the man exhausted himself. He assumed that the Roman had far more stamina than he could endure, and though he knew he could slow down or interrupt time to stop the beating, he just didn't have the energy.

The hits and kicks took on a rhythmic cadence, such that Aori began to anticipate each strike; and yet, he could do nothing to defend himself. When the attacks finally and suddenly broke off, Aori briefly wondered if time had stopped itself in spite of his fatigue.

However, when he managed to open his bruised and swollen eyes, Pettifogger stood atop the Roman soldier's back. Blood dripped from a blade in his hand. Clearing his throat, he said, "Master Timister, perhaps we should go now."

With the gnome's help, Aori struggled to his feet. "Many thanks, Mr. Pettifogger. Perhaps... if you think you remember your stolen abilities, you could... aid me in getting us back to Tweentime."

In an instant, the duo could rest more comfortably within the solitude of the library. As the words "Time heals all wounds" seemed to echo throughout the stacks of books, awareness of his surroundings gradually returned to Aori. Except for the books and the inoperative computer, the library was empty. "Where is everyone?" he hissed through a broken jaw. "Where is my army?"

Pettifogger shrugged. "I will have a look around, sir. Just continue to heal yourself."

Aori reset his jawbone, which was an excruciating task; however, he had the not-quite-so-magical ability to compress all the pain in one short burst, as if ripping off an adhesive bandage. The bones immediately fused together at the fracture, as if they were long-lost lovers reunited at last. His skin stitched together in a fraction of the time it would take outside of Tweentime, and his bruises quickly faded.

By the time Pettifogger returned from his reconnaissance, the young man had almost completely healed from his injuries. "Is everyone gone?"

"I'm afraid so," answered Pettifogger.

"Munder as well?"

"I'm afraid so."

"Any signs of a struggle?"

166

"Munder's style of training consists of brawling with the soldiers on a daily basis. The signs of struggle have become part of the décor."

Aori smiled with only minor pain. "I suppose you're right, Mr. Pettifogger." His brow furrowed once more. "Where could they be?"

Pettifogger scratched his head. "Perhaps Munder took them out... for field exercises? I suppose that's common in the military, right?"

Aori closed his eyes and clenched his jaw as realization swept over him. "No... well, I suppose you're right, but that's not it. Munder took them, but not for training. He took them to battle."

"Battle, sir?"

"He went to rescue the Odestone."

Pettifogger sprang to his feet. "That reminds me!" He sprinted to a cubby-hole hidden behind one of the bookcases. As he touched the intricate locking mechanism on his safe, the metal gears hummed with life. After a few clinks and whirs, the door to the safe opened and piles of treasures sprinkled about the floor.

Once again finding the mirth in the situation, Aori commented, "It seems you're going to need a larger stash, Master Thief!"

Pettifogger took the clay pot from his safe and held it out for Aori to examine.

The teen's recently-broken jaw fell slack. "Is that... Ode? On a Grecian urn?" The pot depicted the Codan elder's near-death in the burning Aeolian House, as well as his subsequent transformation into a rock.

"I believe so. And that's not all."

His mind reeling, Aori interrupted, "How could an Aian be depicted on ages-old pottery in Greece?"

"Wait; it gets better," said the gnome. "There were also pots showing all kinds of other events from Aia."

167

Aori stared at him. "Who was the merchant? Did he look to be Codan?"

Pettifogger thought for a moment. "I didn't see a tail...."

"We must investigate! If there are Aians in Greece, perhaps they know what has become of all the others, as well."

"And Munder, sir?"

Aori grimaced. "I suppose we shall have to trust that he can take care of himself. He is a big boy, after all."

"...A very big boy," Pettifogger elaborated.

At this time, I am sure all my students and/or readers would very much like to hear the tale of Munder's mission to rescue the Odestone from the Temple of Time. However, even as limitless and godly as my temporal omniscience may seem, I am not all-seeing and all-knowing. The veils shrouding the past become thicker in Tweentime, and it is only through a deep and personal connection with Aori that I have been able to recount his experiences there. I know that sounds like a cop-out, but bear with me here.

Back in Greece, Aori and Pettifogger quickly found the pottery merchant, from whom they learned that the urns had been created by a group of Dorian monks in Delphi. Of course, at the reference to the Codan heritage of Dorian, Aori's excitement grew. "These are Codan elders indeed, Pettifogger. We may have found more Aian survivors!"

They managed to hire, or rather, steal horses and traveled to Delphi from Athens. The voyage was rather uneventful, therefore it shall be truncated thusly.

When they found the plain and dilapidated monastery of the Dorians, Aori felt disheartened. "The Dorians of Aia were hardly ostentatious in their demeanor or décor, but they would not have allowed this sort of decay. They must have abandoned this place long ago."

168

A worn, aged statue of a man stood in front of the building, silently and stoically welcoming all visitors. Its palms were open and facing upward, as if holding some invisible book. "At least their decorum did not fall by the wayside with their décor. The Dorians were ever ones to honor their heritage. This must be one of their great heroes."

"Herodotus, to be exact," said a voice. "Meaning he was a hero given to us... by whom? I know not. He is known as the Father of History, as well as the Father of Lies."

Pettifogger and Aori looked around for the source of the voice.

As the voice continued, they heard the crackling, scratching sound of pebbles cast about pavement. "I am Pedant: writer, lyricist, and oft a teacher of wisdom."

The words seemed to be coming from a stone podium on the front porch.

"If you will kindly move me indoors, I will introduce you to the others," said the podium.

"You mean, the podium?" asked Aori, trying to keep the incredulity from his voice.

"Of course, boy. How else will I get inside? Hop on one leg?"

Pettifogger let loose a snicker. The duo wrestled with the heavy stone lectern, and by the time they got it over the threshold of the building, they were both very tired.

"Please, sit," said Pedant. "Make yourself comfortable." Aori began to sit on a long, wooden pew. "Not there," interjected the podium. "That is Ecclesiast, a very old, very ancient religious man. We try not to sit on him. Try the chair in the corner. I believe it is not already occupied."

Aori looked around at the barren, lifeless room. With a wide-eyed look of skepticism at his gnomish companion, he sat in the chair. "Where are all the monks, Pedant?"

"Surely you have heard!" exclaimed the podium. "Alas, it falls upon me to hammer the ignorance out of today's

169

youth." After a bit of a pause, he continued, "Are you seated? Are you comfortable?"

Aori resettled himself in his seat and prepared for a long lesson. If this Dorian was anything like the Odestone, he would, indeed, need to be comfortable. "Please, do go on."

As the podium spoke in its monotone voice, Aori was reminded of his previous childhood as a student in Auldenton Academy. Not all of his teachers were as personable and inviting as his old friend Bertram had been. Most of them taught lifeless, ancient facts that seemed to have no bearing on his life at that time. Ironically, however, Aori read and absorbed any information he could get his mind around, once he became an adult and had a limitless supply of time to read.

Pedant told mostly of his own past as a teacher and writer, briefly touching on how he had followed the other Dorians on a pilgrimage of sorts to Delphi. "The oldest among us remembered when the Oracles were still around. We believed them to remain here still, only in some inanimate form."

"These Oracles, they were Coda as well?" Aori asked.

"Coda? How do you know that word?" The podium shook, and several other objects around the room seemed to vibrate and hum. A harp in the corner twanged dramatically. As Aori spoke, he addressed all the inanimate inhabitants of the monastery. "I know much about the Coda, Dorians. I know that you, or your ancestors, came here from a distant world known as Aia, which has long since been destroyed. I know that you, like my erstwhile companion, Ode, have the ability to sing your souls into nonliving things. You will find, teacher, that I already know much more than my meager age may suggest. However, I do not wish to bore you with the tale of how I became so young."

The room stirred. Wood creaked, papyrus rustled, scrolls brushed against one another, and lit torches flickered enthusiastically.

Pettifogger whispered, "I think this crowd actually would *enjoy* a long, boring story."

Laughing, Aori agreed, "I suppose it is their style. However, we haven't the time."

"Is that so?" boomed another voice from all around them. "Do you not have all the time in the world, Aori Timister?"

The hairs on Aori's neck bristled like a cat's. "Who are you, and how do you know my name?"

"I am Dorian, and this is my house!" the entire building shook with the words.

Aori scoffed, "I think not, old shack. Dorian had to have died on Aia, for I know he did not accompany us on the voyage to this planet. Besides, the oldest and most honored of the Coda would not store his soul in such a ramshackle structure!"

The building shook with such force that several urns crashed to the floor in thousands of shards. Aori silently mourned their loss, for he assumed that Codan people had undoubtedly stored their souls in those pots. Meanwhile, Pettifogger deftly attempted to rescue the other valuable artifacts from destruction.

Trying to return the environment to its calmer, more reserved state, Pedant resumed his monotone voice. "Nevertheless, this is the House of Dorian, and the house *is* Dorian. However, you are right in your assumption that he did not travel with you to Earth—not in his Earthly...er... Aian body, that is. It seems there are facts that you do not know after all, Aori."

Clearing his throat poignantly, Aori continued to listen. At one point, his ego would not have let one so pretentious as Pedant condescend to him. However, over the years he had been humbled by many new and unexpected situations.

"As you may know, the Lord of Time, Tempo, bestowed upon Dorian the gift of singing his life-force into a painting, which he displayed proudly in his temple on Aia."

Aori interrupted, "Surely that painting was destroyed with the temple and the planet."

"Most assuredly," said Pedant pompously. "If I may continue, I will enlighten you."

With a grimace, Aori nodded.

"By the time of Aia's destruction, Dorian the Eldest had many descendants. Each of those Coda carried with them part of Dorian's soul. They put their blood, sweat, and tears into erecting this temple, and so enchanted it with the spirit of the Eldest."

By the end of the story, Pettifogger's attention span had long since waned. Instead, he had taken the initiative to catalog the most expensive-looking artifacts in the building, just in case they were to have to make a speedy getaway with the precious bits of Aian history. Sadly, though he searched high and low, he found no records at all of his deeds. Perhaps his story had evaded capture as well as he always had.

Pedant continued, "Many of us did not have heirs to pass on the Dorian line, so the few remaining monks took up the task of gathering any and all Dorian artifacts to store them here. It has since become a sort of museum for items that have a story to tell."

A long, metal stake on a shelf caught the gnome's eye, and his hands snatched it on impulse. It vibrated in his hand, and he dropped it. It hit the floor with a loud clang, and everyone (and everything) fell silent.

"Be careful! That is a very sacred object!"

Aori picked up the stake. "It appears to be rather ordinary. Is it a Dorian artifact? Whose soul resides within this metal?"

"None, so far as we can tell," said the podium. "We know there is lore trapped inside, but none of us have the ability to listen to it. Its song is foreign to us."

"How did it get here, then?"

"Missionaries from faraway lands brought it, and our monks purchased it. We do sense some strong emotions inside it, but alas! No Dorian has ever been very keen on interpreting or understanding emotion."

"That has been our experience, with both the Odestone and his daughter, Lithe."

"You knew Emmeleia as well?" asked a softer, more feminine voice. It came from an instrument on the wall, and the voice was much more melodious than any of the others.

"Yes," Aori answered. "She came with me on my voyage to Earth. However, we were separated, and I have not seen her since. I thought perhaps one of you might have more information about the other Aian survivors."

"Our lore has been fairly limited to this area. We tend to keep to ourselves, but I do recall some other Coda of note in Greek history. Of course, Herodotus the Historian would know much more about that. His soul has persisted for many more years than mine has."

"Good," said Aori. His patience, which had always been legendary in its brevity, was wearing down to microscopic width. "He's the statue outside, correct?"

The podium sighed. "Yes and no. The statue does depict the famous Greek historian, but it does not contain his spirit. He imbued one of his own history books with his life-force."

"And the book?" asked Aori, losing hope as quickly as patience.

"It was taken, along with around 300 statues, urns, instruments, and artifacts."

Aori felt exasperation boiling inside him. Little did he know, Greeks were famous for this type of rhetoric in which questions spawn more and more questions. Since the time of Socrates, it seemed to be the only way to teach.

With a long sigh, Aori asked, "Who took them?"

"Nero," said Pedant pretentiously, as if dropping the name of some famous friend.

173

"And he is?"

"The Emperor of Rome, of course," the podium answered.

Aori began to understand why Munder always grumbled when Coda spoke or sang. The tedium of carrying on a conversation with a Dorian was like waiting for grass to grow…in winter.

"Then we shall go to Rome," said Aori. "I will bring back your stolen artifacts…"

"…For a price," Pettifogger finished. Aori glanced at him curiously but assumed he had hatched a brilliant scheme of some sort.

"Price?" boomed the entire building, "You dare try to bargain with the House of Dorian?"

"Yes," said Aori. "We will return your lost artifacts, and in exchange…"

"You will give us the book, to be preserved for all eternity in Mr. Timister's library, where it will be safe," Pettifogger finished.

Aori nodded at him and smiled.

The temple rumbled, and all the other inanimate objects vibrated in response. "We accept your offer, Time-Child," said Dorian. "But only because you are Tempo's heir."

Aori decided not to mention how Father Time had all but forsaken, abandoned, and left him for dead. Sometimes, it's best to repress parental issues.

Chapter 2:10

When in Rome...
Stop, Drop, and Roll

Many believe the minutes between three and four A.M. to be particularly supernatural. All those who paid attention in the first book of the *Anachronist Chronicles* might remember that Aori's first foray into Tweentime occurred during that time of night. Those wishing to practice some dark magic often wait around for the clock to strike that hour, and if you really wanted to make the dead rise from the grave, you would need to set your alarm for 3:00.

Through the gray twilight, anyone who happened by the Dead Sea at that time would probably have missed the slightest of ripples in the surface of its murky waters. Despite the availability of water in the otherwise dry and barren desert region, very few organisms lived near the sea. Nonetheless, the sudden appearance of a hooded skull breaking the surface tension of the calm water would have sent anyone running for his or her life.

The grim face rose up from the water, and the twilight faded to black. The Fellfallan Death spirit known as Acheron spread his tattered wings and hovered in a cloud of dust and darkness. The water dripping from his cloak formed icicles as it fell. With dark, soulless sockets instead of eyes, he stared deep into the depths of the sea. Lost spirits cried out to him, and he opened his arms to beckon them into their afterlife. As the phantasmal ether of abandoned lives rose from the depths, Acheron embraced them as lovingly as his cold, lifeless arms could manage.

The dead stillness of the water's surface broke once again with a sudden explosion. Another Fellfalla burst from the abyss with an unconscious body in her arms. She landed on the shore and attempted to revive her fallen friend.

"Daphni!" she called.

Acheron cocked his head to the side, unable to comprehend his wife's actions.

"What does it look like I'm doing?" she answered his unspoken question. The former Fellfallan Imperial guard known as Proserpina stared at him with the icy stare of death. "I am trying to save her."

The slightest murmur of flapping wings served as his reply.

Proserpina yelled, "You know as well as I do that this is not her time. You know how she dies, and it's not like this. Are you just going to stand there?"

Acheron held his palms outward.

"I know you're powerless to help the living, but you know what we have in store for us here. She could help do what we're unable to do."

The Death's Head Moth hovered over them silently. Proserpina pushed down hard on Daphni's chest. With a choking cough, the last knight of the Fellfallan Empire fought her way back to life. She wanted so desperately to be alive, that even passing through a watery underworld could not stop her.

Acheron could not fathom such resolute unwillingness to part with life. Most souls he had carried over recently had welcomed his coming. Of course, many of the ones in this pool had been damned there for eternity. Acheron did not pick and choose; all souls were equal to him.

"Am I alive?" asked Daphni, after she caught her breath.

"Yes," answered Proserpina.

Acheron added a silent, "For now."

Proserpina shot him a cold glare.

"I know," said Daphni, looking straight into the face of the grim reaper. She turned to her friend, who still held her in a firm embrace. "You don't need to soften the blow, Pross. I saw my own corpse, down there, in the void."

The Death's Head Moth murmured.

In a soft, solemn voice, Proserpina said, "He says you've earned the right to know how you will die."

Daphni stared off into the distance, watching the dead calm of the sea. Her hair, with its dark green color, looked like a tangled mess of seaweed. The normally vibrant greens of her armor had faded to a dull, grayish sea-foam.

"Take your time. Think about it. He and I have much to discuss." Proserpina rose and walked over to her spouse, for whom she had chosen to abandon her mortal life. She had followed him to the underworld and agreed to be his bride, but only now did she begin to regret that decision. Their argument, though heated, seemed particularly one-sided, as she was the only one who spoke aloud.

"He is hardly the master you once knew. If he is capable of such evil, we must do *something*," she shouted.

Daphni could not help but overhear Proserpina's words. "Who?" she asked.

Proserpina whispered the name, as if its shame might be lessened as such.

"Finis."

Before Aori and Pettifogger left the House of the Dorians, the instrument with the soft, female voice stopped them. She was a stringed instrument, but unlike the lyre or cithara, which were popular instruments in Ancient Greece, this particular one had a neck, similar to Lithe's mandolin. If one had seen it around the 15th Century, it might have been called a violin. However, its base was a bit wider, its pitch was a bit lower, and somehow, it existed more than one thousand years before its invention.

"My name is Viola," the instrument said melodically.

"Pleased to meet you," said Aori respectfully. He picked the instrument up and examined it closely. Its engineering fascinated him. The strings consisted of horsehair tightened across a metal bridge. Previously, Greek instruments had used tortoise-shells as their sound-boxes, but this design seemed less organic and more refined.

"Please," the instrument whined, "take me with you." Far from annoying, Viola's whine sounded like beautiful, emotional music.

Aori looked around at the others. She hardly seemed to fit in with this crowd of uptight, reserved Dorian artifacts. Whereas they seemed to be chiefly lore-keepers, she had the spirit of the entertainer. "Won't the others miss you?"

The pews, bricks, books, and podium hummed in their characteristic mantra. "They will hardly even notice my absence," she sang. "Besides, I may be of use to you in your journey."

The improved roadway system of the Roman Empire helped expedite their trip, but without a shortcut through Tweentime, it would still have taken a few weeks. Ever the resourceful thief, Pettifogger had managed to acquire a mule and cart, which Aori modified to make the long ride more comfortable. He added a suspension system, wool-padded seats, and a sphere of temporal magic.

Through the bubble of passing time, they could still watch the road ahead of them for bandits or highwaymen, but onlookers would see their rapid travel as just a blur. If he had marketed this safe, speedy means of travel, Aori could have changed the world and made a fortune. However, the self-serving Aori Timister had died long ago with Aia.

An added effect of Tween-travel meant that Viola's soul became visible once again. Though she appeared as a wispy, temporal spirit, they could easily see how beautiful she had once been. Like many Greeks, she wore her hair up, with its length braided underneath in three arcs and curling ringlets falling about the base of her neck. She wore a Doric chiton, which resembled a toga cinched at the waist.

"Though your instrument resonates resplendent beauty, madam," Aori said to her, "it hardly compares to your true form."

Viola smiled. "I appreciate your kind words, Mr. Timister, although my looks faded long before I sang my soul into the instrument."

"Speaking of which, I have never seen such a wondrous invention," Aori fawned. "Did you make it?"

"No," she answered, "It was a gift from Tempo, or Chronos, as the Greeks call him."

"I see," Aori frowned.

Viola noticed his reaction and asked, "I take it you do not share the Dorian's eternal love of your father?"

"Father Time is not my father," Aori insisted. "And I've found that many of his so-called gifts come with a hefty price."

"Now you understand why I wished to leave the Dorian House," said Viola solemnly. "They cared more for worshipping Tempo, and honoring the past, than for creating new music."

"You certainly do not fit in with their crowd," Pettifogger posited.

"You have a keen eye. I am of the Lydian line of Coda, in fact. I sought shelter amongst the Dorian Coda for... many reasons. However, they were not always so stiff and stony. Many of the more youthful spirits of the house either became wandering musicians or were taken..."

"Taken?"

"When the Emperor Nero took the statues and artifacts from our house, he also took several of our living musicians. Apparently, his love for music is even greater than his hunger for power."

With a quick and sudden movement, Pettifogger leapt from the cart and sped ahead of them on the road. When he returned, he was out of breath. "We'll have to stop. They have the bridge blocked ahead. It appears to be some sort of ambush waiting to happen."

"Are they Roman soldiers, or ruffians?" asked Aori. Pettifogger remembered an old saying about honor among thieves. However, another saying indicated that every man, for himself, must fight to prosper. "Ruffians, sir. I've already relieved them of their coin-purses, and it appears, from the haul, that they are good at their jobs."

"And you don't think we could just speed past them, unawares?"

Pettifogger looked uncertain. "They would notice us, I'm sure."

Aori nodded. "Well then, Mr. Pettifogger, do your thing."

Pettifogger had always excelled as a scout and pick-pocket, but he had also become quite accomplished, over the years, at backstabbing and waylaying. With Aori's temporal magic at his disposal, the gnome snuck up behind one of the ruffians, leapt up on his back, and slit his throat. Before any of his companions could respond, Pettifogger bounded from bandit to bandit like some sort of hyperactive squirrel with a blade.

One larger fellow appeared to notice the miniature blur of violence and attempted to stomp him, but Pettifogger managed to dodge and lunge at the man's kneecap with his weapon. The bandit fell to the ground, writhing in pain.

As the mule and cart continued on across the bridge unhindered in its path, Pettifogger jumped back into his seat and went to work at cleaning off his weapons. One of his blades looked like a long, slender spike.

"Pettifogger!" exclaimed Aori. "Did you steal that artifact from the Dorian House?"

Pettifogger's eyes widened. "I thought it might prove useful."

Aori sighed. "While it does seem to be a fairly good weapon, the teacher already said that they could not understand its lore."

"It is difficult, in its rawest forms, to read the emotion recorded in an object," explained Viola. "I believe this makeshift weapon has served some greater violence in its past."

"Perhaps one of the musicians Nero kidnapped may shed some light on its history," suggested Aori. "Did you also say that the Emperor himself is a musician? Could he have Codan ancestry as well?"

Viola crinkled her nose a bit, as if smelling a distasteful odor. "He loves to sing and accompany himself with instruments, but I believe he was not born a musician as the Coda were."

She picked up her viola and began to play a soft, sweet tune. "Much of the lore about Nero is littered with fiction, but I believe in order to truly understand the man, you must hear about his past."

She sang in Greek, which Aori had only recently picked up, and he attempted to translate for Pettifogger. However, like most Codan music, the story seemed to transcend the barriers of language, so that one could understand the lore despite his or her background.

"She says that Nero's father once gouged out a man's eyes for disagreeing with him, ran over a child with his chariot, and was in love with his own sister," he translated.

"Nero's deeds do not cast much better light," she sang.

She continued her tale of how Nero and his mother, Agrippina, were exiled by Caligula, the notorious Roman

181

Emperor, who was also her brother and Nero's uncle. When Claudius became emperor, he allowed them to return to Rome, and he married Agrippina (who was also his niece).

Aori continued to translate, "I believe she just said that Nero married his step-sister, Octavia, because his mother forced her to break off her engagement, and her ex-fiancé committed suicide. Then, it is believed that Agrippina poisoned Claudius so that Nero could become the emperor.

"When his rule was contested by his step-brother, who was, indeed, Claudius's true heir, Nero had his meal poisoned. He later had his mother sentenced to death as well, after accusing her of conspiring against him."

Viola sang of Nero's drunken debauchery, adultery, and duplicity in his personal, family, and political lives. However, the most unnerving part of the tale involved Nero's taking of young male companions. In one horrific case, the emperor had a young man castrated in order to perform a mock wedding ceremony at his side.

At this, both Aori and Pettifogger shuddered simultaneously.

Noticing their discomfort, Viola stopped singing. Rather, she played a melancholy tune on her instrument. The three travelers sat speechless for the rest of the trip. It was not until they reached the outskirts of Rome that she continued her tale.

"I have more to tell, which may be important later. Nero does not like for anyone to outperform him. He had one of his male lovers killed because he was a better actor. One of his wives was forced to slit her wrists, which he called a suicide. He is also prone to fits of rage. It is said that he killed one of his wives by kicking her in the stomach. She was pregnant at the time."

The tragic tale moved Aori to tears. "I was accused of heinous acts of evil on Aia, but at least I never directly took another's life."

Though Pettifogger was painfully aware of the atrocities Aori had committed, he had to agree that Nero's were far more atrocious. He, too, felt emotion swell up behind his eyes.

"You truly do not belong with the Dorians and their lack of emotion, Viola," said Aori.

"I simply state the facts as plainly as I know them, Mr. Timister. It is the instrument that carries the *pathos*."

When in Rome, they say, do as the Romans do. If that meant lying, stealing, or double-crossing every Roman there, Aori and Pettifogger were prepared to do so. Aori developed a plan for getting close to the Emperor without causing him to be suspicious. They joined a musical theatre troupe and began performing Viola's songs. Of course, neither Aori nor Pettifogger could sing or play an instrument to save their lives, so they just held the instrument while Viola played the music herself.

Aori had a wealth of stories at his disposal, having read, written, or translated most of the literature of Aia, Israel, Anatolia, and Greece. In addition, Pettifogger's experience with lying and hiding the truth made him an excellent actor.

They became quite popular within the city and often played to large crowds. It was not long before their performances drew the attention of Nero himself. He called for a special show in his honor and invited a small group of his closest friends, lovers, and advisors.

They scheduled the show for July 15, known as the Ides of July. "Beware the Ides of July," Aori whispered from backstage, anachronistically (and unintentionally) referring to Shakespeare's *Julius Caesar*, in which the Emperor was killed on the Ides of March (in a theatre, no less).

The play they performed was a tale of Finis, the End of All Things on Aia. It was a tragedy, accompanied by Viola on strings and some imperial guest musicians on lyres and panpipes. As you know, Finis was the Living God of Death, until he came to Earth and leapt from the top of the Tower of Babel, presumably to his death.

"What happens," Aori announced after a short introduction, "when a death-deity dies?"

In the play, Pettifogger played the part of Finis, who had lived as a mortal gnome prior to his appointment to the "graveyard shift," as he called it. Finis lived with his family in the mountains, far away from the hustle and bustle of Auldenton. He had three daughters, who were played by local boys in the performance. Life in the country came to be too much for Finis, who longed for the drunken debauchery of his youth in the city.

"With nothing to do but wallow in his own thoughts," Aori narrated as he pretended to play the viola. "Finis soon lost his mind."

The gnome told his daughter that they would go hiking in the nearby caverns. Once there, Finis told her to say her prayers, at which point he pushed her into a dark abyss.

The tale was told and retold, almost two thousand years later, by a musician named Gordon Gano of the musical group The Violent Femmes. The song, which was called "Country Death Song," continued as such:

Don't speak to me of lovers with a broken heart.
You want to know what can really tear you apart?
I'm going out to the barn, with a never-stopping pain;
I'm going out to the barn, to hang myself in shame.

(Gordon Gano, Gorno Music 1981)

After the performance, the audience clapped and cheered, save for Nero. He sat in the darkness of the theatre in pensive silence until the applause ended. Then, he stood up and addressed Aori specifically. "Tell me, boy, what happened to the man then?

"For that story, sir," laughed Aori, trying to lighten the mood, "You will have to wait until our next play."

"I already know the tale, boy," said Nero as he approached the stage. "After he killed himself, he was sentenced to an eternity of committing horrible evils ending only with his own suicide."

Stunned silent and motionless, Aori could only watch as Nero joined him onstage.

Ever quick to escape even the shackles of surprise, Pettifogger found the words that failed Aori: "How could you possibly know that story?"

Nero looked upon the gnome as a lion would look upon an infant gazelle. "I have heard it, before today. Songs of mourning about the many lives of Death even haunt me in my dreams."

He placed a firm hand on Aori's shoulder. With the palm of his other hand, he gently caressed the young man's face. Something twisted and churned in the pit of Aori's stomach. "Now, boy," oozed the Emperor, "Might I play for you the songs I hear in my sleep?"

He stretched his arms open, gesturing to the rest of them, "Or are you the only actors and musicians fit for this stage?"

Remembering Nero's ego, and wishing to keep his meals poison-free, Aori bowed low and stepped down into the audience. Pettifogger and the Roman actors followed him and took their seats.

Alone on stage with the viola, Nero began to play the single most dismal and disheartening dirge in all of musical history. In between intervals of lasciviously fiddling Viola, he sang about the evils of the man who became the Living God of Death. Each part of the song ended with Finis's tragic suicide, and began with a new life of atrocities.

Discomfort and panic quickly spread through the small audience. When Aori checked to see if Pettifogger felt as he did, he caught a glimpse of the gnome running for the door.

185

Some others followed him, attempting to escape the melancholy music. When they got to the door, it was locked and would not open.

As they looked around, all the windows and doors throughout the theatre locked simultaneously. One of the boy actors began to weep, which led the other boys to follow suit.

Behind Nero, two of his advisors carried in what appeared to be a very large hydraulic organ. As he continued to fondle Viola, the pipes of the organ played in synch.

"The hydraulic organ," he explained above the instrumental music, "was invented by an engineer in Alexandria, more than two hundred years ago. This one is my own invention, however."

Aori, who had remained seated the whole time, marveled at the Emperor's design. He had dabbled in manufacturing musical instruments himself, and he had invented Aia's first pipe organ thousands of years before anyone on Earth had the idea. However, despite his own expansive ego, he decided to keep his personal achievements to himself.

As the music swelled and Nero continued the lament, the two advisors approached the front of the stage. As if performing in part of the act, both men removed swords from their hips, held them out at arms length, and simultaneously stabbed themselves in the stomach.

The audience watched in horror, and scrambled toward the other exits. One of the boys tried to climb up to the rafters and escape from a window. The windows, having been created to let light in for dramatic effect in plays (due to the fact that spotlights would not be invented for more than a thousand years), were way up on the ceiling, some forty feet above the stage. As the boy fumbled with the latch of the window, the music swelled again, and the boy simply let go.

One of the women from the audience rushed to the stage, screaming and crying, "He's dead! The boy is dead!" Nero kept playing.

186

Somehow, whether by the power of the music or by some unseen act, a fire ignited within the theatre. Regardless of its conception, the music exacerbated the flames so that they engulfed the curtains and most of the stage. The members of the audience flailed about in terror, most of them wishing for a quicker death than incineration.

Nero kept playing.

Pettifogger, who had always been very adept at picking locks to escape whatever constraints humankind could invent, pulled helplessly at the secure exit. Ripping off some of his tunic, he jammed pieces of fabric into his ears to block out the sound of the music. With a desperate panic, he removed the metal spike from his pack and stabbed violently at the door.

Abruptly, the music stopped. Eerie silence flooded the room.

"Where did you get that?"

Pettifogger wheeled around. Nero was staring a hole right through him. "Me?"

"No, the other gnome with a stolen nail in his hand." Nero sighed. "Never mind; bring it here."

Pettifogger obeyed, though it meant passing dangerously close to the flames. With a quick and heroic thought, he threw the spike right at Nero's head.

Before it could find its target, however, one of the Emperor's soldiers jumped in its path.

"*Dulce et decorum est pro patria mori*," said Nero with a smile. The words were those of Horace, a Roman lyricist. Translated from Latin, the phrase meant, "It is sweet and noble to die for one's country." Of course, in this case, the soldier had died for his megalomaniacal ruler.

As he removed the spike from his soldier, the flames spread to the rest of the building. Holding it in his hand, he rubbed it across the viola in place of the bow one usually uses to play the instrument. The movement seemed somehow perverse and inappropriate.

187

The music that came from the viola issued forth such tragic emotion that few in the audience could remain on their feet. They writhed and moaned upon the floor, stricken physically by the psychological pain.

Nero alone seemed impervious to it all. "Let me tell you about the last life of Finis, End of All Things. In this tale, he was a disciple of Jesus Christ. Some of you may know about the recent death of Jesus in one of Rome's provinces in Israel. Did you know, however, that Finis had a hand in it?"

The flames burst through the ceiling, causing wooden beams to fall and crash into the floor. Above the screams of those left in the audience, Nero continued his elegy.

"Not long ago, Finis went by the name Judas Iscariot. He betrayed his lord and master for thirty pieces of silver. This was but one of the nails that held Jesus to the cross."

As Nero told each and every excruciating detail of the crucifixion, as witnessed by the nail itself, the inferno moved on to a nearby building. The theatre's roof collapsed around them.

Nero kept playing.

"Would any of you, who still has breath to speak, care to venture a guess at the final fate of Judas Iscariot?"

Still in his seat, Aori whispered, "He killed himself."

"Quite right, my boy!" Nero shouted. "A hangman's noose was the weapon of choice, but 'twas his own hand that did the deed."

Several other houses caught on fire, and within minutes, much of the city was in flames.

Nero kept playing.

Pettifogger and a few of the other members of the audience managed to escape the burning theatre, but Aori remained in his seat. Once he reached the relative safety of a canal within the town, Pettifogger remembered his master.

"If he wishes to allow himself to burn, what power do I have to stop him?" the gnome shouted aloud. He sighed

188

indignantly, soaked himself in water, and sprinted back to the theatre.

By this time, all of Rome was ablaze, and very little of the theatre still stood. Pettifogger desperately searched through the wreckage, muttering, "He wouldn't have come back for me, that's for sure. He would have been miles away before he even thought of me."

Through the flames and smoke, Pettifogger could barely identify the devastated pieces of the building, let alone find anyone alive within the ruins. He cursed himself for abandoning his master. From what he could tell, it appeared that Aori, Nero, and the instruments had just burned to ash. He only found a few bodies of audience members, which made Aori's complete disintegration seem highly unlikely. But where were they?

Chapter 2:11

Deus ex Machina

The fire burned for a fortnight—that is, fourteen days and nights. Eventually, it just ran out of fuel to consume. By that time, it had burned up several sectors of Rome, leaving much of the city's population homeless. Imaginably, the citizens blamed Nero, and many believed that he had intentionally set the fire.

Had he perished in the burning theatre that night, history might have altered the story just enough to present him in a positive light. Who knows? With enough popular folklore—or propaganda—on his side, he might have even been hailed a hero. However, he went on to commit several more heinous acts for another four years after the great fire of 64 A.D.

When Pettifogger heard that the Emperor had survived the fire, he first cursed Nero under his breath, and then breathed a sign of relief. If Nero survived, surely Aori did as well.

In addition to finding Aori, there was still the task of retrieving the stolen Dorian artifacts. Despite the fact that many civilians saw Nero as a tyrant and an enemy, Pettifogger still had trouble gathering information about their whereabouts. As persuasive as the gnome could be, it seems the townspeople were kept out of the loop on much of the Emperor's affairs.

Rumors, however, spread rapidly in the Roman grapevine. According to several sources, Nero was busy shifting the blame for the fire to a relatively small religious group, which was the minority in those days: the Christians.

Regardless of whether the Romans actually believed the Christians to be responsible for the fire, they were willing to accept the group as scapegoats. They hardly even questioned the Emperor's treatment of the Christians, no matter how inhumane and unjustified the punishment. Some were tarred and feathered, cremated alive, or thrown to the beasts in gruesome gladiatorial battles. Nero chose to make examples of Peter and Paul, who were well-known disciples of Christ. The Romans decapitated Paul and crucified Peter upside-down.

Taking advantage of the Emperor's latest violence as a distraction, Pettifogger chose to begin his search at the imperial palace. The building consisted of a square-shaped wall surrounding a courtyard, with a dome as the central piece of the complex. Everything Pettifogger knew about the building came from cursory examinations while walking about town. However, he had made one advantageous discovery; while pick-pocketing guards, he came across a key to somewhere within the palace.

On the subject of guards, the palace employed two Centurions per entrance and at least five patrolling the courtyard and exterior areas. He assumed that at least five monitored the interior of the dome-shaped building.

Pettifogger racked his brain for a strategy for getting into the palace, while several ideas had already come to him on escaping. "Aori would know what to do," he muttered to himself. "Of course, he probably wouldn't bother to rescue me."

On his third night of almost-constant surveillance, he finally worked out a plan. It wasn't an elaborate scheme, but he decided to just follow his instincts. He planned to just walk in the front gate. If the guards gave him any trouble, he hoped he could still access the temporal magic he had stolen from Aori. If not, well, the dungeon would be one step closer to his goal.

As it turned out, the Fates were on the gnome's side. One of the Emperor's favorite events, the Circus, planned a performance for that very evening inside the palace court-yard. Nero often chose to participate in the shows, and he would get standing ovations every time, despite his lack of grace or skill.

Pettifogger fit in with the crowd of circus performers seamlessly. There were acrobats, wrestlers, animal-tamers, giants, and dwarves. In fact, most of them were also liars and thieves, undoubtedly. They provided the perfect means for Pettifogger to gain access to the palace.

The performers demonstrated their acts as they traveled down the paved street to the palace, doing cartwheels, handstands, backflips, and other displays of agility. The giants were tossing the dwarves back and forth, while the little people somersaulted through the air amidst the cheers and awe of onlookers.

One of the giants, in particular, looked familiar to Pettifogger. He wore a Centurion's helmet, which hid his face, but two spiraling ram horns protruded from either side of the helm. The sleeveless tunic he wore also did very little to mask the wood of his arm.

"Munder?" Pettifogger whispered as he approached the giant. Before he could get a response, the giant swept the gnome up into his arms and tossed him to another.

"Is…" Pettifogger found himself being hurled back and forth between the giants.

"That…" He wondered how the others could perform acrobatic maneuvers in the air.

"You?" It was all *he* could do just to keep from being sick.

The horned giant caught Pettifogger and answered, "I am a Centurion named Longinus."

Pettifogger stared at his wooden arm, his face, back at his wooden arm, and back at his face. "Munder, be serious. I need your help. Aori is... well, I assume he's trapped inside the Emperor's palace, and I have to rescue him."

Munder, who apparently preferred to be called Longinus, dropped the gnome onto the pavement. He barely noticed as Pettifogger deftly dodged the oncoming traffic of other circus performers. Instead, he looked at his watch, tapped it, and began to walk faster.

Pettifogger sprinted to catch up with the giant's longer stride. "Munder, slow down. Listen to me."

"Can't slow down," he mumbled. "I've got places to be."

The gnome's utter bewilderment stopped him in his tracks. "What is going on with everyone these days? First Aori refuses to leave a burning building, and now Munder's gone and forgotten who he is."

As the last wagon rolled by, Pettifogger jumped onboard and rode through the gates of the palace.

Once inside, Pettifogger made his way into the dome-shaped building using the key he had stolen previously. Inside, he saw a grand staircase winding up the six levels of the structure. In the center of the ground floor stood a marble statue. As he approached it, he could feel sound vibrations emanating from deep within its core.

"This has to be one of the Dorian statues," he said to himself, "But how am I going to get it out of here?" Smaller items could fit in his Timister Totebag, but this statue stood at least twelve feet high. Even if he managed to get it out of the palace without anyone noticing, he would still have to transport it back to the Dorians.

194

"I'll have to find Aori first. He'll figure out something."

Fortunately for the gnomish burglar, many of the guards were preoccupied with either the circus or the execution of Christians, and no one noticed his presence. He moved about the levels of the palace freely, investigating each room for signs of Dorian artifacts or his master.

Finally, he came to what appeared to be an indoor auditorium. At the foot of the stage sat an orchestra of musical instruments but no musicians. Pettifogger dashed over and put his ear to each. If any seemed to resonate all on their own, he stuffed them in his bag.

Eventually he came to a worn and scorched viola. Half of its strings were missing, and one of the others seemed frayed enough to break at any time. "Hello, Viola," he whispered.

The viola plunked back a response, which he interpreted to be a return greeting.

"You look terrible," Pettifogger said. "If I could repair you, do you think you could speak?"

The viola plunked again.

Scavenging around the room for spare parts, Pettifogger managed to find some replacement strings on an instrument that seemed far too dead to be inhabited by one of the Dorians. Quickly, he wound the strings through Viola's bridge and tightened them on her neck. "Is that better?" he asked at last.

"Quite," she sang. Without vocal chords, of course, she had to get her message across with her music. If you have ever heard a wordless tune and understood its deeper meaning, then you understand how it works. Pettifogger was not as adept at interpreting the music as Aori was, but some universal concepts are more easily understood.

"What happened after I left the theatre? How did you escape? Where is Aori? Is he here?" Like a dam that had been storing up for the last two weeks, the gnome overflowed with questions.

195

The viola whined and wound herself into tune. With the accompaniment of other musicians around her (even the ones without Dorian souls could be manipulated into joining such a persuasive Coda), Viola played back the events of that night in the theatre.

"As the flames crept in around us, and the ceiling fell down upon us, Aori Timister seemed to accept his untimely, yet likely, death. It reminded me of the stoic Dorians of old. These days, even the Coda of half my age try to imbue objects with their soul the minute they get their first wrinkle."

Yes, she included her own opinions on Dorian culture in her song. What of it?

"The Emperor continued to play, heedless of the danger around him. It was as if he were waiting for something to happen-- tempting the Fates or the gods to step in with death or some sort of *deus ex machina*."

Deus ex machina occurs in a drama or other theatrical composition when the seemingly irresolvable problem suddenly and miraculously finds a solution by some super-natural means. Literally, it means "god within the machine," which refers to the practice of introducing any given super-natural element in any given play by means of a mechanical pulley system.

"In this case, 'twas not the angel of Death that came for Aori and Nero. Rather, we were spirited away by the most majestic of moths."

"You were saved from the flames by moths?" Petti-fogger questioned.

"Yes. One female wore armor of brilliant shades of green, while the other seemed clad in the dreary shroud of one who has been put to her final rest. The last was a male, though he seemed more like Death itself, or like Charon, come to ferry souls to Hades."

Pettifogger had never seen the Fellfalla of Aia, but Viola's lengthy description of the moth-people seemed to fit with what he had heard in fairy tales as a youth. Only, the

196

Fellfalla were always the scary villains in those stories, while the butterfly-like Fairfalla got the happy endings.

"You're sure they were moths, and not butterflies?"

Viola plunked the affirmative. "As soon as our saviors arrived, I wondered how they could fly, as the flames had already begun to consume their tattered clothing."

Pettifogger heard a sound outside the auditorium and quickly motioned for the orchestra's silence. He looked like a conductor of the symphony, until he darted up the steps to the exit. The hallways remained deserted, while the sounds of the circus continued outside. From a window, he could see that many of the Roman soldiers had gathered around to watch the performers. Curiously, Munder— or Longinus— was missing from the group.

Having decided that the coast was clear, Pettifogger returned for the rest of Viola's story. She picked up where she had left off, with the Fellfalla coming in the nick of time to rescue them.

"At this point, much of the lore escapes me, for it seems as if the flames burned away our bodies. The next thing I remember, we were here, in Nero's palace."

Pettifogger rose to his feet dramatically. "So, where is the dungeon?"

"You will soon find out, thief!"

Pettifogger turned around to find a group of three Roman guards blocking the exit. Before they could move in closer, he lunged for the viola and stuffed it in his bag. Then, he made a break for the door. He managed to make it past the two front guards, but one at the end caught him. As he kicked and flailed about to free himself, the Roman grabbed for his bag.

"Let's see what else this little urchin has stolen from our Emperor!"

Though still struggling to escape the man's clutches, he managed to hold the bag securely with one hand while reaching for his dagger with the other. Rather than letting the

197

Roman gain access to his bag and, possibly, the temporal magic within, Pettifogger chose to destroy it. He stabbed his dagger into its side, causing the other guards to jump back defensively from the blade.

Bright, glowing temporal energy spewed forth from the bag's wound. Thinking he had found his way out, Pettifogger made the hole larger, releasing a burst of energy right at the face of his attacker. The Roman guard let go, seeing as how his face currently existed in that space between time. It was a bit disorienting, no doubt.

Pettifogger seized the opportunity to run up the steps and out of the auditorium. Though he had planned to make his escape into Tweentime, it had worked out just as well to use the temporal energy as a weapon. Besides, escaping to the plane of existence between this minute and the next would not help him rescue Aori.

Behind him, he caught a glimpse of the glowing energy, which had filled the entire auditorium. Assuming the guards were no longer following, he resumed his search for his friend and master. In spite of what his brain tried to tell them, his legs sped down the steps toward the front exit and freedom.

When the doors opened, Pettifogger instinctively crouched behind a pillar connecting the stairway to the floors above. Luckily, his small frame made it easy to hide. From this vantage point, he could see Nero and two of his Imperial guards enter the doorway. The guards were both armed with pole-arms, while Nero seemed to be armed with only an ice-cream cone. Several of his sycophants and advisors followed closely behind. They were all discussing Nero's contribution to the circus, calling him the star of the show.

Behind them, Pettifogger noticed a figure in armor of sparkling shades of green. She wore a flowing cloak that matched her attire and hid her wings from view. "Why would the Fellfalla be working for Nero?" Pettifogger muttered to himself.

The other two Fellfalla that Viola had told him about entered the palace next, followed by a young man around the age of sixteen. He, too, held an ice cream cone. Though the youth had the rather horrible disfiguring scars of a burn victim, the tufts of white hair that remained made him easy to identify. It was Aori.

Pettifogger fought back the urge to call out to his master. Instead, he just watched as Nero turned and walked toward the young man. Astonishingly, the Emperor clasped him about the shoulders-- not in a captor-to-captive way, but in the manner of a father and son. Of course, Nero was not known for taking in young men to act as their father-figure. Undoubtedly, he saw Aori as his next young conquest.

Together, the tyrant and his teen sidekick enjoyed their ice cream and walked toward the throne-room on the bottom floor. Pettifogger wondered if just being around Nero had influenced Aori to return to his megalomaniacal ways of the past. Perhaps Munder was right—maybe Aori was turning into Toki. The apple hadn't fallen far from the tree.

Pettifogger had seen enough. He leapt down from behind the pillar to where Aori and Nero stood, directly below him. Like some sort of monkey, the gnome bounded onto Nero's back and put the dagger to his throat. It was like a rather dangerous piggy-back ride.

"Nobody move!" shouted Pettifogger.

The guards rushed closer to protect their master, but Nero motioned for them to keep their distance. The air between them became very tense. Panic swirled about the crowd of advisors like a breeze.

The two female Fellfalla had served their own empire on Aia as Hawk-Moth Knights of Nerium. Instinctively, they, too, stood at attention, cautiously waiting for events to unfold. The darker, more macabre-looking one just stood and passively observed.

"What is going on here, Aori?" Pettifogger shouted. "Have you completely lost your mind? What are you doing, going to the circus with our enemy?"

"Aori is not my enemy, young man," said Nero, careful not to move his throat against the blade.

"Do not speak to me, despot!" Pettifogger shouted at the Emperor.

"How dare you address the Emperor with such insolence?" one of the advisors spoke.

Daphni, the Fellfalla in shades of green, approached. "You must be Mr. Pettifogger, correct?"

Bewilderedly, Pettifogger nodded.

"I am Daphni of the Nerii. We have much in common, you and I, and I hope that we may get to share stories of Aia one day. However, there is much that you do not understand here, valiant gnome. Put down your weapon, before greater harm comes to you."

Pettifogger looked to the hawk-moths, then to the guards, and finally at Aori. Feeling that his master and only friend had ultimately betrayed him, the gnome's heart sank in his chest. With but a twitch of his wrist, he could save Roman civilians from tyranny and protect the Christians from further persecution at his hands. Faced with the fate of hundreds of innocents at the edge of his blade, Pettifogger could not surrender.

Just as the tension within the room seemed ready to explode, there came an explosion of a different sort. Temporal energy from the burst bag above them had continued to expand beyond the walls of the auditorium, and it now threatened to envelop them all in swirling, purple magic.

Pettifogger looked up for a split second, and one of the Roman guards tackled him, pulling him off the back of the Emperor. He wrestled the gnome to the floor and pinned him like a Greco-Roman wrestler.

With the temporal magic quickly approaching, Aori finally took action. Though he still remained calm and stoic,

200

he managed to keep the energy at bay just by holding up a hand. The enormous sphere shrank until it was about the size of a basketball, at which point it seemed to form an eddy and whirl into itself. Finally, it just disappeared. It its wake, it left nothing but open air. At the edges, where the energy had barely touched the structure, it appeared as if thousands of years worth of decay had suddenly occurred. Roughly half of the dome-shaped palace was either severely dilapidated or completely erased from this time and place.

The guards carried Pettifogger off to the dungeon, and, with his spirit finally broken, the gnome did nothing to try to escape.

Chapter 2:12

The Lance of Longinus

The next day, Aori sat in the Emperor's box-seat in the Roman Coliseum, waiting for the gladiatorial battles to commence. The Emperor had always been a big fan of chariot races, Olympic events, and gruesome battles between prisoners, gladiators, and the occasional bear, bull, or other beast.

Next to Aori sat the spectacularly regal Daphni. Though she still hid her wings from view, she no longer wore her Fellfallan Imperial armor. Her form-fitting dress maintained her various shades of green arranged in an intricate pattern. She kept her hair, which was a dark shade of green itself, braided tightly in order to conceal the antennae that naturally protruded from her head.

Neither Acheron, the Death's Head Moth, nor his mate Proserpina chose to attend the function, for they did not revel in wanton displays of death and carnage. As harbingers of death, the couple had spent most of their lives together rounding up lost souls from the nether and escorting them to the beyond. Their workload had always been considerable enough, what with the wars and invasions on Earth, without the unnecessary death that Nero had single-handedly perpetrated or orchestrated in his short reign.

The Emperor entered the Coliseum with his usual ostentatious fanfare, and even though much of the crowd disliked him, they still cheered. If Democratic President Barack Obama had attended a Monster Truck Rally in the Republican-dominated South, he would have heard the same sort of cheers. Spectators at these sorts of events were eternally enthusiastic.

Daphni whispered, "Do you have a plan yet?"

"Not yet," Aori whispered back. "I am waiting for the right moment, and then I'm sure something will present itself."

"I cannot understand how the despot who we blamed for tampering with Aia's seasons could be the same, patient teenager to my right." Daphni laughed at the irony of it all.

Aori's face remained unchanged.

When Nero approached them, he greeted them effusively. "Young Timister," he said with a smile. "Lady Daphni."

"Hello, Emperor," said the Fellfalla with a respectful salute.

"You two are in for a very exciting day. If you have never seen two men fight to the death, it is truly exhilarating to watch." He turned to the guards on the arena floor and shouted with grand gestures, "Bring in the lions!"

The prisoners who faced the lions in the first battle lasted only a few minutes, much to the dismay of the bloodthirsty crowd and their Emperor. "I assure you, the next fight will be better. Bring out the Centurion, Longinus!"

The gates opened again, and the lions continued to prowl about the arena floor, eyeing their next prey cautiously. The centurion had to crouch a bit to get through the gate, as it had not been created with giants in mind. In one hand, he held a long spear. In the other, he seemed to be holding a large wooden shield. He wore his helmet with the

204

characteristic ram-horns, a motif which seemed to follow him across every life the giant assumed.

"Is that…?" whispered Daphni.

"Munder, yes," Aori whispered back. "He may provide just the timely intervention I've been awaiting."

"Is he still… evil?"

"That will always remain to be seen, in any given moment."

Daphni frowned. "When last we fought, he stole our Emperor's timepiece."

"Yes, that he did. I promise, I will explain it all to you later."

Aori's words did little to satisfy or pacify Daphni's uneasiness. Since she had met him a little less than three weeks ago, he had proven to be much more than the one-dimensional villain she had heard about on Aia. He had demonstrated more considerable compassion than she ever expected from him. However, whenever he shared the room with Nero, Aori seemed emotionless and stiff.

"For now," Aori whispered, "Let us see how events unfold."

As soon as Munder entered the arena, the lions set to their task of exploring and exploiting his weaknesses, as is their *modus operandi*. They acted as a team, crouching low and inching their way toward him. Unfortunately for the beasts, Munder exposed no weaknesses and gave them no opportunity to attack. Instead, he charged the largest of their pride and impaled him with the spear. When another tried to pounce, he blocked the attack with his wooden shield-arm, which knocked the lion to the ground. Before it could regain its footing, it found a spear piercing through its side.

While the other lions cowered in his presence, the gates opened again. Three prisoners entered the arena, saw their opponents, and immediately began scampering for the exit.

The Roman guards prodded at them with spears and yelled for them to join the fight.

While the Romans cleaned up the carnage on the arena floor, Nero took the opportunity to address the crowd. He explained the many misdeeds of the prisoners, just in case anyone in the crowd needed to be convinced that this gruesome manner of execution was justified. He also introduced some of the gladiators who had won matches in the past as well as new challengers.

"As for today's current champion, Longinus, his notoriety should already be familiar to you. He is the Roman Centurion responsible for the death of Jesus Christ!"

The crowd gasped, and smatterings of applause trickled through the audience.

Aori stared at Munder with disbelief. He whispered, "I thought that Jesus died on a cross."

"Yes, the man who many believed to be the Son of God was crucified many years ago. However, it was Longinus who pierced his side with his spear, thus dealing the final death-blow."

The news surprised Aori, who believed that Munder had been too preoccupied with rescuing the Odestone to take part in a brutal murder of a god in mortal form. Munder had performed acts of evil in the past, but even so, deicide seemed beyond him.

His thoughts drifted momentarily to when he first met the boy Jesus in the desert so many years ago. Munder had seen him then, as well, and recognized his divinity. Nothing seemed to make sense to Aori anymore.

With the combination of the prisoners' and the lions' attacks, they almost managed to penetrate the giant's defenses. However, any personal injury only served to fuel Munder's bloodlust. Battles like this, with the odds against him and no gray areas for his conscience, brought him unadulterated happiness. Many of his fights lately had required too much decision-making and morality. In the arena, everyone who was not Munder must be an enemy.

Of course, this mentality would not benefit one prisoner in particular, who currently waited in a holding area with other gladiators and fodder. Though they had taken away his weapons when he was imprisoned, Pettifogger had already managed to equip himself with those of others in the room. Along with an array of clubs and sticks, he had acquisitioned a cat-of-nine-tails, which was something like a whip with metal hooks at the end.

Though he had grown accustomed to avoiding death and bodily harm at all costs, the lifeless bodies of returning arena participants made him hesitate. It seemed unlikely that he would escape a duel to the death; he would have to win.

Even the hardiest of gladiators, with multiple wins under their belts, stood no chance against Munder's might and thirst for blood. They brought in bears, wolves, warriors, and large groups of prisoners, but all fell before the giant.

The crowd loved him, and their cheers invigorated him. Being the main attraction appealed to his ego. Just as the gates opened, however, the Tweenticker 2000 began to chime. Looking at his watch, Munder remembered his purpose for being there. As another wave of prisoners charged at him, he grumbled. Taking up a large battle-axe that had been discarded by one of his fallen opponents, he waited for the group to approach and, to save time, hewed them all down with one swing of the axe.

One of the prisoners remained standing. The blade of the axe had passed far above his head, and he dodged the next few blows with just as much ease.

"Just die already. I don't have time for this," said Munder.

"Really?" laughed Pettifogger. "I've got nothing scheduled. I could keep this up all day."

The gnome evaded another swing, which dug deep into the ground where he had stood. As he leapt to the side, he whipped the nine-tails at the axe and it wound around the handle, near the blade.

With a quick and dexterous movement, he ran up the giant's arm and jumped down behind him. The momentum and leverage combined with the surprise attack created a pulley system across Munder's shoulders, resulting in the axe driving directly up to his face. The blade embedded itself in his helmet, cracking it in two.

Munder's third eye blinked uncomfortably in the bright sunlight. Without the helmet covering it up, the eye darted around to try to focus on the audience. Those in the crowd who could see it returned the gaze with shock and horror.

With his opponent momentarily stunned, Pettifogger seized the opportunity to free his whip from the axe, which Munder had dropped. Briefly, he considered using the whip to escape into the audience, but then he thought better of it. With the crowd stirred up in such a manner, he would never make it out alive.

Instead, he cracked the whip across Munder's back. The metal hooks drove deep into the giant's skin. "Now that I have your attention, Munder, will you please come to your senses? Surely, with three eyes, you can recognize me."

Munder grabbed the whip, the tail of which was still stuck in his back, and jerked the gnome toward him. "I know who you are, pipsqueak; I just don't care. I'm not here for you." He grabbed Pettifogger and hurled him upward, in the direction of Nero's balcony.

Then, with a swift, decisive action, he picked up the spear and launched it in the same direction. It rocketed through the air, hurtling straight towards the Emperor. When it got just a few feet away, however, it froze in mid-air.

Time stood still.

Aori rose to his feet, removed the spear from its potential trajectory, and studied it momentarily. It seemed

208

just like any other spear, but it felt important somehow. He walked over to where a mob had formed around Pettifogger and wrenched him out from under the other bodies. He carried the gnome to the center of the arena, where he surrounded them, and Munder, in a sphere of temporal magic.

It took the gnome and giant a few minutes to adjust to the change. Within Tweentime, however, the three of them could have a conversation without anyone else intervening.

"What do you think you're doing, Munder?" asked Aori.

"No, wait," Pettifogger interrupted. "What are *you* doing, Aori? Are you working with the enemy?"

Anger flashed across Aori's face. "Pettifogger, I brought you here so you could find answers, not so you could interrupt with more questions. Just wait."

Both of them turned to Munder, who just stared at his watch.

"Why would you want to kill the Emperor, Munder?" Aori asked.

Munder grumbled. "He's a god. It's my job."

"Your job is to kill gods?"

"Yup," said Munder. "Remember when I said there had to be some higher purpose for me being thrown all around time in all these different bodies? Well, I found it."

"What about the Odestone?" asked Pettifogger. "We assumed you went to rescue him."

"Oh, I did," said Munder. "Can't you hear him?" He held out the stone, which looked the same as always, but it was missing that familiar vibration of sound. "I found him a long time ago, and I've been hunting gods ever since. You'd be surprised just how many of them don't belong here."

"So you're after Aian gods?"

"Whoever I spy with my extra eye," Munder smirked.

"And that's why you killed Jesus?"

Munder grumbled. "Look, that dude was dead long before I got there. I just needed this Longinus guy's spear to do my job."

"What's so special about the spear?" asked Pettifogger.

Munder grabbed the spear out of Aori's hand and spoke as if he were reading from an encyclopedia. "It's the Lance of Longinus, also known as the Spear of Destiny. It's the only thing powerful enough to kill a god."

Pettifogger tried to wrap his brain around the few answers he had heard, but he just generated more questions. "So... Nero is a god?"

"No," Aori corrected, "Finis is a god. Nero is simply his current mortal form."

"And you knew this, all along?"

"Not the whole time," said Aori. "I had my suspicions, but that night at the theatre confirmed it. All the seemingly unrelated events led us there. I have discovered a plot by the Dorians to assassinate him as well. We were to deliver Viola to him, resulting in his death by fire. Her Lydian command of flames would ensure a spark, if played, and Nero's sinister intentions would fuel the inferno. Apparently, the Dorians and Munder here share the same boss."

Munder grumbled, looked at his watch, and grumbled again.

"Toki?" asked Pettifogger. "Why would Father Time want Finis dead?"

"That's a good question," said Aori.

"And here's another," said Pettifogger. "Why wouldn't *you* want him dead?"

Aori raised his eyebrows.

"I could have killed him last night, when I had my blade to his throat."

"No, but you would have tried, failed, and died," said Aori. "My way was better."

"*Your* way?" shouted Pettifogger. "You just stood there and watched as I got thrown in prison!"

210

"And now you are free," said Aori, "and alive."

Despite the truth within the words, Pettifogger did not like being out of the loop.

Aori stroked his chin thoughtfully, as if he still had a beard. "Your blade would not have killed him, of that much I am sure. The flames also had no effect on him. This Lance of Longinus, however, could work."

"Then let's just go back there, unfreeze everything, and watch it happen," Pettifogger suggested. "After everything the Emperor has done, I don't see how we could allow him to live."

"Agreed," said Aori. "However, I don't know if we can prevent that. Aside from Finis, only Acheron knows anything about this curse."

"The Fellfalla?"

"Yes, the dark one. He was Finis's right-hand-moth for centuries on Aia."

Pettifogger considered their options. "If he lives, he will continue committing crimes against humanity ending only with his suicide."

"At which point, he would begin a new life and do the same thing over again."

"But if he dies today, by Munder's spear…"

"Assuming that it will kill him," Aori continued, "won't we just speed up the curse? He will be reborn today and commence the atrocities as soon as he is able. We face either the devil we already know or the one we don't know who has yet to be born."

Pettifogger sighed.

"Look at it this way," suggested Aori, "If Toki wants him dead today, then perhaps the best option is what I have been doing: wait around for other options to present themselves."

Pettifogger looked at him with disbelief. "For the last twelve hours, I was convinced that you had lost your mind. Now that I have an explanation for your actions, I'm still not sure that you're sane."

211

"At least I'm not carrying around a rock and calling it my friend," Aori laughed. "You know Ode's not in there anymore, right, Munder?"

Pettifogger looked around the room. "He's gone."

"Gone?" asked Aori. "Where could he have gone?"

Munder held the Odestone to his ear and shook it. "Who's next? Where am I now?"

The Odestone offered no response.

Munder grumbled.

"Only children and madmen speak to rocks, Munder," said a voice behind him. "Which of those describes you best?"

Munder wheeled around on his target and pointed the spear right at his head. Though he had arrived unarmed, his wooden arm had quickly taken on the form of the Lance of Longinus. In his current incarnation, Munder was a large aborigine, roughly eight feet tall, with skin as dark as night.

The speaker appeared to be aged in his hundreds. His skin was as worn and weathered as rocks on a windy beach. The voice was monotone and scratchy, like gravel.

"Ode?"

"In the flesh, as it were."

"But, how?"

Ode gave a hint of half of a smile. "Tempo, in his infinite wisdom, has blessed me with another lifespan. Of course, I can return to my stone at any time, if I so choose."

Munder returned the half-smile with one of his own. "Well, let's get to work. I don't have time to just sit around and chat."

"Undoubtedly. Let us go, then, and find the deified mortal in charge of these creatures."

Munder just stared at the beasts, which grouped together to form a pack.

Ode sighed. "Do you remember how, on Aia, each type of animal was governed by a man or woman with the power to change into that animal at will?"

"You mean like the werewolf that used to hang out with Quondam?"

"Yes. They are called Antheri. That one was the demigod of the wolves," said Ode.

They began to walk toward the pack of wild, dog-like creatures.

"And what's so important about this demigod? Why him?"

"*Her*," Ode corrected. "And she is a displaced god in a world that does not need her, Munder. She has become obsolete. If Tempo is ever to become the one supreme being, we have to thin out the ranks of this polytheistic planet."

Munder just stared at the creatures. "Fine. From now on, I'll just kill stuff. I don't understand your fancy explanations anyway."

Ode sighed.

As they approached the pack, each animal began to growl and snarl at them. The beasts looked something like dogs or wolves, but the Tazmanian Wolf was actually a marsupial. Like the wombat or kangaroo, this marsupial had a pouch. Unlike the koala, however, this animal demonstrated less cute and cuddly behavior and more of the violence and scavenging one would expect from the canine family.

The pack began to circle them, and Ode took this opportunity to vanish, presumably retreating into his rock. Munder cracked his neck, pointed the spear at his targets, and grinned wickedly.

The wonton slaughter of her kin drew the attention of Thylacine, their queen. As she stepped out of the bushes, she growled ferociously. Though she stood on two feet like a human, she crouched low as if ready to pounce at any

213

moment. Brown fur covered her whole body, and her head looked something like a wolf or fox. She had stripes, similar to those of a zebra, running down most of her back.

Thylacine barked at him viciously, possibly speaking in some language beyond his understanding. Lunging at the giant's hip, which was still a bit of a jump, she barely managed to break his skin with her powerful jaws.

Despite his many dreadful qualities, Munder had never relished in committing acts of violence against women. More out of pity than respect, he stood and watched as the Tazmanian wolf-goddess scratched, clawed, and gnawed at him, to no avail.

"Ode?" he called to his rock. "Do I have to kill her? She's so cute. Couldn't I just take her as a pet?"

The rock did not respond.

"Fine," grumbled Munder. He grabbed the scruff of her neck with one hand and held her above the ground. Though she tried to scratch and claw her way free, she did nothing but make him angry.

With one quick, merciful movement, he thrust her onto the spear, driving it up through her chest and out through her back. To hasten her death, he then snapped her neck. He did all this without his trademark bloodlust and wicked grin.

As you may have guessed, Tazmanian Wolves are now extinct.

Chapter 2:13

Prolonging the Inevitable

"What happened?" Daphni asked Aori after he returned to his seat in the coliseum. To her, and to all the other spectators, a gladiator had just thrown a spear at the Emperor. However, now both the gladiator and the spear had vanished right before their eyes.

"What do you mean?" Aori mocked ignorance in a voice that Nero could overhear.

"Where did the gladiators go? Both of them are missing now."

The mob that had gathered around Pettifogger were currently looking around at each other, unsure of what to do next. At that point, the gnome in question was actually a few city blocks away and taking the opportunity to prowl around the Emperor's palace.

"Are you sure they didn't just leave?" Aori shrugged.

Nero turned around, looked at him, looked back at the arena floor, and then sat down.

"I'll explain later," Aori whispered to Daphni.

Fortunately, much of the Emperor's palace had already been transported to Tweentime, including the Dorian statue

Pettifogger had deemed unmovable. There were still some odds and ends that had belonged to the Dorians, which Pettifogger stacked up in a secluded, empty room. Since he had turned his Timister Totebag inside out, thereby creating a temporary rift between time, he could no longer use it as a means of smuggling artifacts out of the palace.

"You have returned," said a solemn voice from the shadows of the room.

Pettifogger wheeled around and instinctively reached for his dagger.

"Do not fear us, Pyrite Pettifogger."

As the two Fellfallan spirits of Death stepped out of the shadows, Pettifogger found it a bit difficult to imagine them as anything but fearful. Acheron, the Death's Head Moth, had the appearance of a grim reaper, complete with a tattered cloak and a ghostly skull under his dark hood. Dust and shadow seemed to cling to him inseparably. His companion, Proserpina, seemed a bit more alive in contrast, and perhaps even a bit more human than moth. She, too, wore a tattered, dull-gray cloak.

"I apologize if I startled you," said Proserpina.

Pettifogger cleared his throat. "I'm just a little on edge, I suppose. I just left an arena battle with a giant and escaped a rather intense beating by a riled-up mob."

Proserpina turned to Acheron, somehow understanding his silent communication.

Turning back to the gnome, she asked, "Nero still lives, then?"

"How did you know?"

"Even in the world of the living, Acheron sees and knows much. The Emperor, as you may know, was his employer, in a previous incarnation."

Pettifogger nodded. "Should we have allowed him to die?"

The Fellfalla shared a gaze, as if they were discussing the matter in their own private language. At length, Proserpina

216

answered, "He will most assuredly die, and it is his destiny to die by his own hand. I hope, for the sake of all the living, that Aori made the right choice today."

The Death's Head spoke again, and this time it sounded to Pettifogger like the fluttering of moth-wings. Proserpina nodded to him and headed toward the door.

"We must be going. The land of the living is not for us. However, please relay a message to your master for us."

"Of course," said Pettifogger.

"Tell him, after Nero has died, he should go to the Dead Sea," she said gravely. "He may speak with us there, and perhaps we shall know more at that time."

Aori stood on what used to be a stairway in the Emperor's palace, but since most of the building had been absorbed by a temporal rift, it now served as a rather nice balcony. As he looked out upon the courtyard, the citizens who toiled away at their daily routines seemed to work faster and faster. When the sun began to set, Aori realized he had sat by and watched the entire day roll past before him. He wondered if he had sped up time for the world, or if he had only altered his own personal time.

In the distant darkening sky, he could see the approach of a large, winged creature. When he recognized it as Daphni, an involuntary smile spread across his face. "She's half your age," he mumbled to himself. "Of course, right now, I suppose I'm only a teenager."

She seemed to be flying toward the palace at an extremely fast speed. "Perhaps she has news from Acheron," he said to himself. "Or she's just really keen on seeing me again...."

His answer came like a bullet to the chest. In a whirr of agile movement, Daphni dive-bombed him and kicked him square in the torso. His boyish, infatuated smile shattered with his ribs as he crashed into the banister of the stairway.

In an instant, she had the blade of her seven-foot halberd pinned against his throat. The design of the blade matched her armor, with sleek, sweeping angles and intricately etched patterns. The shaft of the halberd contained spiraling gold braids studded with pale green jade. It had been a gift from Emperor Saturn to his Imperial Guard.

"Give me a straight answer, Aori Timister!" she shouted. "Are you the same villain you were on Aia? Will I do the world a great service by ending your life right now?"

Aori stared, wide-eyed, at his attacker. He tried not to gulp, as it would only bring his throat closer to the blade. "I would hardly call myself a villain, though I may have been painted that way in the past."

"I should have done this days ago, Time-Bender," she said through gritted teeth.

"Look," said Aori, "I didn't mean to speed up time. I was just watching the people pass, and I think the boredom got the best of me."

"What? I was referring to when you froze the gladiator battle."

"Oh. Well then…."

"What were you talking about?" she punctuated her question with the point of her halberd.

"Oh, nothing. I must have just slowed myself down. But, as for the arena, I think you'll find that my actions saved the life of the Emperor, and perhaps many other, more innocent lives."

Only then did Daphni pull her weapon from his throat. "Tell me everything. And, if it is as I think, and you have conspired with that evil giant, I will do nothing to stop my blade from tasting your blood."

"Quite poetic, my dear," Aori gulped. "I will tell you all that I know."

"Start with why you would spare the life of the current incarnation of Finis."

As the story of the arena battle unfolded, Daphni loosened up her Imperial Guard-like resolve. Something in her had trusted him since the night she saved him from the burning theater, but there just seemed to be too many different conspiracies running atop one another. She longed for the simple days of fighting off anyone who was an enemy of the Fellfallan Empire... but as she thought about that, she remembered Gypsy. The exiled Fellfallan wanderer had been an enemy of the empire but a friend to her and much more to her brother. *Nothing is simple*, she concluded.

They talked for the rest of the evening and well into the night. The Fellfalla, by nature, are nocturnal, and since Aori had never liked taking the time to sleep, he definitely did not mind whiling away the hours with a beautiful woman.

"How will we stop the never-ending cycle of suicide and rebirth?" she asked finally.

"I wish I knew, Daphni. I hoped that your friends Acheron and Proserpina could help, but they've gone back to the spirit world, it seems."

Daphni laughed. "At first, I thought you had made them disappear somehow, like you did with Pettifogger and the giant."

He smiled, but his thoughts lingered on Munder. "If he's hunting gods, you and I both may be in danger. Munder, in his finite wisdom, may not distinguish between super-natural entities and mortals with dominion over moths."

For the next few years, Aori served as Nero's chief advisor and thereby prevented acts of violence on the Emperor's part. They provided medical assistance and housing to all those who were injured or lost their homes during the fire. He even allowed people to live within his palace and courtyard. When civilians rebuilt their houses, Nero ensured that they were built with brick in a manner that would prevent future disasters.

In the area most devastated by the fire, Nero commissioned the construction of a larger, more extravagant palace complex. Despite Aori's insistence that such a display of ego would not help his public image, Nero felt that the people needed to see that their leader could rise up from the flames like a phoenix.

During this time, Aori allowed himself to age a bit more rapidly than normal, but not enough to arouse suspicion. He felt that it hurt Nero's reputation to be seen continuously with young men, and he didn't like the suggestive looks he got from the Emperor from time to time.

As Nero still believed Pettifogger to be an assassin and fugitive, Aori had to keep his dealings with the gnome a secret. However, they still managed to ferry out a good deal of Dorian artifacts, as well as a few technological innovations the Emperor had either created or stolen from others. Most importantly, Pettifogger rediscovered the spike from Christ's crucifixion, which made a more than adequate dagger.

Daphni remained in Rome even though her fellow Fellfalla had returned to the spirit world. Gloom tends to breed gloom, so it was far better for Daphni to remain with the living. She had much of her life ahead of her, and it *was* a Roman who came up with the saying *carpe diem*, after all.

Often, she would perch atop the apex of the former palace's dome, which actually looked something like an ice cream scoop missing a bite. From there, she could see much of the city, including the egomaniacal tribute that was Nero's Golden Dome.

"It reminds me a bit of Emperor Saturn's palace, back home," Daphni sighed.

Aori matched her sigh with one of his own. "The Senate disapproves of it, and the nobles are infuriated at the increase in taxes. I've done everything I can to keep him from committing some horrible crime against humanity, but I never thought I'd need to protect him from *them*."

"You have done great things, Aori." The corners of her lips turned up ever so slightly.

He had followed her up to the roof on more than one occasion, mostly due to the fact that he preferred the company of his fellow Aian refugees to the tyrannical leader he served. Though the demigod and the Fellfallan knight had very little in common aside from their home planet, something stirred inside him whenever she was present. It felt like butterflies—or more appropriately, moths—were flitting about in his stomach.

By the light of the fading sun, Daphni's green eyes glinted like emeralds. Her skin showed a lighter hint of the same pattern as her clothing and armor, and it felt as soft as silk to the touch.

"It has truly been a joy getting to know you, Lady Daphni of the Nerii." whispered Aori.

A fleeting smile graced her lips. She stood up to get a better view, and her dress fluttered in the wind. As she stretched out her arms, she let her wings flap with the warm breeze as well.

The sun dipped down behind the horizon, and she folded her arms across her chest. Her wings drooped to their resting position, which gave the appearance of a long, flowing cape. The tone of her voice took on a more somber quality. "I will have to leave here, soon."

Aori had very little experience with displays of emotion. He had always felt them deeply, but many of his companions throughout the years had either been catatonic parents or mechanical slaves. "Why is that?" he cleared his throat of any possible lumps.

What the Fell?

Fellfalla: moth / human hybrids; fell means dark or vicious, even though they're mostly pretty nice

Fairfalla: their butterfly counterparts

Farfalla: the general term for both types of faerie-folk

221

"I came to this world in search of Gypsy, and I have to do that before…"

"…Before your time on Earth is over," Aori finished. "Of course. I'm looking for any and all Aians refugees on this planet. You may find that more of your people came over with us in the ships."

"Some must have, because I have seen larvae and moths in the night sky since coming here." Her fleeting smile returned. "I have even seen some butterflies, which means that Fairfalla must have made the voyage as well. It hardly seems possible, since the Royal Kingdom of the Fairfalla died out long before the death of Aia."

"I believe Time may have manipulated life on this planet, as he did on ours. He may have transported them here eons ago." He stood up, wobbled a bit, and walked over to her once he found his balance. "Nevertheless, I will help you in any way I can. I am a man of many resources."

She turned and looked into his pale, grayish-blue eyes. "You mustn't leave Nero, though. Look at all the evil he spread before you came."

"Of course," he agreed, though he wanted to rebuke the Emperor and leave the Empire to crumble under its own wickedness and evil. He wanted to just grab her and hold her while the city burned around them… so to speak.

As if reading his mind, she whispered, "Whatever has grown between us, Aori, can never be. Fellfalla have very short life spans, and I am considered middle-aged by our reckoning."

"Immortals and ephemerals have shared lives together before," he argued.

"I will die one day. I caught a glimpse of my fate, in the Dead Sea," her voice warbled with emotion.

"I can stop time. I will bend it so that we can grow old together." In desperation, he let his own emotions overflow. He reached out and grabbed her hand.

"Aori…"

222

"Look. The clouds have all stopped moving. The people below are still."

With the sigh of one who has given up an argument, she smiled briefly.

He wanted to kiss her, to stop the smile from leaving her lips, but something told him that he should not rush this, of all things. *Patience*, echoed in his brain.

Within their own private sphere of Tweentime, they could just enjoy that sunset forever. Thoughts of her people, other Aians, Nero, and the future all faded away. Aori had spent most of his life waiting on others, so he felt justified in letting the world wait for him.

Of course, peace in Rome, like the life of the moth, was ephemeral. Before the Golden Dome was completed, the Senate and a group of high-ranking military officers conspired to have Nero assassinated. They believed him to be unfit to rule and, instead, proposed a return to the Republic of old.

As the most qualified for sneaking around and eavesdropping, Pettifogger discovered the plot to kill the Emperor and quickly told Aori about it. "Even his own advisors are in on it," Pettifogger told him.

"Not Seneca, as well?" Seneca had been one of Nero's most trusted counselors and tutors since his very young days of exile during Caligula's reign of terror.

"I relieved him of the money they paid him to betray the Emperor," Pettifogger admitted.

Aori allowed a bit of half-smile. "At least there is justice in that, I suppose." He paused for thought. "Who are we kidding? Upsetting a tyrannical regime is the justice here. Nero *should* be overthrown."

"The Death's Head Moth said he was destined to die by his own hand," said Pettifogger, though he struggled with the idea of letting the despot live.

"Besides, where is the justice in such a betrayal? How can they sleep at night, knowing they will soon stab their master in the back?"

Pettifogger winced, as if he had been wounded himself.

With the knowledge of the conspiracy at his disposal, Nero ordered the executions of nineteen of his former friends, advisors, and appointed praetors. Several others were exiled. For Seneca, who admitted to having spoken with the conspirators, Nero performed a special, private musical piece. Seneca took his own life.

The uprisings and betrayals did not end then, however. Each year leading up to Nero's death, the Roman Empire faced revolts in Judea, Britannia, and many other provinces. His military accepted bribes to undermine and rebel against him, and the Senate hired whoever they could find to assassinate him. Every attempted coup ended with more executions and forced suicides.

Finally, in 68 A.D., the countless rebellions and betrayals took their toll on the Emperor. The Senate finally amassed enough bribed soldiers and state officials to back Nero into a corner. They planned to have him flogged to death, and he had no means of escape.

On the night of June 9, all of his servants, guards, and advisors abandoned him. Though his entire palace was empty, Nero swore that he heard music coming from somewhere in the building. In a panic, he ran from room to room, shouting, "Who is there?" The music echoed louder and louder, and Nero recognized the song as the one he had played in the theatre while Rome burned. It was the song that haunted him in his dreams for most of his life.

"They will come for you," whispered a voice, which could have easily come from inside his own head. "They have all turned against you. You have no way to escape... except Death."

He rushed up the stairs to his personal quarters, opened a locked closet, and took out a weapons chest. After fumbling with the lock, he managed to get it open, only to find all of his weapons missing. Reaching down into the chest reminded him of a deep, dark cavern. At the bottom, he found the nail that had been used to crucify Christ. Cradling it in his hands, he closed his eyes as tightly as he could, gripped the nail, and drove it into his neck.

When the Roman soldiers, who had come to arrest him, found him bleeding on the floor, he gurgled and spat out the words, "What an artist dies with me!"

After his death, Rome went through four emperors in just one year. The Empire fell into chaos, and it would be many years before Rome returned to its former glory.

Aori, Daphni, and Pettifogger left that same year and never looked back. They returned to the Dorian Temple in Greece, which had fallen to ruin in the few years they had been gone. Much of the stonework had worn away, and weeds had grown up all around the building. As they entered, they noticed several broken tiles in the floor, and part of the ceiling had collapsed.

"Pedant?" Aori called to the temple's teacher. "Is anyone here?"

The harp in the corner, though buried under rubble, hummed with its two remaining strings. In response, some of the other furniture vibrated softly.

"What has happened here?" asked Daphni. Though her direct experience with the Coda was limited to her encounters with Lithe and the Odestone back on Aia, she had always been told stories about them as a young larva.

"It seems Tempo has forsaken the line of Dorian, at last," proclaimed Aori in a loud voice. Then, he continued, a bit softer, "It happens to the best of us."

225

Pettifogger removed the burned and damaged viola from his pack (which he had turned right-side-in), and she immediately began to sing.

"Look at what has become of you, in your self-centered pride!" sang Viola. In a softer voice, she spoke to the living: "Their voices are faint. Their life-songs are fading."

Aori chimed in, "Dorian! Instead of dying a mortal's death, you have only prolonged your decay over hundreds of years! Is this what you wanted?"

Dust fell from the collapsed ceiling, as if to symbolize the last of Dorian's spirit finally breaking. Worn pages of ancient texts flapped rhythmically as the wind blew through the building's broken walls.

Pacing amongst the debris, Aori addressed each deteriorated artifact. "I cannot give you back your mortal lives, nor can I lengthen your time on Earth. Decay is an inevitable part of life, even for non-living objects. However, I can release your souls in Tweentime, so that you may reside there for eternity."

The house stood still.

"I will give you time to decide."

The podium of Pedant, though turned on its side and missing pieces, scratched out the sound of chalk on a chalkboard. A pew consisting of rotted wood creaked. Two urns rubbed together, making a squeaking sound.

Soon, a cacophony of noise reverberated throughout the temple, eventually forming a syncopated rhythm. Chairs and tables stomped their legs, doors slammed shut, and the urns knocked against one another.

The thumping beat of the house swelled in crescendo, becoming louder and faster as more inanimate objects joined in the song. Soon, everything in the house shook, which caused more dust and rubble to fall from the ceiling. The walls and floor rumbled, as if an earthquake had suddenly struck.

"The House of Dorian accepts your offer, Aori Timister," bellowed the temple itself.

228

Chapter 2:14

The Dead Sea

When Aori returned to his library, he found it, too, to be overgrown with weeds. The goldenrods Pettifogger had planted, or constructed, had grown to the size of trees. The building itself had increased in size as well, such that he felt it would be appropriate to rename it the Timister Literature and Research Complex.

Aori stood on the front steps and welcomed the newcomers. "I apologize for the current state of the facilities. Our gardener has been away." He smiled at Pettifogger, who immediately went to work tending his mechanical plants.

Much to Daphni's delight, the large flowers had attracted many moths and butterflies, which fluttered around the metal blossoms, looking in vain for pollen. "How did they get here?" she wondered aloud.

"Very interesting," said Aori. "I have not seen them here before. Do you recognize any of them?"

"I believe so, though I am not accustomed to seeing them without their Farfallan masters." She took to the sky and joined the tiny insects in their orbit around the mechanical flowers. "Come, little ones. I will find you something to eat."

The moths and butterflies followed her into Aori's library, where they set up a pavilion for the insects. Daphni brought them sugar-water, as conventional flowers would not grow in Tweentime.

"I think you'll find," Aori explained to her, "That they won't require much in the way of sustenance. I have lived here for extended amounts of time with no food, water, or sleep. It defies all logic, but such is the nature of Tweentime."

For the Dorian Coda, they assigned a special wing, which had specialized acoustics for music, shelves for displaying sculptures, pottery, and other works of art, and, of course, room for an audience to sit.

The Dorians themselves abandoned their inanimate shells and wandered the complex as temporal spirits. As one might guess, Pedant still taught anyone who would listen, Viola entertained audiences with new compositions (with the occasional old standby), and Herodotus continued chronicling the history of Earth.

Aori scoured the available literature for any hints to the whereabouts of Quondam, Lithe, Gypsy, or the various other Aian refugees. However, as adept as Herodotus was at organizing and ordering the library, they had to sort through too many different times and places.

"I'd also like to know where Finis is now, so keep an eye out for evil babies," Aori told Herodotus.

"I have updated them with as much as I know, but I am a historian, not a chronicler of the present. Perhaps you should find a newspaper, if you want up-to-date information."

"Or, if I could just get this contraption to work," Aori huffed as he approached the strange technology growing through the floor. Like the garden outside, it, too, had grown into a tangled mess. The cables connecting its many parts wound around the table and up the walls like vines.

230

However, as full of life as it seemed to be, it provided no information of the future, as Aori had hoped.

Turning back to the hundreds of books that had gone forth and multiplied in his absence, he explained the library's magic to the old Coda. "The books in this library have taken on a life of their own. They are not limited to the words they once held, on Earth. Rather, they change as the building changes. If we wait long enough, I believe your book will update itself."

The historian eagerly moved from bookshelf to bookshelf like a child who has found a new toy. He marveled at the vast amounts of history stored within the books.

Aori left him to his research and walked up a winding flight of stairs to what he assumed had grown up to be his personal quarters. At the top of a tower, albeit much smaller than the towers he had built on Aia, he found the reflecting pools he had created after the destruction of the Tower of Babel.

The pools had become spheres of glowing energy suspended in mid-air like balloons at a child's birthday party. In the spheres, he saw Munder killing the goddess of the Tazmanian wolves, Pettifogger tending to the garden, and Daphni communing with the moths. Several other spheres were dim or completely dark.

By rotating one of the spheres with his hands, he could tune into the current time period on Earth. Since he had built his temple in between time and space somewhere around the fertile crescent, his view was limited to that area.

However, as he bent the temporal energy to his will, he could zoom out to see the bigger picture of present events. There seemed to be a war going on between the Romans, led by a man named Titus, and the Hebrew people in Jerusalem. As he watched the events unfold, time seemed to be moving more rapidly. Armies flowed into one another like tides, houses burned, and people died. All those who fled the city were captured and crucified around the perimeter of the city.

The siege of Jerusalem took roughly a year, but Aori watched it all unfold in minutes.

"Aori!" The spirit of Herodotus shot up the stairs like a purple, glowing firework. "The book is changing before my very eyes! It tells of a war... the Romans have destroyed the Jewish Temple in Jerusalem."

"Yes, I just saw it happen, I believe."

Herodotus's jaw dropped. "Aori... two years have already passed since we came here."

"It's as if I have the world outside on fast-forward," Aori muttered to himself, even though the reference to VCRs of the future meant nothing to him at that point. "Of course, I'm not manipulating time. Let us be very clear on that. That's how I got into trouble on Aia. No, I think I've just slowed down the passing of time here, in Tweentime, so that we are like rocks in the stream of time. The river flows past us, while we stand still and watch."

"That sounds beautiful," Daphni declared as she entered the room. She looked around at all the spheres. "Your mastery of time is amazing, Aori."

"Not amazing enough, I'm afraid. I still can't pinpoint the locations of anyone outside this time and place. If I stretch, I can see places I have been before."

Herodotus, enraptured in his book, decided to leave the two of them alone. He found the books of the library far more exciting anyway.

Like a moth to a flame, Daphni found herself drawn in and mesmerized by the swirling magic. She reached out and touched one of the dimmer spheres with her fingertips. Immediately, the purple sphere shattered into many smaller pieces, which flitted around the room like moths. The swirls even appeared to have tiny wings, and if you could focus on one long enough, it displayed fleeting images of faraway events.

"That's interesting," Aori remarked. "The energy seems to have reformed itself in your image, or at least one familiar to you. Perhaps you can tame them, as you do their real-world counterparts."

Closing her eyes, Daphni attempted to reach out to the temporal moths with her mind. Gradually, they came together to form one, large moth with outstretched wings. Amidst the swirling energy, Aori could see a large body of water.

"The Dead Sea," said Daphni after opening her eyes. "I would recognize it anywhere."

Aori slapped himself on the forehead, as one does when he has forgotten an important appointment. "I was supposed to find Acheron there, after Nero's death."

"We must go there, then. How far away are we?"

"Take my hand," said Aori.

Together, they walked into the temporal moth.

The Dead Sea gets its name from the fact that, due to the salinity of the water, not very much grows there. How did a saltwater sea, with no inlets or outlets to the ocean, come about in the middle of a desert? That's a good question. Perhaps there's a salinity deity with that responsibility. Then again, if that was true, Munder probably would have already killed him or her.

Overlooking the sea, several plateaus or bluffs provided a relatively safe haven for religious groups who had been persecuted by other sects. One such group, the Essenes, has been credited with depositing the Dead Sea Scrolls in a cave around this area, roughly around the time Aori and the others left Delphi for Tweentime.

Another ostracized religious group, made up of Jewish Kana'im and Sicarii, took refuge in the fortified city of Masada. While both the Kana'im, or zealots, and the Sicarii were staunchly, and some might say fanatically, dedicated to their religious beliefs, only the Sicarii, which meant "dagger-men" in Latin, were willing to kill to protect those beliefs.

233

They stabbed backs of both Roman enemies and Jewish allies who did not oppose the Romans fervently enough.

Nevertheless, Masada held a strategically ideal position on top of a plateau, with only three small footpaths that lead up the side of the cliff, which were roughly 1000 feet high. They believed their defenses would keep them safe and secluded enough to avoid Roman confrontation. However, the military of the empire saw the strategic location as a threat and a nice potential base for the future.

From the point of view of a Storyteller, it seems obvious that some exciting, dramatic conflicts must have existed between the zealots and the assassins, and their standoff against the Roman siege would undoubtedly make for an entertaining story.

However, when the Romans got to the city, everyone was already dead.

"You have come too late," Proserpina stated simply as she and Acheron rose from the depths of the Dead Sea. They hovered a few inches above the salt-encrusted sand of the shore and stopped in front of Aori and Daphni.

"Too late?" asked Aori, shocked. "We traveled between time to get here instantly!"

"Nothing more can be done here." Proserpina turned back toward the sea.

"Wait, Pross!" Daphni called to her. "Who has died here?"

"Nine hundred six humans." She looked up at the fortress of Masada. "If you wish to see their bodies, you will find them on that mesa to the west."

Daphni reached out and grabbed Proserpina, who had once been one of her truest friends. "Wait! What has happened to you? You seem so cold and... distant."

Proserpina stared at her with dull, lifeless eyes. "When you have seen as much death as I have, I wonder how you will behave, Daphni of the Nerii."

Aori interrupted. "What could we have done to stop this?"

"Nothing," Proserpina stated flatly.

"Then how is it that we arrived too late?"

"If you had come after Nero's death, as Acheron requested, you might have identified Finis's latest incarnation in time to prevent the deaths of the others."

"Impossible," scoffed Aori. "How many years have passed since Nero's death? I do not believe that a four-year-old could be responsible for this much carnage."

Acheron looked at him with the barren stare of a man with only shadows for a face.

"Finis must be elsewhere," Aori continued. "What evils could a child have committed, so early in life? This child is no King Saul, who I witnessed massacre eighty-five priests. He is not a Judas, who betrayed his messiah to the enemy. Surely, this child could not have equaled Nero in his acts of violence toward humanity."

He stared up at the ruined fortress, which had only recently been abandoned by all but a handful of Roman soldiers. "Let's investigate, to see if we can find any clues to why this tragedy happened."

The three Fellfalla flew up to the fortress, carrying Aori among them. As they approached, the smell was overpowering. Buzzards had begun to circle overhead, and flies had gathered around the bodies. It was all Aori could do not to get sick.

Acheron immediately set to work seeking out stranded spirits from the city, while Proserpina attempted to shoo away the carrion birds out of respect for the dead.

If this had been a crime drama on television, they would have cordoned off the area, and gloved crime-scene-investigators would scour the area for footprints, blood trails, and DNA samples. Obviously, Aori had no forensics equipment or crime lab. He knew nothing of dusting for fingerprints or measuring the angles of their entry wounds.

235

However, he had a gut feeling that they had not perished in battle with the Romans. For one, their attackers would have used arrows or siege weapons to attack from afar. While it appeared a battering ram had been used on the fortified gate, there were no clues to suggest that the people had been killed by catapults or trebuchets.

"Look around for children who could be Finis's age... roughly around age four, assuming he was born into a new life right after Nero died." At Aori's suggestion, they split up to examine the horrific mass of children's bodies. The tragic scene ripped at the hearts of the living, and even Acheron and Proserpina felt a hollow kind of sorrow.

"Do you sense anything from their spirits, Acheron?" Daphni asked.

The Death's Head Moth spread his wings out wider, as if they got better reception that way. The dust from thousands of graves and decomposition fell from his tattered robes. The buzzards suddenly stopped trying to scavenge for food to stare at him. The air around Acheron got very thick, and the high winds that normally blew across the bluffs stopped completely.

While Acheron performs his ritual, which takes quite awhile, perhaps we should take a few minutes to explain the afterlife of these particular followers of Judaism. Many believers in this time chose to focus on life rather than what came after it, but some groups believed in the immortality of the soul. To them, the soul moved on to other beings after death. While this idea of reincarnation contradicts the idea of Heaven and Hell, it does fit rather well with popular Aian beliefs. Souls travel to She'ol, or an underworld similar to where Acheron and Proserpina live, and their life-force is redistributed to other bodies around the planet.

In this case, however, the souls vanished.

"What?" shouted Aori in disbelief.

"The souls are all gone," Proserpina repeated. "They must have been taken."

"Who, other than Acheron, would take souls?" asked Daphni.

"Maybe," suggested Aori, "they're being stored in some objects, as with the Dorian Coda." Picking up one of their clay pots, he called out, "Pettifogger?"

As his gnomish companion was currently in Tweentime, he did not respond.

"Oh, where is my head? I'm just so used to having him underfoot." Aori gathered up some more of the items the zealots had owned, but it seemed that they had not been a very materialistic group.

He placed the items near the body of a young child, who could have been the age that Finis would have been at that time. "I'm just going to run these items to the lab. I'll be right back." In a flash of purple-hued light, Aori, the body, and several of the zealots' meager worldly possessions vanished altogether.

After he had gone, Proserpina took Daphni aside. "Are you certain that you know what you are doing?"

Daphni continued to examine bodies in the city for clues. "What do you mean? I am waiting for Aori to return."

"You know what I meant, Daphni. You are not long for this world, and he is the mortal form of a god of Time. Have you no sense of irony?"

Daphni wandered from body to body, seemingly avoiding the issue. "He has provided me with more in the last few years than I ever had as an imperial knight back on Aia. He loves me, and I…"

"Do you?" Proserpina interrupted. "Or are you making a deal with the Time god, as Emperor Saturn did? Has he promised to give you immortality?"

The green knight of the Nerii lingered in the town's garden, where the zealots seemed to have diverted rainwater into several aqueducts. Despite the arid climate of the Judean desert and the dearth of vegetation around the Dead Sea, this particular garden seemed to be thriving. Aside from the fact

237

that two of the town's citizens had perished here, it made for a very beautiful scene. Even that carnage seemed to have been cleaned up by the plants, which had somehow already grown up around the bodies.

"Daphni?"

She smelled one of the blooming flowers, reveling in that smell that she linked with sustenance and safety. "If I stay with him in Tweentime, then Time's effects will not phase me."

Proserpina looked around at the blooms, which provided her only with memories. Their nectar could not satisfy her, in death. She attempted to smile in order to be positive for her friend, but it came out as a crumpled grimace.

"I know what you're going to say." Daphni stood up and walked to the edge of the garden, which overlooked the sea hundreds of feet below. The wind gusted up the side of the bluff and caught against her wings. She felt as if she were flying.

"Do they have wind in Tweentime? Do flowers bloom there?"

"Yes… in a way. They are metal."

"Metal flowers?" Proserpina's attempts at smiles gave way to a sort of confused frown.

"They still grow."

As if in response to their conversation, a flower bloomed right next to the face of a female zealot. It almost looked as if she wore flowers in her hair.

"If time does not pass in Tweentime, then how is it that you arrived here four years after the time we expected you? One would think that Tempo's demigod would be a bit more punctual."

"I'll answer that," Aori interrupted. He carried the child's body in his arms, and he wore a strange contraption on his head. Part goggles and part helmet, the device made him look like some sort of insect. Spiraling shells of some rather large crustacean hung from his ears, and two long antennae protruded from the shells.

"Is he trying to look more like a moth, for your sake?" whispered Proserpina.

Daphni smiled.

"Time in between time bends to my will. For instance, I left here only moments ago, but I spent months working on this device. I call it the Residual Resonance and Deity Detector, or the Deitector for short. It should allow me to see whether any of these bodies belonged to Finis, and, if any lore has imprinted on the rocks and objects around, I should pick up the vibrations through these antennae."

As he began reexamining the bodies through his goggles, he seemed to be muttering to himself. "No? How about now?"

"Are you talking to someone, Aori?" Daphni asked. She gave a look to her friend that meant, *Don't you even dare call my significant other insane.*

"Oh, I'm sorry. I forgot to introduce you. Daphni, this is Elegos. He's one of the Dorian Coda that live with us now. In life, he wrote poetry for mourning and funeral songs. He seemed the perfect asset to our investigation."

Proserpina looked around and then looked at Daphni with a look that meant, *Your significant other is insane.* "There is no one else here, Aori," she stated plainly.

"The Dorians sing their souls into material things," Daphni explained, with a spiteful look, to her friend. "Obviously, Elegos is inside the device."

"Brilliant observation, my dear," said Aori. "He is the ghost in the machine, if you will."

"Do you hear anything yet?"

Aori listened carefully. "I believe, through my observations and deductions I made both here and in Tweentime, that these people all committed suicide. They were dead before the Romans even arrived."

"Suicide? Then surely Finis is involved."

239

"What? No. I'm sorry; I have Elegos spouting poetry in my ears right now. It's difficult to concentrate. Perhaps I should have brought one of the other Coda along."

Elegos vibrated throughout the instrument.

"Well, then, focus on the task at hand. I need to know what transpired here, and preferably not in poetic form."

"I will tell you, without the aid of your silly contraption," said a strange voice.

The others turned toward the garden, where the corpse of the zealot with the flowers in her hair slowly rose.

"Is it Finis, rising from the dead?" whispered Daphni.

Acheron muttered something inaudible.

"No...." Proserpina answered.

Aori looked her up and down with the goggles. "No, it's not Finis, but it is a deity." He ran over and embraced the corpse, much to the dismay of Daphni and those who already thought he had lost his mind.

"Aori? You are hugging a dead body," Daphni whispered.

Though the body had been decaying in the hot desert sun for days, it seemed rather fresh at that point. Vines encircled its limbs, and flowers seemed to grow throughout its hair. By the time it had risen to its feet, it looked much less like a corpse and much more like something botanical.

"Asalie!" Aori announced with a grin from ear to ear, or from one residual resonance receptor to the other.

"In a manner of speaking," Asalie whispered hoarsely, as if making the vocal chords of a dead woman proved difficult.

"We have been looking all over for you," Aori gushed. "I was afraid you were dead."

Vines pushed up on the corpse's cheek muscles in order to form a smile. Asalie's weak voice sputtered, "No, the Dying Embodiment of Life will go on dying, yet. And you have found me, everywhere you have looked."

Everywhere the corpse stood, flowers bloomed. "It is my job to wander, as you know, Aori. If I didn't, how would Earth have seasonal growth cycles?"

"Perhaps because of the planet's tilt and its annual orbit around the sun?"

Asalie and Aori laughed as two friends who had just shared an inside joke.

"You were always so mundane in your explanations of grand events, Aori."

"And you're like a walking folktale, Asalie."

Asalie laughed. "Nevertheless, I mustn't get distracted. Weeds grow in my brain and make me lose my train of thought from time to time."

"Yes; what can you tell us of Finis?" asked Aori.

"First of all, I'm surprised you didn't find me sooner, Mr. Timister. I have left messages for you in each of his incarnations. Did you not see the tree from which Judas hanged himself? I was there."

"I must admit," Aori confessed, "it took me awhile to put together all the clues. I just assumed that King Saul had acted of his own accord, and that his death was unrelated to any others."

"Nothing is unrelated, Aori. Even now, your path and that of the Queen of the Fellfalla have intertwined like vines. It is beautiful, how living things come together."

Daphni cleared her throat, clearly uncomfortable with the talk of her personal life. "What can you tell us about this tragedy, in particular?"

"I can tell you he's not here."

"What?" asked Aori. "But with this much death, all by their own hands…."

"As you said, Finis could not have committed horrific acts before the age of four. No, something more sinister is afoot here. These people killed themselves to avoid death at the hands of the Romans, but they have been unwitting carriers of a terrible plague."

241

Aori looked around at the bodies, covering his mouth. "I see no signs of illness."

"It is a pox on the living," Asalie wheezed. "It may be Finis's design, but this seems a bit much even for his standards. Though, he always did love a good plague. I remember one epidemic on Aia…."

"Asalie, focus," Aori snapped. "Why would the souls of all these individuals have vanished completely?"

The herbaceous corpse turned to Acheron. "You did not remove their spirits to your realm?"

Acheron murmured inaudibly.

"I see." Asalie held out the corpse's finger, and a flower bloomed at its fingertip. A white moth came, seemingly from nowhere, and gently landed on the flower. As the moth removed the nectar from the flower, Asalie spoke again. "Continue on as you have done. Find this Gypsy you seek, and I believe you will find more Aians along the way. Keep an eye out for deaths by suicide, but do not let this new plague fool you. I believe it is part of Finis's plan to throw you off his trail."

The moth flew away from her finger and landed on Daphni's. As she studied it closely, she noticed that it looked very similar to the Fellfalla named Lymantria Dispar, who she called Gypsy. "Wait, Asalie…" she interjected, "Earlier, you called me the Queen of the Fellfalla. Does that mean that my brother, Oleander…"

"The King is dead. Long live the King," Asalie rasped. "Of course, by that I mean that he lives on in the moths that traveled here from Aia. You will find many who bear your likeness, Daphni Nerii."

Despite Asalie's words of encouragement, Daphni mourned the loss of her brother. She had hoped to find Gypsy and reunite her with Oleander, as the two had always had a tragic, unrequited love. Gypsy had never been one to settle down, and Oleander's higher station among the knights and nobles of the Empire had always kept them apart.

242

As Daphni lost herself in thoughts of her brother, so too did Asalie's mind meander. She muttered, seemingly to herself, about white and pink flowers in the Mediterranean area called Aiwa. In fact, similar to a crazed homeless person on the street, Asalie just repeated, "Aiwa," over and over as she circled the garden.

"Asalie?" Aori gently tapped her on the shoulder, trying to get her attention.

She seemed to respond, but her words were incoherent.

"Asalie, I have more questions. Where is Finis now? What do we do when we find him? How can we stop his curse?"

The vines holding the corpse together had begun to wither and fall away, and many of the flowers wilted. The body collapsed to the ground

Aori drooped his head. "She has a growth... inside her brain. That's why she's the Dying Goddess of Life. Ironic, isn't it, that one who controls growth around the world would be driven insane by it?"

"She seemed to make sense, for the most part," Daphni reassured him.

"I suppose, although it seems illogical to keep wandering around, waiting for the curse to spread, rather than seeking out Finis in his youth. Of course, I wouldn't have found Nero if I hadn't been sidetracked on other missions." He turned to her and smiled. "And, I wouldn't have found you...."

Taking her hand in his, he pulled her closer. She embraced him tightly, wishing he could take away all her pain. "Aori," she whispered through her tears, "Let's leave this place. I can't take anymore death today."

"You should go," Prosperpina agreed. Her voice carried a kind of sympathy and emotion she had not shown since joining Acheron in the underworld. "We will stay behind and give these beings the respect they deserve."

243

The former Fellfallan knights hugged and said their good-byes, and Aori smiled at Acheron awkwardly. "Keep in touch," he mumbled uncomfortably.

Acheron mumbled a similarly strained, yet inaudible, response.

Chapter 2:15

The Oracle of Delphi

Pettifogger dug a hole in the garden's soil, which was soft, malleable, and swirling with purple energy. In the real world, this type of soil would most likely never support life. However, Pettifogger had no seeds to plant anyway. Instead, he planted raw minerals, ore, and scraps of metal he found lying around. Nuts, bolts, nails, or screws grew just as well in Tweentime.

He had just finished planting a long iron rod upright in the ground when he heard a loud crash coming from inside the house. "What happened?" he called out as he ran inside.

Aori had returned to Tweentime in order to build his Residual Resonance and Deity Detector, and he zipped around the workshop in a flurry of clanks and whirrs. The workshop looked as if a natural disaster had struck.

"I don't have time to talk, Pettifogger. I need you to take these items to the lab so that the Coda can try to listen to their lore."

"Lab? We have a lab?"

Aori snapped, "Just find the Coda. I have years of inventing to do in a few minutes of Earth-time."

"I can help," Pettifogger offered.

"Help me by taking those items to the Coda, Pettifogger!"

The gnome backed out of the room and trudged dejectedly to the music room. On his way, he passed by the library, where he heard a strange screeching noise. It came from the computer.

"Oh, hello Master Pettifogger," said an electronic, robotic voice.

Pettifogger stared, wide-eyed and mouth gaping, at the computer. "Did you just talk?"

"Oh, yes. I'm sorry to startle you. This is Dorian, of the Coda. I just decided I might be of some use if I sang myself into this contraption."

"Ah, good!" Pettifogger remarked. "I need to find a Coda, to examine these artifacts."

"If they came from Masada, I can already tell you what happened."

"What?"

The computerized voice explained, "Finis was not there, but they did all commit suicide. You'll see."

"How do you know that?" asked Pettifogger. He examined the computer closely, while at the same time feeling a bit odd talking to an inanimate object.

"This contraption has stored a wealth of information, Master Pettifogger. It is truly amazing. It carries the lore of thousands of Aori's books."

"Incredible."

"Indeed," said Dorian. "However, it still needs some work. Hey, I heard that you are pretty good with your hands. You might be able to fix it."

"At least *someone* around here appreciates my engineering," Pettifogger mumbled.

"What was that?"

"Oh, nothing. Aori just kicked me out of his workshop, even though I could probably make whatever he's inventing in half the time."

246

"Hmm," buzzed the computer's speakers. "Well, I am sure he will be impressed if you can get this device operational. First, we need a source of power. The temporal energy will have to do. Do you think you can get up to the roof?"

Pettifogger took a metal rod, similar to the one he had planted in the garden earlier, and climbed up to the roof. Once there, he could immediately see the crackling, raw energy that Dorian had told him to find. It looked like lightning streaking from clouds of temporal energy.

"I hope this doesn't kill me," he muttered, as he held the rod up as high as he could.

The lightning arced all around the rod, violently flashing and smoking. It snaked down the metal and into a long length of wire that Pettifogger had previously grown in his garden. The energy burst through him, knocking him backwards.

Flashes of light burned in his eyes, and it hurt to open them. He could barely make out hazy shapes of purple light all around him. Rubbing his eyes only made the visions blotchier.

Gradually, one of the purple blobs seemed to take on the shape of a small person. As his eyes found their focus, he recognized the figure. "Daisychain?"

The figure of his sister did not respond. She seemed to be busily tending a garden, similar to the one Pettifogger had made in Tweentime. Soon, other gnomes joined her. Pettifogger recognized some of them, but others seemed much younger than any he had rescued before the destruction of Aia.

As he tried to stand, the images got smaller, as if a camera was zooming out. He saw dense forests, mountains, and large bodies of water spread out before him. The terrain looked very familiar. "Aia? Could it be? Is this the past?"

The wire next to him vibrated. "It worked, Mr, Pettifogger! Come quickly!"

When Pettifogger got back to the library, he found the computer humming with life. It breathed out through a fan on its back, and it even had a face. A painting, just like the one Dorian had always held sacred back on Aia, displayed upon the screen. It showed him in all the handsome, regal glory of his youth.

"You did it, Master Pettifogger," said the computerized voice of Dorian. "You truly are a genius!"

The gnome smiled proudly. "Dorian, when I was up there, I saw images... of my family."

"All in due time, good sir. First, you should go tell Aori about the computer."

"Oh, right," Pettifogger conceded.

In the workshop, Aori was tinkering with the goggles that Pettifogger had stolen from him so long ago. "Are those my goggles?" asked the gnome.

Aori looked up for half of a second. "*Your* goggles? No. I invented them. You stole them." He spoke in short sentences to save time.

"Well, of course, but weren't you going to use them to make me a telescope?"

"Yes, but..."

Hurt feelings filled Pettifogger's voice, along with a tinge of anger. "You said you would build that for me a long time ago, so I could see my family on Aia. I need to see them, Aori."

"Not now, Pettifogger. There are more pressing matters."

Pettifogger sighed with frustration. He grabbed the goggles and two seashells, held them together for a few seconds, and watched as the metal fused to the shells like the bark of two trees. "There," he said. "It's done. Now, can we talk?"

Aori examined the invention in wonder. "Yes. …No. Eventually, you'll have to tell me how you did that, but right now, I need to go find Finis."

"He's not there," said Pettifogger, but Aori had already vanished.

Back in the library, Dorian attempted to console him, as best a computer from the emotionless line of Dorian could do. "I am sure if you had told him about me, he would have been impressed with your ingenuity. Perhaps his own pride blinds him to your accomplishments. I think he is jealous of you, Mr. Pettifogger."

"*He* is jealous of *me*?" Pettifogger shook his head. "I thought you'd see it the other way around. He *is* a god, after all."

The robotic sound of Dorian clearing his throat came out as more of an electronic growl. "He is but the mortal portion of the Temporal Trinity… he is more of a demigod, if anything."

Pettifogger looked around cautiously, as if Aori could hear the heretical words. "He's pretty powerful."

"Ah, but what powers does he have than you have not managed to steal from him?"

Guilt widened the gnome's eyes. "How did you know about that?"

"I am a master of lore, Mr. Pettifogger. Your story is now legend." The screen saver engaged on the computer, and images of the planet Aia filled the screen. Clear mountain streams cascaded in beautiful waterfalls, emptying into rivers and lakes. Wondrous forests blanketed the land in verdant magnificence. The planet seemed so youthful and immortal in those images.

"I had forgotten how beautiful it was."

"*Is*," the robotic voice of Dorian corrected.

"So this is the present? I was right all along? And the images I saw, of my family?"

"Also happening as we speak."

Excitement intertwined with emotion and burst out in tears down Pettifogger's cheeks. "How do I get there?"

The computer remained silent for several minutes. A small hourglass on its screen turned over and over. "I will work on that. The future is buried in many files and folders in here, and I do not have the power to bend Tweentime, as you do."

"Do you think I have the power to get there myself?" asked Pettifogger excitedly.

"Perhaps you will, one day." A box appeared on the screen, with a blue bar gradually increasing across it. The words "One Moment, Please" flashed repeatedly in the box.

After several minutes of "thinking," Dorian continued, "There is one among us who might be able to help. Check among the artifacts you retrieved from Nero. You should find a glass jar filled with water."

Pettifogger ran to the museum, where they displayed the clay pots, sculptures, and other Dorian artifacts. Just as the Codan computer had indicated, he found a glass jar with water inside. The water looked cloudy and no longer transparent.

"I found it," said Pettifogger, "but it's not very clean anymore."

"That's because the future is murky," Dorian remarked. "Every event may change the course of every other event. I have learned that the hard way."

"What do you mean?"

The monitor's lights dimmed, as if Dorian had closed his eyes. "It is not important now. My life just turned out… contrary to how I had planned. Aori took control and changed everything. We must not allow that to happen on Aia again."

Anxiety filled the room. It felt as if events were aligning against Pettifogger's only friend. "We aren't going to hurt Aori, are we?"

"Hurt him? Heavens no. He is, as you pointed out, the Son of Time. How could we hurt him?"

"Well, that's good." Pettifogger still felt a bit anxious.

"We are not staging a revolution against your master, if that is what you were thinking," Dorian cackled. The robotic laugh sounded eerie and electronic. "We have to help him, actually."

"Help him?" Pettifogger felt the skin loosen up a bit on the back of his neck.

"If you would be so kind as to place this wire into the jar, perhaps the Oracle can explain."

"Oracle?"

"The Oracle of Delphi. Once upon a time, heroes and political leaders sought out the Oracle in order to see the future of legendary battles. Of course, Greece has ever been the target of invasions, conquests, and transfers of power. For that reason, we saw fit to remove the Oracle from her pool in Delphi."

"So, you stole the water."

Dorian paused. "In a manner of speaking, I suppose. I prefer to think we were safeguarding her from those who might use the information for ill-gotten gains. You see, the Coda have always been the custodians of the water. To be exact, the Oracle was actually a Coda who interpreted the lore stored inside the water. She stored her essence within."

"You mean, you trapped me there," shouted a woman's voice from the computer's speakers.

"Oracle, your vision of the past is even more obscured than that of the future. Let us not speak of what happened years ago. Our industrious and illustrious friend here needs to see what will happen years from now."

The water inside the jar vibrated, causing ripples in its surface. "I see. Please touch the jar, and I will try to see into your future."

Pettifogger gripped the sides of the glass jar and gazed into the rippling, cloudy water. Similar to the glass

251

harmonica, or glass singer, that Lithe got from Tweentime so long ago, the glass jar resonated a high-pitched hum.

Within the ripples, Pettifogger recognized the figure of Aori, although he looked much older, similar to how he had looked in Aia's last days. Behind him stood a vast army of soldiers, knights, and primitive warriors from various periods of time.

The tinny voice of the Oracle sang through the computer's speakers:

> The winds of change blow cold
> And leave a bitter chill.
> He who takes control of time
> Shall make the seas stand still.
> With the corruption of the power,
> The minute will become the hour.

The ripples and the humming stopped, leaving silence to fill the room.

At length, Pettifogger blurted, "What does that have to do with my family? Or Aia?"

"I see nothing of Aia," said the Oracle. "Didn't it crumble to pieces?"

"Again," Dorian interrupted, "Your sight of the here and now proves inferior to your foresight, Oracle. Aia is growing as we speak, Mr. Pettifogger. However, I believe what the Oracle *could* tell you is of graver importance to us now."

Pettifogger sighed. "Fine. Explain it to me, then. The minute will become the hour?"

The hourglass appeared on Dorian's screen again, along with the "One Moment, Please" message. After several moments, he displayed the Oracle's lyrics on his screen. The font was a simple, boring one.

"As you may know, the word *aori* means 'wind of change' to the Ori and some other people of Aia. Therefore, I believe we can interpret this as a message about Aori, and the

252

detrimental effects he may have on this planet, as well as your sacred Aia."

Pettifogger puzzled over the last line. "The minute will become the hour. Could that refer to the theory that Aori will eventually take over as the Time god?"

The computer paused, and the fan slowed to a soft whirr. "I see; then you already know the future, Mr. Pettifogger. In addition to being an exceptional gardener and engineer, it seems you are also an accomplished seer!"

Pettifogger chose not to mention that Munder had actually come up with the idea.

"You have seen already how Aori amassed the Army of the Anachronist. His recruiting will go on throughout the centuries, and every evil attributed to Tempo will be done by Aori's hand."

"I don't believe he would purposely destroy Aia again," said Pettifogger. "If I hadn't betrayed him..."

"Perhaps you do not truly know Aori," Dorian suggested.

"He should know me by now, as many years as we've worked together." Aori came up the stairs and patted the gnome on the back. "Your invention was a complete success, Mr. Pettifogger. Though Finis wasn't there, I did see Asalie with the Residual Resonance and Deity Detector-- that's what I decided to call it-- I hope you don't mind."

He took the device off of his head and set it down on a bookshelf, still admiring it. "I daresay, I couldn't have done it without you, Pyrite." Turning toward the computer, he remarked, "Now, what do we have here? You managed to get this infernal machine to work?"

Pettifogger smiled proudly. "Yes, but I think it needs some work. It may have some flawed logic circuits. However, it did predict that Finis would not be there... and the people there... they all committed suicide?"

"Yes. It appears we've been tricked. The event was staged to look like his work." Aori began to walk out of the

253

room. "It's becoming more and more difficult to trust anyone."

Pettifogger and the computer exchanged looks.

Chapter 2:16

One Man's Martyr is Another Man's Suicide Bomber

If two people, from opposing religions, are both willing to die for their beliefs, can they both be martyrs? It depends on one's perspective, I suppose. If they wage a holy war against one another, and one detonates a bomb that kills them both, then would they still both be martyrs?

The Islamic religion itself prohibits suicide, but many Muslims believe that dying in a holy war, or *jihad*, is a hero's death—martyrdom rather than suicide. The suicide bombers of the 20th and 21st Centuries, while still technically dying in the name of Allah, were not considered by most to be true martyrs, in the strictest sense.

Let us take an even more radical example: A member of the Satanic Church, who routinely takes human sacrifices to offer before Satan, decides he can make a bigger impact on non-believers by traveling to the backwoods of the Bible Belt. He gives sermons each day at truck stops and Elk Lodges, and eventually, he is strung up and hanged. He achieves his purpose by calling attention to himself and dying for his religious beliefs. By textbook definitions, he is just as much a

255

martyr as St. Polycarp, who refused to renounce his faith and chose death at the hands of Romans in 155 A.D.

Roughly around that same time, the Romans imprisoned Christian women who refused to give up their faith, tied them to the horns of bulls, and let the bulls run around the arena. The cruel and unusual punishment came from the Greek myth of Dirce, who was killed in a similar fashion. As one can imagine, these Christian women were considered martyrs.

When Munder discovered his four cloven hooves, fur-covered skin, and swishing tail, his first thought was, "Moo." However, soon he began contemplating the ethical ramifications of actions he had taken in his past lives. I'm just joking. He mainly thought, "Moo?"

The whimpering of a young woman from behind his head puzzled him. "What are you doing back there? People don't ride bulls... well, except for in the rodeo, but then they don't ride them for more than eight seconds or so. You lookin' to get gored? Got a death wish, lady?"

"I do not wish to die," said the woman, "But I will not concede to their... wait. Did you just speak?"

Munder snorted and beat a hoof against the ground. "It's crazy, I know, but maybe we should go back to why you're dragging alongside me. If you live through this, maybe I'll explain."

The woman paused. "The Romans tied me to your horns because I would not deny my Lord and Savior."

"Oh. So you're one of those crazy religious types?" Munder blurted with a snort. "Sorry. Do you think your Savior is going to save you soon? I'm just wondering, because I have places to be..." Under his breath, he finished, "...and gods to kill...."

"Though I do not wish for death, I am willing to die for my Lord," said the woman.

"What's your name, lady?" Munder mooed.

"Sulplicia," she answered. She tugged at the ropes binding her wrists to his horns.

He tried to turn his head to look at her, but that just added to her discomfort. "I'm Munder… or I was, before I became a bull."

"I wish we could have met under different circumstances. You seem like a rather pleasant person," she commented.

"Oh, I'm actually a deicidal murderer," Munder admitted.

"Oh? I'm sorry to hear that."

"Well, it's a living. Speaking of living, let's get out of here while you still are."

"There is no escape. I have come to terms with my death."

"I wish you'd cut it out with that negative attitude, Sulplicia. When life ties you to a bull's horns, you gotta… wait, are you naked?"

Sulplicia lowered her head in shame.

"Er… sorry," Munder muttered. "Do your best to walk along beside me, and I'll do my best to take it nice and slow."

"My thanks, Munder. However, I think the crowd, and the Romans, expect me to die. They'll make you run, even if they have to beat you."

"Beat me? Let's see it." The bull puffed up his chest, as much as a bull can do so.

Sure enough, the shouts of the crowd suggested that they were unhappy with the event. They threw stones and other objects at Munder and Sulplicia, and the more he tried to dodge, the more he dragged her violently across the arena floor.

One of the Roman soldiers came out with a stick and hit Munder with it. Trying to keep his head as still as possible, Munder kicked at the soldier with his hind legs. He became more and more frustrated with his inability to fight back and keep Suplicia safe at the same time.

257

With a strained snort, he shouted, "I can't keep from hurting you!"

"Munder, please. There is nothing you can do. They will kill me no matter how hard you try. I can only hope that my Lord will bring me home, to Heaven."

Munder drove his head into the dirt, trying to tear the ropes loose. "Your Lord could have given us something sharp to cut these ropes..."

"Munder, please. My faith got me here; I humbly accept what I am given, and I do not question Him. Please refrain from mocking my faith."

"Hrm," Munder grumbled. "Sorry."

The Romans shouted and ran around the arena like madmen. They released another bull into the arena, and it immediately charged in Munder's direction. It, too, had a woman tied to its horns, and she was already bloody and beaten from the torture.

"Listen, Sulplicia. When I toss my head around, I want you to try your best to get on my back. It'll still hurt, but you'll live."

"Munder..."

"You're going to live today, okay? I don't need more innocent deaths on my conscience."

He whipped his head around, which sent her flailing outward in a wide arc. Thinking the bull had finally come to his senses (or lack thereof), the crowd cheered wildly. Above the din of their applause, and much to his dismay, Munder heard the woman's arm snap. Suplicia screamed in pain, but still managed to land on the back of the bull.

"Sorry," Munder snorted. "It'll hurt, but you might be able to get your arms free now."

Before she could try, the other bull charged and rammed right into Munder's side. Horns tore into his skin, and he felt an explosion of pain. He sidestepped to the right, trying to get out of the bull's path, but he knew any sudden movements would mean certain death for Suplicia.

He turned his head toward the other bull, snorted, and tried to look as intimidating as possible. In desperation, he forced his weight to his hind legs and raised his front hooves into the air. If he could keep his body between Suplicia and the bull, he might just keep her alive.

Suddenly, his wooden arm changed from a hoof to a large, wooden barrel. When the bull hit it, Munder was able to deflect the force of the attack harmlessly to the side. Quickly, he took the offensive and rammed the other bull with his horns.

In response to the attack, the other bull seemed to grow more immense. It rose up on its hind legs, and its arms gradually morphed into a more human physique. In place of his front hooves, he grew hands.

"A minotaur, eh?" Munder grumbled. "Looks like I'm gonna get to kill two birds with one stone. You wouldn't happen to be an Aian demigod in control of bulls, would you?"

The minotaur snorted and tore at the ground with his hooves.

"Unfortunately for you, I am more than a bull as well!" Proudly, Munder rose up on his hind legs and tried to turn into a human also. Nothing happened.

The minotaur charged, and Munder barely avoided being trampled. "Ok, Suplicia, I was wrong," said Munder. "It turns out, we're both going to die."

At that point, he noticed that his back felt lighter. She had fallen off his back when he dodged. Turning around, he saw her lying crumpled on the arena floor, clutching her broken arm beneath her.

He stomped over to her and nuzzled her with his head. She didn't move. Behind him, he could hear the hoof beats of the minotaur. Determined to protect Suplicia, even if he had to die trying, Munder lowered his horns and charged toward his enemy.

259

The minotaur lowered his head as well, and when the two bulls clashed, the larger tossed Munder into the air. Unfortunately for the minotaur, this act proved his undoing.

Though dazed from the blow to his skull, Munder managed to regain enough of his meager wits to grow his wooden arm into the Lance of Longinus. As he came down, he pierced the minotaur's skull.

He cut the ropes that had bound the other woman to the minotaur's horns, but she had died long before the fight had ended. As he approached Suplicia, he could tell that she, too, had stopped breathing. "...All in vain," he grumbled.

It took several Roman soldiers to subdue the bull, and by the time Munder left that body, he had taken with him the souls of nearly thirty men.

"My records indicate that several Christians have been choosing death instead of apostasy," the computerized voice of Dorian explained. Images of people being burned, crucified, or killed by animals flashed upon the screen in rapid succession.

"These people *chose* these horrible fates?" Pettifogger asked incredulously.

"Yes. A woman named Apollonia threw herself into a fire when the Romans tried to force her to perform some pagan ritual. Some of these martyrs, as they are called, have even been crucified underwater."

Pettifogger shuddered and turned his eyes from the screen. "I believe I have seen enough. Could any of these martyrs be Finis reborn? They didn't actually take their own lives, did they?"

"That depends on your definition of suicide," said the computer.

"I suppose so," Pettifogger conceded. "Can you find their birthdates? If we assume that Finis was reborn after Nero died...."

"Here is one that was born in 69, which would be less than a year after Nero's death."

"Perfect. Who is it?"

"Saint Polycarp, the Bishop of Smyrna."

Shocked, Pettifogger asked, "He is a holy man?"

"Who is a holy man?" asked Aori as he entered the library. Daphni followed him, and several purple, translucent moths trailed behind her.

"I was doing some research on the computer," Pettifogger explained. He gestured toward it, but the screen had turned dark and lifeless.

Aori studied the contraption. "Has it grown since I last saw it?"

The cords and cables of the computer had stretched out along the floor and walls, creeping along the surfaces like vines or roots. A large network of transistors, chips, and circuits covered the entire surface of the computer desk, which gave it the appearance of a small cityscape.

"I think so," Pettifogger answered. He told Aori about the saint who he believed to be the latest incarnation of the Living Embodiment of Death. The idea that a saint could be responsible for the atrocities normally associated with Finis seemed even more ridiculous than when Dorian had mentioned it.

"I see," said Aori. "But, didn't you say he would die at the hands of the Romans?"

"According to the computer, yes."

"I tell you, it sure seems like the Romans have been responsible for most of this world's evil. Maybe we should all just sit tight and wait for the Empire to fall."

"Aori, we cannot just sit back and let these things happen," Daphni pointed out.

"You're right," Aori agreed. "I know you're right. To Smyrna, then?"

"I believe that's in Anatolia," said Pettifogger. "I'll get my things."

261

Aori pulled him to the side and whispered, "I'd prefer if you stayed behind."

The gnome stared at him in confusion. "But, I'm the one who found out about this St. Polycarp in the first place, and...."

"I know, Pyrite. It's not what you think."

Pettifogger glared in the direction of Daphni. "Then why?"

"I need someone here who I can trust, Pyrite. You know as well as I that bad things tend to happen while we're away. I can't just leave my house under the care of a bunch of ghosts who used to worship Tempo. You're the only one I can trust."

Pettifogger felt a knot in his gut. "Fine. I'll stay."

In the later part of the ninth century, Munder led a crusade under the name Cuerno Del Toro, which meant "horn of the bull," because his companions believed that he had been a bull in a previous life. He became known as the Bull of the Crusade, which was a bit of clever wordplay. The Bull of the Crusade was also a papal bull, or a mandate from the Pope declaring a Holy War against all pagans, heretics, and Muslims in the Holy Land.

Munder predominately fought in and around the area of what was once the Byzantine Empire and is now Turkey. Basically, while the crusaders under his command focused on genocide of all non-Christians, Munder slew their pagan gods.

He even felt good about it. Not only had he been given a mandate from His Holiness to exact justice on pretty much anyone in his way, but he was also getting rid of the extra gods along the way, as Ode had suggested. Without his conscience harping at him, he was free to be as merciless and remorseless as he pleased.

Propaganda put forth by the Roman Catholic Church at this time cast the pagans, Muslims, Gnostics, and those of any faith other than Christianity as the evil enemies. There-fore, any who opposed them must have been the "good guys," right? If you were the one being killed simply for your beliefs, would you see it that way?

Of course, those who faced him in battle and died were not considered martyrs by the Roman Catholic Church. Technically, however, they did die in a Holy War while defending their faith. In that respect, Munder created hundreds of martyrs.

Aside from their religions, were these men who died for their beliefs any different from the Christian martyrs from a few centuries before? The biggest difference here was that the Romans had gone from persecuting and killing Christians in the names of their gods to persecuting and killing non-Christians in the name of God.

Chapter 2:17

The Infinis

"This man cannot be the Infinis." Aori had begun to refer to Finis's never-ending cycle of birth and suicide in such a manner, so as to separate it from the god, who they had known and considered a friend. As with most words coined by Aori, the name stuck.

Daphni looked down from a high balcony on the congregation of Polycarp's church. The bishop sat near the altar and smiled with a warm, inviting countenance. "He does not seem to be hurting anyone."

"Nor does he seem capable of evil." Making sure no one was looking, Aori placed the Residual Resonance and Deity Detector on his head. As soon as he tried to see through the goggles, a beautiful, spiraling light, brighter than the sun, blinded him. He had to remove the device, at which point his vision slowly returned.

"There is a deity present, of that I am certain. However, I'm probably picking up on the Christian God, since this is His church." Aori rubbed his eyes.

Daphni whispered, "We shall have to wait until the service is over, and ask around for more information. Perhaps there is more here than meets the eye."

Aori held the tonal shell of the Residual Resonance and Deity Detector up to his ear. "Elegos believes that Death is here, as well. He says to listen closely."

They listened. The songs of the choir filled the whole church, drowning out any other sounds. The music was beautiful and melancholy all at once.

"They're singing in Codan," Aori remarked. "The audience must be so used to hearing the songs that they just tune out the words anyway. It's like in the old churches on Aia that sang in Elvish, even though no one understood-- it just sounded pretty."

"Do these people not wish to comprehend the songs of their deity?"

Aori shrugged. "Perhaps they worship the mystery surrounding Him, instead."

"Can you translate?"

"Of course," Aori smiled. "Codan was one of the first languages I learned, once I had the time." As he listened closely to the hymn, a whirling deluge welled up inside him. He felt that his heart had floated up to his throat, and the flood poured forth down his face.

Daphni studied him with puzzled concern. "What is it, Aori?"

Though he attempted to pull himself together, his voice cracked, "They sing of the persecution of Coda throughout their time on Earth. Apparently, having a tail, ears, and a Codan birthmark on their foreheads made them stand out as... heathens."

"These singers do not have those traits. Why would they sing in Codan...."

"They are Coda," Aori interrupted. "They have been... disfigured."

"What do you mean?"

Before he could answer, the song ended and the congregation spilled out of the church. The choir followed Polycarp through a door in the back, and Aori followed them. The

266

bishop led them into a small room, locked the door, and walked on down a corridor to his own room.

Once he had passed out of sight, Aori and Daphni ran to the door. "Odd, isn't it, that a choir would need to be locked inside their quarters?"

"They must be prisoners here, against their will," Daphni deduced.

"Alas," whispered Aori through clenched teeth. "If I had allowed Pettifogger to come along, he could have opened this lock easily."

Daphni paced back and forth in the hallway in front of the door. She grew restless watching Aori just study the lock. Sympathetic to her impatience, Aori whispered, "I know how you hate to be idle. I share that feeling."

"Time is precious, Aori."

"I know. Believe me, I know. However, your precious time is in my hands, now."

Daphni smiled. "Perhaps I could be of better use if I looked around a bit. I could ask some questions... gather some clues."

Aori nodded. "Good idea."

"I will leave a messenger with you, should you need to contact me." She spread her hands, releasing a moth. As it landed on Aori's shoulder, Daphni flitted down the corridor.

Once again alone with the lock, Aori watched as ghosts of the object's past and future superimposed upon the present. Though he tried to force the lock into its older, more brittle state, it just remained fixed.

With a long, exasperated sigh, he broke down and returned to Tweentime with a flash.

"Pyrite!" he shouted. "I need your help!" As he ran up the stairs to the library, he heard a strange, electronic screeching noise. "Pyrite? Are you in here?"

The screeching stopped when he approached the computer. Though he had only been gone around thirty minutes Earth-time, the contraption had grown considerably.

Its cable-roots had now penetrated and grown into the floorboards, and wire-vines crept between the ceiling's support beams. The monitor stretched across most of the wall and almost reached the ceiling itself. Likewise, the walls and floor had produced new growth in order to mesh with the computer.

"Ingenious," Aori whispered. "Nature and technology have never coexisted so… miraculously." Remembering his task at hand, Aori shook off the stupefied awe and called out to Pettifogger once again.

"He is in the workshop," said the computer.

Raising an eyebrow in bewilderment, Aori stared at the contraption. "When I have more time, I'd like for you to explain how you just spoke." With that, he ran to the workshop.

Pettifogger busily tinkered away at some invention and barely noticed his master's entrance.

"What are you working on, Pyrite?"

Startled, the gnome stood up and attempted to hide his work. "Nothing important. Did you need another device of some sort?"

Aori smiled. "No, Pyrite. I need you. Your help, that is. I will just have to trust that the house is safe in the ghostly hands of the Dorian Coda."

"I believe I have developed a solution to that problem. While it won't make them any more trustworthy, it might keep out the unwanted intruders."

"Really?" Aori shook his head slowly in awe. "Your ingenuity never ceases to amaze me, Pyrite. When did you become such a grand inventor?"

Pettifogger returned his smile. "Around the time you began calling me by my given name."

"'Misters' and 'masters' just seem too impersonal, now."

"I agree," Pettifogger nodded. "Now, about this security system…"

"Tell me all about it later, Pyrite. There's a matter of life and death that requires your special talents."

Meanwhile, one of Daphni's moths flitted around the heads of some Roman soldiers, who approached the church. Though the moth could not understand their words, it seemed obvious that they had not come to the church to pray. Rather, it seemed that they marched to battle.

Inside the church, Daphni overheard the bishop speaking to one of his clergymen.

"They are coming to take you away, Bishop."

"Let them take me, then," Polycarp stated resolutely. "With the Lord as my guide, I can endure all."

"They will kill you," said the clergyman.

"They will try, Theris, and if my Lord beckons me, I will go."

"But, sir, if you give yourself up for execution, is that not suicide?"

"The power of the Holy Spirit will be with me, Theris. I will join by brothers in martyrdom and find eternal glory with my Lord."

A moth fluttered in through the open window just as the Roman soldiers banged on the door to Polycarp's room.

The instant Pettifogger touched the locking mechanism on the door, the metal began to pulse with stolen life. Clicking and scraping sounds came from within the mechanism, as if the bolts and such were trudging grudgingly along to work. After an audible moan on the part of the lock, the door creaked open.

The members of the choir cringed as light burst in through the doorway. Though they had a small fire built on a metal grate in the floor, the room looked dismal and dreary. Most of the Coda were female, but there was one young boy among them. In this light, Aori could see the scars left from their disfigurement.

269

"Do not be afraid," Aori reassured them in Codan. "We have come to rescue you."

The Coda looked at each other, and at Aori, with uncertainty.

As Aori tried to persuade them as efficiently as possible, Daphni suddenly appeared in the center of the room. She had traveled through the flames of a torch in the hallway.

"The Romans are here," she shouted.

"If they find us here, they will naturally assume that we are members of the church," Aori added.

Pettifogger closed the door and, by touching the lock again, sealed it shut. "That should buy us some time."

"They have taken the bishop," Daphni explained. "If he is the Infinis, and the Romans kill him, what will happen?"

"I don't know," said Aori. "We are currently working under the assumption that it would be bad, since that was Tempo's plan for Nero."

"Then we must get to the stadium as quickly as possible. One of my moths has followed them there."

Aori turned to Pettifogger. "Pyrite, can you steal my power again, in order to get these Coda to Tweentime safely?"

Pettifogger looked hurt at first, but answered, "Of course." In a flash, they were gone.

As Romans beat upon the door, Daphni took Aori by the hand. "This may hurt a bit," she warned. With his body pressed firmly against hers, she stepped into the fire again.

In the seconds between their departure and arrival, Pettifogger attempted to make the Codan choir feel welcome. Though he spoke neither Latin nor Codan, he smiled and pointed a lot. Once they got to the music room, however, they seemed much calmer.

The Dorian ghosts literally came out of the woodwork to meet them. "You must be a Lydian," said Viola to one of

270

them. "I can tell by your red hair. In life, I was a Lydian too, but I got... pressured into joining these old fossils."

Two of the females were, indeed, descended from the Aian line of Lydia, one of the first Coda. As Viola had already demonstrated in Rome, the Lydian Coda had an affinity for fire. Their music was like kindling, and they could also hear the song of the flames.

"And you," said Pedant to another of the females, "Are you Aeolian?"

A wisp of a young woman nodded sheepishly.

The ghost of Pedant took up his favorite position behind his podium. "The Aeolians, as you may know, came from Aeolia, one of the first Coda that Tempo created from the stock of Elves. Their command of the wind and air is only matched by their ability to communicate with that element...."

Pettifogger interrupted, "They have just experienced some horrible trauma, Pedant. Please save your lectures for after we have made them more comfortable."

"Of course," said Viola. "How silly of me. I was so excited to see more Lydians that I completely overlooked the tragedy written on all of your faces. Come. Sit by the fire and tell us your story."

The fire in the hearth, though made of purple, temporal energy, still felt warm and inviting. The young boy sat down first, but immediately yelped in pain. He crumpled up into a ball on the floor.

"Oh heavens!" Viola remarked with shocked dismay. "Your tails!"

The choir gathered around the little boy and tried to ease his pain. They sang, ever so sweetly, a beautiful hymn about better times.

"Their tails have been... amputated?" Pettifogger asked.

"And their ears...." Tears caught in Viola's voice.

"They were surgically altered, though the surgeon must have been blind," said a Dorian named Heliodorus. He had

271

come to Tweentime in the form of a book on medicine. The ghost of the former physician and surgeon sat down next to the boy and examined his injuries.

"Who would do such a thing?" Pettifogger held his hand over his mouth, which had dropped open in horror.

"The church is responsible, I am afraid," said the low, monotone voice of Ecclesiast, the Dorian who had been a church pew before coming to Tweentime. Before that, he had been a priest. "Those who are holier than thou tend to be less accepting of those who are different."

"We always managed to hide our ears and tails from prying eyes," said Viola. "However, I have heard tales of Coda being persecuted or even killed for their appearance."

The choir began to sing, in unison, the song they had sung before the congregation in Smyrna. The lyrics recounted the years of violence against their people, as well as the horrors they had experienced firsthand. Behind them, the fireplace roared in pathetic fallacy along with the tragic tune.

They had been sworn to secrecy by the bishop and his priests, and they believed that if they spoke even a word about their mutilation, their souls would burn in Hell for eternity. However, since their vows of silence hadn't included their songs in church, they had found a loophole. They had interwoven their story into their church hymns, hoping that someone, or perhaps God, would eventually come along and hear their pleas for help.

Though Polycarp himself had never physically harmed them, his dedication to saving them from the heretical nature of their heredity had made him fanatical and oppressive. They were allowed no musical instruments, and if they were caught performing magic of any sort, they were taken away to be tortured.

As if cutting off their tails and carving off the points of their ears was not enough, the Coda who had proven more unrelenting in their indoctrination of Christianity were either killed or worse. To any Coda, the removal of one's vocal chords was always a fate worse than death.

In order to hide the Coda symbol on their foreheads, the priests and clergymen had undertaken various methods of scraping, burning, tattooing, or wholly removing the skin itself. In order to protect the young boy from such a fate, Ignatia and Luciana, the Lydian Coda, had created an illusion around his birthmark, so that it appeared as normal skin.

They could not prevent the mutilation of his tail and ears, however, and for him, the cuts had not yet healed. The boy, who they called Litoro, was an Ionian Coda, from the line of musicians most closely aligned with the oceans and seas. He had grown up in a family of sailors who had always regaled audiences with tales of adventures at sea. When his father did not come back from an ocean voyage, however, his mother and sisters were taken in by the church.

Their hymn pointed mainly at the priest named Theris, who had been chiefly responsible for their mutilation and humiliation. He had taken to Litoro especially in the last few years, and only the boy knew the true depths of his depravity.

By the time their hymn had ended, even the emotionless Dorian Coda had been moved to tears. Viola wept openly, while Pettifogger had quickly left the room.

A large crowd had already assembled in the stadium, where the Romans had built a massive pyre of wood and oil. They intended to burn the bishop alive. When the soldiers arrived with the bishop and several members of the church, the crowd offered mixed cheers and shouts of protest.

They tied Polycarp to a wooden post in the center of the pyre, as he convinced them that they needn't nail him to it. He explained that God would allow him to endure the fire without moving. When the officials in charge asked that he deny Christ and repent, he told them, "The fire I face will burn for but an hour, while the eternal fires of your damnation shall never be extinguished!"

When they lit the pyre and flames surrounded his body, he did not cry out in pain. Rather than scorching in the intense heat, his skin just turned a golden brown, like baked bread. A pleasing fragrance filled the air.

A sudden explosion of flames burst forth from the pyre, and when the flames subsided, there appeared a winged woman amidst the fire. She held a man in her arms.

"It is an angel of the Lord!" shouted someone from the crowd.

"The Lord has come to save Polycarp from the flames!" shouted another.

"Perhaps the angel could have made a less dramatic entrance," Aori whispered to Daphni.

"Sorry," she replied. "We arrived just in time, though. Look; he's not even burning."

Above the noise of the crowd, they could hear singing in the distance.

"Do you hear that?" said someone in the audience. "The angels are singing hosannas of the Lord! Hallelujah!"

The fire seemed to bend and change around Polycarp's body, so that it formed a great arch over his head. It truly seemed that a miracle had been performed to save him from his fate.

However, at that point, a very large executioner came forth and stabbed him in the heart with a long, wooden spear.

"Munder!" shouted Aori.

The executioner looked up at the man in the arms of the angel.

So much blood issued from the wound that the flames died, and Daphni set Aori down next to the bishop. Aori tried to stop the bleeding, but it just kept pouring out of him. "Munder, I believe you may have just doomed us all."

"What'd *I* do? I'm just doing my job."

"Munder, if I could have stopped the Infinis just by killing him, don't you think I would have tried that already?"

"But... Ode said...."

"You seriously need to stop listening to rocks, Munder." Aori let out an exasperated sigh. "You must have rocks in your head! You just killed a saint. I'd like to see what your next life's going to be."

In fact, his next life was that of a bull, and you all have already witnessed it.

"Stop!" shouted a voice from the crowd. "Wait!" A small man weaved through the mass of spectators and leapt down to the stadium's floor.

"Pyrite?!" Aori shouted. "What are you doing here?"

"We've made a mistake, Aori. We were wrong about Polycarp."

"Yes, I know," Aori admitted. "I assumed a saint could not have been responsible for atrocious acts of evil, but you've seen what he did to the Coda. He must have been the Infinis, after all."

"That's just it," said Pettifogger. "He persecuted them, yes, but the true evil here lies in that man!" He pointed up to the priest, Theris, who had also been scheduled for execution that day.

In fact, the officials had already questioned him and managed to get him to deny his faith completely. Of course, he wouldn't accept their gods either, seeing as how, deep down inside, he was a god himself.

Pettifogger shouted, "This priest physically, mentally, and utterly abused innocent women and children, solely because they had been judged as heretics by the church!"

Apparently, the crowd had grown accustomed to such gruesome acts of prejudice, because they all looked at one another and shrugged, as if to say, "So?"

The Romans took the priest and nailed him to the pyre. As they removed Polycarp's body from the stadium floor, a melancholy funeral song played in the background.

"You can stop singing now, Ignatia," Pettifogger said to the choir.

"They aren't singing anymore," said Aori. "By the way, ladies, nice work with the fire earlier. And the way the air just seemed so calm, and peaceful…."

The Aeolian Coda, whose name was Zephyr, lowered her head reverently, but smiled.

Aori glared at Theris and then looked back at his mutilated victims. With a long sigh, he muttered, "We can't let them kill him."

"So this priest is the Infinis?" asked Daphni.

"It does make more sense. By the way, Munder, try not to kill this one."

Munder grumbled.

"Actually, I believe the Coda would be completely justified in setting fire to him right now," Pettifogger stated plainly.

"I know," said Aori. "But I can't imagine what would happen when a god of Death dies. It could be catastrophic."

"Perhaps we would all live forever," suggested Daphni. The idea sounded pretty nice to her.

Aori sighed. "Unfortunately, I believe that Tempo is responsible for the finite nature of mortality, while Death just provides the means of ending it."

"Y'know," Munder grumbled, "If you all just sit around and philosophically debate this long enough, the guy will be dead and my job will be done anyway. By all means, whip out the big words and hot air!"

Everyone looked at the giant. After a bit of a pause, Aori muttered, "Don't you just hate it when he has a point?"

"While you're at it," Munder grumbled, "Could you make that music stop?"

The funeral song had continued long after Polycarp's body had been removed. In fact, it seemed to have gotten louder. As the blood dripped from the nails in his arms and legs, Theris looked down at the choir below him. Though his voice gurgled with the blood in his lungs, he sang directly to

Litoro, "Do you miss your mother? Do you miss your father? Do you miss me?"

The song he sang would one day be written, in a similar form, by the 20th Century musician Gordon Gano. In that form, it was called "Johnny," and asked, most poignantly, of its title character, "Could you tell me what it's like to die?"

The boy ran up and began beating on the priest mercilessly, while screaming at the top of his lungs. As his fists beat against bone and wood, the rhythm echoed through the stadium.

By the time they finally managed to pull him away, the tidal wave hit. By "tidal wave," I do not refer to a metaphoric wave of tearful emotion. A storm in the Aegean Sea caused the waters of the gulf to rise, which flooded most of Smyrna.

While most of the stadium's spectators managed to escape without grievous injury, the priest Theris died. Oddly enough, the wood of the pyre had all floated to the surface, indicating that he had not been held underwater by the nails.

Though some say he drowned due to the natural disaster, others believe he simply chose not to swim. And, though the holy accounts of martyrdom do not list him among their number due to his apostasy in the face of death, one could argue that he died for his god.

In martyrdom, there is a fine line between salvation and damnation.

Chapter 2:18

The Silk Road

After the flood waters had receded, the members of the choir gathered for the last time in Smyrna. Though they had been offered the refuge and all the hospitality of Tweentime, they had refused the offer.

"There are many like us, who have been subjugated, tortured, or imprisoned for being Coda," Ignatia had told Aori. "We are determined to help them, as you have helped us."

It had taken several weeks of the aforementioned refuge before the choir singers had felt comfortable and safe enough to break their vows of silence. Zephyr, the Aeolian, still chose to speak mostly in song, just in case.

Now, at the port in Smyrna, a gentle breeze blew fresh, cool air across them. As they said their good-byes, Litoro tried to fight back tears, so as to avoid a sudden rainstorm.

"Keep moving," suggested Aori. "Don't stay in one place for too long."

"Avoid religious types," Pettifogger told them.

Daphni added, "If, in your wanderings, you ever come across a Fellfalla calling herself Gypsy, or Lymantria Dispar…"

"We will most assuredly send word," Luciana promised.

"I will send one of my moths with you, as a messenger. They have grown quite attached to your flames, as it is." Daphni smiled.

"And we will listen to the songs of the wind and sea for news that will help your quest," offered Zephyr, in her sing-songy voice. She and Litoro climbed into a boat and untied it from the docks.

"Thank you again, for building the ship, Aori," said Litoro.

"Oh, it's just something I threw together in a few minutes," Aori said with a humble smile.

The Lydian women, after saying their good-byes, rode out of town in a wagon, while Zephyr's winds carried Litoro and her out to sea. They would attract less attention in pairs, Aori had believed, and the breeze of the open sea had called to the Ionian and Aeolian Coda. In their voyages, they would come across many of their kind who had suffered similarly. Many had managed to disguise the most conspicuous parts of their bodies, but some had been disfigured in the world's attempt to assimilate them.

Eventually, the remaining Coda would form tribes of wandering musicians and travel in caravans throughout the lands that would one day be Italy, Romania, Turkey, and some tribes even stretched throughout northern Europe. They intermingled with other outcasts in those areas, and their tribes were called by many names. However, they soon came to be called Gypsies by the villagers who understood only a few words of their quest to find the Fellfallan wanderer.

However, their tale will wait for another time.

Following leads provided by the Coda, Daphni and Aori flew to the shores of the Mediterranean Sea, along the southernmost coast of Italy. There, as the sun set in the sea to the west, they found the flowers Asalie had mentioned in

280

her rambling in the ruins of Masada. The flowers seemed to bloom as they approached, and Daphni found herself drawn to their sweet smell.

"I recognize these flowers, Aori," she whispered as she closed her eyes and flitted through memories. "We planted them in the Empress's garden, before the fall of the Fellfallan Empire. Oleander loved them most of all."

As if summoned by saying the name, several moths came to the blossoms seeking nectar. Like Daphni, they bore the regal colors of the Nerium Hawkmoths. Shades of green glinted in the dim light of the setting sun, as the moths fluttered around them.

"Oleander?" she called out to them, and one landed on her outstretched palm.

The moth flapped its wings, and a thin, green dust sparkled in the air around it.

She listened closely to everything the moths had to communicate with her. According to the oldest of their kind, the original Oleander died when he crashed into Aori's other clock-tower, which also provided a means of traveling to Earth. Since then, his spawn had spread throughout the world, seeking out his long-lost love.

"We have been searching for her, too! Have you found her?" asked Daphni.

The moth explained that the soul of the true Lymantria Dispar, his one true love with the Gypsy heart, had spread out as he had. He had found several moths that had come from her kin, but he believed that the original Gypsy still lived.

"Where is she?"

The moth suggested that they head to Asia, where many Fellfallan refugees had gathered and started the silk trade. The larvae of several types of moths spun silk thread to build their cocoons, and the Asians, who had developed a symbiotic relationship with the Fellfalla, peddled the silk across China, India, and as far west as Byzantium, in modern-day

281

Turkey. The Chinese gave the Fellfalla protection in exchange for the secrets of silk production, and the rare fabric became an expensive commodity throughout the world.

While the larvae that came from Gypsy's kin had never made very good silkworms, they had always been notorious for their consumption of fabric. As I have mentioned before, the Fellfalla passed down a folktale in which Gypsy's ancestors had spun expensive thread to make cloth only to eat the fabric they had spent so much of their lives creating.

The Oleander moth offered to join them in their journey along the Silk Road, which lead east towards Asia. Before they set out on the road, however, Aori suggested that they make a detour through Tweentime. "We will need supplies for the trip, as well as protection. I have heard tales of the ruffians that attack caravans along the route, and I believe we may need weapons... and warriors to wield them."

"You may have forgotten, Aori, but I was a knight in the Fellfallan Empire," said Daphni, obviously offended.

"I had not forgotten, dear. But who will protect you, while you are protecting me? We will both feel safer with a giant ruffian of our own."

Pettifogger's garden contained many new additions, which contributed to the overall aesthetic value of the palace complex. During his stay at Aori's, Litoro the Ionian had sung several beautiful waterfalls and fountains into being in the courtyard and palace grounds. A moat now encircled the complex as well, serving as added security from invaders.

Of course, water had not previously existed in Tween-time, or at least not in Aori's palace. Somehow, it had answered Litoro's call nonetheless, and they just wrote it off as another magical loophole in the strange physics that existed in between time.

With the addition of running water, Aori had invented a water clock, which helped him keep up with the time on

Earth. The water moved a wheel, which in turn caused a complex set of gears and pulleys to move the hands of the clock. The same technology enabled several other innovations, some of which Aori had previously invented back on Aia. He retooled his Magicosteam Engine to power many devices around the house, but he made sure not to create any automatons, such as the clockworkers, that might take on a life of their own and overthrow him.

Pettifogger's garden provided much of the raw materials necessary for metalworking, from the silverweed and the ironwood tree, the latter of which had grown from the metal rod he had planted. Sword lilies and arrowroot grew there as well, so Pettifogger had grown a stockpile of weapons and ammunition.

His favorite flower, however, was his looking-glass begonia. With the glass that bloomed from its stems, he had created mirrors, glass for the windows, and even lenses for a new pair of goggles that he designed for himself to replace the ones that Aori had appropriated for his own, personal use.

"I suppose Aori's neglect finally forced you to create your own device for seeing Aia?" the Computadorian mused.

Over time, the computer had overtaken the entire library, and its circuits covered the whole floor. It had become quite difficult to tell where the living, breathing wood of the palace walls ended and the technology of the computer began.

Pettifogger visited the library seldom, as the computerized form of Dorian had begun to annoy him by that time. However, wires from its CPU stretched throughout the palace, so that Dorian was connected to every room in the house. Speakers had grown in the workshop, so Pettifogger could not escape the attempted manipulations of Tempo's oldest disciple.

"I sense that Aori has returned, Mr. Pettifogger. Undoubtedly, he requires your expertise in engineering some

283

device. He's hardly what I would call a leader, let alone the embodiment of Time on Earth."

Pettifogger sighed.

"I'm just saying, he doesn't seem fit to be affiliated in any sort with Tempo, the Time god."

"I know what you're saying, Dorian. You've been saying it nonstop for the last hundred years." Pettifogger tried to block out the noise of Dorian's suggestions and focus on the goggles, which he called his Pettifoggles. At this point, he could use them to see objects that were far away, but they were not powerful enough to see all the way to Aia.

"If you just sit idly by and wait, he will have destroyed your home planet once again," the Computadorian's voice crackled in the speaker.

Pettifogger held the goggles up to his eyes again, but set them down again with a disappointed look. "Dorian, you keep contradicting yourself. You suggest that I need to stop him, but you also say that he'll become the god that you yourself worship. If I stop him, who will you serve?"

"I... I..." The robotic voice seemed to be caught in a loop, like an old record player.

Pettifogger breathed a sigh of relief. Any time the computer's propaganda against Aori became too annoying, all he had to do was present Dorian with the circular logic of the Aori-Tempo connection. If Aori would one day become the Time god, travel back in time, and destroy Aia, he would be in direct conflict with himself, which just didn't make sense. As a side effect, the strategy also gave Pettifogger a terrible headache.

Throughout the years, those who studied temporal energy, time travel, or the theory of relativity often experienced such mental dead-ends. Trying to understand any infinite plane of existence often lead to insanity, which explains the madness of the *Everseers*. For instance, if a teenage boy traveled back in time with a photograph of his family, would his image progressively fade away the further his parents got from pledging their undying love to one another?

284

> Or, if a cyborg from some post-apocalyptic future traveled back in time in order to prevent the domination of the world at the hands of the cyborgs, wouldn't he cease to exist once he achieved his goal?
>
> As one of the only sane *Everseers*, I find that it's best just to ignore such conundrums. I focus on the past, because it's immutable. Of course, I suppose if you went back further into the past, you could change the less-recent past, which would, theoretically, mean that there are an infinite number of possible less-recent-pasts, as well as an infinite number of presents. Oh, dear.

"Pyrite?" called Aori as he ran up the stairs to the workshop. "Oh. I thought I'd find you here, when you weren't in the garden. It looks beautiful, by the way. Daphni particularly loves the new, organic flowers."

"It's strange. We never had soil or water before the Coda came."

"Yes… I try not to think about it too much," Aori smiled.

"Did you need my help?" asked Pettifogger.

Aori told him about the Oleander moths and their proposed journey to Asia. He explained, in some detail, why he believed they would find Gypsy there, including the story of the Fellfalla who eat their own fabric.

As he hadn't heard about anyone who needed to be robbed or assassinated, Pettifogger asked, "How can I help, then?"

Aori answered, "Well, we need protection along the road."

Pettifogger rose to his feet, smiling at the idea of protecting someone almost twice as tall as himself.

"Have you seen Munder?" Aori asked, shattering Pettifogger's proud smile.

"Oh," he muttered. "You only need my help to find the giant."

Sensing the gnome's disappointment, Aori offered, "Your job here is more important, Pyrite. You're the only

285

one I trust. Besides, that computer is getting a little too big, and you're the only one who can control it."

Pettifogger scowled. "I haven't seen Munder lately. I've been busy holding down the fort while you're off having adventures."

Aori returned the scowl. "Perhaps your computer could find him?"

"It's not *my* computer."

"Pyrite, if I didn't know better, I'd think that you were still that stubborn teenager I picked up in Auldenton."

"Fine," Pettifogger huffed. "I'll go ask the computer." He stormed out of the room and up the stairs to the library, grumbling all the way.

Aori called after him, "If you think grumbling will draw Munder out of hiding, it won't work! That's not his mating call, you know!"

As Pettifogger climbed the stairs, the Computadorian whispered in a robotic voice. "Why would he not wish to have you with him, unless he was planning something behind your back? Maybe he's amassing the power to destroy this world also, and he feels like you would only get in his way."

Pettifogger sighed. "Dorian, where is Munder?"

"What evil does Timister want him to do this time?"

"Actually, we're trying to distract him from the evil your god has been having him do!"

The Computadorian fell silent.

"He's gone."

"Gone?" Pettifogger groaned.

"Gone where?" Aori joined him on the stairs. "And is the computer talking to you?"

"It never stops...." Pettifogger muttered.

"Gone where, computer?" asked Aori.

The robotic voice seemed to warble a bit, as if Dorian were trying to disguise his voice. "He had a previously scheduled engagement. However, he has an appointment with you later."

"What's that supposed to mean?" asked Pettifogger suspiciously.

"He will meet up with you soon."

"How would the computer have records of that?" Aori whispered.

"Let's just go," said Pettifogger matter-of-factly. "I'm coming with you."

Aori began, "But…"

Pettifogger stood up as straight and tall as he could manage. "First of all, I am your friend, not your minion. Perhaps more importantly, however, I cannot tolerate that computer any longer."

Aori's mouth had fallen open a bit, but words failed him.

The trio of Aori, Daphni, and Pettifogger could not have picked a better time to leave the Roman Empire. Around that time, soldiers came home from Asia Minor and spread the Antonine Plague. The plague, which was later thought to be smallpox, killed five million people. The pestilence severely handicapped the Roman forces, which eventually resulted in invasion by Germanic tribes. Two emperors, Lucius Veras and Marcus Aurelius Antoninus, also lost their lives to the plague, hence the name Antonine Plague.

A few years later, an earthquake destroyed much of Smyrna. It was commonly believed, mostly among the Dorian Coda in Tweentime, that one of their line had started the earthquake. If so, then it may have been for similar reasons as Litoro's flood and the Great Fire, hundreds of years later, in 1922. For some reason, Smyrna had developed a legacy of Codan persecution and, subsequently, revenge.

With great relief, Aori and company abandoned the Roman Empire forever. The fall of the empire came gradually, partly as a result of the plagues, invasion from the Germanic tribes, poor leadership, and numerous other

287

reasons. Aori always said that the empire killed itself, and that the plague had been an instrument of the Infinis in order to bring about its self-destruction. Whatever the case, not even the Dorians, with their reverence of the past and the dead, mourned the fall of the Roman Empire.

As the road to China covered roughly seven thousand miles, they agreed that Daphni could not fly the whole way. Instead, they chose to travel alongside the caravans that were already heading that direction. During the day, they asked all the travelers and merchants if they had seen anyone matching the description of Gypsy. However, most people don't pay a lot of attention to moths…even those that are the size of humans.

At night, they traveled through Tweentime, so each town or settlement was less than a hop, skip, or Fellfallan flight away. To lessen the load, Aori and Pettifogger took turns riding on a camel with their provisions. While the travel took a bit longer, going through Tweentime cut the time in half. They could easily make it from one town to another in one night, and they encountered very few people along the road, lessening their chance of a run-in with bandits.

Through the years, explorers and merchants had discovered several other routes to connect their settlement with East Asia. Some chose to travel partly by sea and then north through India. Others took a northern route through the Steppes of Asia, as far as Modern-day Russia and Kazakhstan.

The route provided a means of transporting more than just silk; technological, religious, and philosophical ideas traveled along the road as well. Buddhism spread from India to China via the Silk Road, and inventions such as the astrolabe, crossbow, and compass crossed over from China to Europe.

Of course, these inventions sparked the interest of Aori and Pettifogger, but they managed to stay focused on the quest. They could always examine their treasures in more detail once they returned to the palace in Tweentime. However, the lack of information took its toll on their morale.

"You'd think someone would have seen a five-foot-tall moth-lady flying around," Pettifogger complained. "It's not like she blends into this crowd."

The clothing of the crowd included turbans, burkas, fur hats and boots, and togas. Their attire, especially on the females, showed very little skin. Daphni chose to drape herself in her long, flowing cloak so as not to attract attention.

"I think you would be surprised," she replied. "Gypsy is accustomed to making herself at home in foreign cities. I would imagine that she has already picked up the languages of all these people, and she was always highly skilled at making new clothing to suit her."

Aori scanned the crowd, as he had done in every settlement. "Has anyone spotted a giant yet?"

"He's not here," answered Pettifogger. "I may be wrong about Gypsy blending in, but Munder would stick out like a huge, swollen, stupid thumb."

Laughing out loud, Aori agreed. "I know we don't need his help, but I would just feel better knowing he's not out there killing innocent people… or gods."

The Oleander Hawkmoth returned with a group of Daphni's moths. He fluttered around her head, obviously communicating. She told the others, "They scouted out the whole town, and she's not here. However, they believe she must have come through this area, because some of the clothing for sale by merchants has her look."

The moths led them to a marketplace, where they found beautiful rugs, dresses, blankets, and clothing woven from the finest silk. Daphni examined the products closely, looking for Gypsy's distinct style. "Spread out and look for a pattern similar to the bark of a tree," she suggested.

They rifled through the fabric, and the moths fluttered mainly around one table, which caused the shop-owner to go into fits of shouting and swatting. Daphni attempted to apologize as she picked up a black and white garment. The detail of its design outshined all those around it, as most weavers and tailors could not afford to use more than one color of dye in their fabric. As she felt the soft silk, its arching black lines rose and fell like waves. "This is it," she whispered, "Isn't it, brother?"

The Oleander moth rested upon the fabric, much to the dismay of the shop-owner.

Aori stepped in and offered the man several coins, which silenced him. He went back into his tent and spoke to someone in a language Aori had not yet learned.

"Pyrite, will you take this back to the palace and have the Coda examine it? Maybe they can listen to its song and tell us more about Gypsy's whereabouts."

Pettifogger looked up at him.

"Pyrite, please. I'm asking you as a friend, not giving you an order."

With a sigh, the gnome took the garment and vanished into Tweentime.

As soon as he was gone, the shop-owner came out of his tent, shouting and pointing at them. Aori could not make out what he was saying, but several large men followed him out of the tent. They wore fur hats and long beards, but their skin was much lighter than the usual nomads that populated that area.

"They must think that we stole the fabric," said Aori. "I'll try to explain."

One of the men grabbed Daphni first, but she immediately broke his arm and elbowed him in the face. She dodged as he tried to swing a sword at her with his good arm, and her cloak billowed around her as she danced circles around him. The various shades of olive and emerald distracted him just long enough for her to kick the legs out from under him.

Tiny larva worked rapidly behind the scenes to form her thick, chrysalis armor to encase her skin. It was done before the man could rise to his feet. Suddenly, she was a shining knight from another world, covered head to toe in her unmistakable pattern of green hues. Her cloak flapped in the dry wind of the Steppes as she hovered several feet above the ground. The helmet, which looked like something from the future, gave her a view of all her surroundings. With insect-oid vision, she caught a glimpse of Aori laying helplessly on the ground. The other bearded man stood with one foot on Aori's neck. He was armed with a scimitar, which dripped with blood.

Daphni's first impulse was to dive right in and take her chances with the armed men, but she had to think of Aori first. If he died, the temporal magic that lengthened her lifespan would surely fade. His survival was linked to hers.

She spread her wings and dove straight into the chest of the man with the scimitar. He flew backwards and into some racks of clothing. Daphni grabbed Aori and turned him over on his back. He had a large wound in his abdomen that was bleeding profusely.

Daphni had never handled death well. Despite the fact that the lifespan of the Fellfalla was naturally short, and she had watched many of her compatriots die in the battlefield, it never got easier. Her parents had died when she was very young, and Oleander raised her as best he could in the cold, stark reality of the Fellfallan Empire. Since life for her people was so short, she felt a burning anger inside her any time that life was ended prematurely. That burning feeling burst inside her, as she knelt beside Aori in the dirt of the marketplace. It exploded from her heart outward through her whole body, as she held him in her arms.

Several other soldiers surrounded them, and Daphni fought with her desire for revenge and her longing to stay and

291

protect him. She shouted at them in the guttural, growling tongue of the Fellfalla.

The soldiers came closer, undaunted by the curses she spat. Most of them wore armor, but some just wore pointed hats and tunics. The men with pointed hats looked like they belonged in the region, while the armored soldiers were obviously outsiders. The soldiers carried axes mainly, with the occasional sword or halberd in the mix.

As they descended upon her, her armor bore the brunt of the damage. She shielded Aori's body with her own as the heavy axes beat against her back and shoulders. The armor of the Nerii had withstood the onslaught of countless enemies in her days as a knight for the Fellfallan Emperor, but she could feel it splintering under the weight of the attacks.

Eventually, they managed to pry her off of Aori, but as they dragged her to her feet, she fought even more violently. She managed to grab one of their halberds, which had always been her weapon of choice, and took out several of their numbers. As the Fellfallan knight hacked her way back through the crowd to her fallen companion, she caught a glimpse of one soldier who towered above all the rest. He, too, wore armor, but his helm sported two long horns.

"Munder!" Daphni tried to call out, but blood caught in her throat. She must have punctured a lung during the fight. It didn't matter, though; without Aori, she would not be long for this world.

The armor cracked around her helmet, which fractured her vision into shards of images. She saw several other soldiers wearing armor that did not fit the area, or even the time. One of them raised a weapon of some sort. There was a flash of light, a loud banging sound, and then everything went completely dark.

292

Chapter 2:19

Backstabs and Frontstabs

Despite the fact that Aori's life bled out of him in a dusty marketplace in the land of Scythia, his palace hummed with its usual vibrant energy. Flowers bloomed in the garden, and the palace itself had grown so large that it had begun to sprout smaller buildings from its roots. It looked like a small village surrounding the larger palace complex. Inside, wires crept like vines throughout each room. Tangled webs of cords, cables, and connections stretched across the ceilings and doorframes. The wood of every wall now buzzed with an electronic hum, and transistors grew amongst the phloem and xylem.

"Look at the magnificence of your creation, Pettifogger," the robotic voice of Dorian echoed throughout the palace. "For years, gnomes have tried to bridge the gap between nature's creations and those fabricated by man. You have brought balance to the eternal struggle between nature and technology!"

Pettifogger looked around at the amalgam of arboreal, architectural, and artificial growth. In spite of his accomplishment, he felt no joy. "I have work to do, Dorian."

The gnome went straight to the music room to find the other Coda. Viola greeted him warmly. "Hello, Mr. Pettifogger. What brings you here?"

He set the fabric down on a table. "Aori needs this examined. We'd like to know anything and everything about its creator, and where she might be now."

"I see," said Viola. "I'll round up the other Coda."

"And..." continued Pettifogger, "...let's try to keep the computer out of it, okay?"

Viola sighed. "I think you know as well as I do that that is impossible. Dorian has absorbed most of the house. The old relic can hear everything we say."

"I can hear you right now," boomed the robotic voice.

"Oh, I know," said Viola sweetly. "I just don't care."

Pettifogger smiled. "Okay, just be as quick as you can."

"Will do," Viola agreed.

Trying to avoid any of the surveillance equipment he had invented and installed, Pettifogger escaped to the garden, where he had always found peace. Daisies and cinquefoils lined the edges of the walkways, reminding him of his sister and mother, respectively. Back in Auldenton, he had been so preoccupied with the fast-paced world of whirrs and clicks outside that he hadn't truly appreciated the life that went on inside his home.

His father, Gneiss, had been an inventor too, but he had always seemed so grounded... so rooted in the natural world. Of course, Pettifogger had very few memories of his father, as he had died many, many years ago.

Stooping down to smell a beautiful purple hyacinth blossom, he whispered, "I will find you."

Suddenly some trumpet flowers, which were made of brass, of course, turned toward him and bellowed, "To whom are you talking, Mr. Pettifogger?"

Pettifogger sighed. "Leave me alone, Dorian."

294

"What do you suppose Mr. Timister is doing, while you are stopping to smell the flowers?"

"I'm sure he's doing just fine," Pettifogger scowled. "He has Daphni, after all."

Dorian's robotic voice blared out of the trumpet flowers. "Yes, I'm sure you're right. Aori would do whatever it takes to survive, even if that meant altering the world's time. Why, he might even go so far as to destroy a whole planet just to save himself."

"Look, Dorian. Aori wouldn't do that. Besides…"

"How do you know? If you trust Aori so much, why haven't you told him about me yet? He still thinks I'm just a normal computer." A looking-glass begonia turned toward Pettifogger, and Dorian's face appeared it its glass.

Pettifogger opened his mouth, but he could not form a response.

"Maybe it's because you really believe me. Maybe you're afraid of what he might become. Maybe you know what you'll become, as well. Maybe you know, deep down inside your twisted heart that you're nothing but a scoundrel… a cutthroat… a backstabber. You know your destiny is to betray him."

"So…" said Pettifogger with a somewhat weak voice, "I suppose you've abandoned all pretense of trying to save the world from Aori, now. It's all about beating down the Chosen Son of Tempo, just because you were always the unwanted stepchild."

The robotic voice fell silent.

After a pause that was long enough to have restarted his system, the Computadorian retorted, "Tempo chose me. He plucked me from the bosom of the mundane elvish bloodline to be the progenitor of a new race! He chose me to be the Immortal Father of the Dorian line!"

"Fine," said Pettifogger. "You were chosen."

295

"The Timisters were nothing but self-serving thieves! They were like Prometheus, stealing fire from the gods, only they stole time!"

Pettifogger tried to focus on tending his plants. His herbs had thrived in his absence, thanks to the irrigation system he and Litoro had built. Cascading waterfalls and fountains gave the garden the serene ambience of trickling water, which could be heard faintly behind the shouts of an insane computer.

"The world had turned for millennia without Aori's help. Then he came along, this Wind of Change, to break the beautiful cycle."

Pettifogger picked off some dying leaves from a thyme plant. "Dorian, you'll have to face the fact that, yes, Tempo chose you, but he also forgot about you. You were like the leaves on this plant, and pruning you allowed the Temporal Trinity to grow."

The stones in the garden's pathway shook with rage.

"Hey," Pettifogger continued, "I know what it feels like to be left behind-- believe me."

"I was not...left behind," said the computer. "I chose to stay with Aia. If my people had not needed me here, I would have died with my planet... unlike Aori, who chose to escape his guilt!"

"I don't think he's as guilty as you think he is, Dorian. Who gave him his power?"

"Only Tempo, the Time Lord, could bestow such power, of course!"

"Of course," said Pettifogger. "And yet, Tempo allowed me to steal it, and when Aori could not manipulate the world as Tempo desired, he used me as his puppet instead!"

The rocks stopped quaking, and the trumpet flowers drooped.

Pettifogger plucked one of the leaves from his thyme plant, and put it in his mouth thoughtfully. "Look, I don't know why Tempo would want to destroy Aia, or if that's

296

even what happened. It's always been too confusing to me, as if the Time god himself had gotten so convoluted and mixed up that he didn't know his own schemes and machinations."

"I cannot allow such blasphemy...." The computer's voice was softer, almost beaten.

"You're obviously confused too, Dorian. Time works in such mysterious ways that you can't even figure out how to do his bidding."

Pettifogger took a long look at the garden, as if saying good bye. He picked a hyacinth blossom and put it inside his coat pocket. Then, with a slight movement of his hand, he caused the ironwood tree to reach down, scoop him up, and carry him high into the air. It placed him gently into a third-story window.

"It just doesn't make sense," said Pettifogger as he entered the library. "You kept trying to convince me that Aori would become Tempo. Are we to believe that, in the future, Aori will go back in time in order to give himself the ability to alter time and renounce himself?"

A blue bar appeared on the computer's screens, which now took up all four walls of the library.

Pettifogger continued, "And why would you, who always served Tempo, want to stop Aori from becoming that which you worshipped for so long?"

The hourglass displayed on the computer suddenly stopped.

"I know you've been trying to communicate with Tempo since you took over that computer, Dorian. The truth is, you have been praying for years, but your god hasn't been listening."

A message box appeared, telling the user that the computer made a fatal error and would need to be restarted.

"I... oh, I guess *you've* stopped listening now," Pettifogger muttered. "You must've blown a circuit. Let me have a look."

297

The gnome looked back behind one of the central processing units, which now took up several bookcases. "You were right about one thing, though, Dorian," Pettifogger said. "I *am* a backstabber."

Pulling out his reclaimed dagger, he repeatedly and systematically stabbed every bit and byte of the computer.

The dagger had been one of the spikes that had nailed Jesus to the cross, which embued it with sacred power for ensuring that Dorian would stay dead forever. With that sense of finality, Pettifogger left the room and never looked back.

"She's dead."

"What? Who?" asked Pettifogger. His fight with the computer had detached him from his whole purpose for coming here. In fact, Pettifogger himself seemed detached, cold, and emotionless.

"The Fellfalla," said Viola.

"Daphni?"

"No, the one who made this. We," she referred to the Coda behind her, "assume that she is dead, because she was dying even as she wove its threads together."

Elegos added, "It is a death shroud."

"So all our trouble we've gone through to find Gypsy has been in vain?" Pettifogger sank into a chair and buried his head in his hands.

"Well, not exactly," said Pedant in his usual condescending tone. "You may not be aware that when the Fellfalla die, they leave behind their souls in the moths that bear their names."

Elegos added, with his flair for the dramatic, "You may still find her, and we may know where to look."

"Not me," said Pettifogger. "I'm done here."

"What do you mean?" asked Viola.

"One of you will have to explain it to them. I have to go."

Elegos began to tear up. "Go where?"

Gazing down at the flower in his coat pocket, he whispered, "Home."

The land of Scythia stretched across what would later be known as Iran, Georgia, Kazakhstan, and Ukraine. The Scythian people were nomadic herders of cattle and Bactrian camels, and they profited for years from selling their livestock on the Silk Road. They invaded civilizations east of Asia Minor, but they never conquered quite enough to withstand the might of the Roman Empire.

However, just a few days before Aori and the others arrived in the Scythian Neapolis, the Goths invaded Scythia and drove out the Romans. Since the Scythians had never actually enjoyed being part of the Roman Empire, they all but welcomed the Goths with open arms. You see, by giving the shop-keeper Roman coins, Aori had labeled himself as a Roman sympathizer and, therefore, an enemy of the state.

Of course, it didn't help that Munder and the Army of the Anachronist had also joined the Goths that day. For around a year, the giant had used the excuse of invading new territories to further his personal quest for deicide. The civilizations that the Goths came across always had their own primitive pantheons of gods, which were really just cheap knockoffs of the more well-known Greek, Roman, or Babylonian gods. No one missed them, because no one was around to worship them.

The Scythians themselves were polytheistic, and they believed Munder to be the folk hero Kolaksay, who had been based on Hercules. They didn't even seem to mind when he killed off all of their gods. They had always seemed like throwbacks to the Roman days anyway.

Just as the soldiers were gathering their fallen, Gypsy's death shroud appeared out of nowhere on the dusty ground. A sudden gust of wind blew it onto Aori's bleeding body.

The Goths were known for their brutal treatment of prisoners of war, and the appearance of Roman arms and legs in the trees around Scythia testified to that. However, when Aori woke up in a dark, stone tomb, he found that all his limbs were still attached.

Since the Scythians were nomads, they rarely built extravagant houses or other structures. Therefore, they had no castles and no dungeons. However, they did honor their dead with monuments and intricately designed tombs. When the Goths needed a place to put their new prisoners, the mausoleum seemed like the best choice.

As Aori breathed the stale, thin air of the tomb, he felt intense pain in his gut. He pulled the shroud off of his face, but the room remained just as dark. Though he could barely see, he could feel a warm wetness just below his ribcage. He called out to the darkness, "Daphni?"

"Aori? You're alive!" She prodded around in the darkness with her antennae, but she could not find him. "Where are you? Say my name again."

"Daphni," he tried to shout, but the pain tore through his stomach. He crawled toward the sound of her voice, and she pulled him closer to her.

"You lost so much blood, Aori. I thought you were dead. Of course, I thought I was too."

"Well, we do appear to be in a tomb," he said, picking up the remains of a long-dead Scythian.

"I noticed that," she said weakly.

"One second. I'll get us out of here." Aori spread his arms as if pushing two heavy walls apart, but his attempt to reach between time had no effect. "That's odd," he muttered.

"What happened?"

"Nothing," said Aori. "I can't open a portal to Tweentime."

300

"Maybe you're still weak from your…injuries." She strained on the last word, as if speaking it aloud made her own injuries hurt worse.

"Are you okay?"

"I have some broken ribs, and they fired at me with some weapon that my armor barely repelled. I have the projectile here."

"Was it a gun?" Aori rolled the bullet over between his fingers. "It must have been. I didn't know they had been invented yet."

"Munder was there, too."

Aori felt the silence of the tomb wrap around him. "Then he must have the Army of the Anachronist with him, now. But, why would he betray us?"

"Isn't that all he's ever done?"

He thought for a moment. "I suppose so. I just don't understand why Tempo would have waited this long to send in his biggest mercenary. He could have killed me long ago."

"Maybe he just wants you out of the way, so that Munder can kill everyone else."

"Of course. He doesn't want me to die, but he doesn't want me to interfere either."

Daphni took a labored breath. "I'm afraid we *will* die, though, unless we can get out of here."

"You're right." With much effort, Aori managed to stand. He used the wall to support him as he explored their tomb. "It doesn't seem to be very big. That means our oxygen is very limited. I'm sure we'll suffocate before either of us die of old age."

"Is that supposed to make me feel better?" asked Daphni.

"Sorry." He grabbed the shroud and wrapped it around her. "Are you cold? You're shaking."

"I…yes… thank you."

He pulled her closer towards him, so that the warmth of his body might ease her shivering.

301

Daphni whimpered, "I'm not good with death, Aori. This tomb…."

"I know, Daphni. I know." He held her as tightly as he could, determined to fight off the oncoming doom. She had almost died protecting him, while he had just crumpled on the ground bleeding to death. He owed her, and he would fight off Death itself, when it came.

She turned her head just enough that they touched cheeks. Even in the pitch darkness, his lips found hers. They kissed until their heads swam in the thin air.

"You're still shivering," he said.

"I feel quite warm. I think the blanket is vibrating."

"What? Vibrating blankets haven't been invented yet."

"No, look, Aori. It's the fabric we got in the market-place! I can barely see its pattern, but there it is!"

The blanket continued to vibrate in successive pulses.

"It's Elegos!" Aori exclaimed. "He says he would have spoken up sooner, but he didn't want to ruin our beautiful moment. Let me see if I can pull out his temporal ghost."

The act seriously weakened Aori, but he managed to conjure a thin specter that looked as if it were made up of tiny particles of dust. Fortunately, the purple glow of his temporal energy illuminated the room to some extent. His ghost had the appearance one would expect of an ancient Greek, complete with laurel circlet and toga. He was mostly bald, and he had no beard.

"It is good to see you both alive," said Elegos.

"The dying amongst the already dead," Aori mused. "You must appreciate the poetry in that, Elegos."

"It is beautiful, but it pales in comparison to the exchange I just witnessed between you two." The Codan ghost sniffled.

"Where are we, Elegos?"

"This is a Scythian tomb, I'm afraid. We're underground … several meters, it seems. The dead here have wonderful stories…."

"Perhaps we could save them for another time, Elegos," Aori said with strained patience. "We're in a bit of a hurry."

"Of course! You need to get out of here. It's been so long since I've breathed, I forgot how necessary it was!" The ghost wandered around the room, listening to the resonance within the stone walls.

Realization struck Aori suddenly. "Elegos, where is Pettifogger? Why did he send you back in his stead?"

The ghost began to sob softly, and he sank to his knees.

"Elegos?" Daphni tried to pat him on the back consolingly, but her hand passed through him.

"Did something happen to him?" The concern broke Aori's voice a bit.

"I don't know," sobbed Elegos. "He just left."

"What?"

"He told us it was important that you got the shroud-- Oh! I almost forgot about the shroud!"

"First, tell us about Pettifogger," said Aori. "Then, the shroud."

"Well, he said he was going home." The ghost sniffled. "Of course, I took that to mean that he was dying, but the others disagreed."

All Aori could do was stare at the floor, lost in thought.

"And the shroud? Is it Gypsy's?" asked Daphni.

"Yes, definitely. However, its story is not a happy one, I warn you."

Daphni swallowed hard. "I assumed as much. Then she is dead, I suppose? I could not hope, after all these years, that she would still be alive."

Elegos looked up at her with tears glistening in the pale, purple light. "We believe there may be gypsy moths in China, however. I think I can lead you there."

"First, we'll have to get out of this tomb," said Daphni.

The ghost placed a hand on the wall of the tomb again. "I sense nothing but more earth and rock beyond this wall."

He turned to Aori. "Can't you just whisk us all away to Tweentime again?"

Still staring at the floor, Aori seemed to come back from some far away place. "What? Oh, I tried. I think I'm too weak. I was stabbed."

"This wall is solid as well. Miles and miles of earth…and bones," said Elegos.

Standing caused a searing pain in Aori's stomach, but he rose and examined the ceiling. It was roughly six feet tall, so not much taller than he was. His face fell with his spirits. "If Pettifogger were here, I am sure he would find a way to escape."

Pettifogger stood at the edge of a cliff consisting of swirling matter. He gazed off into a void of purple energy. "This is where you found me, waiting for my eternity of penance to pass. Here I stand again, on the precipice of my own misdeeds, waiting."

"That wasn't me, who found you. Well, not exactly." The figure of an old man stepped up behind him. Temporal energy crackled all around him, and he glowed with a purple light.

Pettifogger didn't even bother to turn around. "Not exactly? You're not Aori, but you're not really Quartz Thymegarden, are you? Whatever. It hurts my brain to think about it."

"Wiser men than any of us have lost their minds contemplating it."

Through the haze of purple swirls, Pettifogger could almost see a beautiful, blue and green orb. Something fluttered past his face, but it was gone before he could see it. "It's done. Just like you said would happen."

The face of the old man flickered, and another elderly countenance took its place. Like a grainy film projection, it continuously wavered between the forms of numerous senior citizens.

"Sometimes my memory serves. Of course, when it comes to recollections of the future, I find it's less of a pain in the brain to just forget."

"Was the computer's attempt at manipulating me really necessary?" asked Pettifogger.

"I wasn't sure if you'd come around."

"Well, I don't like it."

"You're saving the world, Pettifogger. It may not seem like it now, but you'll be the hero one day."

"Whatever," muttered the gnome. "Just let me see my family."

Chapter 2:20

Forsaken Again

The air inside the Scythian tomb reeked of death, and its dearth gave Aori a headache equal in intensity to the wound in his stomach. Even Daphni felt light-headed, in spite of the fact that she had grown accustomed to thin air in high altitude flights.

"When Oleander and I were training to become Knights of the Nerii, we had to undergo all sorts of tests of endurance. We were taken to the depths of the sea and up to the heavens. Oleander could always hold his breath longer than I could, though." Daphni moved her antennae around, listening to the silence of the tomb. "I wonder where the moths are, now. They must have flown away when we got captured."

"Maybe they will send for help," suggested Elegos, trying to remain positive on behalf of his living companions.

"I don't know who they would find to help us," Aori replied. "Everyone we know is either miles away, in Tween-time, or the reason we're in this predicament."

"Don't the Dorian Coda have some power over rock and stone?" asked Daphni.

Elegos fed off of Aori's negativity. "If I were a true Dorian, perhaps. Then, I could cause an earthquake and knock down these walls! Alas! I am just a poet. I hardly think my words could move mountains worth of stone."

"Then you may be writing poems for our funerals as well," Aori muttered.

Daphni huddled close to him for warmth. "If we had a fire…."

Elegos began to cry again. "One of the others should have come instead. Viola could have started a fire, or Dorian could have just told the rocks to get out of the way. I'm useless!"

"Most likely, Dorian would have left us here to rot," said Aori.

"Yes," Elegos sniffled, wiping his eyes. "I've been meaning to tell you…."

"I know. He infected the computer, and he's taken over the house."

"You knew? He said if you found out, you'd destroy him. Sometimes I wish you had."

Aori sighed. "I knew he'd eventually try to overthrow me. I guess I should have just left him in that temple in Delphi."

"Your heart was in the right place, Aori." Daphni rested her head on his chest.

A loud *boom* echoed through the mausoleum.

Daphni stared at Aori's chest quizzically.

Boom.

"I think it's coming from outside," whispered Aori.

Boom.

"And above us," added Elegos. "They are footsteps."

They heard rocks scraping above them.

"That is the sound of rocks scraping above us," Elegos offered.

"Thank you, Elegos."

Dust fell from the ceiling. A thin ray of light, no bigger than a pinhead, shot down to the floor. Slowly, as the scraping continued, the light grew larger. When the sound stopped, it left behind a round circle of light, roughly the size of an orange, upon the floor.

Aori stood under the hole and looked up into the light above. It appeared that a long, thin shaft stretched up to open air. From what he could tell, he estimated their depth to be around twelve feet.

"Hello?"

The booming voice echoed through the tomb.

"That's the voice of…"

"We know, Elegos," Aori interrupted. He yelled, "Munder?"

"Hey there, old man," said Munder. "How's life in the grave?"

"You should definitely try it. Soon."

Munder laughed. "Nah, my work's not done yet. By the way, sorry you kids got all roughed up and stuff. That wasn't really part of the plan."

"You had a plan?"

"Well, me an' Ode, yeah."

Aori sighed. "So you and a rock that hasn't talked for years made a plan to lock us up, but you didn't intend for us to get stabbed, beaten, and shot?"

"Yup."

"The road to Hades is paved with those sort of intentions, I've heard," Elegos added.

"Indeed," Aori agreed. "And why, might I ask, did you need to lock us up?"

"You're the bad guy," said Munder.

"I see." Aori gritted his teeth. "Have you been talking to Quondam again?"

"No. Well, a bit, but everyone knows you're evil. You said yourself that you'll probably become the Time Lord some day."

"That was your idea."

Munder shouted, "Whatever. I'm doing the world a favor."

"Munder… when you said 'everyone knows…' did you mean you and your rock?"

"He's not a rock anymore. Ode's a real boy now. Well, he's an old man, but that was a Pinocchio joke. You wouldn't understand, because you've never seen a cartoon."

Aori turned to Daphni and whispered, "Tempo must be manipulating him through Ode. I guess I never should have trusted that rock, either."

"I apologize on behalf of all Dorian Coda, sir."

"Thank you, Elegos."

Munder yelled, "The computer said you're evil too, so it must be true. Computers know everything."

"Does he seem more child-like than usual, to anyone else?" Aori commented.

"He never had much of a brain," said Daphni.

"It hasn't been that many years since we saw him in his previous life. He must be very young."

"And yet, still the size of a house?" asked Daphni.

"Well, maybe he's a young ogre," Elegos contributed.

Aori laughed.

Munder yelled, "The computer even had your little runt friend convinced."

The smile left Aori's face, and time seemed to stand still.

"Come on," yelled Munder. "You pal around with a bloodthirsty giant and a backstabbing scoundrel, and you're surprised when they sell you up the river?"

To Aori, the air seemed even thinner, as if he were suffocating.

"We're villains, Gramps! All of us. You, me, the runt…even that computer. Heck, I bet that little fairy chick you got there is just waiting for the right time to double-cross you."

Daphni yelled, "I would never…"

"Oh, give it up, fairy. You know if Tempo said you could live forever, you'd stab him in the back just like old Pettifogger."

Aori clutched at his gut. The tomb seemed to get smaller, as if the whole world were crashing down upon him. On Aia, everyone seemed against him for a hundred different reasons, but he knew, deep down, that he deserved their ire. He had taken Coda, Ori, and Agypsians forcefully from their homelands. He had destroyed miles and miles of forest land. Seasons passed by, while he complained about not having time to take care of his own parents. On Aia, he *had* been a villain...with the best intentions paving his way to hell, of course.

He had changed, though! On Earth, he had worked for the brighter tomorrow. Of course, he did steal some books and texts along the way, and he still hadn't managed to stop a crazed, suicidal despot from committing horrible crimes against humanity in an endless cycle....

Daphni put a hand on his shoulder. "Aori," she whispered, "You know he's lying."

"No, he's right." He closed his eyes, unable to look the others in the face. "I should have sacrificed myself to Tempo long ago, just to get it over with. I can't change who I am. No matter how hard I try to do the right thing, I'm still just the god of Time in human form. I'll always be his puppet, and people like Munder will just be the strings."

"You can't believe that," said Daphni. "You're not the same person you were on Aia."

"Munder!" he yelled. "I'm the one you want. Just let Daphni go."

Elegos sobbed heavily in the darkness.

"And Elegos, although he's a ghost, and probably isn't even confined to this space."

"No, my lord," the Coda sniffled, "I was only weeping because of this beautiful moment."

311

"At least turn off whatever bewitchment is keeping me from using temporal magic. I promised Daphni a long life in Tweentime, and I intend to hold to my word."

Daphni reached for his hand and held it firmly. "I'm not leaving you, Aori." Tears were streaming down her face as well. "I've borrowed too much time as it is. I am prepared to die, here, with you."

"That's touching an' all," shouted Munder, "But I didn't take away your powers, old man. You gave them away."

Aori rubbed the crinkles in his forehead disconsolately. "Pettifogger."

"There's an old saying: Don't leave your house unlocked, if you don't want to get robbed. I don't know; something like that. You even *told* him to steal your power. Did you think he was just going to give it back? When somebody steals something, it's gone, pal."

"Just like before…." said Aori, shaking his head.

> ### Moths and Death
>
> Many cultures link moths with death. If a white moth enters a house, it is believed in some countries that someone in the house will die. In Christian art, the pupa of the moth serves as a symbol of death. Throughout the world, the moth carries with it an ill omen. This may be due to the fact that moths fly mostly at night, or because most moths do not display the bright, vibrant colors of the butterfly. Of course, it could also have something to do with the eight-foot-tall grim reaper that is Acheron, the Death's Head.

"Yup. That's the best part! He stole from you, I betrayed you, and you *still* trusted us! And you say I'm the dumb one!" Munder's laugh thundered through the mausoleum, causing dust to fall from the ceiling.

Aori sunk to the floor of the tomb, unable to lift his head.

As the laughter died away, silence filled the tomb once again. Aside from the occasional sniffle from Elegos, it seemed as if they had joined the hushed denizens of the hallowed halls.

Days passed without a sound within the tomb. Possibly because of that deep connection with the spirit world, the silence of the tomb was broken by the sound of fluttering wings.

Daphni's antennae shot straight up, aching for that familiar noise, or for any noise, for that matter. She looked up through the hole in the ceiling, and though she could see nothing in the night sky, she called out to them in the guttural speech of the Fellfalla.

The fluttering got closer, and soon it sounded as if they were right overhead. A group of moths spiraled down the narrow shaft into the tomb. They landed on their Fellfallan mistress with the unmistakable joy of a child reunited with its lost mother. Relief filled her voice, but it mixed with sorrow as she told them all that had transpired.

Immediately, one of the moths flew back up the shaft to find help. The others gathered around to hear the rest of Daphni's story. She told them about the betrayal, the accusations, and the feelings in her heart. If Elegos had been able to understand the Fellfallan tongue, he would have wept again.

"There is hope," she said, finally, in a language the others could comprehend. "They will bring us all the food they can carry, which I know doesn't sound like much, but they are also going to find someone to get us out of here."

Having lost all hope entirely, Aori could barely look up at her. He didn't have the heart to remind her that any humans above them who would be sympathetic to their cause would be just as confused by their mode of communication as he was.

She told the Oleander moth everything Elegos had relayed about Gypsy's shroud. He took off at once, flying up

313

the shaft with the speed of a bullet. After the last of her moths had left the tomb, Daphni sat down beside Aori and grabbed his hand for the first time in days. He gazed at her, still tongue-tied.

She whispered, "I told him to go on and find Gypsy alone. He will make it there before we ever could-- that is, if we manage to get out of here."

The dim light of Elegos's specter shone in her eyes. Aori let himself smile, and he felt a warmth buried deep inside him. "You will get out of here. You will find her."

"That's just it," she said. "I've had a lot of time to think, down here, at the edge of oblivion. I've spent most of my life serving others, seeking out love for others, and I've finally realized that I should have just focused on the love that's right here."

Elegos sniffled.

"I don't need to find Gypsy, and I don't need to live forever, Aori. I just need to be here, with you, for whatever life I have left."

Aori rubbed the tears from his eyes. "I... I'm sorry." His head fell to her chest, and she cradled him in her arms.

"I know," she whispered in his ear. "But, I don't love you for your power, or for your promise of eternal life. You are a good man, Aori."

The sound of singing reverberated off the walls of the tomb.

"Elegos?"

"Don't let me interrupt," he sniffled.

"What are you doing?" asked Aori.

"I'm singing my soul into these rocks. I'm going to get you two out of here, even if it kills me."

Though it was a long flight, and he had to stop many times along the way, the Oleander moth eventually made it to Qianshanyang in the Zhejiang province of China. There, he

314

found Gypsy, or one of the moths that bore her soul for the rest of eternity. Though she still made him chase her, she did settle down at last. Once he caught her, they never parted again.

The song that Elegos sang to the stones and rocks that imprisoned them was a long and personal one. He sang for many days, and the moths made several trips down the shaft to bring tiny morsels of food and drops of nectar for Aori and Daphni. Their stomachs were never full, but they got enough to keep them alive.

They were happy, or as happy as one can be in a lifeless tomb. Even the most self-pitying, sorrowful song in the world could not cast a shadow between the two lovers, which was fortunate, because Elegos actually sang that very song. They tried not to listen, which wasn't hard considering how wrapped up in one another they were, but the bits and pieces they heard explained why Elegos cried so often. When you spend your life writing poetry to lament the dead, the song that represents your very soul doesn't include a lot of rainbows and puppies...except dead ones, of course.

After several days, one of the moths returned. It whispered something in Daphni's ear, and concern spread across her face. She translated, "The city above has been deserted. The soldiers are gone, and any remaining citizens are dead."

With a labored sigh, Aori nodded. "No help will come from the Scythians, it seems."

"But," Daphni added, "we aren't too far from the main road. If any travelers come through, perhaps they can come to our aid."

He took little solace in the hope that some traveler would follow a moth to their location, but he wrapped his arm around her waist and smiled, nonetheless. "When we get out of here, we can find Munder and use his watch to get back to Tweentime. We may have to drop a house on him in order to get him to cooperate, but perhaps we'll manage."

Daphni smiled. "Maybe we could start a family."

"I've always wanted an heir... and one with wings would be nice."

They laughed the carefree laugh of a couple with no worries, no stress, and no tomb imprisoning them. He pulled her body closer and held her firmly, hiding his hopelessness deep inside him. Even if they did escape, any children they had would be shunned from any of the societies he had witnessed. The Earth was a cruel, unforgiving place. He wondered, briefly, if Tempo had made it that way; perhaps he had manipulated history such that horrible things would happen to the best of people. *No*, he thought. *It's me. I've somehow caused this world to fall into ruin, just like I did on Aia. Perhaps I am cursed as well.*

As if Daphni could read his thoughts, she whispered, "The future will be brighter, Aori. Our children will never have to endure what we have experienced." She kissed him softly on the neck. "I know what you're thinking, Aori."

"That I love you, and never want to lose you?"

"Well, that I already knew." She grinned. "You know, the Farfalla have married Coda, in the past."

"Did they have children?"

"I don't know," she admitted. "I've only heard fairy tales, and they don't usually go into that kind of detail."

"I supposed they lived happily ever after, nonetheless," Aori smiled, but it quickly faded as the reality of their situation resettled. "Daphni, who are we kidding? Even if it were possible, I'd make a horrible father. I tried to kill my nephew, and look at how I treated my own parents! I completely neglected them, and I've never even tried to find them in Tweentime!"

"Aori, that's just the pity talking. We've been listening to Elegos sing for almost a week now. His song is just making you doubt yourself."

316

Her words made some kind of sense to him, but the stark reality of the tomb encased him. "Maybe you're right," he conceded. As he kissed her, he tried to block out the soul-song of Elegos.

Moths and butterflies rarely live more than a year in the adult stage of their life cycle. Most adults die within a week or two of leaving the cocoon, so they have a very magnificent, but painfully ephemeral prime. The tragedy of their existence is what drew Elegos to leaving Tweentime via Gypsy's death shroud in the first place. The ancient Greeks always loved their tragedies.

Farfalla, being that they were both Homo sapiens and Lepidoptera, shared some of the characteristics of each species. They rarely lived as long as the average human, whose life expectancy ran approximately eighty years at best. The Timisters, of course, lived much longer than that. Most Farfalla who did not die of illness, accident, or violent death met their ends after around twenty years.

By Farfallan standards, Daphni had lived a long life. At age ten, she joined the Fellfallan Imperial Guard. By the time of its fall, she was seventeen. Since coming to Earth, almost one hundred years had passed. Of course, she had spent a good deal of that time living in the cracks between the years.

Daphni knew that she had cheated Death. Long ago, when she crossed over from Aia to Earth, she passed through the Dead Sea. In that void between the physical realm and the spirit world, images in air bubbles showed her all of her fallen friends and family. She had seen Gypsy there, but hope had driven her forward in her quest, nevertheless.

She saw herself there, too. When she asked Acheron about it later, he gave her the choice of knowing when she would die.

Now, as she held Aori in her arms, she wondered if she had made the right choice. She had chosen ignorance, but now she desperately needed to know how much longer she

317

had left. It wouldn't matter, in the long run, because she had already been treating these precious minutes as if they were her last. However, for Aori's sake, she wished she could prepare him.

"Aori," she whispered, "If someone could tell you the exact time of your death, would you want to know?"

He sat down on the coffin that took up most of the tomb, so as to give the question his full attention. She sat on the floor facing him, with her knees pulled up between his. After a minute of deliberation, he concluded, "No."

"I was given the choice, and now I wish I knew."

"Once in my life," Aori explained, "I would have gone to any lengths to find out my own future. I even tried to invent spectacles that could see into the future."

"It seems, with all your command over time itself...."

"That I would have the gift of foresight as well? Perhaps I do, and I just haven't discovered it yet. Asalie told me once that she believed I was descended from the writer of the future."

"Someone just wrote the future?" asked Daphni.

"That's just it. At some point, it was written, but I changed all that. At least, I was supposed to, or so Asalie said."

"That's confusing."

"I know. Was I supposed to tamper with time, leading to the destruction of Aia? Or, was I supposed to change the world by saving it? I've never been too sure."

Daphni cocked her head to the side and smiled, as if she had suddenly cracked the code. "If the future is unwritten, then you weren't *supposed* to do anything. You were destined to do whatever you did."

"Hmm. That's a pleasant thought. That way, I can just go on living, minute to minute, without worrying about what I should do next."

"Welcome to my life," Daphni smiled.

Aori smiled too, but she could tell he was deep in thought. "It would be nice to know if we make it out of here, though."

"My thoughts exactly," she agreed.

Her voice had become scratchy, presumably from all the dust and mold within the tomb. She had developed a cough, which rattled through her broken ribcage with all the fervor of an earthquake.

Speaking of earthquakes, Elegos finally finished his song, after six whole days of nonstop singing. His specter had vanished, as his soul now resided inside the walls of the tomb. His first attempts to break down the stones had been unsuccessful, but he was weary from days of singing. The discussion of death amongst his companions had driven him to try again.

As soon as the walls began to vibrate, Aori and Daphni looked at one another anxiously. After the last few unsuccessful attempts, they had learned not to get their hopes up. Instead, they braced themselves for the inevitable shower of dust.

More dust than usual fell upon them, which seemed like a sign of progress. It got so thick, though, that they both began to choke. "Elegos! We can't breathe!" shouted Aori.

The vibration in the walls ceased, but the cloud of dust remained. It seemed to swirl about the room, as if it had a mind of its own. "Elegos, are you controlling the dust, now?" asked Daphni.

Soon, however, the answer to her own question struck her with cold terror. She had seen dust as black as night in her nightmares, as a child in a pupa stage. As the cloud of dust gathered into the forms of small, brown moths, Daphni gasped and clutched Aori tightly.

She buried her head in his chest, and he tried to swat them away like bothersome flies. The moths landed on the coffin, and they were joined by more and more dust-ridden

319

companions, until the entire coffin was covered in tattered, dusty wings.

The insects spiraled around in a giant mass, until they reached the ceiling of the tomb. At that point, they stopped fluttering their ragged wings, and the already stagnant air around them stood still.

The wings took on the form of a worn and faded cloak, which seemed to draw in the dust like a magnet. Darkness filled the void between its folds, billowing out with the clouds of dust. Suddenly, in the nether of the cloak's hood, a decrepit and decayed skull peered down at them.

In a weak voice, Aori tried to sound pleased. "Acheron. Good to see you again. Although, next time you don't have to scare us to death!"

Daphni swallowed hard. She buried her head further into Aori's chest and pulled herself as close to him as physically possible. Tears burst from her eyes.

"It's okay, Daphni. He's probably just here to tell us more about the Infinis."

The Death's Head just stared down at them with the unblinking coldness of Death itself.

"No," Daphni sobbed.

Aori kept trying to comfort her. "Then he's here to get us out of here! The moths must have asked him for help!"

Daphni choked back her tears. "He can't help us." Taking deep breaths, she managed to continue, "He's forbidden to help the living. That's why he left us to deal with Nero."

"But..." Aori refused to accept what he knew as the true reason for Acheron's presence.

"I thought, since I had traveled with him, and since Proserpina had fallen in love with him and everything, that he wouldn't be as...frightening...when he came...."

Aori's face fell into the soft tangles of her hair. Gently, he kissed her on the top of her head. The harder he tried to squeeze his eyelids shut, the more pneumatic pressure built

320

up behind them. When he finally gave up, the tears cascaded from his eyes and splattered into her dusty hair.

Slowly, laboriously, he raised his head, as if the force of all the rocks around them held it down. He stared up into Acheron's hollow eyes and whispered, "Please. It's not time yet. We haven't had enough... You can't."

Acheron just stared.

"Take me instead," Aori bargained. "I bet your boss would love to have me. How fitting would that be, if Time passed on with Death?"

Daphni felt the years pile up on her, as if she suddenly *were* over a hundred years old. Clutching her wings in her fist, she could see scales flaking off and joining the cloud of dust. The vibrant, green hues of her wings faded to a dull grey, and her skin looked wrinkled and weathered.

"No!" shouted Aori. He rose to his feet defiantly, resting her gently on the floor. Standing between the reaper and his objective. "You don't want her, Acheron! I'm way older than she is. I'm probably past a thousand now."

He lunged at Acheron with all his might, but cold, bony hands held him at bay. Swinging wildly, he managed to strike at only ethereal wisps of darkness and dust.

"You can't stop him, Aori. Death cannot be stopped," Daphni whispered in a raspy, weak voice.

Aori clenched his fists, threw his shoulders back, and puffed up his chest. "I am the god of Time. I can stop Death! You have no power over me, Shade!"

The tension in the tomb thickened. Aori knew his powers were too weak to fight off Death's chief emissary, but he refused to back down. Just as he felt his will wavering, the walls began to shake.

Rocks and dust fell from the ceiling, pelting off of their bodies and bruising their skin. The tension between the two godheads snapped like a bowstring, and Aori fell backwards into the wall.

He slid down next to Daphni and pulled her closer. As she could no longer lift her head, he gently raised her chin and pressed his lips against hers. They shared their final moments, heedless to the rocks piling up around them.

Elegos had felt such strong emotions and such an intense need to aid his friends that he shattered the earth all around them. The rocks above them, having no support, caved in on top of them.

Acheron stood alone in what had once been the thriving marketplace of the Scythian Neapolis. He opened his arms wide, and the souls of the fallen citizens sped to the safety of his billowing cloak. With a long sigh, he looked over at the collapsed tomb.

As he stared unblinkingly at the rocks, he detected the subtlest of movements. In a sudden burst of green dust, hundreds of *daphnis nerii* moths issued forth from the cracks between the stones. As they spiraled up higher and higher, Acheron began to walk back the way he had come. He turned, and his stare lingered on the collapsed tomb, but a feeling of powerlessness ached in his decayed bones. A gust of wind blew through his cloak, and he slowly disintegrated into dust, moths, and shadows.

Daphni felt her soul climb into the open air, and the feeling of freedom carried her higher and higher. She felt the clean, fresh air whipping against her wings, and she wondered why she had ever feared death. Worry gave way to weight-lessness, and all her worldly concerns crashed to the ground below her.

The winds that had blown through Acheron also scattered Daphni's moths across the Earth. Some soared to the heavens, others explored the highest peaks, and a few climbed up to the stars.

Only one moth stayed behind. She could not leave the tomb that had proven her undoing.

Time moved on around the collapsed tomb, and every once in awhile the rocks would vibrate with the Elegy of the Fellfalla. Elegos felt at home in the mausoleum, and he decided to stick around for the indefinite future.

When archaeologists excavated the tomb a thousand years later, in 1932, they found the remains of an old Scythian king inside a coffin, but they discovered no other bones inside the tomb.

Part Three

Zeitgeist,
The Spirit of the Times

326

Chapter 3:00

Retrospective Perspectives
by the Historyteller

Scholars believe that the word *zeitgeist* originated from the German words meaning "Spirit of the Times." While one cannot refute the translation of the word, it's obvious that the Temporal Spirit predated the German language by, oh, about a million years. I've seen it with my own *Eversight*.

Society, with its culture, morals, and ideals, reflects the spirit of the time in which it exists. That's the idea behind the word zeitgeist, but it also permeates the character, choices, and morals of the Temporal Spirit as well. We are a product of the time in which we live.

The cultural shift from one time to the next also demonstrates a shift in historical perspectives. For example, most people would agree, in modern times, that slavery is wrong. It's deeply engrained in our collective consciousness and conscience that a human cannot own another human. However, the general consensus for hundreds of years passed judgment very differently. Some slave-owners may not have been as evil as we depict them in movies and books; some may have just been caught up in the spirit of the time.

Often, when a massive cultural or moral shift happens,

the older generation gets left behind. People excuse blatant bigotry and racist comments from their elderly grandparents, saying, "That was okay to say back then," or, "That's just how things were done in those days." It's almost as if the spirit of one time period can excuse any behavior as long as it's the spirit of an earlier time period. "It seemed like a good idea at the time," we say.

In the spirit of King David and Solomon's times, marrying multiple wives fit the generally accepted norm (at least for kings). However, when looking back on it from a more modern zeitgeist, one might begin to wonder why God favored them so highly. In another Biblical example, the part of the zeitgeist for Old Testament times involved the heavy use of animal sacrifices to appease God. Slaughtering and burning a lamb was so important back then, in fact, that Cain's paltry offering of an entire growth-season's worth of crops just didn't compare to Abel's animal sacrifice. In later years, God seemed to stop caring as much about that particular ritual. According to a more modern zeitgeist, Cain's offering actually seems more humane. The sins of the father aren't always sins to the son, or vice versa.

Any era, age, or epoch requires distance and hindsight to truly understand. It's like a lobster boiling in a pot; when you're in the moment, you don't realize you're in it. And by the time you recognize it, the moment's passed (or, in the case of the lobster, you're dead). I'm sure that's how the Nazis felt during World War II, as they got all caught up in the spirit of those times. They didn't realize how momentous that time period would be, any more than the rest of the world did, but from a historical perspective, it was revolutionary.

Speaking of revolutions, they're often the harbinger of a major shift in the cultural mindset, but again, it takes hindsight to fully grasp the change. Historians labeled the Bronze Age, Iron Age, Renaissance, Age of Reason, Industrial Revolution, and other divisions of time hundreds of years after those particular zeitgeists faded away. The first blacksmith who smelted iron never thought, "I bet this is going to change not only the way we make weapons, but our entire way of life as we know it."

In each era or age, people get swept up in the spirit, and it carries their generations through a roller coaster of highs and lows. Empires rise and fall, power changes hands, and the cult of personality finds a different person to follow. The zeitgeist, as do most things in this universe, follows a cyclical pattern. Periods of prosperity precede pitfalls into poverty. It's like Asalie said, "If you don't like something, just wait around long enough, and it'll eventually change."

Chapter 3:01

Organized Chaos

The instant Aori shuffled off this mortal coil, a singularity of sorts appeared inside his tomb. Like a black hole, only purple, it defied the natural laws of physics. Time itself gravitated toward that point, such that yesterday, today, and tomorrow squished together into one.

In that purple hole, Tweentime merged with the real world (and possibly the next world, if you can wrap your brain around that existentially). Violet visions of the archaeologists that would one day excavate the tomb superimposed upon the slaves who removed the first piece of soil to bury the dead there.

Gradually, over some arbitrary measure of time, the singularity condensed into the recognizable apparition of a human body. With another flicker and flash of temporal energy, the ghost donned a stylish top-hat, goggles, and a Van Dyke beard, modeling the latest fashions of the final days of Aia. To the phantom, the wardrobe change felt familiar, and yet from days long gone by.

The spirit hovered with arms outstretched, as if beckoning the rest of its kind to join it in the collapsed tomb. The singularity pulled all dislodged temporal spirits toward it—that is, the souls of all those who had died and gone to Tweentime. Elegos struggled at first, as he had already grown accustomed to the comforts of the sepulcher, but eventually he gave in to the inevitability.

Other Dorian Coda joined him, wrenched away from their books and auditoriums in Tweentime. Pedant tried to explain, as condescendingly as possible, what had happened to them. Unfortunately, he knew as little as the rest of them.

Luckily for the Timister family, the purple hole contained an infinite volume of space, so everyone, all the way back to Aori's Great-Great Grandfather August Timister, could fit comfortably.

In the next instant, the ghost looked like Ode, or as the Codan lorekeeper had appeared in the sunset of his life on Aia. In fact, the faces of every soul present appeared as an elderly man or woman. Like some strange stop-motion animation, the shape of the specter shifted from one soul to the next.

To an *Everseer* such as myself, the Zeitgeist represented a compilation – or mixtape, if you will—of Tweentime's greatest hits. Anyone who sold his or her soul to Tempo now flickered in and out of a mixed-up, animated collage of wrinkled faces.

Horace Timister, grandfather of Quondam and father to Aori, shimmered with a purple glow that lit up his son's final resting place.

"Aori?"

"He's dead, Horace," said Aori's mother, Eve. "The tomb collapsed on top of him."

"Yes, I'm really sorry about that," Elegos apologized.

"Que sera sera," sang Dolente the Coda, even though the song post-dated him by thousands of years (and light-years).

"Don't beat yourself up about it, Elegos. Aori's in a better place now," said Ecclesiastes.

"Um… this isn't a better place. This is the same place."

332

"Ah, but it's a better time," said Horace. "In fact, there's never been a better time than *any*time."

Though the crumbling stone filled the tomb and blocked off all escape, the Zeitgeist knew that, not long ago, the way had been clear. It also knew that, in the future, the archaeologists would put a ladder in for easier access. So, using the power of the Dorians to enter inanimate objects, the spirit traveled through time via the stone, climbed the ladder, and exited the tomb in the year 1932.

A green-tinted moth fluttered around the Zeitgeist's head, calling forth more familiar emotions. Memories bubbled close to the surface, but the Dorian Coda lacked the sentimentality to feel anything. A spark of something smoldered deep within the Zeitgeist, thanks in part to the Viola part of the spirit. However, the majority smothered those romantic feelings and moved ahead according to schedule.

"No time for love, Dr. Jones," said a part of the Zeitgeist that people once called Ekisha. She had been an Orien fortune-teller on Aia, an *Everseer*, and a pawn in Toki's chess game.

The Zeitgeist slid fluidly between time and space, traveling to and fro to places of temporal convergence. The *axis mundi*, as they would one day be known, called out to the spirit like powerful radio antennas, and the moth tagged along to each time and place.

Across time, the Temporal Spirit ran across other refugees from Aia. In most instances, the spirit witnessed events with the emotional distance of a casual observer. As it noticed Munder endure all manner of strange and brutal near-death experiences, however, a twinge of a smile crept across its translucent face.

In a Mayan temple, the Zeitgeist saw a werewolf Antheri fighting jaguar gods, an Orien girl with a suicide goddess, and the Infinis as it insinuated itself into ancient cultures. The former living god of death seemed to have transcended life,

333

as the Infinis plague infected and ended countless lives.

Nearby in South America, the Zeitgeist watched hundreds of innocent people drink poisoned Kool-Aid at the suggestion of the Infinis. Other cults, such as the Order of the Solar Temple and Heaven's Gate, took similar ways out in the decades that followed, with the Infinis calling the self-inflicted shots at the center of each.

"It's an epidemic," the Zeitgeist stated plainly.

"Don't be so dramatic," interjected Heliodorus, the Dorian physician.

"Oh, it's worse than that," Elegos said dramatically. "It's a pandemic!"

The Zeitgeist backed away to get some perspective and watched the Earth rotate and revolve years at a time. Each instance of Infinis-induced suicide appeared as a tiny dark spot in the Zeitgeist's view of Earth's history. Within a millennia or so, the shadows covered every inch of the planet.

"Wherever we go, Doomsday follows. We can't leave the house without destroying the world."

"At least it's not our fault, this time. It's the Infinis."

"Maybe, or maybe it's all part of Toki's greater plan."

"Tempo."

"Priori."

"Whatever."

"The Spirit shall not speak against the Father."

"Who is speaking? Who am I?"

"We are the Zeitgeist. We are the Temporal Spirit."

"Am I talking to myself?"

"There is no 'self' anymore. There is only the Zeitgeist."

"What if there is no greater plan, though? What if nothing is set in stone? That means we can prevent these horrific mass-suicides from happening. We can still save this planet."

"You just watched it happen. It happened."

"No, but time is like a river, and it can be dammed up, dried up, or diverted."

334

"I don't think you understand time."

"I don't really think any of us do, which is scary, since we're the Spirit of Time."

"There is no 'us.' There is just the Zeitgeist."

"Shut up!" the spirits shouted as one.

.

Chapter 3:02

You Might Not Like What You Find

For the rest of the journey through time and space, the Zeitgeist enjoyed the solitude (or multitude, to be precise) of quiet reflection. The various entities that made up its unified gestalt kept their collective trap shut and just contemplated the history of the world.

Nations rose, fell, and in many cases, whole groups of people committed suicide to avoid capture or death at the hands of their enemies. The outlook, with both foresight and hindsight, proved rather grim. The Zeitgeist began to understand why *Everseers* chose to focus on finite time periods rather than the entire span of past, present, and future. The view overwhelmed and depressed even the most stoic of the Temporal Spirit's parts.

As a whole, the Zeitgeist decided that a change of perspective would do a world of good. Aori's sisters, Morning and Tomorrow, had been more cheerful and optimistic than the rest of the family, so the Zeitgeist deferred to their judgment.

Instead of following the trail of bodies, they chose to let

the green-tinted Daphni moth lead the way. It fluttered its way through Tweentime, across oceans and continents to the land of China, which actually went by several other names and was only called China centuries later, by foreigners. At any rate, the moth somehow followed the path of its brother, the Oleander hawk-moth, to a village known as Qianshanyang.

There, the Zeitgeist discovered a thriving silk trade, and though the chief producer of the thread was the larva of a moth called *Bombyx Mandarina*, the region seemed to be a haven for all types of moths.

The Temporal Spirit searched for a Fellfallan presence in the village, as the human-sized Antheri normally watched over and protected the moths of their species. The Zeitgeist briefly worried that all Fellfalla on Earth had met the same fate as Daphni.

"What if these moths are all that are left of the Fellfalla?"

"They've never been favored by Tempo—that's why their lifespans are so short. Perhaps it is natural selection at work."

"Perhaps it's time for that to change."

The Zeitgeist reached out a finger and a white, furry moth with black spots attempted to land but passed right through its hand. The spirit caught the moth in a sphere of temporal energy. Immediately, the Gypsy moth was joined by an Oleander moth. The Zeitgeist managed a smile. The sphere of temporal energy acted like a fortune-teller's crystal ball, revealing the future of the moths.

As the years passed, dynasties shifted power in that region, and control of the silk trade changed hands numerous times. The industry itself waxed and waned depending on supply, demand, and disease in the populations of the silkworm and the mulberry tree it eats. Throughout the states of flux, Oleander and Gypsy remained alive, well, and inseparable. They bore many offspring, and the Zeitgeist blessed them with unnatural longevity as well.

Somehow, one of the larva grew up to be a Farfallan girl.

338

She looked like Gypsy, with the speckled white coloring, but her father's regal air passed down to her as well. The Zeitgeist watched as she grew to be the Matriarch of a tribe of gypsies, outsiders, and Aian refugees that wandered throughout Europe and Western Asia.

The Matriarch would also go on to found a very important group of women known as the Sisterhood of the Spiral. The main purpose of the sect was to slow the spread of the Infinis plague and try to prevent the unnecessary deaths of innocents. Members included such illustrious names as Asalie, Asia, Lithe, and Caitlyn, to name a few. Despite its inner longing to remain with the more familiar faces, the Zeitgest felt a stronger force tugging it to other times and places.

When the images of Lithe appeared within the time-bubble, the Zeitgeist paid special attention. Future events flashed by quickly, which made it difficult to focus on any one instance. However, since Ode and Lithe shared a familial—albeit non-emotional—bond, the Zeitgeist felt a similar link to her. As if pulled by some unseen rope, the spirit hurtled through time and space to her location.

As the purple hue of temporal magic washed away like a watercolor painting, the bright light of a blazing inferno took its place. The perspective from inside a burning building warped and twisted as visions of the history and future of the building flickered amongst the flames. The effect disoriented the Zeitgeist, making it all but impossible to navigate the flames.

The scorching conflagration did not burn the Zeitgeist's skin, but the intensity of the images seared its collective soul. In the visions from across time, hundreds of women were tortured throughout the history of the building, which had been converted from a church into a prison for the Inquisition. The Zeitgeist watched helplessly as Lithe and two other Coda endured unspeakable acts of cruelty. When the agony reached a fever pitch, the building exploded.

The Zeitgeist darted towards Lithe's position and finally managed to find her despite the jarring scenes dancing between the flames. As the spirit bent down to pick her up, however, its translucent hands passed right through her body.

Suddenly, the flames sputtered out like a candle in a jar, and the Zeitgeist stood inside the lobby of a modern, expensive-looking hotel.

"Lithe?" The Zeitgeist could feel the concern slowly dissipating, as the less-sentimental majority inside the spirit ruled. After a few minutes passed, the memory of Lithe's burning body had all but faded away completely.

"No sense dwelling on the past."

"Lithe would want us to move on with our lives."

"I'm sure she'll be fine. Time heals all wounds."

"She is half-Dorian, after all. Perhaps she's already sung her soul into something."

With flickers of a grimace, an eye-roll, and a shrug, the Zeitgeist floated on like a leaf in the stream of time. It passively let the current steer the way, while numerous acts of aggression occurred throughout the historical events depicted just below the surface. Ghettos filled with persecuted unfortunates, bombs dropped all around, and the streets of Prague ran red with blood, but the Zeitgeist just casually wove its way through centuries' worth of tumult and traffic.

Chapter 3:03

Phantom Minutes

As the years whizzed by the Zeitgeist's face, so too did the traffic of myriad modes of transportation. Cars of various makes and models wove between bicycles and horse-drawn carriages. A sleek, expensive sports-car zoomed right through the Zeitgeist's body, permitting brief glimpses of technology across the ages. For a few seconds, the car's passengers somehow simultaneously listened to an 8-track player, rocked out to a cassette deck, boomed CD audio through sub-woofers, and wirelessly synced music from their mobile phones.

The Zeitgeist just took it all in, absorbing and absolutely loving the perspective on technological changes. Even the paving of the street flickered and shifted from dirt to cobblestones, bricks, and asphalt. Nothing remained the same for too long. Gaslights grew into electric streetlamps, and shop windows advertised televisions of all different shapes and sizes alongside other gadgets such as telegraphs, radios, kinetoscopes, computers, printing presses, typewriters, iPads, and something from the future called a HaNGDiVMoG, which played hallucinations of movie games, or some such nonsense.

Each device took the Zeitgeist on a tour of the time and place in which it was invented, which then led to visions of new machines, locations, and decades. The Zeitgeist witnessed how changes in technology led to shifts in the spirit of the times, and each new contraption evolved from the ones that came before it. From that viewpoint, it almost seemed as if artificial creations grew and progressed like living things.

The Zeitgeist traveled all the way to Japan and back in time through an intricate, web-like network of video game consoles, VHS players, televisions, and radios. A bullet train carried the spirit across the country, until it gradually regressed into a steam train and then a more primitive wagon train. By the end of the jaunt through time, the Zeitgeist had lost all orientation and direction.

The massive, snowy peak of Mount Fuji loomed to the southeast, casting a shadow over the surrounding area. The dim twilight before dawn crept across most of the Aokigahara Forest, which was so dense with trees that darkness lingered even on the sunniest of days.

The morning air carried a chill that might have penetrated to the bone, had the Zeitgeist possessed a corporeal form. The air fell heavy amidst the twisting and impenetrable branches, as no wind could blow through the concentration of trees. Elegos and several of the other Coda could hear the silent, yet deafening, songs of death reverberating among the wood and leaves. It seemed that the eerie stillness absorbed all other sounds of the forest.

Despite the contorting, mossy roots that jutted out of the ground, the earth itself appeared black and lifeless. The soil consisted predominantly of volcanic rock, left there eons ago by Mount Fuji itself. Almost in defiance of the rocky terrain and the emanating aura of death, life continued to break through and thrive in verdant glory. Perhaps the dead fertilized the living growth. As Asalie would say, it is all part of the cycle.

Regardless of the majestic and ancient presence of the forest, the ominous gloom permeated all of the folklore, legends, and factual information reported about the area. The Zeitgeist soaked in the lore of the place, which stretched back centuries, and every story involved grisly death. In modern times, Aokigahara is known as the Suicide Forest, and its reputation stems from a lengthy and twisted history of tragedy.

Even though much of Japan's culture grew around the honorable samurai, taking his own life in ritual *seppuku*, the sheer number of suicides among the trees in this forest carried a heart-wrenching sense of dread that far outweighed any sense of honor. As the Zeitgeist explored, and the various parts of its whole soaked in the lore, even the most stalwart and stoic among them recoiled at the frequent and ghastly sight of bodies hanging from branches. Occasionally, the bones of the deceased could be found among the other litter left behind by visitors.

It didn't take a forensic scientist and a crime lab to draw connections between these deaths and the eternally self-destructive embodiment of death known as the Infinis. Of course, these multiple untimely ends could have resulted from any number of causes, from mental illness to attention-seeking, but no matter what brought these victims to the forest, the Infinis undoubtedly provided the catalyst for combustion.

As the Zeitgeist wandered deeper into the sea of trees, the overgrowth gave way to barren branches and rotten wood. Black roots insinuated themselves throughout the cold ground, creeping like the tentacles of some monstrous creature from a dark abyss. Long-dead leaves littered the forest floor, only slightly covering the corpses, which seemed far more plentiful in this neck of the woods.

The trapped and tortured souls of the humans who took their own lives wailed in a song that only the Zeitgeist could hear. The mourning songs reverberated in every dead and

343

decaying tree. The moans, cries, and screams overlapped in such cacophony that the Zeitgeist understood the desperation of those seeking an ultimate escape. A few more minutes of this, and even the Spirit of Time would be calling it quits too—that is, if it weren't already a ghost.

As the trees thinned, visibility increased, and the Zeitgeist saw the source of all the decay. An enormous tree with a trunk that spanned a city block towered over the decrepit and lifeless husks that surrounded and fell at its feet. However, as the Zeitgeist studied its prodigious growth, the tree's history and future sprouted like leaves, literally in some cases. At one point in its life, the tree had been a World Tree, or a type of axis mundi that acts as a conduit between parts of the world (or, as some believe, other worlds).

The Zeitgeist filtered out the extraneous timelines and focused on the here and now. The fate of the giant tree gradually revealed itself as a huge stump with a circumference of at least a thousand square feet. Right in the center of the tree stood a man with a familiar, yet unrecognizably aged face.

"I know you, don't I?" asked the Zeitgeist.

"Senken?" asked the old man.

"Is that your name? Senken?"

"That depends on how old I am," the old man answered. "To the Ori, it means 'ancient sage.' Do I look ancient to you?"

"Actually, yes."

"Ah, but so do you. I think I'll call *you* Senken, instead."

The Zeitgeist just stared blankly. "This is ridiculous. Are you an evil tree or what?"

"What?" the old man remarked defensively. "I'm the one who killed it, about a hundred years ago or so." He hobbled around on the massive stump, stopping occasionally to tap against the wood with his walking stick.

"You're not the Infinis, are you?"

"No. Are you?" The man looked up from his intense

344

focus upon the wood.

"No. This has got to be the most confusing conversation we've ever had."

The old man shook his head with a smile. "Every conversation with you is confusing. Would it help if I said that you're me, from the future?"

"What?! Why would that possibly help? That's exponentially more confusing!"

"Well, what would you say if I told you that's exactly how you explained it to me, centuries ago?"

The Zeitgeist just sighed and watched in dumbfounded silence as the old man stooped low and began to scratch some words into the tree's remains. Somehow, his walking stick had grown a sharp point at the end. In fact, upon closer inspection, it looked more like a wooden sword. Suddenly, pieces fell in place in the Zeitgeist's collective consciousness, and he realized why the old man looked so familiar.

With the warm feeling of a family reunion, the Zeitgeist smiled and replied, "I guess I'd say, 'Hello, Quondam.'"

.

	?? BC	c. 1020 BC	1010 BC	33 AD	54-68 AD	c. 73 AD	156 AD	c. 200 AD
Earth History	Tower of Babel destroyed	David killed Goliath	King Saul died	Jesus crucified; Judas betrayed Jesus and hanged himself	Emperor Nero ruled Roman Empire	Mass Suicide at Masada	St. Polycarp Martyred	Scythian Empire Ended
Vague Plot Points	Aori et al scattered throughout time and Earth	Munder started getting beaten by every little kid in history	The Timister Tweentime Library began construction	Aori's Big Fat Greek Vacation	Aori met Daphni, among other things	Aori did some Crime Scene Investigation	Aori got a front row seat to the action	The Zeitgeist became a bit more crowded

.

ABOUT THE AUTHOR

 Jared Kitchens cannot foresee the future. His gifts, though extraordinary in their own right, do not include *Eversight*. He's not a Historian or anything like that. He doesn't even own a watch.

While writing his previous book, *Seasons of the Wither*, the first book of the *Anachronist Chronicles*, he discovered the uncanny ability to squeeze an extra day out of every four years. This permutation of time allowed him to then start part two, *The Temporal Trinity* in addition to working as an elementary school teacher.

After completing that book, he met and married his sensible and beautiful wife, who explained to him that everyone has the Leap Day power, and that it's not so much mystical as arbitrary and mathematical. That took a bit of wind out of his sails, but he still managed to continue writing the next few books of the *Anachronist Chronicles*, which should be published within this century (again, he cannot foresee the future).

Mr. Kitchens continues to work as a Gifted and Talented teacher, enjoys raising two brilliant children of his own, and desperately scrapes together every free millisecond in order to work on his favorite pastime, writing.

While you're patiently waiting on the next installment of the *Anachronist Chronicles*, be sure to follow us on Facebook under KitchensInk at Facebook.com/AnachronistChronicles

Made in the USA
`Columbia, SC
31 August 2022

65768135R00214